"Want to come inside with me?"

Justin was on his feet in an instant to open the screen door for her. "Love to. Do you like to party?" he asked. "We could go to the Rusty Spur some Saturday night if you do."

Emily carried Gussie to the end of the sofa and eased down carefully with the cat still in her arms. "No, thank you. That's not my idea of a date."

"What is?" Justin removed his hat and coat and laid them on one of the recliners and then sat on the other one.

"Anything but a noisy bar full of drunks," she answered.

"Candlelight dinner, a movie?"

"A picnic and a long talk in front of a fireplace." She smiled.

"That could be arranged." An instant visual of the fireplace at the old cabin flashed through his mind.

"Justin, are you asking me on a date?"

"If I did, would you accept?" he asked.

High Praise for Carolyn Brown

"Carolyn Brown makes the sun shine brighter and the tea taste sweeter. Southern comfort in a book."
—Sheila Roberts, *USA Today* best-selling author

"Like a good piece of chocolate, there's nothing more delicious, memorable and addictive than a Carolyn Brown story."
—Fresh Fiction

"Carolyn Brown's cowboys are as real as they come."
—RT Book Reviews

"Carolyn Brown writes about everyday things that happen to all of us and she does it with panache, class, empathy, and humor."
—Night Owl Reviews

THE LONGHORN CANYON SERIES

"A slow-simmering romance...that's sure to please fans of cowboy romances."
—*Publishers Weekly* on *Cowboy Honor*

"Western romance lovers are in for a treat. This wickedly saucy series is unputdownable. There's no one who creates a rancher with a heart of gold like Carolyn Brown."
—RT Book Reviews on *Cowboy Bold*

"Lighthearted banter, heart-tugging emotion, and a good-natured Sooner/Longhorn football rivalry make this a delightful romance and terrific launch for the new series."

—*Library Journal* on *Cowboy Bold*

"Everything you could ever ask for in a cowboy romance."

—The Genre Minx on *Cowboy Bold*

THE HAPPY, TEXAS SERIES

"Wonderfully charming characters...This sweet, heartwarming romance is sure to increase Brown's fan base."

—*Publishers Weekly* on *Luckiest Cowboy of All*

"Goes down like a cup of hot cocoa—warm and sweet."

—*Entertainment Weekly* on *Long, Tall Cowboy Christmas*

"A truly romantic cowboy story...full of love, hope, loss, and second chances. Top Pick."

—Fresh Fiction on *Long, Tall Cowboy Christmas*

"One of the best feel-good reads I've had the pleasure of reading yet this year! It tugged on your heart strings and had you cheering for true love."

—Once Upon an Alpha on *Toughest Cowboy in Texas*

Also by Carolyn Brown

The Longhorn Canyon series

Cowboy Bold
Cowboy Honor

The Happy, Texas series

Toughest Cowboy in Texas
Long, Tall Cowboy Christmas
Luckiest Cowboy of All

The Lucky Penny Ranch series

Wild Cowboy Ways
Hot Cowboy Nights
Merry Cowboy Christmas
Wicked Cowboy Charm

Cowboy Brave

A Longhorn Canyon Novel

Carolyn Brown

FOREVER

New York   Boston

Copyright © 2019 by Carolyn Brown
Preview of *Cowboy Rebel* copyright © 2019 by Carolyn Brown
Second Chance Cowboy copyright © 2018 by A.J. Pine

Cover design by Elizabeth Stokes
Cover copyright © 2019 by Hachette Book Group, Inc.

Forever
Hachette Book Group
1290 Avenue of the Americas, New York, NY 10104
forever-romance.com
twitter.com/foreverromance

First Edition: January 2019

Forever is an imprint of Grand Central Publishing. The Forever name and logo are trademarks of Hachette Book Group, Inc.

The publisher is not responsible for websites (or their content) that are not owned by the publisher.

The Hachette Speakers Bureau provides a wide range of authors for speaking events. To find out more, go to www.hachettespeakersbureau.com or call (866) 376-6591.

ISBNs: 978-1-5387-4493-2 (mass market), 978-1-5387-4491-8 (ebook)

Printed in the United States of America

OPM

10 9 8 7 6 5 4 3 2 1

This one is dedicated to my cousin Jan Edwards Barker—for all the love and support you shower upon me!

Dear Readers,

As I've said before, I tend to drag my heels when it comes to finishing a series. This one was no different. I spent several months with these cowboys and their sassy ladies. I got to know them so well that it was difficult to let them go. Then my fantastic editor Leah suggested that we add a few more books to the series, and my heart skipped a few beats. That's when Tag and Hud Baker showed up with their friends, Maverick and Paxton Callahan—their hats in their hands and asking me to tell their stories, too. So keep your reading glasses right handy and don't put your cowboy boots in the closet. This is not the last of the Longhorn Canyon series.

I have a sign in my living room that says *There's always, always, always something to be thankful for.* I look at it every day, and today I'm sending bushels of thanks to my editor Leah Hultenschmidt for continuing to support me and make this process of taking a book from an idea to a polished product such a delight. And thank you to my whole team at Forever—y'all are the best! Hugs to my agent, Erin Niumata: We've been together twenty years. That's longer than most Hollywood marriages, folks. Also I have to thank Mr. B, my husband, for his love through my career. Romance isn't always flowers and candy; sometimes it's washing dishes, doing laundry, or going to the burger shop for supper so I can write one more chapter.

I love to hear from my readers, so let me know what you think of Justin and Emily's story.

Until next time,
Carolyn Brown

Cowboy Brave

Chapter One

Emily Baker rarely dressed up for anything. But this was an important occasion, and she wanted to make a good first impression. Judging by the applause from the Fab Five, as the quintet of residents called themselves, she'd succeeded. Of course, they usually only saw her in scrubs, so perhaps the bar hadn't been set that high.

"Go get 'em, and don't take no for an answer," Otis encouraged.

"Tell 'em we'll take up a collection and pay the big bucks." The two long gray braids that wrapped around Bess's head were the only thing that distinguished her from her redheaded twin sister, Patsy. Bess waved a lace hanky at her as Emily stepped out into the brisk Texas air.

"Two bits, four bits, six bits a dollar. All for Emily, stand up and holler." Patsy did a few snap movements like a cheerleader, and all five of them shouted like they were at a football pep rally.

Then Sarah, tall and thin with chin-length gray hair, put a key chain with a rabbit's foot in Emily's hand. "For good luck."

"Okay," Larry said. "We got to let her go. Let's go to my place, get out the dominoes to pass the time while we wait for her to come back with the good news." Every bit as tall as Sarah, he herded the bunch of them away from the door and down the hall.

When the Fab Five had come up with the idea for a "field trip," she'd tried to talk them out of it, but ever since they'd read in the newspaper last summer about underprivileged kids going to the Longhorn Canyon ranch, they'd been begging to spend a week there too.

After a twenty-minute drive, Emily found the ranch with no problem. She parked her red Mustang in front of the house and checked her reflection in the rearview mirror. She fluffed up her long, dark brown hair, and reapplied her bright red lipstick.

She took a deep breath and wished that she'd figured out a better plan than just flying by the seat of her pants. Trying to figure out what to say first, she wasn't watching where she was going, and her heel sunk into a gopher hole. She regained her footing just in time to avoid falling face-first, but in doing so, she stepped in a pile of fresh cow manure.

"Shit!" she muttered.

Amen, her grandmother's voice popped into her head.

And if that wasn't embarrassing enough, just then a tall cowboy with steel-blue eyes opened the door and stepped out on the porch. Lord, have mercy.

"Can I help you?" he asked.

She opened the gate into the yard and said, "I'm Emily Baker. We visited on the phone last evening." She looked up into blue eyes.

"My brother, Cade, is the one that you talked to. He forgot that he had another meeting this morning in Wichita Falls. I'm Justin Maguire. Please come right in." He stood to one side and motioned her inside.

She couldn't track cow crap inside the house, so she kicked off her high-heeled shoes, leaving them on the porch. She glanced down at her chipped toenail polish and wished that she'd taken time to redo them. But not even ugly toenails would keep her from her mission—not after that send-off at the center.

"Should've been a little more careful about where I was steppin'," she said.

Justin grinned. "That's part of ranch life, darlin'. Evidently you haven't lived on one."

Oh, honey, you are so wrong about that, she thought.

As they crossed the foyer and entered a huge living room, she studied him from the corner of her eye. Scruff covered his square jaw, but she could see a very slight cleft in his chin. He walked with the cowboy swagger and confidence that would have women falling all over him. And he'd called her darlin'—did he flirt with everyone?

"We can talk in here, Emily. Have a seat anywhere. Sorry about the mess."

"Thanks. I work at the Oakview Retirement Center in Bowie. Cade and I were going to talk about renting your bunkhouses for a week. Did he let you know if y'all have made a decision?" She spit it all out at once without taking a breath as she sat on the edge of the sofa, legs crossed at the ankle and back straight.

"He only told me that someone from the retirement center was coming by to visit about something as he was walking out the door fifteen minutes ago, but this is the first I'm hearing about it." His forearms bulged beneath the rolled-up sleeves of his black, pearl snap shirt, and his hands were huge.

She had to look at him to talk to him, but when she did she noticed that the top two snaps of his shirt were undone, giving her a peek at light brown chest hair. She couldn't get her thoughts together looking right at him. She'd expected the Maguire brothers to be her dad's age. "There are five elderly folks at the center. They have some problems, but basically they're pretty spry to be in their seventies." She glanced down at the coffee table, where papers were strewn about. "You're building a house? Are you an architect? I thought the Maguires were ranchers."

"We are, but I'm trying my hand at drawing up the plans for our foreman and his new wife," he answered.

Emily leaned forward. "Doesn't look like it's going to be very big."

"Not here at first, but the design will make it easy to add on later." He chose a chair close to the coffee table where the plans were laid out. "So tell me more about this idea you've got, Miz Barker."

"Baker, not Barker," she corrected him.

"Sorry about that. I'm better with faces than names. Might not be real good with names, but I never forget a pretty face." He raked his fingers through light brown hair that had definitely had a cowboy hat settled on it not long ago.

Don't flirt with me, cowboy, she thought.

"I'm the senior activities director at the Oakview Retirement Center and we try to have an outing for our patients a couple of times a year. One elderly gentleman asked that we visit a ranch for a week this spring. He had a big spread up near the Red River when he was younger. I can tell he gets homesick for all this." She motioned with a flip of her hand.

"For the smell of fresh cow manure?" Justin chuckled as he glanced down at her feet.

A slow burn crept from her neck to her face. "And hay and baby calves and all that goes with ranchin'. Like I said, there are five of them who are interested, and they're all in their seventies. They've got some arthritis problems, but none of them need wheelchair facilities. Otis was the rancher and his buddy, Larry, owned a construction business. Then there's Sarah, Patsy, and Bess, who want to get away for a while. Sarah was a schoolteacher but grew up on a farm. Patsy and Bess are twins who were raised on a ranch back in the 1940s and 1950s."

"Will there be medical professional folks to stay with them? And if this could happen, we'd have to have some paperwork showing we weren't responsible for accidents," Justin asked.

"I'll stay in the ladies' bunkhouse and will give their meds each day, and I'll be in direct contact with the on-call nurse at the center. And we'll be glad to sign a disclosure freeing you from all responsibility," she answered. "Would it be possible for me to see the bunkhouses?"

"Sure, but I'll have to talk to the rest of the family before I can give you an answer. You got a coat? It's not far from here to the bunkhouses, but that north wind is pretty cold."

"Just this jacket." She looked down at the lightweight sweater that matched her dress.

"You can borrow one of ours. Be right back." He whistled as he left the room.

Most of the time she was comfortable in her size-eighteen skin, but suddenly she was self-conscious. It would be so embarrassing if he brought back a jacket that wouldn't even close over her more-than-ample breasts. But one look at the canvas work coat he held out to her when he returned had her wondering if there was a giant on the ranch.

"Excuse the stains. The coat belongs to my brother, Cade, but he won't mind you using it," Justin said.

She slipped her arms into it. The smells of ranch life lingered and made her a little homesick, but she brushed the feeling aside and headed for the door.

"Thought you might need these." He handed her a box of tissues. "Or if you've got some boots or other shoes in your car..." He paused.

"I have work shoes out there, and I'll change into them," she said, quickly.

"Great. Can I get them for you?" he asked.

"I'll take care of it." She slipped her feet back into the shoes waiting on the porch. Thank goodness she'd left her oldest pair of Nikes in the trunk. She sure made a picture wearing a cute little dress, a work jacket, and her sneakers, but how she looked didn't matter—what mattered was convincing the flirty cowboy to rent the bunkhouses. She couldn't bear to go back to the center and tell the Fab Five that she'd failed.

He met her at the bottom of the porch steps and walked beside her to a bunkhouse and swung the door open. Years ago both bunkhouses were filled with hired hands, but these days most of the help on the ranch lived in town and commuted to work. Even though it was used only once a year now—when the ranch opened up to a few inner city, underprivileged kids—it was well kept and warm inside. And absolutely perfect for her ladies.

"Four small bedrooms." He pointed across the living/kitchen area and then swung his hand around to the other side. "And one big one for the supervisor. Look around if you want."

"It's perfect." The small rooms had individual vanities with sinks.

"Take a peek in the bathroom of this one." He led the way through the bigger bedroom.

"Oh. My. Gosh!" She clamped a hand over her mouth when she saw the enormous tub. Had it been built for Cade? He'd need something that big if he filled out the coat she wore.

"Back when the bunkhouses were built, we had this six-and-a-half-foot, big burly foreman. I shouldn't say we, it was long before my time. All he asked for was a tub big enough to soak his tired bones in at night, so my grandparents had this special made for him," Justin explained. "Before we go on to the boys' bunkhouse, let me ask a few questions."

She couldn't take her eyes from that tub. "Sure. Ask anything."

"What kind of activities will the ranch need to provide for these senior citizens?"

"I don't think you'll be expected to entertain them. They just want to be on a ranch, maybe be allowed to take walks and feel the freedom of being in the country." She brushed past him on the way back to the living room. "Does the boys' place look like this?"

"Exactly, only it doesn't have the big bathtub. Just a nice-size walk-in shower," he answered.

"I won't actually need to see it then, but a walk-in shower is great. Larry has a bad hip, and Otis has a bum knee, so that'll make things easier for them. Do you have a price in mind for the week?"

Justin shook his head. "Can't even begin to think about that until I talk to the family. There's all kinds of things we'll have to consider."

"I understand. When do you think you might have an answer?" she pressured.

"What week did you want to book the bunkhouses?" He led the way outside. "And you did say that you would personally oversee most of their stay here, right?"

"Next Monday would be great. Then they'd be back at the center for the Valentine's Day celebration. But if that's too soon, then maybe the week after Valentine's?"

"I'll talk to the family about both times and let you know," Justin said. "So you've been working at Oakview for five years."

"Yes, as the activities director. I plan things to keep the residents busy. We do Bingo Mondays. Craft Tuesdays. That kind of thing. And then there are outings, but this is a big thing. I've never had a week-long trip with any of them. It's mainly just day things like a trip to the Dallas Zoo or maybe to the mall over in Wichita Falls around Christmastime. We did go down to McKinney for their light festival last year," she answered. "And I'm talking too much. I just get so excited about my job. Helping the elderly is so rewarding."

When they reached the car she pulled a card from the pocket of her dress and handed it to him. "Thank you, Mr. Maguire. I'll be lookin' forward to hearing from you. Here's my card. I've written my cell phone number on the back."

"I'll definitely let you know by morning and possibly tonight." Justin tucked the card into his pocket.

Growing up, Emily had never been a petite little slip of a girl. She topped out at five feet eight inches, and with the high heels that she loved but seldom got a chance to wear except for church on Sunday, she was up close to six feet tall. She glanced over at Justin and wondered if he flirted with all women.

Like a gentleman, he walked her to the car and opened the door for her. Tipped his hat and then turned to go back inside the house. She started up the engine and turned on the heat, then realized she was still wearing Cade's coat. Leaving the car running, she jogged back to the fence surrounding the house and bunkhouses, opened the gate, and dashed up onto the porch. She rang the bell and waited.

She held the coat out to Justin when he opened the door. "I forgot to give this back. Thanks for letting me borrow it."

"Darlin', you can wear my brother's coat anytime you want to visit the ranch." He winked.

Thank God he'd already gone back inside, because as she was walking from the porch to the car, she stepped in that same cow patty—again.

"Well, dammit!" she swore under her breath. "Nobody rattles me like that."

She stopped at the back of her car and got out a reusable grocery bag. She sat down in the driver's seat, put her shoes inside it, tied the top shut and tossed it to the back, and hustled her bare feet inside the car.

She always talked to herself when she was agitated. Slapping the steering wheel, she was determined that she wouldn't say another word, but it didn't work.

"I'm an independent woman. I paved my own way. I proved that when I left my folks' ranch and made my own choice about life."

Her phone rang. She picked it up from the passenger seat and put it on speaker. It was crazy to think that it could be Justin calling to say that he'd made a quick phone call and everything was set on go, but she crossed her fingers anyway.

"Hello."

"Hey, sis, I know you're at work." Her brother's voice sounded agitated. "Are you in the car? I hear road noise."

"Yes, I am, Taggart." She went on to tell him why.

"You must be aggravated. You never call me by my full name unless you are," Tag said.

"I wanted this resolved right now," she said.

"Join the club." Tag sighed.

"What's goin' on?" she asked.

"Matthew is driving me crazy. Hud and I think we should invest in the property up for sale right next to our ranch, but he won't even hear us out. We even offered to manage it on our own. Our big brother wouldn't have to do anything more than he does now. But oh, no, he says the ranch can't spend the money," Tag said.

"Buy it on your own," she said.

"We could, but then we wouldn't have operating capital," he said. "When you come home next month for the reunion, will you talk to him?"

Dammit! One of the many reasons she'd left West Texas was because she didn't like being the only sister, who had to settle arguments among her three brothers. Matthew, the oldest, had always been the bossy one, and the twins, just a year younger than Emily, were always in some kind of trouble with him.

"I'll see what I can do," she agreed. After all, she'd only be there for a weekend. Maybe she'd even enlist her parents' help in settling the argument. They'd have a much better insight into whether the twins would be ready to take on that responsibility.

"Thanks, sis. So you're going to spend a whole week on a ranch? That doesn't sound like you." Tag chuckled.

"Hey, I like ranchin'," she said. "I just don't like all the paperwork, and as the girl in the family, that was about to fall right in my lap. I wasn't sure I wanted to do that the rest of my life. I'm pulling into work right now so I've got to go."

"Will you talk to Matthew about buying the property while you're here?" Tag asked.

"I promise," she said.

"Lookin' forward to seein' you," Tag said.

"Me too. Bye now."

She hurried across the parking lot in her bare feet, leaving both pairs of soiled shoes in the back seat of her car. The Fab Five were waiting in the lounge for her.

"So?" Sarah asked. "Did he say yes and knock your shoes plumb off your feet? I heard that both of them Maguire boys look like sex on a stick, but the older one is married. So which one did you talk to?"

Otis sniffed the air. "Hell, no, he didn't. She stepped in cow crap. I'd recognize that smell anywhere. Was it going in or coming out?"

"Both," she admitted.

"Well, darlin', when you live on a ranch, you learn to watch where you're puttin' your feet. I remember when we graduated from high school our principal told us that we could wear our cowboy boots to the ceremony but he'd better not get a whiff of bull shit or he'd send us home." Otis's round baby face beamed every time he got to tell a story about his past.

Patsy poked him on the arm. "Enough reminiscing. What did they say? Do we start packing?"

"He has to talk to his family about it first," Emily answered.

Sarah clapped her hands. "That's not a no, so we've got hope."

Patsy hugged Emily. "We're goin' to break out of this joint for a whole week. There's no way he could refuse someone as beautiful as you."

"Break out," Bess said. "Like you did when we were kids

and you got thrown in jail for tryin' to sneak in the window at daylight?"

"It was your fault. If you hadn't gone and called the police before I got inside, I wouldn't have got caught," Patsy argued.

"Did you flirt with him a little?" Larry asked. "We should have told you to do that."

"I did not!" Emily exclaimed. "I just stopped back to tell y'all because I knew you'd be anxious. Hopefully, he'll call tomorrow and let us know for sure. I'm going to gather up my stuff and go home."

"Fair enough," Sarah said. "Let's go pray."

Emily stopped in her tracks and turned around to look at them. "Pray?"

"Yep, if all else fails then give it to God." Sarah grinned.

"Pray, nothing." Otis moved over closer to Emily and inhaled deeply. "That smell of fresh cow patties is better than any women's perfume in the world. If he says no, I'm going to offer to double whatever he wants to rent them cabins to us."

"You'd think they were in prison." Nikki pushed a medicine cart around the corner and met Emily coming down the hall. "Where are your shoes?"

"Smelling up my car. They're probably ruined. I stepped in a pile of cow manure."

Her best friend for the past five years was stifling a giggle. "Before or after you talked to the Maguires."

"Technically, both."

"What?" Nikki's giggle turned into a full-fledged laugh.

"It's not funny. I saved up for weeks to buy these shoes. And it was so humiliating. Here, Justin Maguire is waiting to invite me in and I have to kick off my smelly shoes at the door."

"Oooh, I hear Justin is pretty cute. What happened after that?"

"I managed to step in the same cow pile on my way back to the car, but I was wearing my old work shoes. I can wash them," Emily answered.

"You really went inside in your bare feet? Did you get cow crap on your pantyhose, too?"

Emily walked along beside her. "Yup. I didn't wear hose today. I was there to get him to let the Fab Five stay on the ranch, not impress him. Besides, what choice did I have?"

"Bullshit! You would've worn your scrubs and work shoes if you didn't care about impressing him."

"I was trying to be professional." Emily headed toward the break room to change into scrubs.

"Whoa! Hold the horses!" Nikki laughed. "I'm your best friend. You're all flushed. If just meeting him does that to you, how are you going to be when you are around him for a whole week if he does say yes?"

"Very careful," Emily threw over her shoulder.

*   *   *

Justin heard the kitchen door squeak, but he didn't look up until Levi entered the living room. Levi was like a second brother to him. His adoptive mother, Mavis, had been the ranch cook for years. And his father, Skip, was the ranch foreman before Levi took over the job.

Levi leaned over Justin's shoulder and pointed.

"Claire wants a bigger closet and a bathroom big enough to put in a garden tub," he said.

"Yes, I do." Claire looked down over Justin's other shoulder. A short blonde with a big heart and a sassy attitude, she'd stolen Levi's heart last November when she got stranded on the ranch during a winter storm.

"I thought that if we extend this wall out six feet"—

she pointed to an outside wall—"that should do it, and the rest of the room could be given to the kitchen for a bigger pantry. Is it doable?"

"I don't know. That will sure enough cause structural problems." Justin slid a sly wink at Levi. "This started out as a little house and it just keeps growing and growing."

"Don't tease me, Justin Maguire!" Claire shook her finger at him. "This is doable."

"Of course it is." Justin grabbed her finger. "But remember, once the foundation is laid, you can't keep changing your mind."

Her other small hand closed over his. "But you said we could knock out the closet at the end of the hall and add on later when we have a dozen kids."

Justin chuckled. "Levi, I see why you married this woman. Those big blue eyes are irresistible."

"Don't I know it." Levi slipped an arm around her waist and kissed her on the forehead.

"Hey, we got news!" Retta yelled from the front door.

Cade's arm was draped around Retta. "We had the ultrasound done and..." He smiled.

"There's going to be a little girl on the ranch at the first of summer," Retta said.

"Mama is going to be over the moon." Justin beamed.

Claire moved away from the plans and tiptoed to hug Retta. "Congratulations! Have you started thinking of names yet?"

"I want to know when we're buying her a pony," Levi said.

"Longhorn Canyon hasn't had baby girls in years," Justin said. "I'd buy her a pony for her first birthday, but I bet her daddy brings one home when she's born."

"I'm already thinking about the quilt I'll make her,"

Claire chimed in. "Maybe something in gingham with an eyelet lace border."

"That sounds adorable," Retta said as she eased down into one of the recliners.

"We had a visitor while you were gone," Justin announced.

"Who? Oh, that woman from the retirement center, right?" Cade sat down on the arm of Retta's chair.

Justin shifted his focus from the drawings to Cade. "That's right. Emily something from that Oakview Retirement Center in Bowie for elderly folks."

"You plannin' on checkin' into a nursing home?" Retta teased.

"Would you please finish our house plans before you check into the retirement place?" Levi said in mock seriousness.

Justin set his jaw. If they were teasing him this much just because a woman came to the ranch, the week she was there they'd really act up. "Y'all don't deserve to know what she wanted."

Cade laid a hand on his shoulder. "Oh, come on, brother."

Justin went on to tell them, ending with, "I told her I'd have to talk to the family before I gave her an answer."

"Why would these elderly folks want to visit a ranch?" Levi asked.

"Some of them are former ranchers or farmers and they miss the life. I thought we could hire Mavis to come out and help with the cookin', but if y'all don't think this is a good idea, then..." Part of Justin wanted them to nix the whole thing right then. The other part wanted them to vote unanimously to say yes. The downside was that Levi and Cade were so happily married that they'd immediately start playing matchmaker.

Justin could sidestep all of that for a week. At almost

thirty, he still had a few years left in him to sow lots of wild oats. He liked hitting the Rusty Spur bar on weekends and bringing a different woman home with him. If a woman even mentioned anything longer than a one-night stand, he jerked on his boots and got the hell out of Dodge.

Besides, as soon as he finished the plans for Claire and Levi's place, he intended to draw up a set for his own house. There was plenty of room in the ranch house, but a new baby would sure enough cramp his love life. Nothing would send one of his weekend women running quicker than a baby's cries through the whole house. Not that he didn't love kids—he couldn't wait to be an uncle. But Cade and Retta needed the space to be parents, and it was time for him to move out.

The cabin! He thumped a palm against his head when he thought of the little house on the back side of the ranch. *Why didn't I think of that before? It's plenty big enough for a bachelor, especially since it's so private.* It wasn't a five-star hotel, but it was livable. Claire and Levi had stayed in it for a day or two during that bad snowstorm a few months ago. And sometimes friends of the family used it for a hunting cabin. It would be perfect for him until he could get his house built.

"Are you listenin' to a word I've said?" Retta raised her voice.

"I'm sorry. I was thinking about house plans," Justin answered.

"Cade thought we could ask Mavis to help out that week, but I can manage breakfast and lunch for six extra people." She glanced over at Claire. "Could you help out with supper after you close up shop too?"

"No problem. I can even make the dessert for each evening and bring it with me," Claire said.

Justin looked at his brother and Levi. "So what do you two think?"

"I want to know what Emily looks like," Levi said.

"Tall as Retta." Justin frowned, trying to think of details to give them. "Remember Gretchen, the bartender at the Rusty Spur until last year. Well, give her brown hair, blue eyes, a curvy body, and take away about thirty years."

"Pretty, then?" Cade asked.

"Yep." Justin nodded.

"Lookin' back over the last year, you got to be one crazy cowboy to invite a woman here, even for a week," Cade said.

"Just because you fell in love with Retta and Levi did with Claire when they came to the ranch don't mean—"

Levi butted in before he could finish. "Be real careful. Fate has a way of kickin' a cowboy in the seat of the pants when they say *never*."

"All teasing aside," Cade said. "I'm for it. But we won't charge them for anything," Cade said. "We don't make the kids pay, so I wouldn't feel right making the elderly pay. I just don't want them to be disappointed in their little trip."

"Why would they be?" Levi asked.

"This is a busy season with calving going on, so we won't have much time to entertain them," Cade answered.

"Emily says that they won't need to be entertained. I imagine that they'll eat, sleep, maybe walk out to the barn to see the animals, and then come back for another nap." Justin laughed.

Chapter Two

Excitement filled the Oakview van that Monday morning as the Fab Five found seats behind Emily, who was serving as the driver. Derek, the orderly who often assisted Emily, had loaded their luggage, and Emily had given him a few final pointers for the next week's activities. So now the trip was a reality, and Emily was the only one who had reservations about spending a whole week on a ranch.

"Wagons, ho!" Otis shouted from the middle of the van.

"Wagons, my royal butt," Patsy said. "We're on tour and this is our tour bus. We're off to do shows."

"And what are you going to do?" Bess poked her sister in the arm. "You never could carry a tune, so it can't be anything musical."

"Oh, but, honey, I can dance, and I've been practicing my striptease dance. I bet Larry can figure out a way to fix me a pole so I can do my best work," Patsy shot back.

Larry's grin deepened the wrinkles. "I'll get my dollar bills ready to stuff inside your under britches, darlin'."

"Everyone buckled up?" Emily called out as she started the engine.

"Yep!" they all said in unison.

Emily put the van in reverse, popped the clutch, and spun out, leaving a skid mark on the concrete parking lot. "Then get ready for a ride. If you see flashing red lights, yell at me and I'll go faster."

"This ain't a tour van, it's a race car. When we get to the ranch, we should do some street racin' in the pasture," Sarah yelled from the back. "I love to drive fast."

"You love anything fast. Did you take your heart pills this mornin'?" Patsy said.

"Did you?" Sarah shot back. "I just have to take one to keep my ticker goin'. You have to take three, so don't be fussin' at me."

"Both of you hush and enjoy the fast ride," Bess demanded.

"You got it, darlin'." Sarah's blue eyes glittered. "I'm like fast food. Hot, cheap, and ready in a minute."

"That's like Patsy in college," Bess said.

"Oh, the sweet memories." Patsy sighed.

"Turn on the radio," Larry called out. "When I was workin' in construction, I'd play it even louder than the teenagers did. Only they liked rock music and I like country."

"That's probably why you have to wear hearin' aids," Sarah told him.

"Worth every minute of it." Larry chuckled.

"I wish we could roll down the windows and pretend we're in a convertible," Patsy said.

Emily intended to give them the best time she could. She found a country music station and turned up the volume.

Then she opened the window next to her, so some of the brisk morning air could flow into the van. Maybe when it blew Sarah's gray hair around in her face, it would make her happy.

The DJ on the radio said, "And now it's time for our five-in-a-row contest. After I play the songs, the fifth caller who has the song and the artists of all five will win two tickets to see Blake Shelton at the Win Star Casino next month."

"Remember When" started to play.

The whole bunch of them yelled out the name of the song plus, "Alan Jackson."

"If one of you win, who are you takin' with you to the concert?" Emily asked.

"Ah, honey, we won't win because we ain't goin' to call in. If we all can't go, then ain't none of us interested," Otis said.

"Besides if we want to go see a concert, then we'll play a game of poker and the one with the most money at the end will have to pay for all five tickets," Patsy said.

That song ended and "Marry Me" by Thomas Rhett started. They yelled out the artist and title before the first words were sung.

"I know this one by heart. Y'all sing with me," Larry said.

They sang off-key and out of tune at the top of their lungs, not only with that one but also with every song that was played. By the time the five songs ended they were in Sunset, and a few minutes later she turned down the lane onto the ranch.

Otis unbuckled his seat belt and made his way to the seat right behind Emily. He stuck his face as close to the open window as possible and inhaled deeply. "I'm going home, darlin'. For a whole week, I'm going to be on a ranch. Thank you so much for gettin' this all arranged for us."

"Are we there yet?" Patsy hollered.

"Three minutes and I'll be parked in front of the bunkhouses," Emily yelled over the top of Conway Twitty singing "Lay Me Down."

"If I was thirty years younger, I'd get one of the cowboys on this ranch to lay me down." Patsy giggled.

"Honey, you'd still be old if you was forty years younger," Bess told her.

"What about you, Emily? Would you let a ranchin' cowboy whisper pretty love words to you like Conway is sayin'?" Patsy asked.

"Never," Emily answered as she brought the van to a stop in front of the bunkhouse with GIRLS written on a swinging sign between two porch posts. Strange that she hadn't noticed that before. "We'll unload the ladies here and then move on down to get the boys' stuff out of the vehicle."

When Justin had called to tell her that the family had decided to let her residents have the bunkhouses for the week, she'd asked several questions. Bedding and towels were provided. There would be an assortment of snacks and drinks ready for the guests, but their meals would be shared with the family in the big ranch house. And it had been decided that there would be no charge, which was very generous of the Maguires.

Justin had said that he'd leave the bunkhouses open, so she wasn't expecting him to be there when they arrived. Yet there he was, leaning on the porch post like a cowboy in a whiskey commercial—dark cowboy hat settled just right on his head, tight jeans hugging his butt and thighs, and work boots that showed enough wear to prove he was a real cowboy and not one of those Saturday night wannabes. He swaggered from the porch to the van, opened the door, and poked his head inside.

"Welcome to the Longhorn Canyon ranch. I'm Justin Maguire and you'll meet the rest of the family at dinner. That's the noon meal here on the ranch. Supper is in the evening." He smiled. "We hope y'all have a good time while you are here and enjoy the week."

Suddenly Emily's jacket was too warm. She wished she had one of those church fans with a funeral home advertisement on one side and a picture of Jesus on the other. But right then she couldn't even get a cool breeze to flow through the open window.

"Proud to meet you, son," Otis said. "I'm an old rancher who is right happy to get to feel like he's going home for a week. And if you need an extra set of hands for anything, you just say the word, and I'll be more'n happy to help out. I got a bum knee but that don't mean I can't throw hay out to the cattle."

"Thank you," Justin said. "I might just do that."

Emily brushed against his side when she stood up and that heated up the van even more. "Let me introduce the rest of the Fab Five." She pointed at each one as she called out their names. "Patsy, Bess, Sarah, and Larry."

Each of them held up a hand or waved at him.

"Whew! Darlin' are you married?" Patsy smiled as she slid out of her seat with Bess right behind her.

Bess winked at him. "Strong as you are, I bet you can help us get our luggage inside."

"Yes, ma'am, Bess, I sure will give you lovely ladies a hand. And no, Miz Patsy, I'm not married." He chuckled.

"Can you two-step?" Sarah followed behind the other two ladies.

"Been known to give it a try a few times," Justin said.

"We'll see how good you are some evenin'. Me and Larry is the best at the center. You can dance with Emily and we'll see if you're as good as us," Sarah said.

"A ranch party! I love parties," Otis said. "Justin can bring the tequila."

"Wine," Sarah said.

"Jack Daniel's," Larry declared. "But first we better get ourselves settled in, hadn't we?"

"Nonalcoholic punch. Alcohol does not mix with your meds, and you know it," Emily said. "And yes, you need to get settled in."

Justin helped each of the ladies out of the van and they all flirted with him as if they were in their twenties.

Otis reached out toward Justin. "I'll take a little of that help. This old knee don't like steps after it's set a spell."

Justin gave him a hand and then turned to grab Larry's arm as he maneuvered the steps down to the ground.

Emily had helped every one of them onto the bus, but it was nice to have a big, strapping cowboy make them feel so much at home.

"Next." He smiled up at her.

"I'm able to climb stairs all on my own," she said.

"I'm sure you are, darlin', but it's not often a rough old cowboy like me gets to help a lovely lady down the steps." His grin grew bigger with every word.

After all that, she couldn't very well refuse him. She eased out of the driver's seat and put her hand in his.

"There shouldn't be any fresh cow piles inside the fence," he said.

When she reached the ground, she let go of his hand. "I hope not, but then again if you turned a few calves loose in this area, you wouldn't have to mow."

"A little on the sassy side, aren't you?"

"My family says so," she answered.

"I bet they do," he said and then turned his attention to the new guests. "If y'all will follow me, I'll show you the bunkhouse."

"Oh. My. Goodness!" Sarah squealed when she stepped inside. "This is better than a fancy hotel."

"Is the boys' place like this?" Otis asked.

"Exactly, except the girls have a big bathtub. We had a really big foreman when the bunkhouse was built and all he asked for was a tub that he could stretch out in. You boys have two bathrooms with walk-in showers. I'll bring in your things and you can show me where to put it all." Justin waved a hand to include all five of the rooms. "You ladies pick out which bedroom you want."

"We want the one with the big tub," Patsy and Bess said at the same time.

"That's usually the counselor's room," Justin said.

"They can have it. They're used to sharing a room," Emily said.

Patsy peeked into the room. "One bed. I can't sleep with Bess. She kicks and talks in her sleep."

"We could take the big bed out and put in two of the twins from the other rooms," Justin said.

"That's so sweet," Patsy all but purred.

"Thank you. While you get the baggage in, I'll strip down the beds and get them ready to change out."

"That would be great," Justin said.

"You go help him get our stuff," Patsy said. "We know how to strip down beds. Between the three of us, we'll have it all done before y'all get our things in the house."

Larry poked Otis on the arm. "Let's go on down to the boys' bunkhouse and choose our rooms. I ain't sleepin' in the same room with you. You snore like a hungry old grizzly bear."

"Fine by me," Otis said. "Justin said we got us five rooms over there. I want the one across the house from you. You can outdo me when it comes to snorin' any day of the week."

*   *   *

Justin followed Emily out to the van and caught bits and pieces of the argument as Otis and Larry crossed the lawn separating the two cabins.

"What's the dog's name? Looks like he's got some Cata-houla in him," Emily said.

"His name is Beau and you must know your dogs. He's a Catahoula and bluetick hound mix. Looks like he's about to make friends with the guys," Justin answered.

Otis and Larry eased down on the porch steps of the boys' bunkhouse and had already begun to pet the dog when Justin looked that way again.

Emily shifted some of the luggage around, explaining, "The black ones belong to the guys. All these bright colors are the ladies'. I'll take in theirs and you can have the guys." She picked up two heavy bags and started across the lawn.

Justin had hired hands who weren't that strong. He stacked up several pieces of luggage and hefted them up on his shoulder. "Got a cat named Gussie that'll probably come around soon as she realizes we have guests," he called out as he headed down to the boys' place.

"Sarah will be over the moon," Emily yelled back. "She had a cat and waited until it died before she would leave her home. And Larry talks about his pets too. So the cat and dog might get spoiled while we're here." Emily set her load inside and went back for more.

Justin set his suitcases on the guys' porch and hurried back to the van. "I'll help with those. Gussie loves people. We don't care if she stays in the bunkhouses—as long as the guests are okay with it—so the folks can spend as much time with her as they want." He took in the last three bags and set them on the living room floor.

Sarah pointed toward the three bright pink bags. "Those are mine and I'm stayin' in that room."

Justin tucked the smaller one under his arm and carried the other two into the room Sarah showed him. "There you go, ma'am."

Sarah patted him on the arm and slid one eyelid shut in a wink. "Thank you, darlin'. I could have got those, but there's somethin' about watchin' a strong cowboy haulin' something, whether it's suitcases or bags of feed—well, it does an old gal good."

"Thank you, I think." These folks were feistier than he'd expected them to be.

Sarah was almost as tall as Emily, but she was thin as a rail. She could probably use some rocks in the pockets of her baggy jeans to hold her on the ground in a north Texas wind.

"Let's get these beds changed around before we take Patsy's and Bess's stuff to their room," Emily said.

Justin hoisted the mattress off the bed in one motion and carried it to the living area. He stacked it against the wall and went back for the box springs.

"I'll help with that." Emily beat him to the room and was already wrestling with the big item.

"Stand it on the side and grab hold of the end," he told her.

They moved it to the living room and then worked together to relocate a couple of twin beds from the other bedrooms. "They don't look like twins," he whispered.

"It's the hair. Think of them with no hair and they really are alike," Emily said out of the side of her mouth.

He squinted, and sure enough, Emily was right. Bess had wound two thick braids of gray hair around her head like a crown. And Patsy's hair was dyed red and kinked up all over her head, reminding him of steel wool pads used for scrubbing. Both women were short and stocky and had the lightest blue eyes Justin had ever seen, and if it wasn't for their hair, they would look identical.

"Where were you when I was thirty?" Patsy teased.

"Good God, sister," Bess scolded. "He wasn't even born when you were thirty. You're old enough to be his grandmother."

Patsy waggled her finger at Bess. "But I'm not too old to wish I was young again, so don't fuss at me."

Once the beds were changed out, the sisters took charge, putting sheets on them and then unpacking their things.

"And now, we should go check on the guys, right?" Justin asked.

"Right," Emily agreed.

She was downright cute in jeans that hugged all those curves and with her dark brown hair pulled back into a ponytail. She looked more comfortable and more at ease too than when she'd been dressed up on her first visit.

"That's a lively bunch of ladies back there," he said as they made their way to the next building.

"That could be the understatement of the century," Emily said.

"You sure get along with them good. Is there anything else in the van we need to take?" he asked.

"The Fab Five are my favorites at the center. Actually, they're more like family than residents, and we've got everything taken in now. Should I move the van or is it okay to leave it there?"

"It's fine right where it is," he answered. "Did you give them that Fab Five name?"

"Not me." She shook her head. "They were already known as that when I came to work there five years ago. When I asked if my predecessor had tagged them with it, Otis said that they'd come up with it on their own. They're best friends and are always in and out of each other's places."

He set the luggage on the porch and opened the door for her. "I hope they don't get too bored out here in the country."

"Those five?" Emily laughed. "Bored is not in their vocabulary. They're always into something."

"Hey, did you get the old hens situated?" Otis looked up from the table where he and Larry had a card game already going.

"We did," Emily said. "Y'all got rooms picked out?"

"Yep, and we hauled the suitcases in from the porch so we get to rest a few minutes," Larry said. "I hope it's all right that we let the dog in. He's curled up beside my bed. I think he's going to like me the best."

"It's fine. His name is Beau," Justin said.

"I heard you tellin' Emily that, and it's a fine name. But he likes me better than Larry. He's just sleepin' in there by Larry's bed for now. Tonight, he's going to spend the night in my room. I understand ranchin' dogs more than Larry does."

Otis and Larry were complete opposites, and reminded Justin of that old cartoon strip "Mutt and Jeff." One was tall and lanky. The other so stocky that a class five tornado couldn't budge him.

Larry raised a bushy gray eyebrow. "Beau. Strange name for a dog."

"Named after a Texas Longhorn football player," Justin said.

"Well, then, I'd say it's a fine name to give the feller. I'm glad he gets to come inside with us. I missed my ranchin' dogs when I had to give up the place," Otis said.

"I had a dog too. He was a bluetick hound, named George after George Jones," Larry said. "And my cat was named Dolly after Miz Parton. Are we on our own until time to eat? Me and Otis want to go out to the barn soon as we finish this card game. We need a nice long walk."

"I'll drive you out there," Emily said.

"No, we really want to walk," Larry told her. "Don't worry. We'll take it slow and watch for gopher holes. I ain't wantin' no hip surgery at my age, and Otis's knee ain't goin' to let him go too fast."

"Promise?" Emily asked and went on before they could answer. "Are your cell phones charged in case you need to call me?"

"Yes, mama," Otis teased.

"You better be careful," Larry said. "She's liable to treat you like a son if you call her mama."

Emily raised both eyebrows. "You might do well to listen to him."

"Okay, okay, get your coat back on, old man. I saw the barn when we was going from the henhouse to this one." Otis shifted his gaze over to Justin. "What's for dinner?"

"Retta's got a pot roast in the oven. And I think I saw a couple of pecan pies on the cabinet," Justin answered.

"In that case, I'll be sure I'm washed up and have my hair all combed pretty by noon. And I'll see to it that Larry has his half a dozen hairs in place," Otis teased. "Man, this is wonderful. Thank you for letting us come to your ranch, Mr. Maguire."

Justin shook his head. "I'm just plain old Justin. Mr. Maguire is my dad. You'll meet him and my mama at dinner today. They don't live here permanently, but they've come for a long visit."

"That'll be real nice," Larry said and then turned to Otis. "Think we ought to stop by and see if them women want to go with us?"

"Hell, no! They're still busy lining up all their makeup shit and perfumes on their dressers." Otis laughed. "Let's take Beau with us instead."

"And then we'll brag about it at dinner." Larry whistled, and Beau came out of the bedroom, tail wagging and ready to go.

"Sarah's goin' to be mad that we got a dog and she didn't." Otis chuckled as the two of them donned their coats and left, with Justin and Emily right behind them.

They stopped on the porch and Emily watched the guys for a few minutes. "I'd feel horrible if one of them fell."

"You can't put them in a cage," Justin said.

"I guess not." She sighed.

Justin was used to barhopping on the weekends, doing some two-steppin', some beer drinking, and getting lucky most of the time. He hadn't met many women that he couldn't charm right into bed with him and talk them into making breakfast for him the next morning. But suddenly, he didn't have anything to say and the silence was more than a little awkward.

What was the matter with him? He was never without words when it came to talking to a woman.

"So what now?" he finally asked.

"Well, the ladies are unpacking and getting all dolled up

for dinner. You know where the guys are. I'm not needed here right now. Think whoever is in the kitchen could use some help?" she asked.

"That would be Retta, my sister-in-law, and my mother, Gloria. They've probably got things under control, but I'd like for you to meet them."

"I'd like that."

They stepped off the porch at the same time. "So how are the house plans coming along?"

Justin didn't even have to shorten his stride so that she could keep up with him. "Just about done. The contractor is coming the first of next week, so we need to have everything decided for sure by then."

He found himself wondering how it would be to hold her hand. As if his brain sent the message to his hand, his fingers brushed against hers. She quickly tucked her thumbs in her hip pockets. He couldn't tell if she felt that little jolt of heat or not—perhaps she didn't even realize that he had touched her.

"You should have Larry take a peek at the house plans," Emily said. "He was a contractor. It'd sure make him feel important to be asked for advice."

A sudden north wind whipped her ponytail around in her face and sent his hat blowing toward the porch. Hopalong, the cotton-tailed rabbit that came around every spring, hurried from under a dormant rosebush and sat down on the brim.

"Looks like our resident bunny made it through the winter." Justin chuckled.

"Is that a pet or something?" Emily asked.

Justin bent down and rubbed the rabbit's ears. "He's one of Levi's strays. He came up here a few years ago with a broken foot. Levi nursed him back to health and then turned him loose. He usually brings spring with him when he comes back each year. You can pet him if you want. He don't bite."

Emily sat down on the porch step, and Hopalong made his way up to sit beside her. She rubbed the spot between his ears, and the rabbit laid his head over on her leg. "He's so tame."

Justin sat down beside her. "Levi has a way with animals. Beau, Gussie, Hopalong, all came to us broken, and he made them whole again. Right along with Little Bit, the donkey, and Hard Times, the turtle."

"Is Levi another brother?"

"Not by blood, but as you girls say, by the heart. He's the foreman of the ranch. He and his wife, Claire, are the couple that I'm designing the house for," Justin explained.

The bunny hopped under the rosebush, and Emily rose to her feet. "It takes me a while to get names straight. I'm better after I meet the folks."

"Well, it won't be hard to keep Retta and my mama straight. Retta is tall and Mama is a little short woman." Justin ushered her into the house, through the foyer and back to the kitchen. "This place sure smells good. I brought Emily to meet y'all. Emily, this is Retta Maguire and this is my mother, Gloria."

"It's a pleasure to meet you." Retta smiled.

"Yes, it is," Gloria said. "Son, we really should be goin'. The Cattlemen's Association meeting is at ten o'clock."

"Yes, ma'am. See y'all at dinner." He smiled at Emily as he and his mother disappeared out the back door, leaving her alone with Retta.

*   *   *

"When is the baby due?" Emily asked when they were gone.

"End of May or first of June, but the doctor says that she's going to be a big girl. Cade is six four, and I'm sure no petite, fragile little rose," Retta answered.

As tall as Emily but not nearly as curvy, Retta had pretty brown eyes and hair that probably had a lot of chestnut in it when she was in the sun.

"I hear you on that note," Emily said. "I never was a tiny girl either. If you'll tell me what to do, I'll be glad to lend a hand."

"Can you make a good batch of hot rolls?"

"I can make them. I'll let y'all decide if they're good or not," Emily said.

"Do any of our new guests have diet restrictions?"

"Their motto is that they'll eat what they want and die when they're supposed to. They've all got some issues, but hey, they're all past seventy. Bess is borderline diabetic, but she takes a pill a day and is careful about her sugar. She wouldn't want anyone to go to special trouble, though," Emily answered.

"So why are they in a nursing home if they're in that good of health?" Retta asked.

"They aren't actually in the nursing home," Emily explained. "They call the wing they live in independent living. If and when they get to where they need more help they'll move into the assisted living and then later into the nursing home or hospice wing."

"Why aren't they living in homes of their own?" Retta asked.

"Because they don't have family, and they were lonely. Show me where the pantry is, and I'll get that bread started."

"I can relate to that business of not having a lot of family." Retta opened a door into a huge room lined with shelves and food. "But I sure got adopted into a big, loving bunch when I married Cade, and I love it. How about you? Got siblings?"

"Twin brothers who are a year younger than me, and an older brother who is four years older. Then I have enough cousins to fill a third world country." Emily picked up the flour bin and a container that was marked YEAST. "When they all come in for Thanksgiving it's a zoo. My grandmother still has it at her place, and there's usually over a hundred people there."

"For real?" Retta gasped. "How do you seat them all?"

"Out in the barn. It's still set up for the winter cattle sale party so there's plenty of tables and chairs. Granny does the hams and turkeys and everyone brings the sides and desserts." Emily opened two cabinet doors before she found a big mixing bowl.

"That sounds amazing." Retta put the teakettle on a burner. "I'm craving hot chocolate. Want me to make one for you?"

"That'd be wonderful, thank you."

If Retta had ever had that much family all gathered around her, trying to fix her up with the nearest bachelor or tell her what to pursue in college, or that she should buy a truck instead of a car, she would have changed her comment from *amazing* to *smothering* in an instant.

Chapter Three

Well, what did you think of Emily?" Gloria asked that evening when she and Justin were alone in the living room.

"What did you think of her, Mama?" Justin fired right back.

"She's good with those old folks," Gloria said.

"Do I hear a but?"

"Of course not." Gloria's answer didn't convince him. "Walk with me out to the trailer. I'll make us a cup of coffee."

"I'm way too full from that supper to drink a cup of coffee. I need to go visit with Larry about these house plans for Levi and Claire. I'll walk you out there, but I'm not going inside."

"Get my coat for me. I'm going to wrap up two pieces of the leftover pie for your dad's bedtime snack," Gloria said.

"Yes, ma'am." Justin followed her to the kitchen and

went on through to the utility room for both their coats. His mother had always been independent as hell and spoke her mind without a second thought about how it might sound. She'd never been clingy, so why had she had a personality change that day? Did the older folks being underfoot during meals make her realize that she wasn't far from their age?

"You never did answer me about Emily," Gloria said on the way across the backyard to where the RV was parked.

"She reminds me a little of you," Justin answered.

"Oh?" Gloria turned around at the door.

"Outspoken and funny. The way the old folks banter with her is downright entertaining." He chuckled.

"And her looks?" Gloria asked.

"Beautiful woman," Justin said. "See you at breakfast. North wind is pickin' up. You and Dad stay warm."

"Good night, son," Gloria said as she slipped in the RV.

Justin tucked the house plans into his coat and buttoned it. With his mind on the last details of the house, he started toward the guys' bunkhouse. Getting Larry's opinion wasn't just to make him feel good. Justin really wanted to talk to him about a few of the finer points.

"Well, good evening." Emily's voice startled him.

He whipped around to find her sitting back in the shadows on the porch of the ladies' bunkhouse. Light flowing from the window lit up half her face, leaving the other part in darkness. Had he been an artist instead of a draftsman, he would have asked her to pose for him, just like that. The picture would be one of those immortals that lived on for decades.

"Evenin' to you. It's pretty cold to be sittin' outside," he said.

"Probably, but I like the sounds and the smell of the

night," she answered. "It's different on a ranch than it is in the city, even a small one like Bowie. What are you doin' out this evening?"

"I was just going down to talk to Larry about those house plans. Sounds pretty quiet around here. Are the ladies already asleep?"

"They're all down at the boys' place. Said they were going to play cards and didn't invite me, so I'm trying to give them their space. Want something to drink? They keep a pot of coffee going. Patsy is addicted to it."

Justin shook his head. "Naw, I don't usually drink it after supper. Can't sleep if I do. See you at breakfast."

"Reckon Retta could use some help? Or how about you? Need someone to do more chores with y'all? I'm an early riser," she said.

"I don't imagine that she or Mama would turn down help, but if they do, we sure don't. Things start hoppin' around six o'clock," he answered. "You always been one to get up and around early?"

If Retta and his mother didn't want her in the kitchen, he'd sure take her with him to help feed. After the way she'd handled those suitcases that morning, he didn't have a doubt that she could take care of fifty-pound bags of feed with no trouble.

"Oh, yeah. My older brother is an old bear until he gets at least two cups of coffee, but my younger ones and I are bright eyed and bushy tailed, as the old saying goes. I'll be up at the kitchen at six and y'all can put me wherever you want. The Fab Five will show up for breakfast at seven, right?"

He sat down on the porch step. "Seven is breakfast time, but it's always on the bar, but if they're a little late it's no problem. So do your brothers live in Bowie?"

"No, they're still out in West Texas," she answered.

"How long have you lived in Bowie?"

"Five years. Have you always lived on the ranch?"

Five years within twenty minutes of the ranch—and he'd never seen her before. Surely he would've noticed someone that pretty if he'd run into her in the Rusty Spur on Saturday night, or even at the ice cream shop some evening.

He rose to his feet. "Born and raised right here."

"Except when you went to college?"

"Didn't go to college." For the first time, it made him uncomfortable to admit that. "Levi and I graduated one Friday night and the next Monday we went on a full-time payroll right here on the ranch. It's all either of us ever wanted to do."

"But you're a draftsman," she said.

He shrugged. "I had a couple of classes in high school. It's more like a hobby. I've designed a couple of barns, but this is my first house. They'd have to fit me with a straitjacket if I had to sit in an office all day long."

Emily shivered and pushed up out of the rocking chair. "Me too. I like to be out or at least doing something. I'm not a paperwork person. The night wind is getting colder. Want to come inside?"

"Better go on and talk to Larry. Want to go with me?"

"I probably should check on them. They've been gone a couple of hours now." She made her way down the three porch steps and started that way.

He walked along beside her. "So do you live at the retirement center?"

"No, it's an eight-to-five job," she answered.

"But you do live in Bowie, right?"

She nodded. "Yep. Got a little garage apartment that's real private. It works well for one person."

"Pets?" he asked when Beau greeted them from the other bunkhouse porch.

"Nope. I like cats and dogs but…" It was her turn to shrug. He knocked on the door. "Pets need room, right?"

"And lots of care," she answered.

"Come on in and join us," Otis yelled out.

Justin opened the door and let Emily go in before him. His focus was on the way her waist cinched in from those well-rounded hips, and he didn't realize that she'd stopped walking until he ran into her backside.

"Sweet Jesus!" She gasped.

Sarah giggled. "I don't think Jesus would want to play strip poker with us, but y'all are welcome."

Justin peeked over Emily's shoulder. Like watching a car wreck, he couldn't take his eyes off the sight before him. Patsy was down to white cotton panties and a bra; Sarah still wore a shirt and her underwear; Otis was wearing red satin boxers, and Larry had on tighty-whities. Evidently Bess was winning because other than being barefoot, she was fully dressed.

"What in the hell…" Emily blurted out.

"Don't be a prissy butt," Bess said.

"We play all the time. We got rules, and they say that we don't take off our underwear," Patsy said. "If we was younger we might, but it's just downright depressin' how everything hangs when you get to be our age."

"It don't raise our blood pressure, and it don't hurt my hip or Otis's knee," Larry put in his opinion.

Emily turned around so quick that she had to throw up her hands to keep from falling. They flattened out right on Justin's chest and he put his arms around her to maintain his own balance.

"We're all over twenty-one," Otis said. "And, Justin, if

you'll pick up a bottle of tequila next time you are in town, I'll pay you double for it. We want to play with shots instead of money while we're here."

"I'm going to win that game. I can hold my liquor better than any of you," Sarah said.

"In your dreams," Patsy told her.

*   *   *

Emily was so embarrassed that an ice water bath wouldn't take the crimson out of her cheeks. She dropped her hands and raced outside with Justin right behind her. She expected him to tell her that if she couldn't control her residents better than this, then they'd better just go on back to the center.

Justin chuckled. "Lord, I hope I'm that ornery when I'm their age. They're a hoot."

"I had no..." she started.

"Hey, don't worry about it. Like Larry said, all of them are of age, so it's their business what they do. I thought all they'd want to do is sleep and eat and maybe pet the dog. Boy was I wrong."

"I need a drink," she muttered.

"What kind and how much? Come up to the house with me, and I'll pour us both up a shot of something strong. We deserve it after that, and don't go all bossy mama on them. They're adults, and they do this all the time at the center," Justin said.

"See you at breakfast." She went inside the bunkhouse and slid down the back of the door. She blinked several times, but she couldn't unsee what her eyes had taken in. She shouldn't have been so rude to Justin and left him standing on the porch after he'd been so sweet to offer her a drink, but she couldn't look at him without blushing.

A soft giggle escaped and quickly turned into full-fledged laughter. Justin was right—she wanted to be that full of life when she was in her seventies. She looked down at her double-D's and laughed even harder. "When gravity gets you, girls, I certainly won't be losin' my bra in a game of poker with the boys, either."

She finally rose to her feet, removed her jacket on the way across the floor, and tossed it on her bed. She'd barely gotten turned around when she heard a soft knock on the door.

"Come on in," she called out, expecting to see one of the ladies returning for another piece of clothing from their stash. She just hoped whoever it was had the good sense to put on a coat and wasn't out wearing nothing but her underwear in the cold night air.

"Everyone decent?" Justin's deep drawl preceded him into the room.

"Yes," Emily said. "Did you reconsider and decide to send us all packin' tonight?"

"Not one bit. You said you needed a drink. I didn't know if you were a wine or whiskey girl, so I brought both." He kicked the door shut with the heel of his boot and held up two bottles.

"Wine, please. I don't even care what kind it is." She answered at the same time a big yellow cat jumped into her lap. "I owe you an apology. I didn't mean to be rude, but I was blushing, and I didn't want you to see my red face."

"Apology accepted, but I have a confession. It took several splashes of cold water to cool down my face. I can't remember the last time I blushed." He chuckled.

"Me, either." Gussie sniffed at the wine bottle.

"Does she drink?" Emily asked.

"No, but she's never met a stranger." Justin fished two

stemmed glasses from his pockets and set them on the coffee table before removing his coat and tossing it over the back of a recliner.

He poured two glasses and handed her one.

"Cowboys don't drink wine," she said.

He took a sip and sat down in the soft leather recliner facing the sofa. "This cowboy happens to like blackberry wine."

Emily had never had that flavor, so she barely tasted it on the first sip, and then took a bigger gulp. "This is some good stuff. I could get used to this in a hurry."

She sat down in the other recliner and glanced at the full bottle of Jack Daniel's sitting beside the wine. "That could be a disaster if the ladies found it."

"Yep, that's why we'll either hide it or I'll take it back with me when I leave," he told her. "Do they get to drink at the center?"

"No, sir! They all take meds that liquor would interfere with, but now I'm wondering just what they buy when they go to the mall or out shopping for food," she said.

He finished off his wine and poured more.

Emily tossed back what was left of hers and held her glass out to him. "Just half as much as last time."

"Can't hold your liquor?" Justin teased.

"Honey, in case you didn't notice, I'm a big girl, and I come from good Irish stock. I could drink a cowboy like you under the table," she said.

"You'll have to prove that sometime." He shared the remainder of the bottle between the two of them.

"Not while the Fab Five are around or they'll want to indulge right along with us." She smiled.

Justin's grin looked downright mischievous. "Then after the week is over, we'll meet up and see if you can outdo me.

I'll bring the liquor. You bring a basket of food, and we'll have us a picnic."

"Where's this contest going to be held?"

"Out in our barn. In a motel room. Right here in this bunkhouse. You call the place and bring a basket of fried chicken, and we'll just see if your brag holds true. You name the place, and I'll be there," he said.

She imagined him all stretched out on a king-size bed in a motel room, his muscular body all tangled up in the sheets.

You've only known him one day. Be careful. Nikki's voice popped into her head.

I can handle him, she argued with her best friend.

"You're on. In this bunkhouse the weekend after the Fab Five goes back to the center. I'll meet you here with the fried chicken at eight o'clock on Sunday night." The minute the words were out of her mouth, she wanted to shove them back inside. But she'd never been able to back down from a challenge.

Comes from having three brothers. Now it was her mother's voice talking to her.

"I'll be waiting with the booze," he said.

"Listen," she whispered. "I hear them coming back."

Justin was on his feet in a flash and had his coat on before she could blink. He tucked the empty wine bottle in one pocket and the whiskey in the other, leaving behind the two wineglasses. "You might want to hide those."

She nodded and carried them to the kitchen. He left by the back door just as the ladies opened the front one. She downed what was left in her glass and quickly rinsed it. She started to pour out the rest of what Justin had left, but she'd always thought it was a sin to waste good wine, so she turned it up and drank that too.

By the time the ladies had removed their coats, Emily

had stashed the glasses behind the cereal boxes in the cabinet.

"Are we in trouble?" Patsy giggled.

"Should you be?" Emily asked.

"A cat!" Sarah squealed. "What's her name? She's goin' to have a litter, isn't she? Come here, you precious thing and let me pet you."

"Her name is Gussie, and Justin says that she can stay in the bunkhouse anytime she wants," Emily said.

"She's mine while we're here, and she gets to sleep with me." Sarah picked her up and held her close.

Bess went straight for the refrigerator and opened it. "I'm hungry. Anyone want ice cream before we turn in for the night?" She sniffed the air. "I smell fermented black-berries. Hey, if we find them, we could make some more wine."

"More?" Emily asked.

"We made a lovely concoction at Christmas in Sarah's room. We bought blackberry wine at the store. At least that's what we thought we were buying, but it turned out to be a cordial. It was right good with a little sparkly club soda in it," Patsy said.

"Good glory!" Emily gasped.

"I wish I had some of it." Sarah carried Gussie to the kitchen. "A few tablespoons would be real good on ice cream. Do you like ice cream, pretty kitty? Or are you just a plain old milk drinker?"

"How did I not see this side of y'all in five years?" Emily asked.

"We're really good at hidin' things from Mama and Daddy." Sarah grinned. "I found some chocolate syrup and whipped cream."

"Precious Memories," Patsy started singing.

"Hush," Bess scolded. "You'll make Emily blush."

"Too late for that. I'm already there," Emily said. "I'm going to take a shower. See y'all in the morning. Justin says breakfast is at seven, but it's served buffet style, so if you're a few minutes late, don't panic. I'll have all your morning meds with me. And I've put your night pills on the vanity in each of your rooms."

"Take a cold one to help in case you dream about Justin tonight," Patsy teased. "I'd like to dream about what I could do with whipped cream and chocolate and a cowboy like that."

Chapter Four

Emily awoke the next morning hoping that her charges had gotten their rebellious streak out of their blood and the rest of the week would go smoothly. She put on her coat and yelled across the bedroom, "Hey, girls, I'm going up to the ranch house to help with breakfast. When y'all get your hair and faces all fixed, come on up there."

"Will do," Sarah yelled back. "I got a text from Otis that said he and Larry are already up there. We won't be long."

Up at the big house, she wasn't sure whether to knock or walk right in. But the decision was made for her when Justin opened the door.

"C'mon in. We're all in the kitchen going over the house plans. Retta and Mama are making breakfast. Just follow me," he said. "Dad helped me with the feeding chores this morning, so that's all done."

A wave of disappointment washed over her. She'd loved the day-to-day work on the ranch. Liked the smell of early morning as she helped her dad feed, and the sounds of newborn calves bawling in the pasture. What she didn't like was being cooped up in an office all day, taking care of the paperwork on the computer. Matthew did a fine job of it, and had let it be known that he couldn't wait for Emily to get her business agriculture degree so she could take over.

The gents were all bent over the kitchen table, studying the house plans. As serious as their expressions were, no one would know that they'd been down to their boxers the night before in a game of poker. Larry's thin face was drawn down in a frown as he moved his finger over the graph paper.

"Son, you might consider making a storage closet here at the end where you have some dead space. If they decide to build on later, they can always relocate it into the new addition. And be sure to put in lots of electrical outlets. Claire will blame you if she has to run an extension cord to dry all that pretty blond hair every mornin'," Larry said.

"That's good advice." Justin nodded.

"And one other little thing. Instead of cabinets that make an ell, consider using the corner for a pantry. It's tough for a short lady to get to top shelves, and I think she'd enjoy being able to walk right into a pantry," Larry said. "Other than those small details, you've done a fine job. What are you working on next?"

"My own place," Justin answered.

"What did you say?" Cade asked.

"I've decided to move into the cabin in a couple of weeks, and then start thinkin' about plans for my house. I'd like to put it back there where the old well is."

"But..." Retta caught the last of what he said.

"That's downright crazy. You've got a home right here.

The cabin is far too rustic to live in." Gloria came in right behind her.

Justin turned his attention to his mother. "I've made up my mind."

The tension in the room went from a zero level to a ninety-nine in seconds. Emily wished the ladies would rush in right then to break it, but they didn't.

Justin took a deep breath and let it out slowly. "Y'all need your space to raise the new baby girl. Levi and Claire are stayin' at her quilt business until their place is done. And it's time for me to be out on my own too. I'm going to spoil that baby too much as it is. Y'all don't need me interfering with everything you say or do, and believe me, I will if I continue to live in the house."

"Oh, come on, son." Gloria finally smiled, but it didn't reach her eyes. "We're only going to be here a month. You'll put off moving until we leave, won't you?"

Justin shook his head. "No, I want to go pretty soon. Since you're here, you can help Retta turn my old room into the nursery."

"Only if you don't try to take over, Mama," Cade said.

"I'd never do that, but I was thinking pink walls with a princess theme," Gloria said.

Retta rolled her eyes. "I was leaning more toward yellow walls and a unicorn theme."

Glad to have something to take her mind off the still rising tension, Emily worked her phone from her hip pocket to find a text from Tag: *Where the hell are you?*

She quickly typed: *At work.*

Another message appeared instantly: *Called work. You're not there.*

She sighed as she wrote: *On a field trip. Will call home later tonight.*

The room had gone quiet, and everyone was staring at her. "Sorry about that. Family."

"We was afraid there was something wrong with the girls," Larry said.

Otis let out a long breath in a whoosh. "They're all right, aren't they?"

"I'm sure they are," Emily said. "I think I hear them on the porch, now."

"Are you all right?" Retta whispered as she pulled Emily around to the other side of the bar with her.

"Oh, yeah." Emily lowered her voice. "Family—the other *F* word."

Retta nodded seriously. "You got that right. Too little is sad. Too much is horrible."

"Don't let Gloria intimidate you when it comes to the nursery," Emily said.

"Oh, honey, that isn't goin' to happen," Retta told her.

"Hey, darlin'." Cade joined them. "Want me to set the table?"

"Yes. I thought we'd do buffet, but I've changed my mind," she answered.

"We're here," Patsy called out as she and the other two women entered the house.

Bess went right to the table. "We'll set the table if that big handsome husband of yours will bring the plates and silverware to the dining room. We miss being able to help out. This will be like we belong here rather than bein' visitors. My mama used to say that you really get to know someone when you work with them."

"Want me to make the pancakes?" Justin asked.

"What can I do?" Emily asked.

"Help Justin with the pancakes," Retta answered.

Gloria moved around the counter. "I'll help him with

that. You can put out the jams and jellies and butter, Emily."

Emily headed to the refrigerator. "I'm on it."

Retta patted Cade on the shoulder as he carried the plates into the dining room. "I won't even argue, and thank you all."

"You've got to put those plates closer to the edge or Otis will never reach his food," Sarah said, fussing at Patsy.

"Are they always like this?" Retta whispered to Emily.

"Sometimes it's worse," Emily said out of the side of her mouth.

"Justin told me this mornin' about their card game. God, I hope I'm that full of life when I'm their age," Retta said.

"I'd just like to be able to keep up with them at the age I am now," Emily said.

When Justin and Gloria had filled a platter full of pancakes, Emily carried it to the table and set it on one end. All of the Fab Five were beaming. Then it dawned on her. Food at the center was always served buffet style. Each resident got a plate, filled it with whatever they wanted, and either carried it to their table or someone did it for them.

Sitting around a table with food that would be passed was like going back in time for them. It was reminiscent of their childhood days on the ranch or even in their homes. No wonder they all looked like cats with canary feathers sticking out of the corners of their mouths.

"We were wondering," Otis said as he put two biscuits on his plate and passed them on to Larry. "If me and Larry might take the four-wheelers out for a little spin this morning? We both used them before so we know how to drive 'em."

"Don't see why not, but it's not my call. You need to ask the boss lady here." Justin moved his knee over to touch hers under the table.

There were definite sparks, but she chose to ignore them. "Be careful and keep your phones with you," she said.

"Yes, Miz Emily." Larry nodded and pointed toward the pictures hanging on the dining room walls. "Did you do all these, Justin?"

"Not me. I can draw a straight line with the help of a ruler, but Benjy drew those for us. He was one of the kids who came for our summer camp until this last year," Justin answered.

"And then his grandmother died, and there was no one to take him, so Levi's parents adopted him. Y'all will meet him this weekend. He works for us on Saturdays," Cade said.

"He's a damn fine artist," Sarah said. "How old is he?"

"Twelve," Justin told them.

Emily listened to the conversation with one ear as she studied the framed drawings on the walls.

Justin's knee touched hers again. "Pretty good, huh?"

"Better than that. He captures their happiness," she said, softly. "Does he want to pursue art?"

"It's a hobby. He wants to be a rancher," Justin answered.

"Too bad," Emily muttered.

"Why's that?" Justin frowned.

"He's really good. He could go far with his work," she answered.

"Probably so, but his heart is in ranching. Has been since he first came to stay with us for part of the summer. In a few weeks, he'll be showing a sheep at the Montague County Livestock Show, and he's already sketched it for Mavis and Skip, his new parents," Justin said.

"Oh, wow," Otis exclaimed. "I would love to go to a livestock show. Haven't been in years and years."

"I'll be glad to take you if it's okay with the center," Justin said.

"Me too?" Larry asked.

"If y'all are going, then we want to go too," Sarah said. "I remember going to those events when I was teaching school. Several of my kids showed animals."

"Where'd you teach?" Justin asked.

"Petrolia, up near the Red River," she answered.

"I know some guys who graduated from there, and we go to a cattle sale up there in the fall," Cade said.

Sarah put two pancakes on her plate. "Small world."

"Well? Can we all go to the livestock show?" Patsy asked.

Emily's brothers all showed cattle in the livestock show and had a wall full of trophies and medals to show for it, plus a pretty hefty bank account from the premium sales.

"I'll get it on the calendar when we get back," Emily said. "One day, right?"

"Actually, it's one full day of showing and then the next night there's the premium show," Justin said.

"Maybe the boys will let me help shear and powder the sheep." Otis's eyes went all dreamy. "Or wash down the cattle."

"Or maybe they'll let you sit in the announcer's box, since you had one of the biggest spreads in the state before you retired," Cade said.

Otis raised an eyebrow. "How'd you know that?"

"Anyone who's a rancher in this area would recognize the name Otis Green." Justin chuckled.

Emily was glad that her last name, Baker, didn't bring up any thoughts of the ranch she'd grown up on. Passed down on her mother's side of the family, it was known as the Big Sky Ranch and ran a Rocking B brand. It was a family joke that Emily's grandmother told her mother she couldn't date anyone who didn't have a last name beginning with *B*. And then her mother, Anne Bennington, married a neighboring rancher, Frank Baker. They'd already begun to tease Emily about marrying a cowboy with a *B* name when she was in high school.

The whole bunch of them were deep in conversation—the guys were discussing the aspects of a good steer or sheep from a bad one, and the ladies were talking about a shopping trip to the mall to buy new boots for the event.

Justin turned to face her. "So are you buying new boots too?"

"Not me. My sneakers will do just fine."

"Ever worn boots?" Justin asked. "Maybe for a little two-steppin'. You grew up in ranchin' country. Surely you did some dancin' at your granny's barn for the sale parties."

"I can dance in shoes as well as boots." It wasn't a lie, but it was skirting the truth. She'd left all but one pair of her cowboy boots in the closet when she went to college.

*   *   *

Emily couldn't remember the last time that she had time to read a book. Monday through Friday she was usually working. Saturday was for cleaning her apartment. After church on Sunday the rest of the day was set aside for laundry and grocery shopping. But that afternoon she picked up the romance novel she'd been trying to finish for a month and stretched out on her bed to read. The guys were off playing around on four-wheelers and the ladies had taken a walk out to the barn to see a mini-ature donkey.

She fell asleep with the book in her hands and awoke with a jerk when she heard her phone ringing.

"Hello." She answered on the fifth ring.

"We need help!" Otis said frantically. "She's down and I tried to help her. We're out here close to an old cabin. Come quick."

Otis hung up before she could get any other information.

Emily's heart was pounding in her ears as she threw the book to the side and raced to the house. No one was there and she didn't have Justin's number to even ask how far it was to the old cabin or how to get there. So she jogged out to the van and called Otis back as she drove past the first barn.

Patsy answered the phone in a panic. "Are you on the way?"

"Yes, I am. What's going on? Give me some directions."

"Follow the trail. It's all the way to the back of the ranch, and the trail ends right here. You'll see us. It's maybe five minutes. Got to go. Otis is yellin' at me."

Again, the phone went quiet. Emily saw the path before her and pushed down on the gas pedal a little harder. She hadn't even taken time to put on a jacket, but she was so worried she didn't even feel the chill in the air. Was it Sarah or Bess who was hurt and how in the hell did they get that far back on the ranch anyway?

She saw the two four-wheelers and braked hard not far behind them. Once she bailed out of the van, she could see them all on the ground, either sitting or on all fours. What if Sarah or Bess had had a heart attack? Or what if Otis had fallen in a gopher hole and busted up his knee, or Larry's cranky hip had finally given out? She could scarcely breathe as she parked and ran toward them without even thinking about where she was stepping or the brambles tearing at the legs of her jeans.

"What's happened?" she asked.

They all moved back a little and Otis pointed at a heifer

that was down. "She's goin' to lose that calf if someone with long arms and know-how don't go in there and pull it out. She's too tired to push anymore. I can walk you through it, but…"

Emily was already rolling up her sleeves as she plopped down on the ground behind the cow. "What can you tell me?"

"It's breach and my arm isn't long enough to turn it around," Otis said. "You have to…"

"I know how to pull a calf, but you could have told me that a heifer was down." Emily shoved her long arm into the animal and found the calf. "Now come on, darlin', and work with me." She talked to the heifer as she got a firm grip on the calf and tried to turn it. Even with her strength, the calf slipped out of her hands, and she had to reach for it again. Another contraction created even more pressure on her arm, but she held on and maneuvered the baby around to the right position. "Now, sweetheart, give me a couple of real good pushes, and we'll get this birthing done."

"How'd you know how to do that?" Otis asked.

"It takes a butt load of power to turn a calf," Sarah whispered.

"Save your applause," Emily said, panting as she held on to the calf's front feet and tugged with the next contraction. "That's good. One or two more and we'll be done with the hard part. Don't give up on me now," she crooned to the heifer.

Two hooves came out and then the calf's head. Then a big bawl from the heifer and the shoulders emerged. After that it was just a whoosh, and the baby was lying at her feet. Birthing gunk covered her legs, her arms, and her shoes, but by golly there was a live baby. She hadn't pulled a calf since she left the ranch, but she hadn't lost her touch, and there was a fair amount of pride in her as she looked down at the new baby.

She wasn't even aware that Justin had joined them until he stepped in with an old towel and swabbed out the calf's mouth. It let out a whimper and its mama was instantly on her feet, licking it and taking over the responsibilities. "You did an amazing job. Pulling a calf takes a lot of power and sometimes even a rope. You did good."

"You talkin' to me or that heifer?" Emily asked.

Justin tossed a clean towel toward her. "I'm talkin' to you. We'd have lost the cow and calf both if you hadn't been here."

"We found her," Otis piped up. "We was ridin' the four-wheelers and saw her. We didn't know how to get a hold of you, Justin, so we called Emily."

She wiped her arm as clean as possible and pulled her shirt sleeve down. Then she turned toward the Five and asked, "Did you ladies walk all the way out here?"

"Wow, where'd you learn to do that?" Patsy asked, evidently hiding something.

"I helped out a couple of times on my grandmother's ranch," Emily answered.

Otis grinned. "You're a natural. Justin should hire you to work for him."

"No!" Patsy gasped. "We need her at the center."

"If she moves out here, I'm comin' with her. I bet y'all wouldn't charge as much to rent the bunkhouses as they do at that place anyway, and this is a lot better," Sarah declared.

"I'm not going anywhere," Emily said. "I thought you were going to see the little donkey."

"We did, and we petted him, and I even kissed him on the

nose," Bess said. "But then Otis and Larry got on the four-wheelers, and we wanted a ride. So we all came together and we found the cow and called you."

"How?" Justin asked.

"Look at that big old boy. He could be a breeder for you, Justin." Otis sidestepped the question.

"You guys take the four-wheelers back to the barn. I'll take the ladies home," Emily said.

The women all hurried toward the van. The guys hopped on the four-wheelers and were gone before she could blink. The new baby wasn't on its feet yet, so Emily knelt beside Justin and started rubbing her towel over it.

"Thank you, again," Justin said. "You were amazing."

"You're welcome. Look, he's trying to stand up," Emily said.

It took two tries, but soon the little calf had its feet under it and was head butting his mama's udder to find his first meal.

Justin slung an arm around Emily's shoulders. "Nothing like this feeling."

"Fresh new life. It's pretty awesome." Emily had forgotten how wonderful it was.

"Goin' to have a sore arm tomorrow?" Justin drew her closer to him.

"Probably, but it's worth it," she whispered. "Otis is right. He's going to be a keeper. Look at those shoulders." The moment was surreal, as if she and Justin were the only two people in the universe and had just witnessed a miracle.

"Looks like it, but how do you know so much about—"

"I told you," she butted in. "I used to spend a lot of time on my grandma's ranch. Guess I'd better get these ladies back to the house."

He stood up and extended a hand. She put hers in it and he pulled her to her feet. "I should get my phone and take a picture."

He pulled his from a hip pocket. "Stoop down here beside the baby, and I'll take a selfie of the two of us with him." Justin held the phone out with his long arm.

"Send it to me so I can share it with my brother Tag. He won't believe it without a picture," she said as she headed back to the van and then turned. "How'd you know we were out here?"

"I didn't. I was going back to the cabin to make sure the water was turned on, and to see if it needed cleaning before I move in. I just happened upon all this." He caught up to her and walked beside her.

She got into the van. "See you later."

He waved at the ladies and then jogged to his truck.

"I would have puked if I'd had to do what you did," Bess said the minute Emily was settled into the driver's seat.

"Are you going to make us go back to the center?" Patsy asked before she could even start the engine.

"We saved a calf so no, but after I wash up, y'all owe me some answers." She drove to the bunkhouse without hearing another word from the ladies. When they were inside she went straight to the bathroom, stripped out of her clothing, took a shower, and washed her hair. Then she donned a knee-length terry bathrobe and went out to the living area to find them on the sofa.

"Okay, how did you all get out there on only two four-wheelers? I know y'all didn't walk that far. It's got to be more than a mile."

Two minutes ticked off the clock on the wall. Not a one of them said a word.

"Okay." Patsy finally sighed. "I'll tell you what happened, but I still think it was pretty neat the way you knew how to deliver that calf. I had no idea you ever lived on a ranch."

"You are beatin' around the bush. I'll tell it," Bess said. "It's like this. Otis and Larry had permission to ride the four-wheelers and we wanted to go too. So I got on behind Otis, and Sarah got on behind Larry."

"And I rode on the handlebars with Otis and Bess, kind of like when we were all kids. Only then it was a bicycle, and it wasn't nearly as much fun because it didn't go as fast," Patsy said. "And I pretended I was in a convertible with the wind blowin' my hair. I don't care if you make us go back to the center now that you know. It was worth it, because it was the most amazin' thing that's happened to me in ten years. I felt young again. I loved it so much that when I get bored, I'm going to shut my eyes and pretend I'm doin' it again."

Emily shivered at the thought of the four-wheeler hitting a gopher hole and sending Patsy butt over kinky red hair out into the pasture to break her fool neck. But what could she say? This might be the last time they ever got to be free and young again.

And nobody got hurt. Her grandmother's voice said softly. *Go easy on them. Getting old is a bitch.*

"I would have carried the burden with me the rest of my life if one of you got hurt. But since no one did, I'm not taking us back to the center. You have to promise me that you won't do such a fool thing again." Emily felt like she was dealing with rebellious teenagers rather than five people who were all over seventy.

"We promise," they said in unison.

"And I promise I'll hold her down and call you if she even tries it," Bess said.

Patsy bowed up to her. "I'd like to see you try. Let's go tell Otis and Larry that we get to stay. They're probably back at the boys' bunkhouse by now."

"No strip poker either!" Emily called out as they picked up their coats and headed outside.

"How about strip gin rummy?" Sarah giggled.

Emily shut her eyes and prayed that the rest of the week would go smoothly.

*   *   *

Justin took his seat at the supper table beside Emily, his mother and father seated across from him. "Y'all hear that Emily's been holdin' out on us? She pulled a calf today, so she's got some ranchin' experience."

"My grandparents have a little spread. I spent some time there until I went to college," Emily explained.

Otis put two scoops of mashed potatoes on his plate and passed them on to Sarah. "Emily was amazin'. A vet couldn't have done a better job. She knew just what to do and didn't even flinch one time."

"Yes, she was." Justin smiled at her.

"I guess this isn't your first time at that job, since you did so good," Vernon said.

"No, it's not," Emily answered.

Justin expected her to tell them a little more about visiting her grandmother's ranch, but she didn't.

"I could never do that," Gloria said. "I was more of a stay in the house and take care of the social duties and books. Like what Retta does."

What in the hell was wrong with his mother? She'd taken to Retta and Claire both from the beginning, but she was looking at Emily as if she had horns and a spiked tail.

Emily smiled at Gloria and changed the subject. "I love sitting down to a meal like this."

Very good, Justin thought. *Mama was baiting you and you sidestepped it. Do you feel the little barbs she's throwing your way?*

"Me too," Sarah said. "Y'all ever want to put in a retirement center on the farm, I bet you'd have a list a mile long of folks waitin' to get into it. I'd be number one. I'd even be willin' to double what I'm payin' to stay at that center. It ain't half as much fun as this place."

"Thank you." Justin took a biscuit and handed the basket off to Emily. There were definite vibes when their fingers touched, and he looked forward to seeing her for their drinking date in another week.

"We all thought Emily was a big city girl." Larry went back to the subject of the calf. "We just called her so she'd bring some help from the house."

"I am a city girl," Emily said.

Justin wondered just what soured her on ranching life, but her short answers said that she didn't want to talk about it. Maybe later, when she'd had a few drinks, he could get her to tell him more.

"How did all five of you get out there to begin with?" Levi asked. "We've only got a couple of four-wheelers. Did you ladies walk that whole way?"

Justin appreciated Levi changing the subject. "I was wonderin' about that myself."

Patsy dabbed her mouth with a napkin and said, "I'll tell you the whole story." She embellished it even more than she had when she told Emily. "Since that ride, I've been thinkin' that ridin' a bull would be fun. Y'all got one that we could try our hand at?"

"No, ma'am!" So many people answered at once that

Justin could've sworn the ceiling raised up a couple of inches.

"Then can we have a picnic at that old cabin tomorrow?" Sarah asked. "We'd like to spend the day exploring back there."

"That can be arranged," Justin said.

"I'll get a sandwich picnic ready," Retta said. "Gloria and I have hair appointments in the morning. Any of you ladies want to join us?"

"Thank you, but we'd rather have a picnic. We got a beauty operator that comes in on Friday every week at the center," Sarah answered.

"And you can bet your sweet little butts that I'm going with you ladies," Emily told them.

"I guess that leaves out skinny-dippin'," Larry said. "I noticed a little creek back there, but..." He shrugged.

"Good grief!" Emily sighed.

"I'll go along with y'all," Justin said.

"I was thinkin' that you and I could go to lunch after Retta and I get our hair done. We really should stop in at the fairgrounds and take a look at what's needed for the show." Gloria shot a sweet smile across the table.

"We can do that another day. Or y'all can do a walk-through at the fairgrounds and take notes. I'm going with this bunch," Justin said.

"Aha! Mama's favorite is turning her down," Cade teased.

"I don't have favorites," Gloria protested. "And if I did, today it would be Levi."

"Why's that?" Cade asked.

"Because he's not buggin' me about favorites," Gloria said. "And getting back to the picnic tomorrow. It's way too cold to even wade in Canyon Creek. We don't want y'all gettin' pneumonia."

"Been sixty years since I got to go skinny-dippin'." Patsy sighed.

Claire laughed out loud. "Y'all remind me of my grandmother and her friend Franny, who lived right beside her. They were always into something. But I don't think they ever went skinny-dippin'."

Bess pointed her fork at Claire. "Honey, you might be amazed at what they did in their young years. We didn't have all this fancy technology stuff, so we made up our own fun, and human nature ain't changed since Adam and Eve got kinky after eating that big red apple."

Justin glanced over at Emily. That pink glow in her cheeks was adorable. He could envision her, with all those luscious curves, dropping her jeans and all the rest of her clothing on the banks of Canyon Creek. Wearing nothing but a smile and maybe those cute little gold hoop earrings that she had on that evening, she'd wade out into the water and crook a finger to invite him to join her.

She turned, and her eyes locked with his. "What are you grinning about?"

"Just a picture in my head," he answered honestly. "Wouldn't you love to have had a photo of Patsy on the handlebars of that four-wheeler?"

"No, thank you."

"Oh, come on now. You could tuck it away, and when we're their age, we could see if we could reenact the whole thing," he teased.

"I reckon you'll have long forgotten about me by then," she said.

He leaned over and whispered, "I don't think so."

After the kitchen was cleaned up, Emily said good night to everyone. Levi and Claire didn't linger long before they left to go home. Retta and Cade were cuddled up together on the sofa.

Vernon yawned and looked over at Gloria. "Darlin', it's past our bedtime. We should be gettin' on out to our place. These boys have plumb wore out this old man today."

Justin had been sitting in a recliner, but he popped the footrest down and said, "I'm going out to the barn and check on Little Bit."

"I'll go with you," Gloria said.

"No, you won't. He's been walkin' out to the barn in the dark now for years, and sometimes a man needs to be alone with his thoughts," Vernon said.

"You don't tell me what to do." Gloria glared at him.

Justin caught his father's wink as he slipped out of the room and grabbed his coat. He was on his way around the house when he caught a flash of light in his peripheral vision. When he glanced that way, he could see Emily's silhouette a brief second before the door closed. She sat down in one of the two rockers, and he changed his course.

"Hey," he called out when he was a few feet away. "Want to take a walk?"

"I don't think I'd better get too far from them. After the past two days, I probably should be down at the boys' bunkhouse watching movies with them."

Justin rested his elbows on the porch railing. "They took *Quigley Down Under, Steel Magnolias,* and *The Cowboy Way.* I think they're safe for tonight. Mind if I join you for a spell?"

"Not at all." Gussie jumped up in her lap and started to purr. "Well, hello, pretty girl. Sarah's been worried about you all day. Where have you been?"

"Probably out in the barn." Justin eased down into the

other rocker and propped his feet up on the railing. "Do you ever feel like a fifth wheel?"

"Just all the time when I go home. My oldest brother is engaged, and the twins, Taggart and Hudson, are always... well, let's just say that they like to party... Tag is the rebel, bad-boy twin and Hud is the good boy, life-of-the-party twin who's usually with Tag to keep him out of too much trouble," she said.

"Here—hold my beer and watch this." Justin laughed.

"You got it." Emily nodded. "I've actually heard that too many times from my brother Tag."

Justin could sure understand her younger brothers. Most Saturday nights found him at the Rusty Spur. The majority of the time he either went home with a woman or brought her to the ranch.

"Oh, really?"

She picked up Gussie. "It's colder out here than I remembered. Want to come inside with me?"

He was on his feet in an instant and opened the door for her. "Love to. Do you like to party?" he asked. "We could go dancing at the Rusty Spur some Saturday night if you do."

She carried Gussie to the end of the sofa and eased down carefully with the cat still in her arms. "No, thank you. That's not my idea of a date."

"What is?" Justin removed his hat and coat and laid them on one of the recliners and then sat on the other one.

"Anything but a noisy bar full of drunks," she answered.

"Candlelight dinner, a movie?"

"A picnic and a long talk in front of a fireplace with a Jack and Coke in my hand." She smiled.

"That could be arranged." An instant visual of the fireplace at the old cabin flashed through his mind.

"Justin, are you asking me on a date?"

"If I did, would you accept?" he asked.

She didn't have time to answer because all three ladies rushed in the front door. Sarah was holding her jacket together and shivering. "It's damn cold out there. This gettin' old is for the birds. Circulation is bad, and my feet are freezing. Next time the guys are coming to our bunkhouse to watch a movie."

"Then we'll have to listen to Otis complain that the cold is affecting his knee and Larry fuss about his cranky old hip," Patsy said. "You just need some fat on your skinny body to protect you against the cold."

"I've got plenty of cellulites, but I'm shivering too. Oh, hello, Justin," Bess beamed when she realized he was in the room.

"Did we interrupt anything?" Sarah asked and then rushed over to the sofa to gather Gussie up into her arms. "You came home to me."

Justin rose to his feet, settled his cowboy hat onto his head just right, and then put on his coat. "I was out for a walk. I should be getting on with it. You ladies have a nice evening."

Chapter Five

Emily couldn't decide if the Fab Five looked like they'd geared up for an African safari that Wednesday morning, or if they were going to a hobo convention. Patsy had a daisy on her straw hat. The guys wore floppy canvas hats that strapped under the chin. Bess and Sarah each had a head scarf tied around their heads. The ladies carried yellow plastic tote bags. Otis and Larry each sported a camouflage backpack.

Emily lined them all up and took a picture before they climbed into the van. "Hey, what's the baggage for?"

"For whatever we discover while we're exploring today. Maybe we'll even find some arrowheads to show everyone at the center," Patsy answered.

Justin got into the van and chose a seat directly behind Emily. "Watch out for snakes. This is the time of year they like to come out of their caves and hidey-holes to get a little sun, and this is a beautiful day for that."

"If I see one, I'll scream loud enough that the whole county will hear me," Patsy told him.

"And I'll come rescue you." Justin smiled.

"She's not afraid of snakes, but if she sees a worm, she'll start hollerin' just to get you to come runnin' out to rescue her," Bess said. "If you hear me carryin' on like I'm possessed, you get your sexy little butt out to kill a spider. God, I hate them things."

Emily drove past the barn and down the same path that she had the day before, but when she got to the spot where the cow had needed help, she braked and asked, "Which way now?"

Justin pointed out the front window. "Straight ahead. Just follow the trail. It leads you right up to the cabin."

She drove a little slower around a slight curve, and there was the place. It didn't look so much like a cabin to her but more like a small house with a nice front porch. She parked, and the Five were on their feet in an instant.

"Whoa!" She held out a hand to block the door. "Has everyone got your cell phone and is it charged?"

"Yes, ma'am," they chimed in together.

"My number is in it, but have you all programmed Justin's now, too?"

Five nods.

Justin pointed out the side window. "About two city blocks that way you'll find the barbed wire fence separating this ranch from the next one. That's your first border."

"Anything past that has lions and tigers that'll tear us limb from limb, right?" Patsy giggled.

Bess shivered. "Enough of that or I'll be checkin' behind every mesquite thicket for a big mean cat."

"Might even be bears on the other side of that barbed wire," Larry teased.

"I'm meaner than lions and tigers and bears. I'll protect you ladies. I'm like Indiana Jones. What's the other borders?" Otis asked.

"Remember seeing that big twisted tree lying off to the side of the path on the way back here? That will be your boundary in that direction," Justin answered.

Larry nodded. "Old scrub oak. Bet the last windstorm took her down."

"A tornado got it a couple of years ago. Dinner will be served inside the cabin in two hours, but you can always come back anytime before then. Have fun and call us if anyone gets in trouble or needs a ride," Justin said.

The seniors filed out of the van, met outside under a big tree for a powwow that included lots of hand gesturing and decision making, and then went straight ahead on their first exploration.

Justin waited for Emily to get out of the van and whispered, "How far behind them should we stay?"

"Oh, no! Like you told me, they're adults." She threw up her palms. "They've got their cell phones. If they run naked in the woods, I don't want to know about it. Besides it's too chilly for that, isn't it?"

"It is for me, but they're tough old birds." Justin chuckled. "I'll get the sacks of food and carry them inside. Would you please hold the door for me?"

The old wooden screen door reminded her of all the times that she'd run through one just like it at her grandmother's place—and she could still hear her grandmother yelling at her for slamming it. She continued to hold it until he'd brought in the second load and then followed him inside.

"Don't slam the door." He chuckled. "Guess you never heard that."

"Oh, yes I did, like twenty times a day, along with 'stop runnin' in and out.'"

He laughed out loud. "And 'were you born in a barn?'"

"All of the above." She stopped and scanned the whole place.

A well-worn leather sofa faced a fireplace that had a brightly burning blaze in it. That meant Justin had gotten up early enough to drive out here and make things comfortable for them. A table with four mismatched chairs was between the back of the sofa and the kitchen. And to her right was a nice big king-size bed covered with a colorful patchwork quilt.

"Is that one of Claire's?" she asked.

"Yes, it is. She and Levi spent a few days here before they got married. She gets all the credit for the feminine touches, like the curtains and that quilt."

"It's so cozy and quiet. I can hear birds singing but no traffic noise. No wonder you want to live here."

"It's not much, but it's real private, and it's got plumbing. Bathroom is through that door." He pointed and then nodded toward the other end of the cabin. "Kitchen will do for what cooking I'll do."

"What kind of cook are you?"

"I make a mean bologna sandwich and I'm a pro at heating up canned soup or chili. And I can flip pancakes like a chef. Most of the time I'll eat dinner at the ranch house anyway. It's our usual time to discuss what we need for the afternoon jobs. And sometimes I'll even have supper there." He picked up a quilt from the back of the sofa and spread it out in front of the fire.

"We've got a couple of hours of one-on-one time before the children return to tell us all about their exploration trip." He motioned for her to sit down.

"Children?" She eased down gracefully.

He kicked off his boots and sat in front of her. They were so close that she could count his thick, dark eyelashes. "Didn't you feel like a parent when we were giving them their orders?"

"Maybe a little," she admitted. "But it's my job to see to it that they're taken care of. After the four-wheeler thing, I'll probably be worried every time they walk out the door, so yes, I guess I am a little like a parent. Otis and Larry have bone issues, and the other three take blood pressure meds. If something happened, one of the guys might not be able to walk and one of the ladies might wind up with a stroke. But I have to remember that they all have sharp minds, and they'll call if they need us."

"Who are you trying to convince? Me or you?" He chuckled.

"Me, if I'm honest," she admitted.

"I thought I heard Otis say that he has a car. Do you worry about him when he drives?"

She nodded. "Every time he takes all of them to the movies or out to eat, I worry until they get home. Dammit! I didn't realize it, but I do act like a mother, don't I? I've got to stop that."

Justin stood up and started for the kitchen. "Want something to drink? There's a couple of beers in the fridge. We can hide the bottles so no one will know."

"Love one."

He popped up on his feet and went toward the refrigerator. With that chiseled face and those dark lashes above those bedroom eyes, he wouldn't even look right in anything but tight jeans and boots. A three-piece suit would be as out of place on his muscular body as a nun's outfit on a hooker.

"Did you go to college to be an activities director?"

Justin twisted the tops off two bottles of beer and handed one to her before he sat down in the same spot.

"Yes, I did. I have a degree in social work from Cameron University in Oklahoma," she answered.

"Why'd you skip over the border?"

"They gave me a full scholarship," she answered and then turned the questions toward him. "You ever regret not going to college?"

"Not one minute. Ranchin' has been in my blood my whole life," he answered. "Skip says that it don't matter if you dig ditches or sit in the Oval Office, if you enjoy what you do, you're a success. If I apply that definition, I'm a huge success."

"Then I suppose I am too. You know you don't have to babysit us out here today. I'm capable of making sandwiches for their lunch, and I wouldn't want to keep you from your work."

"One of the reasons I love my job so much is that I get to be my own boss. Thought I'd stay until after we eat our sandwiches. Truth is I want to hear how excited they all are when they get back from their safari. Then y'all can have the cabin to yourselves."

"Now who's actin' like a parent?" She smiled.

"I guess I was." He chuckled. "This kind of reminds me of when the kids come for the summer."

Emily drew her knees up and wrapped her arms around them. "Tell me about them. Are they scared when they first arrive? This has to be so different from where they live."

Justin took a long drink from his beer. "At first, they probably are, but after a day or two, they adjust. Kids are like that. They adapt better than older folks. Maybe I better rephrase, because the Fab Five, as you call them, sure fit right in here."

"Probably because, except for Larry, they are all former ranchers or lived on a farm when they were young. They really are having a wonderful time," she said. "So eight kids? Four boys and four girls? I'd love to work with kids like that, again."

Justin leaned forward a little. "How much vacation time do you have? We pay real good, and I'll hire you on the spot right now."

"I sure don't have five weeks," she said. "But I think it would be great to work with kids again. What y'all are doing here is awesome, Justin."

"Again? I just figured you'd started at the center when you were right out of college," he said.

She took a long sip of her beer. "I worked part-time for an after-school program for underprivileged kids while I was in college, and then for social services in Austin two years before I took the job at the center."

"From children to elderly. I bet that was an adjustment," he said.

"It was." She sighed. "I was the caseworker in a bad situation. Drug addict father, abused mother, three little kids. I did something we're not supposed to do. I got involved. That woman and those kids became more than numbers on paper. I got them all the help I could, but that father was a piece of work."

Tears welled up in her eyes, but she didn't let them fall. "He was taking their food stamps and selling them for drug money. The last thing I did before I left was talk her into leaving him. I got her into a women's shelter with the kids, and they were ready to send her to a safer place."

"But? I hear a but," he said.

"The husband found her and promised her the moon and stars if she'd just come back to him. I begged and pleaded with her not to go, but she kept saying that she loved him and he'd changed. That's when I couldn't take it anymore. At least working with the elderly in a nice little retirement center, I don't have to see that kind of abuse and know there is nothing I can do about it." She swiped the back of her hand across her eyes. "Sorry, that just brought up so many feelings of failure."

He laid a hand on her knee. "I can't even begin to imagine, but I can sympathize. When the kids leave the first of July, the place feels empty, and I worry about them."

Suddenly, everything in the cabin went still. She couldn't hear the birds singing outside anymore or even the crackle of the fire. She moistened her lips and leaned slightly forward, and then his lips were on hers. The kiss started out as a sweet brush, but it soon deepened into more. His hands cupped her cheeks. She opened her mouth slightly to invite him in. The chemistry between them was so hot that it put the fireplace blaze to shame. He broke away to scoot closer to her and put his arms around her. Before their lips could meet in another kiss, they heard what sounded like a herd of wild bulls nearing the house.

"I guess that's the cue for our date to end." Justin chuckled as he stood up and extended a hand to help Emily.

She took it and was only mildly surprised when he was strong enough to pull her to her feet. "Date? I didn't usually kiss on the first date."

"But I'm irresistible." He grabbed the quilt and tossed it over the back of the sofa.

Emily picked up the two empty beer bottles and headed toward the kitchen to throw them away.

"Hey, we're starvin'. Can we have an early dinner?" Patsy was the first one inside with a tote bag filled to the brim with all kinds of earthy treasures.

"We'd have stayed gone until noon but them two got to complainin' about their bones." Bess pointed toward Otis and Larry.

"Well, y'all was fussin' about gettin' short-winded," Larry said.

"Bathroom?" Otis came in doing a dramatic dance across the floor.

"Man, you got a thimble-size bladder," Patsy said. "I bet he had to stop and find a bush every ten minutes while we was out."

"Only the strong get to grow old and, darlin' Patsy, when a man gets old, his bladder shrivels up to the size of a raisin. You ladies get to keep great big ones," Larry said.

"Yeah, big ones that lose their pucker power," Patsy shot over her shoulder on the way to the table.

Emily headed toward the kitchen area. "There's nothing that says we have to wait until noon to eat. We'll get out the food and I'll make sandwiches and pour drinks."

"Aww, come on, now." Sarah looked around the room. "Let us pretend like this sweet little cabin belongs to us and we're makin' our own dinner."

Bess went right to the table and began taking food from the bags. "Just what we wanted—white bread, mustard, chips, cookies. Bologna and mayo in the fridge?"

"And Retta fixed a big bowl of fruit salad. It's in the refrigerator." Emily wondered if her lips were as bee-stung as they felt. One touch let her know that they were actually cool. "Y'all sure you don't want some help?"

"Y'all can make your own, but we've got ours," Patsy answered. "You know how long it's been since I had a bologna sandwich with mustard and dill pickles? Oh, and you brought onions and tomatoes. This is better than a fifty-buck steak."

"Don't expect me to kiss you good night if you eat onions. I hate them," Larry said.

"Oh, come on, darlin', ain't I sexy enough to kiss even with onion breath," Bess teased.

Larry removed four slices of bread from the bag and started making two sandwiches. "Nope, wouldn't even kiss my wife if she ate those things, and you ain't nearly as sexy as she was. She looked like Dolly Parton when she was young. Big chest, little waist, round hips. All the boys was after her but I was the lucky one who got her, and she gave up onions for me most of the time."

Justin leaned over and whispered softly in Emily's ear, "Would you give up onions for me?"

His warm breath sent delicious little shivers through her that she hadn't felt in years. Then her phone pinged and she moved away. "I hate onions, so I can't answer that," she said as she checked the text.

It was from her brother Hudson: *Have date for you for the family gathering.*

She hurriedly typed: *No thank you.*

One came right back: *Too late. Already arranged.*

She typed back: *Break it or I won't come home.*

The next one said: *Party pooper.*

She turned her phone off and put it back in her pocket.

"Sorry about that. My brother…" She let the sentence hang.

Justin leaned in again and whispered, "Would you wear a blond wig and pretend to be Dolly for me?"

"Dolly is way too old for you, darlin'." She looked him up and down like she was assessing him naked for a modeling gig. "And I'm not sure you could keep up with someone like her, anyway. She's a firecracker. And besides, I'm a brunette. Never wanted to bleach it blond or make it black either one. Looks like you're just out of luck today."

"That's life." Otis slapped him on the shoulder. "Some days you get to be the pigeon. Some days you have to be the statue. Today is your statue day, son."

"Ain't it the truth." Justin draped an arm over the short man's shoulders. "Let's go make ourselves a sandwich and sit in front of the fire to eat."

"Us old folks can't sit on the floor. The gettin' down ain't too hard, but oh, my, that gettin' up is a bitch." Otis laughed. "I'll just clean me off a section of the table and you two kids can sit on the floor in front of them embers."

Emily caught Justin's gaze across the room. One eyelid slid shut in a slow, sexy wink. That comment about him being irresistible was pretty damn close to the truth.

Larry carried his food to the coffee table and sat down on the sofa. "And when we get done, we'll show y'all what we found. I got a perfect squirrel skull. I'm going to put it on my desk and use it to hold my favorite pen. I used to have a 'gater head but somehow in the move I lost it."

"So, Miz Emily, did you ever have a weird pen holder?" Justin asked as he made his sandwiches, with no onions.

She spread mayo on two slices of bread and then added everything else. She was surprised that the old folks hadn't commented on the sparks flying between her and Justin. Maybe they were so interested in food that they didn't pay attention to anything else.

"Only if you call a Cameron Aggie cup weird." She finally answered Justin.

"You went to Cameron?" Sarah took her plate to the living area and sat down in the middle of the sofa. "You never told me that. We'll have to talk college someday. That's where I got my teachin' degree. I stole a glass from the cafeteria to keep my pencils in."

Emily crossed one leg over the other and with the grace of a seasoned ballerina, sat down beside the fireplace. "Do you still have it or did it get lost in the move like Larry's 'gater head?"

"Sittin' on my desk right now. One of the few things I couldn't get rid of. I found some really nice dead leaves today. I'm going to spray paint them gold and have them mounted in shadow boxes to go above my little sofa," Sarah answered. "Otis, come on over here and sit on the sofa with us. Bess and Patsy can have the table."

"Thanks but I'm too messy for a plate in my lap. I'll just stay back here with the ladies," Otis said.

Heavy footsteps on the porch caused everyone's eyes to go toward the door. Levi poked his head inside and asked, "I heard there was a party goin' on in here. Has anyone made bathtub gin yet?"

"Naw, we'd have to make shower gin," Otis said. "There ain't no bathtub in this place, but that's a good idea."

"I know where there's a really big tub," Patsy said.

"And it's for taking baths, not making liquor," Emily warned.

Justin bit back a laugh.

"Get on over here and make yourself a sandwich. There's plenty," Otis offered.

"Don't mind if I do, and then I'm stealing Justin. We've got a whole afternoon of workin' cattle. Want to join us, Otis?"

"You bet your sweet ass, I do." Otis chuckled.

"I'll take good care of him and won't let him get hurt," Justin whispered.

Emily shot a smile his way. "Good luck."

Emily didn't think that she'd ever seen such a spring in Otis's step when he put on his safari hat and joined the younger two cowboys on the way out of the cabin. But it was Justin's swagger that took her eye a helluva lot more than Otis's.

"Okay if me and Bess get our afternoon beauty sleep on that bed? Shame that the covers ain't even ruffled," Patsy said. "We left y'all alone, hopin' that you'd have a little hanky-panky story to tell us when we got back."

Emily rolled her eyes. "There's absolutely no hanky-panky story between me and Justin."

"What if fate says he's your soul mate?" Patsy kicked off her shoes and sat down on the bed. "You can't fight fate or you'll regret it forever."

"How could I even know if he's my soul mate? I've only known him a few days," Emily said.

"Ah, honey, you'll know," Sarah said and then turned to Patsy. "Y'all ain't gettin' that big old bed all to yourselves. I get the middle pillow. And I don't want to hear a bunch of bickerin', either. We're goin' to take our afternoon naps like good little girls."

"Yes, teacher," Bess teased.

Larry tucked a pillow under his head and pulled the throw from the back of the sofa down over his body. The moment he shut his eyes, he was snoring. Poor old guy—the morning had worn him plumb out. They may act younger than their years, but today their age had sure caught up with them.

"What about you, Emily?" Patsy asked.

"I'm going to catch up on some work, since I brought my laptop. Y'all have a good sleep and when you wake up, I'd love to see all your prizes from this morning."

"Can't do that." Sarah yawned. "We got to wait for Otis

to get home so we can all be together and tell our stories. But after supper we're all meetin' up in the girls' quarters, and we'll tell you about them then. Why don't you invite Justin to join us?"

"We'll see about that," Emily answered.

"I hated it when Mama said that," Bess said as she shut her eyes and joined Larry in the snoring business.

Emily cleared off the table so she'd have a place to work. After she'd set up her laptop and discovered that she didn't have Wi-Fi in the cabin, she pulled her phone from her hip pocket, and hit Nikki's number.

Her friend answered on the first ring. "Emily! I thought you'd fallen off the face of the earth. I swear this week just hasn't been the same without you. Derek is doing all right with the activities you left him to do, but the place is like a tomb without the Fab Five."

"Hello to you too," Emily said softly so she wouldn't wake anyone.

"What is that horrible noise?" Nikki asked.

"I'm in a small cabin with four of the Five, and they're taking their afternoon naps," she answered.

"Man, that's a lot of snoring. So tell me all about what's been going on. Have you changed your mind about Justin Maguire?"

Emily took a deep breath and paced the floor. "He's sexy as hell, a great man, and he's kind to everyone."

"And I hear in your voice that he's gotten under your skin," Nikki said.

"I had a case of chiggers once and I got over it. I guess I can get over this too. Besides, I've only been here three days. Nothing romantic has happened, but let me tell you what this group has gotten into." Emily changed the subject and went on to fill Nikki in on the Five's antics.

"You pulled a calf?" Nikki's voice went all high and squeaky.

"That's all you got out of that story?" Emily asked.

"No, the rest is funny. That's why we miss the Five here at the center. But you actually birthed a calf. I knew you'd lived on a ranch, but I figured you were the prissy type who never got her hands dirty."

Emily stopped pacing and sat down in a kitchen chair. "My parents insisted I learn the business just like my brothers."

"I just can't imagine you doin' that. Got to go now, job calls. Just three more days and y'all will be home and things will liven up around here. Tell everyone hello for me."

Nikki didn't give her time to say good-bye. One minute she was talking, the next the phone went dark. Emily opened up her laptop and began to list everything she'd need for the Valentine festivities at the center. After last Christmas, the craft closet was nearly bare, so she'd need lots of things for the residents to make their Valentine boxes and cards to each other.

I wonder what kind of card Justin would give me, she thought as she added construction paper and glitter to the list. Growing up, she'd loved turning a shoe box or a cereal box into a masterpiece to take to school. But she would never look at her cards until she got home. She'd race from the bus to her bedroom and dump them all on her bed. She'd hold her breath, hoping that just one of them would have a lollipop with it because boys only gave a special girl that kind.

But she never got one.

Chapter Six

Not just no, but hell no!" Emily popped her hands on her hips.

"But it ain't a wild rodeo bull. It's pretty tame," Otis argued. "If Larry woulda helped me, I think I could've ridden him like a horse."

Emily sent a dirty look toward Larry and shifted her gaze toward Otis. "And you, no amount of talkin' will make me change my mind."

"Okay then, how about horseback ridin'? It ain't the same and it won't impress the ladies, but at least I'll be ridin' something," Otis asked.

Justin wasn't a bit of help, standing over there in the corner of the ranch house, arms crossed and with one boot propped against the wall. He should've nipped this crazy notion in the bud when the two guys came to him with it. Some father he'd make! Whoever he married would have to wield the heavy hand while he'd be the good parent in the relationship.

Not a whole lot unlike Emily's daddy. She could always talk him into anything, but not her mama. When Mama said no, it was definite, and a herd of wild bulls couldn't change her mind.

"We could've just done it without askin' nobody, but we gave you our word after the four-wheeler thing," Larry said.

Justin straightened up and said, "I've got an idea. There's a mechanical bull at the Rusty Spur. The bar doesn't open until evening, but I know the owner, and she'd probably let us use old Demon if Emily would give the okay." He looked her way and winked.

One wink and all her resolve went right out the window.

His eyes held hers without blinking. "You can even go with us to be sure that Demon don't buck too hard. The ladies can spend some time at the ranch house, either with a movie or helping Retta pick out a color for the nursery."

Otis begged with his eyes. Larry's big grin and twinkling eyes said he would be so disappointed if she said no. Surely, it couldn't hurt for them to ride the bull on a very low speed, but what if one of them fell off and broke a hip on her watch? The thought almost made her change her mind, and then the door burst open and a cold wind blew all the ladies into the ranch house.

"What are y'all doin' in here?" Patsy asked. "Are you plannin' something without us, Otis? Did she say y'all could ride the bull? We done told you that you couldn't do something we can't. I ain't goin' to stand on the side-lines and be a cheerleader. I'm going to ride the bull if you are."

"Just like them to go behind our backs, ain't it?" Bess frowned. "Well, we're here now and we got on our jeans and boots and we're doin' whatever you get to do."

Sarah raised her hand toward heaven. "Preach on, sisters."

"We're goin' to ride the mechanical bull at a saloon," Otis said.

"If Emily says yes," Larry added.

"Yee-haw!" Patsy squealed. "I ain't done that since we went to Billy Bob's for my fiftieth birthday. I rode that sumbitch for eight seconds with a tequila in my free hand, and I didn't spill a drop."

"But only after she'd had five shots and a couple of margaritas before she mounted up." Bess tilted her chin up defiantly. "I stayed on eight seconds, and I was sober as a judge."

"Oh, hush!" Patsy nudged her on the arm. "I should've brought my cowboy hat. Can we go by the center and get it?"

"No, you can't," Emily said.

"Do we get to drink, since we're in a honky-tonk?" Patsy asked.

"No, you don't." Emily raised her voice. "The only way I'm saying yes is if you promise you won't drink. All of you are on meds that warn against drinking while taking them."

All of them raised their right hands. "We promise."

Justin was on the phone when she glanced his way. She couldn't hear a single word he said for all the chatter and bets going on around her, but he finally nodded and gave her the thumbs-up sign.

"Okay, but only for one ride each. Justin will have to draw a map for me," Emily said. Thank goodness the week was almost over. She shuddered to think of what they'd request next.

Justin pushed away from the wall. "I have to go pick up some supplies half a mile from the Rusty Spur. I'll drive ahead of y'all and show you the way."

"And afterward we can go out and eat at the Mexican place in Bowie," Sarah said.

"Y'all want to break Retta's heart," Emily asked. "She put a ham in the oven and she's making baked beans and sweet potato casserole, and she's done all that because Larry and Patsy mentioned it being their favorite at supper last night."

"Ride the bull and come home." Patsy made the decision for all of them. "We can go out to eat any old time. Retta's cookin' is far better."

Otis sighed. "I wish this was home."

Larry laid a hand on Justin's shoulder. "I'm dead serious about this. Anytime you want to rent out these bunkhouses to us, we'll pay you what we give the center. You could make a lot of money and we'd be very happy living here. I'd even supervise any construction that you've got goin' on and Otis would help on the ranch."

"And we'd help Retta in the house and we'll be damn fine babysitters." Sarah clasped her hands together. "I always wanted to be a grandmother."

Bess raised her hand. "I call first dibs on rockin' the new baby."

"Over my dead body," Patsy said. "I'll fight you for the first time."

Justin raised an eyebrow toward Emily, as if he might actually be thinking about their proposal. He'd better not encourage them or he'd never hear the end of it.

"We'd better think about the present and see what happens in the future. Y'all get your cowboy boots on and meet us outside," Justin finally said.

The sun was bright, but a chilly wind whipped her hair across her face as Emily headed outside. That didn't prevent her from staring at Justin's backside when he hurried ahead of her to open the van door. There was no justice in the universe. Making a man that fine and then turning him into a cowboy so she couldn't have him was an unforgivable sin.

She settled into the driver's seat. Justin stood outside the open door.

"I thought you were going to lead the way in your truck," she said.

"I am," he answered. "I just want you to know that we'd never bring five seventy-year-old people on the ranch permanently. But if we did, could we hire you to do the same job you are doing now?"

"Oh, no! I've got a job," she said.

The Five were decked out in as much western attire as they could muster, but Otis was the only one who had a cowboy hat. They were all laughing and talking about how he had to share it.

"Ever ridden a fake bull?" Sarah asked Emily.

"One time and I stayed on the full eight seconds. But that was just to show my brothers I could do anything they could," she answered. "Everyone strapped in and ready to go?"

"You bet we are," Patsy said.

"Okay, let's get on the road. I'll lead the way." Justin winked at Emily as he left the van.

"I brought a purse full of quarters," Patsy said. "I'm going to plug them into the jukebox so we can dance before we leave. I ain't been to a honky-tonk in more'n twenty years, and I'm sure goin' to make the best of today."

"What if you drop graveyard dead right in the middle

of a dance? You damn sure ain't no spring chicken any-more, sis." Bess folded her arms over her chest and glared at Patsy.

"Then my prayers will be answered." Patsy slid into the seat beside her. "I ain't plannin' to go out with a whimper. I'm finishin' up this life with a bang and then I'm goin' to slide into heaven shoutin' at someone to open the doors. I won't have the energy to do it myself because I done used up every bit of what the Good Lord done gave me to live every moment of my life. Remember what that preacher said when he came to the center a few weeks ago. He said we ain't supposed to waste our talents."

"And your talent is riding bulls?" Larry asked.

"Hell, no!" Patsy exclaimed loudly. "My talent is dancin'. You'll see. I got lots of quarters." She patted her purse.

"What if nobody wants to dance with you?" Bess asked.

"I don't need a partner. I just need a pole and I bet there's at least a support beam in that place," Patsy teased.

As she drove behind Justin's truck, Emily wondered how she'd go out of the world. Would it be with regrets or would she have used up all her talents? Would Patsy be waiting at the Pearly Gates to guide her into heaven?

Granny used to say that when you're faced with a fork in the road always take the one that looks like it would make you happy and never think about the other one again. If Emily had two paths of life before her right at that mo-ment, she wondered which one she'd take, and would there be regrets.

The Five were so excited when they saw the honky-tonk that they'd left their seats and were waiting at the door when Emily came to a stop. They hurried out of the vehi-cle and even beat Justin to the door and then inside the old weathered wood building.

"I hope they're not disappointed," Justin said as he walked beside her.

"It could be a corrugated steel building with a dirt floor and they'd be happy," Emily said.

A tall blond woman yelled from behind the bar, "I'm Vivien and I set the rules in this place. You got to have a drink before you can conquer old Demon."

Emily's eyes widened and she started to say something.

"It's just root beer," Justin whispered. "I called Viv on the way here and told her the rules. No liquor, and Demon is tired this morning, so he's only going to buck on slow speed."

"I'll have a double shot of Jack?" Otis said.

"Honey, I can spot a fake ID a mile away and there ain't no way a one of you is over twenty-one, so it's root beers all around. But Demon is waiting for you, and the jukebox is hungry for quarters, so you can dance after the rides. But first a drink because you got to loosen up to ride my bull."

"She's good," Emily said.

"Yep, best therapist in the whole world as well as bartender. She'll take lots and lots of secrets to her grave."

Emily wondered how many of Justin's secrets she'd be taking to the grave with her. Maybe the count of all the women he'd been with, along with their names?

"We're the Fab Five," Larry said. "This here is Patsy, Bess, Sarah, and Otis is already on a barstool.

"And I'm Larry." He turned up the root beer and took a long gulp, then wiped his mouth with the back of his hand. "I reckon we'll be gentlemen and let the ladies ride Demon first."

"There's plenty more root beers where those came from, so y'all drink up, and then we'll wake old Demon up," Vivien said.

Patsy took a sip and then headed toward the jukebox. "Let's get us some music goin'. I've been out of honky-tonks too long. I used to get six songs for a quarter. Now I only get one. But I don't care. I'm goin' to put every one of these coins in this thing."

"If you run out, I've got some in my pocket," Larry said.

"Well, would you look at this? They've got our kind of music, Larry. There's some of the old stuff on here. First of all, 'Looking for Love.'"

Larry raised his bottle.

Justin held out his hand to Emily. "May I have this dance, darlin'?"

She'd danced at Christmas with a cousin or two, but it had been years since she'd two-stepped with a cowboy. The last time was at a high school dance, and it had not been a pleasant experience. The guy only danced with her because he'd lost a bet to some other kids, and that was his penance.

"I ain't never seen her two-step, or dance at all for that matter," Patsy said.

Emily put one hand on Justin's shoulder and tucked the other one into his. He pulled her close and began to move around the dance floor with her. She was sure glad that two-stepping, like riding a bicycle, all came back to her because Justin was an excellent dancer.

When the song ended, he stepped back and bowed slightly to kiss her knuckles. "Thank you for the dance."

Her voice came out in a whisper. "You must've had lots of practice."

"Little bit." He grinned.

The Fab Five applauded like they were judges on a real-ity TV competition.

"Okay, who's first?" Vivien called out when the noise

died down. "Demon says he's ready to buck someone off on their ass this mornin'."

"Me," Patsy yelled. "I played this song special for my ride."

"Ring of Fire" started as Larry got into the ring and helped her up on the bull.

She pointed at Otis. "Give me your hat or else that empty bottle."

He threw his hat like a Frisbee. She caught in on the fly, looped her fingers through the rope around Demon's neck, and held the hat up with her right hand.

"Let 'im out of the chute." Patsy nodded at Vivien.

Vivien pushed a button and Demon started to buck. Emily held her breath. If that was a slow speed, she'd never want a single one of them to try the fastest speed. Eight seconds seemed to last three hours, and when Vivien ended the ride, Emily blew out all the air in her lungs in a whoosh.

Justin laid a hand on her shoulder. "It's okay."

"One down, four to go," she whispered.

Bess reached for the hat. "My turn because 'Achy Breaky Heart' is my favorite, and that's what is playin' next. I'll think about Billy Ray when he was young while I'm on the bull."

Emily sucked in another lungful of air and covered Justin's hand with hers. About halfway into the ride Bess almost fell off, and Emily squeezed his hand hard.

"Breathe, darlin'," he whispered.

"I can't," she gasped. It wasn't until the next four seconds had passed that she refilled her lungs. "Why did I ever agree to this?"

"Look?" Justin pointed to the dance floor, where Patsy was dancing all by herself.

"And this one is mine," Sarah yelled. " 'Tennessee Whiskey' is startin' up. If I'd ever found a man who'd sing this song to me I might not be an old maid today. Give me that hat, Bess."

"Don't worry, honey," Vivien said. "They'll all make their eight seconds and live to tell the stories about it." She pointed toward the dance floor. "And I'm guessin' that the way Patsy is dancin', this ain't her first honky-tonk."

Sarah slapped the hat down on her head, grabbed an empty bottle, and held it up the whole time she was on Demon's back. "Yee-haw! I got this, Emily. Take a picture. The folks at the center ain't never goin' to believe it. They'll be beggin' for you to take everyone to the ranch."

"There will never, ever be another ranch vacation," Emily muttered as she snapped a picture.

As soon as Sarah finished her ride, she joined Patsy and Bess on the dance floor, and the three of them swayed to the next song on the jukebox. Thank God, there were only two more days of this vacation. If the Five stayed at the ranch any longer than that, Emily's hair would turn gray.

When Otis finished up his ride, he settled his hat on his head and took a bow. "I still got it."

Vivien led in the applause and then said, "I think it's time for another root beer to wet the whistle. Y'all did a fine job."

"Yes!" Patsy yelled. "Give me another beer! Emily, can we dance for thirty minutes before we go?"

She checked her watch. "That'll be the limit."

"Oh, oh!" Sarah pointed at the jukebox. "This one is for you and Justin. Y'all got time for one more dance."

Justin raised an eyebrow and opened his arms.

She walked into them, and they moved together across the floor. "You know that they're playin' matchmaker, don't you?"

"Oh, yeah, I know." He laid his chin on the top of her

head. "We might as well make them happy. I've never danced with a woman like you."

"You mean a big girl?"

"No, ma'am. Besides being sexy, you're tall enough that I don't have to bend to put my cheek next to yours. And you know my every dance move before I even make it. I could stay on this floor with you all night."

"I bet you say that to all the girls," she said.

"No, ma'am, I don't."

She leaned back and locked eyes with him. "You're serious, aren't you?"

"Yep, I am, and I'd like to see you again after you leave the ranch. Would you go to dinner and maybe a movie with me?"

She wanted to say no. She really did, but somehow the word wouldn't come out of her mouth—he'd called her sexy, and he'd meant it. That deserved at least a possibility, right?

"I thought we already had a date in the cabin," she said.

"You don't kiss on the first date, so that one don't count," he teased.

"Okay, then, call me sometime and we'll see."

"You can depend on it, and now for the grand finale so they'll have something to talk about." He bent her backward and planted a scorching hot kiss on her lips.

When the kiss ended, he brought her back to a standing position. The Fab Five were staring at her with big grins on their faces, but her cheeks felt as if they were on fire.

Justin picked up his hat from the bar, settled it on his head at just the right angle, and waved as he left the bar. "I'll see everyone at noon."

"Why don't you do that to me after a dance?" Sarah asked Larry.

"Because I'd pop my hip out of place, and besides one of

my kisses would shoot your blood pressure so high, you'd stroke out. I don't want to go to jail for murder." Larry chuckled.

Emily's knees still felt weak, so she backed up and sat on a barstool. She could fully well expect them to want to talk about that kiss on the way home, and she needed to think about how she'd answer them. Something cold touched her arm, and she jumped like she'd been burned.

"Sorry about that, sweetie. Didn't mean to startle you," Vivien said. "I poured you up a double shot of Jack Daniel's. It'll cool you down after that kiss?"

That was her favorite whiskey. Vivien had even put one cube of ice in it. How did she know exactly what Emily liked?

"I shouldn't. I have to drive them back to the ranch." She stared at it longingly.

"Honey, no offense meant here, but a woman your size won't be in trouble with that much whiskey. And let me tell you a secret. I've been servin' Justin Maguire drinks since before he was twenty-one. He was one of the first kids who had a fake ID that I didn't catch. By the time I caught on, he was old enough to buy it legal. I've seen him drive home after a night of doin' nothing but dancin' the leather off his boots and only one beer in him. And then I've seen him talk some cute little bar bunny into going home with him. But I've never seen his eyes light up when they looked at any woman like they did when he danced with you."

"But..." Emily stammered.

"He's a good man with a big heart who makes his livin' runnin' his ranch. Now I ain't runnin' your business, but, sweetie, think about it real hard before you slam the door on an opportunity." Vivien wiped down the already clean bar with a white cloth. "I know that man," Vivien said. "Now you do what you want with that information. From here on, it ain't a bit of my business, but you can trust him. I'd swear to that on my mama's grave."

Emily took a sip of the Jack, held it in her mouth a few seconds, and then swallowed. There wasn't a doubt that she could trust Justin. But could she trust herself? It would be so easy to fall for him.

Chapter Seven

A cool night breeze moved the tree branches as Justin walked toward the barn. He remembered Cade telling him how he'd be one crazy cowboy to invite a woman to the ranch for a week. But Justin didn't feel crazy—not one bit. Then again, Cade probably hadn't felt foolish either when he hired Retta to work as a counselor for the girls' bunkhouse last summer. Levi might have thought he'd done something a little crazy when he rescued Claire and her cute little niece, Zaylie, during a blizzard. Both Retta and Claire had stayed in the girls' bunkhouse, so maybe that damned place had magical powers.

"And now Emily's in the bunkhouse." He suddenly felt a presence behind him, and whipped around to make sure he wasn't about to be head butted by a bull or cold nosed on the hand by Beau. He saw a large shadow, but before he could focus, Emily was right there and taking the last step before she would run smack into him.

She didn't see him until it was too late, and he had the choice of wrapping his arms around her or letting her knock both of them to the ground.

"Whoa, darlin'. Shall we dance?" Should he hum the tune to a country song so they'd have music?

"I don't feel like dancin' right now." She spit out the words.

"Where are you goin' in such a hurry?" he asked.

"Anywhere. Everywhere. Nowhere. I had to get away and get some fresh air. Thought it might erase the pictures in my head, but it's not working," she said.

"You want to talk about it?" Justin asked.

"Hell, no!" she said. "I can hear my granny goin' for the soap in the kitchen to wash my mouth out for sayin' bad words, but dammit! I swear, my brain is never going to be the same."

"What's got you cussin'?" He took a step back even though he'd rather have stood there with her in his arms until daylight.

"You'll never guess what they're doin' right now," she fumed. "I thought I was home free. They rode the bulls and played dominoes until bedtime last night, all quiet and well behaved. I wish they were children. I'd ground the whole lot of them."

"More strip poker?" he guessed.

"Worse!" She covered her cheeks with her hands.

He took her hand in his and led her toward the barn. "Come on, girl. You need to cool down before you explode. Want me to go have a talk with them?"

"God, no! They'd make you blush, too. Hell, they'd make the devil turn a darker shade of red."

She matched his long strides until they were inside the barn. Her hand in his was comfortable, and the sparks were almost as bright as the stars above them. He led her all the way to the tack room, where he switched on the light and then pulled her down beside him on a well-worn sofa.

"Now tell me what they've done now," he said.

"Larry and Sarah are playin' strip poker like you said. He's down to his shirt, boxers, and socks. She's lost her shoes and socks and shirt. The other three have gone skinny-dippin' in that big bathtub. When I walked in on them, they invited me to join them," she said. "None of them have a bit of shame."

He laughed so hard that he had to drag a handkerchief from his back pocket and wipe his eyes. "I know it's not funny—but it is."

"It might be to you, but it damn sure wasn't to me. God, I wish I could unsee that sight."

"You ever been skinny-dippin'?" he asked.

"Not with boys," she answered. "Have you?"

"Want to be my first? We can find us a lake or that big bathtub." He grinned.

She jerked her hand free and slapped him on the arm.

"Guess that means no. Well, if you ever change your mind, then just give me a call, and I'll get the water ready. Do you like bubbles?" he teased, but the vision in his head wasn't a joke. He could imagine running hot soapy hands down her sides, touching her voluptuous body in places that would make both of them pant with desire.

"Don't hold your breath," she said.

"Oh, honey," he started to say something really smart-ass but his eyes landed on her full lips. Half the lipstick she'd applied had been chewed off, probably from worrying about the antics of the Five.

He leaned forward, cupped her chin in his hand, and brought her lips to his in a fiery hot kiss that came close to knockin' his socks right off. His tongue gently touched her upper lip, asking permission to enter her mouth. She opened it slightly, inviting him inside.

*   *   *

Emily ignored the pesky voice in her head telling her to run, not walk, back to the bunkhouse, that things were getting out of control. She leaned in and wrapped her arms around his neck.

One of his hands went to the back of her head to hold it steady. He was no novice at this business of making out because his other hand found its way up under her shirt and massaged her back. She pressed closer to him, liking the way his hard chest felt on her breasts, the way his lips felt on hers, and most of all his hands on her bare skin.

Finally, he broke away and kissed the sensitive place on the inside of her neck. If he'd started there, she'd have already undone her bra for him. By now she'd be as naked as those three were in the bathtub. She moved back and blinked a few times. If she focused on something in the room, maybe the scorching desire for hot sex would leave her body. She should've looked across the room instead of down at his belt buckle. A deep crimson blush dotted her cheeks.

"We can't be trusted any more than the Fab Five, can we?" she asked.

"Whew!" He leaned his head back on the sofa. "I ain't never got this stirred up over a few kisses."

"Me, either," she admitted. "But maybe we better take a lesson from it and not let it happen again."

His head jerked around to face her, and suddenly, they were kissing again. When he finally pulled away, he grinned. "Well, it's not *just* the first one that leaves me breathless. Second one made even more sparks. There's something between us, Emily. We shouldn't ignore it but give it a chance to see where it might lead."

Vivien's words about him being a good man who happened to work on a ranch came back to Emily's mind. "We'll see how things go when I'm not here all the time and you've got your bar bunnies to keep your bed warm," she said.

"And who's going to keep your bed warm?" he asked.

"I scarcely have time for dating, but when I do, it's usually someone..." She hesitated.

"Someone like who?"

"Let's just say it's been a long time since I've been in a relationship. I know I'm a big girl, and I'm fine with that. It's a 'take me as I am or go to hell' situation for the most part. But my last boyfriend kind of soured me on getting serious with anyone for a long time. He wanted to change me into his image of the perfect woman," she said. "He wanted me to join a gym, go on a strict diet, and have some cosmetic surgery. Let's just say on that last issue that I hate needles so I wasn't willin' for his suggestions. It ended the whole thing. The next year he married a tall blonde who looked like a runway model."

"He was an idiot. You're already perfect," he said.

That melted her heart. "Thank you for that." She leaned over and kissed him on the cheek. "We'd better get on back. I'm just hoping they haven't gotten into something even worse than skinny-dippin' when I get there."

His phone rang before he could say anything else. He snapped it off the holder on his belt and answered, "Hello, Mama. No, I'm at the barn."

A few seconds later he said, "I'll be there in a little while." He ended the call and shoved the phone back in his pocket. "Now where were we? Oh, what could be worse than skinny-dippin'?"

"Oh, maybe streakin' from the bunkhouse to the barn in this weather. I'd have to call 911 to come get them for heart attacks. And heaven forbid if Larry or Otis stepped in a gopher hole and busted up a hip or knee." Her pulse still hadn't settled down, so her words came out between short breaths.

"They're pacing themselves and saving that for tomorrow night after the party. Think about it, Emily. They've done one ornery thing a day. So they're saving the best until last." Justin tucked her hand back into his as they left the tack room.

The shiver that made its way from her neck to her toes had nothing to do with the weather. Or with the embarrassment the Five had put her through that week—the rascals would be lucky if they ever got another vacation away from the senior center. The sparks flying around her had to do with Justin and the fact that he'd said she was perfect. No one, other than her grandmother and her parents, had ever told her that.

"Need my jacket?" Justin asked.

"Nope, just need tomorrow to be over so I can take this crew home and get back to normal," she said.

"What's normal?" Justin asked.

"Good question." Emily squeezed his hand.

Justin pointed at the ranch house. "Levi and Claire are back. Mama said they were on the way. Want to come in with me?"

She shook her head slowly. She'd rather go inside the ranch house for sure and avoid the ladies a while longer. "I should get on back to be sure no one drowned or fell getting in and out of the tub, and it sounds like you're supposed to be doing something else, anyway."

Justin stopped at the edge of the bunkhouse porch. "Tell me again why these spry folks are in a home anyway?"

"Loneliness," she said. "Pure and simple. They don't have family. Each of them have their own little apartment, and since Otis still has a driver's license, he has a car, so they can leave pretty often for a movie or to go out to eat. They have some problems but not too many for folks who've passed the seventy milestone."

"Poor old darlin's. I'd hate to come to the end of my life and not have family around me. I want kids and grandkids and hopefully even great-grands." He kissed her on the forehead. "Good night, Emily."

"Night," she muttered.

She didn't go inside right away but stood in the deep shadows of the porch and watched him until he reached the house. With a long sigh, she finally opened the door to find the three ladies lined up on the sofa. They were wearing chenille robes of various colors, and their wet hair gave testimony that at one time or another, they'd all been in the tub or shower.

"Where you been? Out kissin' on Justin?" Patsy giggled.

Bess poked a bony finger on Patsy's shoulder. "Ladies don't kiss and tell."

Emily took a deep breath. "I want you to promise me that there'll be no shenanigans tomorrow."

"We was talkin' about that before you caught us skinny-dippin'," Patsy said.

"Just so you don't put all the blame on the short folks." Sarah ran a comb through her chin length hair and tucked it behind her ears. "Me and Larry had our turn when the water went cold and they got out. Had to run another tub full. It was so freeing that I thought I was a teenager again. My boobs even floated! First time they've been lifted up without support in years."

"We've had so much fun this week, it's been like we were stars in that movie *Cocoon,*" Bess said. "Did you notice that me and Patsy didn't even argue as much as usual?"

No matter how hard she tried, Emily couldn't keep the grin at bay, not even by biting her lip. Nor the guilt from her heart for being judgmental about what they were doing. They were, as one of them said early on, over twenty-one, and no one forced them to do anything. So what if they'd done some pretty risqué and crazy things. It had made them happy.

"And if I die tomorrow, I'll go out with this big smile on my face that the undertaker won't be able to undo." Sarah sighed. "This was better than going to Disneyland as a kid."

"Hell, honey, this was better than a chocolate brownie with chocolate chip ice cream and pecans on the top," Patsy said. "And now I'm going to bed to dream of all the fun we've had. Thank you, Emily, for giving us old folks some precious memories. And—" She lowered her voice. "If I die before Sarah, promise me you'll put all the pictures you took in my casket with me. Even in eternity, I don't want to take a chance on my memory going bad and forgetting what this has meant to us."

Now Emily was getting all misty eyed. "Y'all are..."

"Family," Bess said. "And you're our precious baby girl."

"Thank you." Emily blinked back tears. "Now you'd best get some beauty rest. I hear we're meeting Skip and Mavis and Benjy tomorrow evening. We'll spend the day getting ready for the party. I'm volunteering to do nails and hair."

"Thank God!" Bess said. "Patsy's hair looks like an old mop that's been hung upside down on the clothesline to dry."

"Well, yours looks like a pot full of spaghetti," Patsy shot back.

"Oh, both of you stop your bitchin'," Sarah said. "Emily will you do my makeup? I always look like a clown when I do it."

"Of course I will. And I'll French braid you hair."

"Mine too?" Bess asked.

"Sure thing," Emily agreed. "And we'll use a curling iron on Patsy's to make her beautiful. Now I'm going to bed. Sweet dreams to the bunch of you."

"Come on, girls. We've got to go get our snorin' done so we can par—tee." Sarah dragged out the last word like a teenager.

After a quick shower, Emily stretched out on the twin bed and laced her hands behind her back. She'd experienced more emotions this week than she had in years—from aggravation, to embarrassment, to tears, to downright steamy hot desire. And now after that make-out session in the barn, she had mixed feelings about what she would say to Justin when and if he ever did call and ask her out.

Chapter Eight

Just as Emily and the three ladies were about to leave the bunkhouse and go to the ranch house for breakfast on Saturday morning, her phone rang. Seeing that it was her grandmother, she answered it as she stepped out onto the porch. "Hold on, Granny. I need to get something done right fast and then we'll talk." Emily turned to the ladies. "Y'all go on. I'll catch up."

"Honey, you talk to her as long as you need to," Sarah said. "I'll keep these two in line."

"Hmmph!" Patsy snorted. "As if you could ever make me behave."

"I may not be the hussy you are, girlfriend, but I'm bigger than you, and if all else fails, I'll just knock the shit out of you," Sarah told her and then smiled. "We'll all be sweet little old ladies, Emily. Talk to your granny."

"Okay, Granny, I'm here," Emily said.

"Who was that talkin'?" Opal asked.

"Sarah and Patsy. Bess is with them. Remember I told you last week that I was bringing them to the ranch for a field trip," Emily answered.

"I'd forgotten. So you're still there?"

"Yes, ma'am. What's goin' on at the Big Sky Ranch?"

"We're busier than ever. We could use your help. I wish you'd get over this fancy notion of yours and come home," Opal said. "Lost a calf last night. If you'd been here, it would've lived. I just know it."

"Granny, we've been over this a hundred times." Emily sighed.

"We'll go over it some more before it's all said and done," Opal said. "Maybe you'll get so tired of hearing it that you will get your fanny back here."

"Granny, I love you, but I've got a job to do here. Can we talk later, like tomorrow or some evening next week?" Emily asked.

"Of course, but I hate that I got to make an appointment to talk to you." Opal sighed. "But you go on and spend your time with the other old ladies that you take care of every day. I'll just take a number and wait."

Your guilt trip won't work on me. I'm happy where I am and with what I'm doing.

"I love you, Granny. Sending hugs and kisses," Emily said.

A long, noisy sigh. "I guess I'll take what I can get. Have a good day, honey."

Emily tossed the phone on the sofa, grabbed her coat, and jogged all the way to the house. She took a moment to catch her breath before she followed the conversation to the kitchen. She peeked around the corner to find all of her five folks plus the rest of the family ready to sit down to breakfast.

"Hey, come on in here and meet Mavis." Sarah motioned toward her.

She took a couple of steps inside the room. "I'm so sorry, Retta. I had a phone call from my granny and..."

"No problem. Talk to your grandparents every chance you get. I wish mine were still living so I could visit with them. I've had plenty of help this morning. Everyone needs to grab a chair. Emily, this is Mavis. That tall feller is Skip, and the boy over there by him is Benjy. Now let's eat before the gravy gets cold." Retta lowered her voice. "Don't know if anyone has told you but Benjy is autistic."

He was a cute kid, kind of big for his age. Emily had dealt with similar kids in her previous job so she knew that they didn't like to be hugged or pressured into conversation. Benjy's issue had to be minor because he was sitting beside Otis and talking a mile a minute about ranching.

"You were a rancher? Why did you quit? That's the best job in the whole world," Benjy asked.

"Yes, sir, I sure was." Otis nodded. "I quit because I got too old to do the work by myself, and it was lonely on the ranch after my wife died. I agree with you, son. It is the best job in the world, and I'm mighty proud that we got to spend this week on the ranch. It was like goin' home to us. Are you goin' to be a rancher when you grow up?" Otis asked.

"I'm one now. I have a goat and a sheep that I'll show in the Montague County Livestock Show in a couple of weeks. Did you know that goat meat is lower in fat and cholesterol compared to beef, pork, mutton, and poultry? Goats' milk is easily digestible and less allergenic than cow's milk. Goat milk is higher in calcium, vitamin A, and niacin than cows' milk."

"I did not know all that. I've never eaten goat. Have you?" Otis asked with a perfectly straight face.

Benjy shook his head. "And I'm not going to eat Dolly, either. She will be a breeder after the show. But I will try the milk if she ever gives any. Goats were domesticated by man in 10,000 BC and were the first animals to be used for milk by humans. And since it is high in all those vitamins, it will be good for me. You and I can be friends, Otis. We can talk about goats and sheep, and you can go with me to the barn to work when we get done eating. I like you."

Justin almost dropped his fork, and Cade stared at the boy like he had horns sprouting out of his red hair.

"I like you too, and I'd love to be your friend. You are very smart. Maybe you can teach me a few things." Otis passed the biscuits to him.

"And maybe you can teach me too." Benjy put two on his plate. "I have to muck out the stables and brush Little Bit, the donkey. He looks forward to his grooming once a week. Miniature donkeys have intelligence that is superior to all other farm animals. They're easily trained."

"I would love to go with you," Otis said. "Would you mind if we invite Larry to go with us?"

Benjy studied Larry for a while before he spoke. "Skip says that you draw things."

"Yes, I do, but I'm not the artist that you are. I draw plans for houses and barns and buildings." Larry waved to take in all the pictures on the dining room walls. "You have a very good eye. These pictures are amazing."

"Thank you." Benjy stared at his plate. "You can go with us, Larry. Maybe you can help me draw plans for my new sheep building. It should be big enough for Dolly and her friend, Emmy Lou. Sheep are like family. They need more than one to be happy."

"I'd be glad to help you with plans." Larry nodded.

Emily laid a hand on Justin's leg under the table. He jumped like he'd been shot and raised an eyebrow.

"What's happening here? I thought Benjy didn't make friends," she said.

"Be damned if I know. Must be the age thing. Only one he ever made friends with that fast was Skip," Justin said out of the side of his mouth. "It's a good thing. He'll keep Otis and Larry occupied all day, and they won't get into trouble."

"Thank God," Emily whispered.

"Okay, let's talk about what all we've got to do today," Gloria said from the other end of the table. "Justin and I will be spending the day in the office, getting the taxes all ready to go to the CPA."

"I've already done that," Retta said. "Took all the paperwork in the week before you arrived."

"Well, then Justin and I have some errands to run," she said.

"We need him on the ranch, Mama," Cade said. "You know how busy we are right now."

"Then he shouldn't have taken the whole day off yesterday," Gloria snapped.

"I didn't," Justin said. "I was gone all of two hours, and I picked up supplies while I was in town."

It didn't take a genius to know that Gloria didn't want Justin spending so much time around the Fab Five. Especially when she pushed back her chair and said in a tone so cold that it could have turned the devil's pitchfork from red to blue, "Then I'll go to Wichita Falls by myself." She laid a hand on Justin's shoulder and sighed as she left the room. In a couple of minutes, Emily heard the noise of a truck engine.

Mavis took a deep breath and let it out slowly. "She's not happy, and you know what that means."

Vernon chuckled. "If Mama ain't happy, ain't nobody happy."

"You got it." Mavis had the same kinky hairdo and the same twinkle in her eyes as Patsy.

"Shopping always makes her feel better," Justin said.

"Makes all of us happy," Mavis agreed and then leaned around Skip and asked Retta, "Hey, where's Claire and Levi? I got so involved with meetin' all these new folks that I just realized we're missin' two."

"Levi is on his way. They had breakfast at home," Retta said. "But she'll be here for the pizza party tonight."

"Good," Sarah said. "I haven't gotten the chance to talk to her about coming to the center and giving us a quilting lesson. I used to do a lot of that so it'd be fun if she can work it in."

Mavis sent a platter of bacon and eggs around. "Why don't y'all just go down to the shop on the fourth Thursday of every month? She's lined up free quilting lessons for everyone. I'm going for sure."

Patsy turned to Emily. "Can we do that?"

"Of course you can. I'll drive you and me, and Larry will wait outside for you or else drive on out here to see what's goin' on," Otis said.

"You'll have to check with the supervisor. Rules state you can have a car but you have to stay in the county, and if you go another mile or two south of Sunset, you'll be out of the county, so you'll have to be careful," Emily said. "If our supervisor says it's all right for Otis to take y'all, then I'll get out the two sewing machines in the activity center and you can work on your quilt tops from one lesson to the next."

"And if the supervisor says no, just call me," Mavis offered. "I'll be glad to drive over and get the ladies for the afternoon. We can have the lesson and then maybe have some coffee or ice cream before I have to take you back."

"That's sweet and we'll sure take you up on it," Bess said. "It'd be fun to get out for a day."

Mavis buttered a biscuit and reached for the strawberry jam. "I'll be sure you have my number before you leave. Are y'all stayin' for church tomorrow? We're having our Valentine's Day potluck after services. You'd all be welcome to join us."

"We need to go to church to atone for our sins for this week." Patsy sighed. "The reason we got into so much trouble was because we ain't been to church in a long time. The services they have at the center ain't the real deal. We need to have singin' and testifyin' and some real preachin' to get us back in line."

"Well, I can certainly agree with that, so yes, we can go to church as a group tomorrow." Emily nodded. "We'll need to be back by mid-afternoon at the latest. If y'all would have everything packed and in the van before we leave we could go from the church to the center, and you could spend a little more time at the potluck."

Otis saluted smartly. "Yes, ma'am."

"Were you in the military?" Benjy asked. "A salute is the sign of respect. But if a sniper is suspected, it is forbidden, because the enemy could use that to recognize officers as targets."

"No, son, I wasn't in the military," Otis answered. "But I do respect Miz Emily very much. Larry was in the army during the Vietnam era. He did two tours over there."

"Vietnam was the second longest war in our history. Thank you for your service, Larry," Benjy said, seriously.

Larry's eyes misted over, but he sat up a little straighter and taller in his chair. "Thank you, son. I appreciate that."

"How does he know so much?" Emily whispered to Justin.

"He reads all the time, and he has an eidetic memory. The doctors say that some autistic kids have it, but it's very rare. Guess he's one of the few," Justin answered.

She shot a look across the table at the boy, big for his age—if she were just a few years older, he could be her son. Her grandmother was constantly telling her that her biological clock was ticking loudly, but even looking at that precious child didn't make her regret not getting married right out of high school and starting a family. She glanced around the table. Why did she even need to think about children? She hadn't gotten the Fab Five raised yet.

*   *   *

Justin picked up the tablecloth on one end, and Emily gathered up the other one. They carefully folded it so that the crumbs all fell to the inside, and then carried it out to the back porch to shake it.

"What's on your agenda today?" he asked.

"Got to get ready for the party tonight. The ladies want me to do hair and makeup," she answered.

He dropped the cloth on the porch and tipped her chin up with his knuckles. "I've wanted to kiss you all morning."

Her lips were so soft, and every single time he kissed her, he felt a deep stirring. Call it sparks, chemistry, electricity, or whatever other word folks used when two people were drawn to each other, but Justin could feel it all.

"Since we've already done this several times," he whispered softly in her ear, "are you going to leave me at the door on our first date without even a good night kiss?"

"Never know until we have that date," she teased.

"Remember that I'm irresistible." He grinned.

"Yep, you are." She picked up the tablecloth and carried it inside to the utility room.

"Are you serious?" he asked right behind her.

"You said it. I believe you."

"Now *you're* joking."

"Maybe. Maybe not." She brushed a sweet kiss across his cheek. "Now, I've got to get down to the bunkhouse. I don't have to tell you what happens when the Five are left alone, and this is their last day. What if they're saving the worst thing of all until now?"

"Then we'll keep them separated. Benjy can entertain the guys and you can entertain the ladies with all that hair and makeup," he said.

"Sounds like an excellent plan to me," Emily said.

Justin hummed all the way from the house to the barn, where he found Benjy, Larry, and Otis talking about the morning chores, and a shot of jealousy hit him. Sure, Benjy always talked to Justin and didn't flinch if he laid a hand on the boy's shoulder every now and then. But the kid had just flat out taken to Otis like they were long-lost relatives.

Ever think it's because the old guy reminds him of his grandmother? A voice in his head asked. *You're also jealous of Cade because he has a baby on the way, and Levi because he's found someone. What are you waiting for?*

If settling down was what he wanted, he realized suddenly, then it was time to get on with the program and do so. And this newfound feeling he had for Emily might mean that she was the right one to do it with—but if she wasn't, then what? One of them might get hurt really badly. His mind was still chasing itself like a dog trying to catch its tail when he reached the barn.

"Hey, Justin." Benjy waved. "Otis and Larry are helping this morning. And then I'm goin' to show them how to groom Little Bit. Did you know that Hopalong has made him a bed in the back of one of the stalls? Are we getting things ready in case a heifer has trouble calving?"

Justin made his way back to the area where they were working. "That's right. We like to keep things ready, and Levi mentioned Hopalong had showed up again. Was he happy to see you?"

"Oh, yeah." Benjy flashed one of his rare smiles. "We all got to pet him and now he's sleepin'."

"Well, don't work Otis and Larry too hard. Emily will shoot me if they get sick over this," Justin said.

"Never happen. Benjy here is a fine boss." Otis chuckled. "He's letting us pace ourselves."

"That's good," Justin said.

Benjy pushed a full wheelbarrow outside to dump it. "Be right back, boys."

Otis leaned on a shovel. "That's a good kid, there, and he loves this kind of work. He's already a good hand, but with his smarts, he'll be a fantastic one in a few years. He could probably work out in his head how many rolls of barbed wire you'd need."

Larry propped a heel on the lower board of a stall. "I ain't never seen a kid that intelligent. He's such a delight to be around."

"We think so too. I'm so glad that he's made friends with y'all," Justin said.

"Hell, son, we're glad he let us be friends with him." Otis grinned.

"Got to go." Justin removed his cowboy hat, combed his hair back with his fingers, and resettled it on his head. "See y'all at the party."

"Lookin' forward to it," Larry said. "What're you off to do today?"

"Got a field to plow," Justin answered.

Beau followed Benjy from outside and stopped to let both Otis and Larry rub his ears before he headed toward the tractor. When Justin didn't follow right then, he turned around and barked at him.

"I think Beau wants to plow with you today," Benjy said.

"Looks like it." Justin nodded.

Justin opened the big green tractor door and jumped inside. Tail thumping against the leather seat and his paws on the dash, Beau was ready to go. Justin settled into his place and turned on the radio to his favorite country music station.

Plowing a big field in a tractor while listening to country music was usually Justin's definition of a good day. A month ago the only thing that would have been on his mind was whether or not he'd get lucky that night at the Rusty Spur. But all through the morning all he could think about was a party with seven elderly folks, a thirteen-year-old boy, and six adults. Pizza and Pictionary were on the agenda, and he couldn't wait for time to pass so he could be in the middle of it all.

At noon he turned the engine off, got out his sack lunch and thermos, and sat down on a fallen log under a big scrub oak tree. Beau rushed out to find the nearest bush and then chased two squirrels up a pecan tree. When the dog realized Justin was eating, he sat down at his side and put a paw on his leg.

Justin pinched off a chunk of his sandwich, fed it to Beau, and then tipped up his coffee and let the dog have a sip of that. "I like Emily. There I said it. There's just something about the way she is with those old folks, and the way she looks at Benjy, and now she's got me thinkin' about settling down. She's got a good heart and damn it, Beau, she's one sexy woman with all those curves."

Beau whimpered and looked up at the tractor.

"You're no help at all. You could at least wag your tail. I get more reaction out of you when a song that you like comes on the radio. Don't you like her?"

Beau's tail thumped against the brittle grass one time.

"Well, thank you for that tiny little vote of confidence," Justin growled. "Let's just get back to work."

Beau yipped.

"I guess that means I have to figure out things for myself, right?"

One more thump of the tail and Beau made two fast runs around the tractor. By the time Justin had shoved all of his trash back into the sack, the dog was waiting at the door. Beau hopped into the passenger seat, curled up with his paw over his nose, and went to sleep.

His phone rang before he could even start the tractor back up. The ID said it was his mother, but he took a moment to get the engine going so he could turn on the A/C.

"Hello, Mama," Justin answered.

"Where are you?" she asked, bluntly.

"In the tractor, plowing up a field so we can get it replanted," he answered.

"Where's Emily?"

"I have no idea, but I'd guess that she's at the bunkhouse getting things ready for the party tonight. You're coming to it, aren't you?"

"Of course."

"Mama, what's the matter with you? You've been acting strange ever since y'all got here," he asked.

"It's Emily," she said.

"What about her?"

"What do you know about her? What if she's just a gold digger after part of this ranch?"

"Good grief!" Justin raised his voice. "She hasn't even agreed to go out with me yet, and besides she's not that kind of person."

"She's not for you, Justin. I didn't feel like this with Retta or with Claire, but something isn't right about Emily. They'll be leaving tomorrow. I want you to stay away from her."

"Mama, you've never put up this kind of fuss about any of my girlfriends," he said.

"There's something different in you. If she were a one-night stand I wouldn't say a word, but with Levi and Cade both settling down, you've changed. Don't deny it. I can see it, but Emily is not the one."

"What if she is?" Justin asked.

"Trust me, she's not," Gloria said and the call ended.

No good-bye or anything. She simply hung up.

"Dammit!" Justin slapped the steering wheel.

It was going to be a long afternoon. Then he remembered something that Claire's little niece, Zaylie, had told him about time passing when they traveled. According to her, it was measured in songs. It took five songs to go from the ranch to the ice cream store in Bowie. But it took a whole bunch of songs to go from San Antonio, where she'd lived with her father, to Randlett, Oklahoma, where she stayed with her Aunt Claire when he was deployed.

It was 12:20. That meant a lot of songs before he got the field plowed and could call it quits. One song after another played, but he wasn't listening. One minute he was trying to make heads or tails out of the way he felt about Emily; the next he wondered what basis his mother had for what she'd said. Emily hadn't been anything but nice to her.

"I'm acting like a high school kid rather than a feller who's almost thirty," he muttered. "Emily probably isn't goin' to say yes when I do ask her out. And if she does, Mama is going to pitch a hissy fit. Why can't she just love Emily, like she did Retta and Claire?"

The sun was settling down on the horizon when he finally finished the job and parked the tractor in front of the barn. He still hadn't figured out a blessed thing, but at least the day was done, and he could go see Emily. Beau hopped out the minute the door opened and ran toward the house. Justin jogged along behind him and went straight to the bathroom. After a quick shower, he dressed in clean jeans and a shirt, pulled on a better pair of boots, and headed for the bunkhouse.

He didn't realize that he needed a coat until the north wind blew through his damp hair, but he didn't go back to get one. He just picked up the speed and hurried toward his destination.

The buzz of several conversations filled the room when he slipped inside. He searched the room, looking for Emily. Open pizza boxes covered the table, and the countertop was serving as a soft drink bar. Retta and Claire had their heads together. Mavis and the other elderly ladies were sitting around the table, talking about something that required a lot of hand movements.

No Emily anywhere.

His mother waved from across the room and made her way over to loop her arm in his. "I've been waiting on you to arrive. Mavis is talking quilting with the ladies. Retta and Claire are finalizing nursery plans. Your father is over there with the men and Benjy, talking about that silly donkey. I'm the only one here that doesn't fit into a group."

He scanned the room one more time and found Emily coming out of the bathroom. She was wearing a pretty blue dress that matched her eyes and skimmed her knees, and the sight of her took his breath away. Her hair lay in soft waves down to her shoulders, and he longed to bury his face in it like he had the night before in the tack room.

"Emily is right there. You could talk to her," he said.

"I'd rather talk to you," Gloria said.

Justin looked over the top of his mother's head and his gaze locked with Emily's. There was definitely chemistry, and it felt right.

"Hey, Justin is here now!" Patsy raised her voice. "Let's eat and then play the game. I want Benjy on my team."

"Oh, no!" Otis argued. "We get Benjy."

Claire pushed her blond hair behind her ears and headed toward the table with the pizza. "I'm hungry so make way."

Retta picked up a paper plate and began to load it with slices. "I'm right behind you, Claire. I get double tonight because I'm eating for two."

"I'm your friendly bartender." Justin began to fill red plastic cups with ice. "Y'all come on by here when you get your food, and I'll fix you right up."

"You do the ice and I'll pour," Gloria said.

Emily was the last in line and whispered, "Sweet tea is fine."

"Comin' right up. I'll join you. Mama, you can pour your own, right?"

"Of course," Gloria huffed.

"Want a little Jack in that?" he whispered when they were away from his mother.

"That might prove dangerous," she said. "I'm already gettin' daggers shot at me by your mama. Did I do something wrong?"

"No, honey. Mama is just bein' overprotective, but gettin' back to the idea of something being dangerous. It could be a lot of fun."

"What could be fun?" Patsy asked.

"She's got hearing like a bat," Emily said.

"Watchin' you ladies lose. We've got Benjy." Justin quickly covered his comment.

"And we've got Sarah," Bess said. "She can draw real good."

"Yes, I can," Sarah said, which set off an argument among the Fab Five.

While they fussed about who was going to win the games, Justin brushed a strand of hair away from Emily's face. "You sure do look pretty tonight. I want to kiss you so bad right now that it hurts. Think we could slip outside?"

"If we did, your mama would probably shoot me. So we'd better stay right here."

*　　*　　*

Emily hadn't had a man look at her the way Justin was in— she cocked her head to one side and tried to remember—in like ever.

"Thank you. You clean up pretty good too," she answered.

"This has been a really great week. I hate to see it end."

When he lowered his deep voice into a whisper, it was even sexier than usual. And his bedroom eyes, with the thick dark lashes, drew her to him like a bee to a honey pot.

"In spite of all their antics?" she asked.

"I'm not talking about them. I'm talking about us, but it's been fun having them here. I have to admit that I had my doubts about this type of thing, but it turned out really good. I'd let them come back in the fall or next spring if they want to," he said.

"No, thank you. I'll develop heart failure if I try this again." She smiled.

"I'll give you mouth-to-mouth resuscitation if you pass out," he offered.

His eyes roamed over her snug-fitting dress. Suddenly, the room was entirely too warm, and the thoughts of his lips on hers again filled her with even more heat. She took a long drink of the icy cold sweet tea in her hand, but it didn't cool her down a bit.

"First, I don't pass out. And second, I'm not sure you're strong enough to handle me if I did," she said.

"Oh, honey, you just give me a chance, and I'll show you exactly what I can do for you." He flirted with his eyes and body language as much as with his words.

Emily's heart was thumping around in her chest and she could feel her pulse in her ears. "You better go get some pizza because the game is going to start soon. I've got a five-dollar bill that says the girls win."

"If the boys win, you can keep your money and agree to go out with me." He brushed past her on the way to the table.

"If the girls win, you can just give me the five bucks." The touch of his body against hers sent visuals to her mind that were definitely X-rated.

"You're breakin' my heart," he teased as he followed her across the room.

"Yeah, right. You'll be at the Rusty Spur next weekend, and I won't even be a blip on your memory. Eat your pizza, and get ready to fork over a bill when we win this game."

"Will I be a blip on your memory?" He nudged her with a shoulder.

"Of course you will, darlin'. You're irresistible, remember?" she said.

He laid a hand on his chest. "You're a tough woman, Emily Baker."

"You just want to go out with me because I'm probably

the only woman who's ever refused you when you asked," she told him.

"Oh, darlin', you give me way too much credit." Justin chuckled.

Gloria dragged a folding chair across the room, put it at the end of the two remaining chairs left, and sat down in the middle.

Justin motioned for Emily to sit down in one, then he moved the other one over beside her. "There, now we can sit together."

Gloria's smile was sarcastic instead of happy. "I'm so sorry. I didn't realize that I was gettin' between y'all."

"It's okay," Emily said. "I'm glad that we can sit together so I can get to know you better. We haven't had much one-on-one time. Which side are you bettin' on tonight?"

"The boys, of course. Benjy is a crackerjack artist and so is Justin." Gloria's tone was icy.

"So is Sarah. They sure had a good time this week."

"And you? Did you have a good time too?" Gloria's blue eyes, so much like Cade's, bored into Emily's.

Emily didn't blink. "Yes, I did. I used to spend a lot of time on my grandmother's ranch when I was young and it has been fun to get to spend some time in the country. So thank y'all for a lovely week."

"I'm just glad that I've got family so that when I get old, they'll be around to take care of me," Gloria said.

"That's nice," Emily said sweetly. There was no way she'd let Gloria get the best of her.

"And your family? Will you step up to take care of them when they're old?"

"Of course," Emily said. "Family is precious."

The first game of Pictionary began, and Gloria didn't have anything more to say. Emily let the other ladies take center stage in guessing what Benjy was drawing. The living/dining room was filled with laughter, and all she had to do was look at the Five's expressions to see how much fun they were having. Maybe after a year, she'd be willing to bring them back to the ranch. It would give them something to look forward to.

All of the ladies were dolled up and as comfortable in their skins as Emily was—or would be if it wasn't so hot in the bunkhouse. Otis had changed into khaki pants and a button-down shirt instead of his usual jeans and T-shirts. Larry had even donned a pair of gray slacks with a bright red polo shirt. She hadn't seen them so dressed up since the Christmas party.

The boys won.

Benjy high-fived Otis and Larry.

Sarah poked Emily on the leg and whispered, "We let them win that last round to make Benjy happy."

"I had a bet riding on this." Emily groaned.

"Yep, and there was that too," Patsy giggled.

Justin lingered at the door after everyone else had left. "So what night next week is good for you? And I'll need your address."

"I'll have to check my calendar, cowboy," Emily said. "And when I've got a free day, I'll meet you somewhere for dinner."

"She lives out on Belcherville Road," Patsy yelled.

"White house with a detached garage and an apartment above it," Sarah added.

"The lady who owns the house drives an older model white Caddy, but she can't park it in the garage because she's a hoarder and it's full. She'd like to move to the retirement center but she couldn't bring all that crap with her." Bess put in her two cents.

"Thank you all for the clues. And I will call next week to check on that calendar of yours. See you in the morning at breakfast, and then we'll be going to church together." Justin grinned and then gave Emily a peck on the cheek as he left.

"That's a date, right? So we don't have a drinking contest on Sunday evening?" she called out.

He turned around on the porch. "No, ma'am. That's church and a potluck. It's only a date if I pick you up at your house, bring you back there, and hope for a good night kiss."

"Awww, that's so sweet," Patsy said. "I wish I was your age. I'd damn sure give him more than a good night kiss. I'd drag him into the bedroom and do things that would put that *Fifty Shades* book to shame."

Emily's hands went to her crimson cheeks. "I've blushed more this week than I have in years."

"All that blushing means you feel something for Justin." Bess patted the sofa beside her. "Now come on over here, and sit beside me. We need to have a woman-to-woman talk."

"About?" Emily crossed the room, kicked off her shoes, and sat down.

"Why you are so hard to catch. A girl can just run so long before it's time to stand still and get caught."

Emily laid a hand on Bess's shoulder. "He's too good-lookin' to be serious about a girl like me. Right now I'm here, and since I'm not fallin' at his feet like he's probably used to, he's intrigued. He'll forget me when we leave."

"What if you're wrong? He looks at you like he could have you for breakfast, dinner, and supper," Sarah said.

"I'm not wrong. I lost the bet, so I'll go out with him. I honor my bets, and now it's time for bed. We have to get up early to get our packing done before church." Emily thought of the way his kisses turned her knees weak and hoped that the date was just the beginning of many more—but she wasn't about to admit it—even to herself.

"And then it will be over. I could die in my sleep tonight and go out a happy woman." Bess sighed.

"Don't you dare!" Patsy shivered. "If I woke up to a dead woman in the bed with me, I'd probably join you."

"We should do that," Bess declared. "We should all three make a pact to die together on the same day so we don't leave anyone behind to grieve."

They piled their hands on each other's.

"To finishing this life together," Patsy said.

"Yes!" Sarah and Bess nodded, seriously.

A cold chill made its way down Emily's back as she stood up and headed toward her bedroom. It was the last night she'd have to sleep on a twin-size bed. Tomorrow she could sprawl out on her California king without fear that she'd fall off onto the floor if she turned over in her sleep. She had counted down the nights she'd have to spend on the ranch, but now that it was the last night, she dreaded leaving.

"My sweet little old folks are going to be depressed." She talked to her reflection in the mirror as she removed her makeup and took off her earrings.

What about you, Emily Renee? Are you going to be depressed? Her mother's voice was so clear that she jerked around to see if she was actually in the room with her.

"Why are you second naming me?" Emily asked.

If she was totally honest with herself, the answer to her mother's question would be yes, but it was a bitter pill to swallow. It had been fun visiting the ranch, reacquainting herself with everything that she'd grown up with. But all good things must come to an end—and the feeling of nostalgia—right along with this physical attraction that she had for Justin, would pass.

"One date and then it will definitely be over," she said out loud as she crawled into bed.

She closed her eyes only to dream of Justin. In the dream they were slick with sweat after making love on a twin bed. He held her close so that she wouldn't fall off. She awoke the next morning and reached behind her, but there was nothing there but a lumpy pillow. She threw it against the wall.

Chapter Nine

If there'd been a test after church that morning on what the preacher's sermon had been about, Emily would have failed miserably. Somehow she and Justin had wound up side by side, plastered against each other in a crowded pew. Not even a thousand angels flapping their wings could cool her down with that much heat next to her. So God would just have to understand why she couldn't focus on what the preacher had to say.

When Skip delivered the benediction and the final amen was said, everyone stood up as if on cue, and she finally had some breathing space to think about something other than making out with Justin right there on the church pew. Patsy bumped her on the thigh with her hip.

"So where was your mind during the services? I know if I'd been that close to a sexy cowboy like Justin, I would have been thinkin' of how many positions I could get him into," Patsy said.

"You're making me blush again," Emily whispered.

Mavis tapped Emily on the shoulder as they made their way to the fellowship hall. "Would it be all right if I offer to go get all of them and bring them to church on Sunday mornings from here on out? I'd love to do that and to take them home with us for Sunday dinner. Benjy has talked nonstop about Larry and Otis ever since yesterday, and to tell the truth, I really enjoy spending time with those three women. They're a hoot and they remind me so much of my mother's younger sisters."

"What a sweet idea. I'm sure they'd be ecstatic to get to spend Sundays with y'all," Emily said. "Just tell them what time to be ready, and I'll make it right with the supervisor."

Mavis nodded. "Someday me and Skip might be in their shoes. I'm glad we'll at least have Levi and Benjy and hope-fully some grandchildren who'll pop in and see us when that time comes. Be all right if I ask them now, or should you clear it first?" Mavis asked.

"It's perfectly all right to ask them now."

"And you're welcome to join us too," Mavis offered. "I heard your lovely voice when we were having congrega-tional singing. It'd sure be nice to have you in our choir."

"Thank you," Emily said but she wasn't committing to anything. Saturday and Sunday were her days off, and she was selfish with every hour.

When they got inside the hall, she caught sight of the ladies near the kitchen. All three of them were putting on colorful bibbed aprons and taking their place behind the long tables full of food.

"Oh, no!" Mavis started that way. "They're guests. They don't have to work."

"Good luck," Emily said.

When Mavis spoke, they began to shake their heads in unison. "But, we want to help," Patsy said. "It makes us feel like we're young again and back in our own little church."

"And it helps us to feel like we're fittin' in. We sure wish we could come here every Sunday. I've never felt so much at home since I left Berryville," Sarah said.

"This spread reminds me of all the potlucks we had in Bells," Bess said.

Mavis grabbed an apron and joined them. "We'd love to have you as part of our church family. I just asked Emily if I could come get all five of you on Sunday and bring you to church here. Then you could go to Sunday dinner with us."

Bess rolled her eyes toward the ceiling. "I've died and gone to heaven."

"Can we come to Sunday school too or just church?" Sarah asked. "We can be ready right after we have our breakfast."

"We'd love to have you in our senior Sunday school class," Mavis answered.

Emily turned around so no one could see the tears threatening to string black mascara down her cheeks. And she ran smack into Justin. Her palms shot out to his chest and his arms went around her waist.

"If you want a hug, just ask. I'm more than willin'," he teased.

She pushed back from him. "You are the biggest flirt in Texas."

He reached out with a forefinger and brushed away a tear from the corner of her eye. "And that makes you cry? Why?"

"It's not that," she said.

"Got something to do with the way the Five fit in with the church family and how excited they are that Mavis has offered to bring them over on Sundays? You could join them," he said. "What time should I pick you up next Sunday mornin'?"

"Does that count as the date I owe you?" she asked.

"It could," he said.

"Then okay. Church is at eleven. I'll meet you here," she answered.

"On a real date, I pick you up at your door, not meet you somewhere," he said.

"Okay." She sighed. "Call me the night before, and I'll give you instructions on how to get to my apartment."

Justin took a step forward. "Hey, I'll let you off the bet if this is going to be a chore."

"I pay my debts. I'll be ready." She felt bad for the way she was acting, so she said, "Besides, my mama will be so pleased to know that I'm going to church two weekends in a row."

"Honey, don't pressure Emily if she's got things to do," Gloria said sweetly as she moved between Emily and Justin. "Besides we're only plannin' on stayin' at the ranch a couple of more weeks, and Sunday is family day."

"Gloria, darlin'." Vernon got her by the hand. "Skip has saved us a place in line. I know how much you love your peach cobbler, and it's going fast. So let these kids bring up the rear and come with me."

With a hand on her back, Justin led Emily to the back of the line. "You said your mother would be happy that you are in church two weeks in a row. What about your brothers? Don't they go every Sunday?"

"Matthew does, but the twins are CEO Christians." She smiled.

"And that's what?"

"Christmas and Easter Only Christians, and that's

because Mama makes them go twice a year, in hopes that it'll count for something. They've been pretty wild," she answered.

"And how about you? You been wild?"

Before she could answer, a short, round cowboy took his place in line behind them and said, "Darlin', I'm Buddy, but you can call me anything you want to. I don't care if you've been wild or not. You're about the prettiest thing I've ever seen, next to my sweet Allison." He held up the hand of a brunette standing right beside him.

"Oh, really. What do you know about a wild woman?" Emily smiled down at the man. Not only was he short, but he was also stocky, and his smile reminded her somewhat of a cartoon possum eating grapes through a barbed wire fence.

"I done roped me a wild one and intend to keep her forever." Buddy kissed Allison on the cheek and looked up at Justin. "We're getting married this summer."

A glance between Allison and Justin told Emily that the woman would have rather been hanging on his arm than Buddy's.

You're jealous, aren't you? Her grandmother was back in her head.

"Am not," she muttered.

"Am not what?" Justin asked.

"Did I say that out loud?" Emily's blue eyes widened.

He nodded.

"I'm glad there's so much noise that only you heard it." She smiled. "I was arguing with my grandmother."

"I do that sometimes, only it's usually with my mama." Justin's hand on her back moved her right up to the end of the table, where they both got a disposable plate. "I love potlucks."

"Me too. I always want to eat some of everything, but that would be impossible with a spread like this," she said.

"Do y'all live in this area?" Emily glanced over her shoulder at Buddy and Allison.

"I've got a little auto shop, and Allison works at the vet's place over in Bowie." Buddy beamed.

"Did I hear it right, that you're leaving the ranch today?" Allison asked.

"Yes, we are. It's been a fun week, but now it's time to go back to the center."

"I bet it has." Allison glared at her.

"You have no idea." Emily met her gaze and didn't blink. Then she turned around and asked Justin, "So does our church date next week include dinner afterward?"

"Of course." Justin nodded. "Just name the place. Your favorite restaurant or back at the ranch, either one."

She could feel Allison boring holes in her back, but Emily was willing to bet that if the woman and Justin did have something in the past, he'd never taken her to church.

*   *   *

Justin piled food on his plate until nothing more would fit, and then he looked around for a place with two empty chairs. Then he saw Skip waving and pointing at all the chairs they'd saved.

"Y'all want to sit with us?" Buddy asked.

"Looks like the family has saved chairs for us. But thanks anyway." Justin was glad that he had an excuse. More than once Allison had gone home with him from the Rusty Spur, enjoyed a bit of hot sex, and made breakfast the next morning for the two of them. Justin sure didn't want to jeopardize what could happen with Emily with his wild past.

They'd barely gotten seated when Otis asked, "Did you hear? We get to come over here for church every Sunday. It's just barely inside the county line so we could drive there, but Mavis is going to check us out for the day. Ain't that just the best news ever?"

"And Otis can look at my sheep," Benjy said. "He knows about show stock because he raised some when he had a ranch."

"I saw you talking to Buddy." Mavis leaned forward and put her hand to the side of her mouth. "Did you hear that he's proposed to Allison?"

Justin broke open a hot roll and reached for the butter packets in the middle of the table. "He told us, but he was flirting with Emily."

"That boy will be flirting with the nurses the day he takes his last breath." Skip chuckled. "It's the way he is. They're having their rings special designed, I'm told. They'll be ready next week, and then they plan to make the big public announcement."

"Good for him." Justin didn't sigh, but he felt like it. Buddy was another of his friends he wouldn't be seeing at the Rusty Spur on Friday or Saturday nights.

"Weren't you and Allison a hot little item at one time?" Gloria sat down across the table from them. "Seems like I remember you saying she made some really good sausage gravy." She was talking to Justin but looking right at Emily.

"Sounds like Buddy is a lucky man to get a wife who can cook." Emily looked Gloria in the eye and smiled sweetly.

Otis nudged Justin's shoulder and whispered, "Never interfere in a catfight."

"What?" Justin frowned.

"They're establishing their territory, and in case you're

wonderin', the property is named Justin Maguire. I went through it before I got married."

"Married?" Justin gasped.

"It's the end game. Might take a while for them to get there. And you might have to go through a few women to get there, too, but right now your mama is jealous of Emily. Don't worry, Emily is holding her ground," Otis said.

"Hey, y'all saved us a place," Patsy said as she, Sarah, and Bess brought their plates to the table. "That's so sweet. I can't tell you what this whole week has meant to us."

Justin tried to listen as the Fab Five talked about their vacation, but his thoughts kept going back to what Otis had said. His mother had already voiced her opinion of Emily, but could it be possible that Emily was really interested in him?

"You're awfully quiet," Emily said.

"Hating to see the week end."

"I don't think it is ending. The ladies are discussing quilting and Sundays, and Cade invited the guys back to the ranch anytime they want to visit," she told him.

"How about you?"

"We've got a date for next Sunday," she reminded him in a whisper and then raised her voice. "Okay, it's time for good-byes and for us to get on back to the center."

"I don't like it but we do have next Sunday to look forward to," Patsy declared. "We'll bring dessert to the dinner."

"Thank you," Mavis said. "I'll be there at nine thirty on the dot. And you've all got our phone numbers, so call anytime you want to talk."

Justin walked them out to the van and helped the ladies up the steps. Larry was the last one to get inside, and he lingered for a second. He laid his hand on Justin's shoulder and said, "Son, anytime you need some advice on building your house, you come on to the center and we'll go over your plans together. And thank you for everything. This week has been the best time we've had in years."

"You are very welcome, and I'll sure take you up on that offer. I'll start drawing up plans for my own house tonight, as soon as I get my things moved to the cabin," Justin said.

"Anytime you want to sell that cabin, I get first chance," Otis yelled.

"Oh, no you don't. Me and Bess have more money than you and we'll outbid you." Patsy shook a fist toward him.

"Wagons ho!" Sarah yelled.

"See you later," Justin told Emily as he shut the door.

He stood in the parking lot and waved until they were completely out of sight. When he turned around and started toward his truck, Buddy was right there, so close that he almost ran into him.

"Didn't mean to sneak up on you," Buddy said. "But I wanted to talk to you about Allison. I know you and she..." He cleared his throat. "Well, that y'all had a thing a while back, and I don't want things to get all stupid between us. We've been friends since first grade."

Justin clamped a hand on Buddy's shoulder. "What was between us has been over for a long time so there won't be anything weird going on."

"Good," Buddy said. "Now tell me about Emily. Man, she's a looker, but my friend, it'll take some kind of cowboy to tame that woman. She and Allison almost got in a little catfight right there in the buffet line."

"Who says I'm interested in Emily?" That was the second time someone had mentioned those words in the past hour.

"Can't hide it. I could feel the vibes between y'all. They was almost as hot and heavy as what me and Allison got."

Buddy flashed another one of his signature grins. "Got to go. Allison is waiting in the truck. I never thought I'd get a trophy wife like her. And a word of advice. You'd better seize the moment with Emily."

"Got to have a moment before you can seize it," Justin said.

"Make one." Buddy waved over his shoulder as he walked away.

Justin went straight home and had loaded his personal things in his truck before Retta and Cade arrived. He'd picked up a few snacks from the pantry and was about to head out when they drove up. This would definitely be a change. He'd had the same bedroom since he'd gotten out of his crib, sharing it with Cade until they were in elementary school.

Justin opened the door and then leaned on the fender of his truck and waited for them to get parked. He'd hoped to be gone when they got home. It would have made leaving easier. "Hey, I thought I'd get out before you got home so it wouldn't be all weird."

"You don't have to do this." Retta hugged him tightly. "You can live with us forever and we'll be happy."

"She's right, brother," Cade said.

"I know but..." He paused. "You went away to college, and Levi has moved into town until his house is built. Y'all need to get on with making a nursery, and I want to live at the cabin for a while. This isn't really one hundred percent on my own, since I'll be in and out all the time for meals."

Beau came out of nowhere, hopped right into the truck and curled up on the passenger seat. "Looks like I got custody of the dog." He smiled at Cade.

"Yeah, right. Everyone knows that mutt belongs to Levi."

"Hey, wait a minute." Gloria came out of the RV and

opened the passenger door. "I still don't think this is the thing for you to do, but I'm willing to go help you move in."

"I got it, but thanks for the offer," Justin said.

She lowered her chin and looked up at him. "Is Emily going to help you?"

"What is it with you? You've been after me to settle down for more than a year and now that I take a woman to church, you're all pissy."

"You didn't take her. You just sat with her, but gossip is already spreading like wildfire," Gloria argued.

"I'm taking her next week and then to dinner afterward. I don't give a damn about rumors." Hc slid behind the wheel and started the engine. "And again, why are you so dead set against her?"

"She's..." Gloria drew in a long breath and let it out in a whoosh. "She's a big woman for one thing, and..."

"And what, Mama? I happen to think Emily is gorgeous."

"Oh, go do whatever you want. You will anyway. Just don't expect me to like it." Gloria slammed the door and stormed back to the trailer.

He drove slowly, keeping a watch in the rearview. Cade slipped his arm around Retta's shoulders, and together they went into the house—their house for the first time since they got married, and rightly so. Cade should have it, since he was the oldest son. Besides, Justin was really looking forward to building something brand-new to pass down to his oldest son.

He shifted his focus back to the path going around the barn and to the back of the ranch. The truck nearly drove itself over the familiar path, and he wondered if his son would have the Maguires' blue eyes or if they would have Emily's lighter color? Would his mother ever like Emily if sometime in the future, they did get past one date?

He glanced over at Beau. "What do you think, ole boy? I had to practically get down on my knees and beg her to go out with me, and now it's a church date rather than a nice evening alone. Think there's any way that we'll ever share children?"

Never say never. His father's voice was so clear that he checked the rearview mirror to be sure that Vernon Maguire wasn't in the bed of the truck.

Chapter Ten

Emily had to cram two days' work into one evening. At least she'd kept her laundry caught up at the bunkhouse, but there was so much more than just that, and she was tired, both physically and emotionally when bedtime finally came on Sunday night. She slept poorly, even though she was in her own king-size bed. When she awoke on Monday morning she couldn't wait to get back to her routine. Unfortunately, the day turned out to be a Murphy's Law day.

Dark clouds covered the sky when she went out to get in her car. Lightning split the sky and thunder rolled before she could get out of the driveway. By the time she reached the center, rain was coming down in sheets. She got her umbrella from the backseat and carefully opened it. Then she reached for her briefcase, and a hard gust of wind grabbed the umbrella, turned it wrong side out, and ripped it out of her hands. It got hung up in the naked limbs of one of the oak trees. By the time she reached the door, she felt like a drowned rat. She'd taken time to curl her hair that morning, but now it hung limp in her face. She quickly poked in the code to get inside, but the door wouldn't open. She hit it twice more, with rain blowing in her face.

Finally, she removed her phone from her purse and called Nikki. "What's the code? Did y'all change it while I was gone?"

"Nine, nine, one, one," Nikki said. "I'm on my way to the lobby."

"Grab a couple of towels as you come past the laundry." Emily pressed the numbers as she talked. The little light above the keypad went from red to green, and she wasted no time dashing inside. The soles of her shoes were so wet that she stumbled on the edge of the rug and sprawled out on the floor. Her briefcase flew open and papers flew every which way, skittering under the sofa and touching the ceiling fan before they fell back to the floor like oversize confetti.

"Well, that's a lovely way to start out the week, but it is Monday." Nikki held out a hand toward her.

Emily took it and raised herself up to a sitting position. "Murphy's Monday."

"Don't say that. So far my shift is going well." Nikki laughed.

"Then I'm the only one with bad luck. God must hate me."

"Are you hurt? Legs working all right? Arms okay? Did you hit your head?" Nikki asked.

"Only thing that's hurt is my pride," Emily answered.

Nikki handed her a couple of towels. "I'd loan you a set of my scrubs but..."

"As if I could wear a size four petite. Lord, girl, I was born in a bigger size than that. Thanks anyway but I've got a spare set in my locker. I'll just slip in there and get changed, soon as I gather up all these papers. At least I didn't slip and fall outside and get them all wet. They're my financial reports for the week we were gone," Emily said.

"I'll pick them all up for you. Go on and change into dry clothes." Nikki began to gather up all the papers.

"Thank you." Emily picked up the small makeup bag she carried in her briefcase and hurried off toward the employees' break room.

She toweled her hair dry, brushed it out, and pulled it up into a ponytail, but she still groaned when she looked in the mirror. She stripped out of the soaking-wet light blue scrubs and then her underpants and bra. Thank goodness she'd learned to keep a complete change of clothes in her locker, including underwear. She used the second towel to dry her body, which was every bit as wet as if she'd just stepped out of the shower. She had no intentions of taking the time to apply fresh makeup, and usually avoided looking at herself when she was naked, but she caught her reflection in a floor-length mirror. "What on earth does Justin see in me when he could have any woman in the state?"

She'd hoped to have a meeting with the supervisor and go over the reports for the last week, but she was on the clock to play bingo with the residents in ten minutes. So she rushed out of the room and headed that way, only to turn a corner to see Justin coming right at her.

"Well, hello." He smiled.

"What are you doing here?" she asked.

"Is that any way to treat a man who just helped pick up

a bunch of papers that were strewn all over the lobby?" He pulled her behind a partition and kissed her. "I might live now. You're on my mind all the time, Emily."

"You are either a hopeless romantic or the biggest flirt in north Texas."

"Maybe I'm both." He grinned. "A short brunette told me about your fall and where you'd gone. I'm glad I found you and got a life-saving kiss. But I do need to see Larry. She said he's on this wing."

Emily pointed down a hall. "That way. Number one two seven four, but he's probably in the activities room. We're playing bingo this morning and his candy dish is empty in his kitchenette."

"What's that got to do with anything?" Justin asked.

"We give candy bars for winning. When he gets low he never misses a game. Just follow me," she said. "I'm going that way."

He fell in behind her. "Are any of them so poor that they can't afford what they want?"

"Not by any means. The Fab Five are all richer than Midas and have no one to even leave it to or spend it on, but they're tight with their money. They clip coupons and have contests about who can save the most money when they go shopping for snacks each week." She slung open the door, and several people yelled out greetings.

The Fab Five squealed Justin's name and left their spots to hurry across the floor. Gathering around him, they patted his arms and back as if he were a long-lost son they hadn't seen in a decade. Emily felt a sudden flash of pure jealousy.

"Seems like y'all been gone from the ranch for a month instead of a day," Justin told them. "But I was wonderin' if I might have a word with Larry about construction."

"Sure you can. Let's go to the dinin' room where it's quiet," Larry said.

Justin winked at Emily. "See you Sunday if not before."

*   *   *

"So what's your problem?" Larry led the way to a table in the corner and nodded for Justin to sit down across from him.

"I had no problem designing Levi and Claire's place, but this is for me and I don't know what I want."

"It was easy because Claire and Levi knew exactly what they wanted. When me and Sally Ann, my precious wife, built our place, we made sure we both had everything we wanted. So you're askin' the wrong person, son. You need to ask Emily," Larry said.

Justin thought for a minute that he'd choke to death before he could speak again. When he finally got past the coughing, he said, "Why would you say that?"

"She'd be able to give you a woman's view on things."

"What about Retta or Claire?"

Larry shrugged. "What if you do something in your house that Claire wishes you'd done in hers or makes Retta feel bad because she don't have her own brand-new place? You really need an impartial woman's opinion."

"But what if she tells me she likes it all designed one way or blows me off and then pushes me away, and when I settle down, my new woman wants it another way?"

Another shrug. "It'll give you a start and then between us, we'll decide what to keep and what to toss out."

"Well." Justin rubbed his chin. "We're having dinner after church on Sunday. I could ask her what she thinks, but what if she thinks I'm pushing for something more and…"

"More than what?" Larry asked.

"Nothing," Justin said, quickly. "I'll be thinking about the outside dimensions. I'm thinkin' of something that could be added on to, like Claire and Levi's place."

"Smart idea. Hey, you want to come play bingo with us? You might win some candy and you could give it to Emily for Valentine's Day."

"Thanks for the invitation, but I'll pass. I've got to go to the tractor supply store and then pick up a few things from Walmart for Retta," Justin answered.

"Our Valentine's party is at six o'clock. That's after supper on Thursday. You should come join us. We make us some Valentine boxes to put cards in." Larry stood up and started down the hall. "You think about it. Other people's kids come. You could be our relative for the evenin'."

"I'll see what we've got going at the ranch." Justin headed for the door.

"Try to make it. Everyone here makes a box, but you don't have to bring a card for them. Just me." Larry turned around and grinned.

Justin gave him a thumbs-up and left by the door off the dining area. The rain had stopped but the sun still wasn't out. He should go to the party, he thought, because no one should be at an event and not even have a relative there. But would Emily think he was stalking her if he did?

He pondered over that the whole way to the tractor supply store and was still thinking about it at Walmart when he was picking up the few things that Retta needed from the grocery section. He was almost to the checkout counter when he passed a display of valentines. The kind that kids give each other at school parties. Was that the kind Larry was talking about or did they make fancy ones with glitter and glue? If he decided to go he needed to be prepared, but he had no idea what to buy.

Finally, he picked up a box and tossed it in the cart. There was simply no way he had time to make cards, and if he did, what on earth would he write in them? He checked out, went back to his truck, and tossed the box into the backseat.

When he got back to the ranch, he took Retta's things in and put them on the cabinet. Then he went right to the barn, hefted sacks of feed onto his shoulders, and stacked them in one of the clean stalls. That done, he went back to the truck, got the box out, and took it to the tack room. The box contained twenty cards plus envelopes plus a special card with a red lollipop attached to it.

Justin's mouth turned up slightly at the corners. Josie Mae Turner almost beat him up on the playground after their first grade party because he didn't give her the card with the lollipop. She told him that she'd chased him all over the place at every recess for a week so he should know that she liked him. So why didn't she get the special card? When he told her that he'd given it to his mother, she hit on him some more. He chose the one with the lollipop, picked up a pen and drew a heart with a simple J in the center of it. If he went to the party, he'd slip that one into Emily's box when she wasn't looking. Surely that wouldn't be misconstrued as stalking. Then he sorted the rest of the cards into five stacks of four, put them into their little envelopes, and filled in the *to* and *from* lines on the front—Larry got the ones with bulldozers, tractors, and cars; Otis the ones with farm animals; and the ladies got all the cute kittens and dogs.

Now he was ready. He returned everything to the box and carried it outside to his truck. A lot could happen in three days, and if he didn't go to the party at the center, he could always toss them into the trash. No one need ever know that he'd worried over which valentines to give to which of the Fab Five—or that Emily was supposed to get the special one.

Chapter Eleven

"Hey, did you buy out a shoe store?" Larry peeked around the door at all the boxes set on the tables in the recreation room.

"No, but I wish I could. I love pretty shoes. How are you going to decorate your Valentine box?" Emily put out stickers and cutouts on each table, along with glitter, scissors, and glue for the residents whose hands were still limber enough to use them.

"I'm going to make the outline of a skyscraper. I always wanted to design one of them things, so today is my chance." Larry sat down at the first table.

"Sounds great." Valentine's Day had never been her favorite holiday, but the residents loved a party for any reason.

"Speaking of skyscrapers, what's your dream house, Emily? I see you in a big old two-story with a wide front porch," he said.

"Oh, really! And where is this located?"

"It ain't in town, maybe a suburb or on an acre or two with lots of lawn where the kids can romp and play. Maybe even a ranch." He sat down at the table and picked up a piece of dark blue construction paper.

"Why would you see me in that kind of a house, and not a long, low ranch style?"

He shrugged. "I got here early for bingo one day and you were lookin' at a magazine. You left it open on the plans for a two-story. It was painted white and had a big porch with pretty flowers hangin' in baskets in between the porch posts. Maybe you was just thinkin' about the place where you grew up in out there in the panhandle?"

"I lived in a rambling ranch house, but it did have a wide front porch with two swings, one on either end. I loved that porch," she said. "But it's funny that you mentioned that picture. I'd forgotten about it until now. The house was so pretty and yet it wasn't oversized, so cleaning wouldn't be such a job. If I remember right, it had three bedrooms and a bathroom on the second floor and a master bedroom downstairs. Did working with Justin on Claire's place put that on your mind?"

"I guess so. It was real nice to get to do that. Your granny didn't have a two-story either?"

She thought about her grandparents' house south of Tulia, Texas. She'd spent lots of time there as a little girl. Maribel, the housekeeper and cook, had babysat her often before she started to school. Especially on the days when an extra hand was needed on the ranch and her mother filled in. There wasn't anything Mama couldn't do, and like Emily, she really enjoyed getting her hands dirty so she spent a lot of time outdoors.

Larry's chuckle brought Emily back to the present. "My

wife thought she'd like a two-story, so I designed her one but then life got in the way and by the time we were ready to build something new, we decided we liked where we were. Besides, she'd gotten bad knees and my hip was acting up, so we didn't need them stairs. One thing she did say was that she wished she had a closet for all her pretty shoes."

"And that makes you laugh, why?" Emily went on about her work.

"She never went shoppin' with her friends that she didn't bring home a pair of shoes. She always bought at least two pair, sometimes more, but she'd leave the others out in the tool box of the truck."

"Why?" Emily asked.

Another chuckle, only this one was louder. "She knew I'd tease her about buyin' more than she could ever wear out. So she'd bring in the one pair, hide the rest, and then bring them in secretly. I wish I'd built her a closet with shelves and a nice bench so she could just sit in there and look at all them pretty shoes. Several months after she passed, I found a pair of shoes in the truck and sat down and bawled like a baby."

Emily stopped what she was doing and patted him on the back. "I'm afraid I'm just like your wife. Shoes are my downfall." She held up a foot. "I work in these. I wear boots when I go home. I go very few places where I can wear high heels, but every time I see a shoe sale, I buy another pair. I can only dream about a house with a closet like you described."

Larry sighed. "Well, honey, you should have it and a two-story house too, if that's what you really like."

"With a garden tub." She set out a bottle of water at each place. Getting the older folks to drink enough was always a problem.

"So you can go skinny-dippin'?" Larry winked.

"Hey, now!" A vision of sharing a Jacuzzi with Justin popped into her head and immediately she was flushed.

"We're early!" Bess, Patsy, and Sarah arrived.

"I got here first," Larry bragged.

Emily shook the vision from her head and said, "Find a seat and look through all the decorations. There's cupids and hearts and cute little arrows."

"I wanted a four-wheeler and a cow." Otis came in behind them.

"I found one special just for you." Emily pointed to an oversize sticker. "It's set inside a heart frame."

"Ahh, thank you, Emily. I know I'm your favorite." He pulled out a chair.

"No, you aren't," Patsy argued.

"Y'all don't start in fussin'," Larry said. "Me and Emily been talkin' about houses."

Patsy clamped both hands over her eyes. "I'd rather talk about kissin' good-lookin' cowboys and *s-e-x*."

Bess slapped her on the arm. "We can't talk about that in here."

"Why? Valentine's is about lovers and all that delicious stuff." Patsy set two bottles of glitter beside her box.

"Anyway, we were talkin' about her dream house and what she'd put in it." Larry sat down beside Otis and opened a small jar of royal blue paint.

"Well, me and Patsy had ours built when we was forty," Bess said. "We figured we could run the ranch from a pretty little place in town, close to our church and our friends. We lived in it two months before we admitted we were miserable and went back to the ranch house."

"I missed the big pantry in our new house when we went back." Patsy sighed. "It was one of them walk-in kinds with all different-size shelves to hold our supplies and cookware. But giving it up wasn't so hard when we thought about going back home to the place where we'd been born and raised."

Emily pulled out a chair behind the wrapping paper table and sat down. "What'd you do with the house?"

"We donated it to the church for a new parsonage," Bess said. "They're still usin' it for that purpose today and everyone loves the pantry and the little special touches we put in it."

"So would you want somethin' like that in yours?" Larry asked.

"I love to cook, so that would be amazing," Emily said.

"That pantry at Longhorn Canyon was awesome." Patsy drew in a lungful of air and let it out slowly. "For a little while, I pretended me and Bess were back on the ranch while we were there."

"What about you, Sarah?" Larry asked.

"I lived in a two-story until I came to this place. Loved it but it was built when my folks first married, so the closets were small and there was only one bathroom and it was on the second floor. Mama wanted a house full of children, but it didn't happen. Daddy died first and then it was just me and Mama. Then she passed, leaving me to ramble around in it all by myself. It got lonely." She picked up a cutout of a cupid. "I'm going to do layer painting with markers so there will be shading. What kind of cards did y'all buy? I got the kind with a little package of three sweethearts on each one."

"Better be careful which one you put Henry's name on. He's got a crush on you, and if you put one of them conversation hearts that says BE MINE on it, he'll take that as a sign," Patsy said.

"That's a crock of bullshit," Sarah said. "He's got the hots for you."

"That's just because you told him I was wild." Patsy giggled. "I might give him a BE MINE just to put some glitter in his old eyes."

Emily's thoughts went back again to when she was a small child and she wanted so badly to get a valentine with a piece of candy attached to it. Preferably one of those heart-shaped lollipops because she was convinced that it had to taste better than any lollipop she'd ever eaten.

*   *   *

Guilt pricked Justin's heart as he passed by the Oakview Retirement Center on his way to the vet's place that Tuesday morning. What if there were other folks who lived there who didn't have relatives to put cards in their boxes? He couldn't take them all to the ranch, but he could be sure they had a few cards to spice up their Valentine's Day. He needed to get back to the ranch with the supplies, but he could take five minutes to dash into a store for another box of cards.

He had that on his mind when he walked into the vet's office and found Allison behind the counter. In the past, he would have put a little extra swagger in his step and flirted with her, but that day he was in a hurry. "Mornin', Allison. I've got a list of things I need right here in my pocket."

She held up her hand. "Look at my ring. I just got it yesterday."

"Gorgeous." He handed her a short list. "I'm in a little bit of a hurry."

"One word is all I get for a two-carat diamond," she fussed. "I waited on you to do something for two years. I made you breakfast a dozen times, and I still have at least three of your shirts that I kept because they smelled like you."

"I thought we were just havin' a good time. I didn't mean to hurt you or mislead you in any way. Throw the shirts away. The ring is awesome. I hope you and Buddy are very happy. He really loves you. Don't hurt him," Justin said.

After another look at her ring, Allison dropped her hand. "I would never hurt him. You ever goin' to settle down? Does that big blue-eyed goodie-two-shoes know that all you're interested in is having a good time?"

Anger boiled up from Justin's heart. "She has a name. Emily. And I think she's damned sexy."

"Well, I'll be damned. If I'd known playin' hard to get would put stars in your eyes, I would've tried it. Thank God, Buddy loves me the way I am." She picked his supplies off the shelf, entered the information into the computer, and printed a receipt.

He signed it, picked up the small bag, and turned around when he reached the door. "I truly wish you and Buddy a long and happy life together."

"Thank you for that," Allison said, sarcastically.

From the vet's place he went to Walmart for more cards so he could give one to everyone at the nursing home. He was in and out in less than ten minutes. But his mind wasn't on valentines. The idea of Emily playing a hard-to-get game kept circling back around through his mind.

He drove straight to the barn where Levi and Cade had put two ailing cows in the stalls. He met Levi coming out of the tack room with two syringes and a bottle of alcohol.

"Good timin'. But what's the matter? Are you gettin' sick?" Levi said.

"I'm fine." Justin handed off the bag to him.

"Come on and help me. Cade is next door." He nodded toward the west. "He's talkin' to Eli Johnson."

"So did Eli decide to sell after all?" Justin was glad that the topic had changed from him to something else.

"Maybe. But, seriously, what's bothering you? Is it Emily?" Levi pressed on.

"What's that got to do with us thinking about expanding the Longhorn Canyon?" Justin asked.

Levi removed the medicine from the bag and drew up a syringe full. "A lot, but we'll get into that later. Right now I want to know why you look like a sad sack."

Justin told him what had transpired at the vet's office, ending with, "Do you think Emily is one of those women who just plays games?"

"Nope." He carefully gave the first cow a shot and moved on to the next stall.

"Why?" Justin asked.

"She's genuine. You saw her with those old folks and with Benjy. She's not a gamer. We both know all about those kind of women. We've had to outrun too many of them to count. Don't judge Emily by their half bushels," Levi said.

"I remember Skip sayin' that but I never understood what it meant before. I think I do now. It simply means not to judge one person by another," Justin said.

"I've always wondered what the half bushel meant. Maybe it's just what they've got in their lives." Levi gave the second cow a shot. "What does it matter anyway about Emily? You think you might like her?"

"Maybe." Justin kicked at the straw scattered on the floor, expecting Levi to tease him about another woman coming to the ranch and another cowboy biting the dust.

"Then work for it, man. I worked my ass off to get Claire

and it was worth every single effort." Levi patted him on the back. "I'm putting this stuff away, but we can talk more if you want."

"I'm good. Thanks, though. See you at noon?"

"Yep." Levi's head bobbed. "Claire is having lunch with Mavis today, so I'm stayin' on the ranch."

Justin was left to wonder if he'd ever drive into Bowie to have lunch with Emily or if that was nothing more than a pipe dream.

*   *   *

Emily put away all the art things before she joined Nikki at their usual table in the dining room. Most of the residents had eaten and gone back to their rooms, so they had the area to themselves.

"I envy them right now." Emily yawned as she set her tray down.

"Who?"

"Our residents. They're probably taking a nap," she answered.

"Have you heard from Justin since yesterday?" Nikki asked.

"How did your mind go from a nap to Justin?" Emily sat down and ate a bite of her grilled cheese sandwich.

"I saw the way he looked at you. His expression said that he'd like to take naps with you." Nikki put finger quotes around the word *naps*.

Emily dipped a spoon into her soup. "His mother doesn't like me."

"Is he a mama's boy?" Nikki asked.

"Don't seem to be. Maybe it's because he's her baby, and she doesn't want to lose him? Maybe she doesn't want to see him married to a big woman? I don't know what her issue is," Emily said.

"You can win her over, girl, if you're interested enough. It's crazy thinking that anyone wouldn't love you," Nikki said.

"Thank you," Emily said.

"Okay, now 'fess up. What's really wrong? You haven't been the same since you got back from the ranch. I'm your best friend. I can tell you're on edge. I'm not pushin' you to marry Justin Maguire tomorrow but maybe you ought to do whatever it takes to get him out of your system. Take a 'nap' with him." Her hands went up for more air quotes. "Or go out with him a few times. Kill it or cure it, so you have peace in your heart."

"It shows that badly, does it? The Fab Five haven't mentioned it," Emily said.

"They're too wound up about the party day after tomorrow," Nikki said. "You know how they all get at Valentine's. It's even bigger than our Easter egg hunt out on the back lawn. My time is up. Got to go deliver meds. Call me later and we'll hash this out some more."

"Will do. I'll get your tray." Emily finished her soup and went over exactly what they'd been discussing again. One sentence that Nikki had said kept playing in her head—cure it or kill it.

At the end of the workday she didn't feel like cooking, so she stopped at the burger shop and got one of their Tuesday night specials. When she got home, she toted her things up the steps and inside her little apartment. The jacket and briefcase landed on a recliner. The sack with her food was left on the table while she fell backward on her bed.

Her phone rang and the ring tone told her that it was her mother. Rolling her eyes at the ceiling, she pulled her phone from the pocket of her scrub top. "Hello, Mama. What's goin' on in your world?"

"Just callin' to remind you of the Bennington reunion in three weeks. The barn will be set up for the dinner after the spring sale. We won't tear it down until after our get-together," Anne said.

Emily crossed her fingers behind her back. "Of course I didn't forget. I'll drive up on Friday after work and then leave right after church on Sunday."

"Reunion is March second. Go put it on your calendar while we're talkin'. I haven't talked to you in more than a week, so tell me about your Fab Five."

Emily dutifully went to the calendar in her tiny galley kitchen and put a note on the date. "It'll take a while to tell you what all they got into on the ranch." She went back to the bed and stretched out with a pillow under her head.

"Ranch? Tell me everything. I've got a plate of your grandmother's peanut butter cookies and a whole pot of coffee. I don't care if it takes until midnight," Anne said.

"Okay, you asked for it. It all started..." Emily went on to tell her mother all about the first time she went to the ranch and ruined a brand-new pair of shoes, up to the time they got back to the center. She omitted the part about Justin kissing her and about the Sunday date.

"I can tell by your voice that y'all had a wonderful time. Now tell me about this Justin Maguire. I've done business with his father in the past. The Longhorn Canyon is a well-known ranch in Texas," Anne said.

"He's a cowboy," Emily said.

"I know that. Tell me what he looks like."

"He's taller than me by an inch or two. He has brown hair and steely blue-gray eyes."

"I remember his mother being a little bitty thing, but

she sure was bossy. No one walked on Gloria Maguire. She could hold her own against any rancher in the state, and she knew her cattle."

Well, she hasn't changed a bit, Emily thought.

"Are you still there?" Anne asked after several seconds.

"I'm here. I was just thinking that my burger and fries are probably cold." Emily sighed.

"Go eat, girl. You get cranky when you don't eat. We'll talk when you get here," Anne said.

"Love you, Mama." She hit the END button.

She was surprised to find her hamburger still slightly warm when she opened the sack, but the fries were limp and soggy. As she chewed her first bite of burger, she topped off the fries with a few tablespoons of chili and added grated cheese, and then popped them into the microwave. While they heated, she poured herself a glass of sweet tea.

She'd just finished the last bite when her phone rang again. Nikki's picture popped up on the screen, and that always made Emily smile. It was of the two of them being silly at the Christmas party.

"Mama called," she answered.

"Is she already planning a wedding?" Nikki asked.

Emily sighed. "Probably and I didn't tell her about the kisses or that we have a church and Sunday dinner date."

"Whoa!" Nikki's voice shot up a dozen octaves. "You didn't tell me that, either."

"It's no big thing. I lost a bet and the date is paying for it. And I hate to burst Mama's bubble, but I have kissed a few men. And I didn't marry any of them."

"Were any of them cowboys?"

"Oh, yeah."

Nikki giggled. "You do realize that you're giving your mother hope for the first time. And she probably hears your biological clock tickin' too, so she's thinking in terms of grandchildren who will love ranchin' even if you don't."

"I'm twenty-eight. It's not time for any ticking noise yet," Emily said.

"You don't have to convince me, girl. I'm the same age you are," Nikki told her. "But your brothers aren't doin' jack squat about getting your mama some grandbabies, are they?"

"Matthew is engaged, so he can do that for her." Emily put her food trash away, wiped down the table for two, and then set her briefcase on it.

"Does she like the woman Matthew is engaged to?" Nikki asked.

"Not so much. I'm not sure Mama will like any girl the boys bring home. But Darcy is high maintenance and she's not…" Emily hesitated.

"A ranchin' woman?" Nikki asked.

"Nope, and that poses another question. What if, and it's a huge, colossal what if, Justin and I did date and fall in love? I could never come between a man and his family, especially a close-knit one like the Maguires." Emily sighed.

"You don't strike me as a woman who'd let anyone intimidate you about anything. So why do I hear hesitation in your voice now?"

"Crazy, ain't it? I'm stressing about something that will probably never happen, and that's not me at all," Emily said.

"No, it's not. Get over it. That's an order."

Emily snapped a salute even though Nikki couldn't see it. "Ma'am. Yes, ma'am. I will do exactly that."

Nikki giggled. "I've got to study. I really, really want to pass the RN test on the first try, and it's coming up next month. See you tomorrow."

"You'll do great," Emily said.
"And so will you. Bye now."

*   *   *

Justin tried reading a book, but he couldn't keep his mind on
it. He made a package of microwave popcorn, but ate only a
few bites before pushing it away. He'd thought about having
the television cable company run a line to the cabin, but he'd
be there so seldom that he couldn't warrant it. He'd brought
a small television and DVD player, so he popped a movie
in, thinking that might help.

Tom Selleck in *Quigley Down Under* didn't hold his attention more than fifteen minutes, so he removed it and tried
Hatfields & McCoys. When his favorite two older movies
didn't work, he began to question his decision to move out
of the ranch house.

His phone rang and it startled him so badly that he spilled
half a glass of sweet tea down the front of his shirt. He
headed to the kitchen, grabbed a towel, and sopped up as
much as he could, and finally answered the phone on the
fifth ring.

"Did I catch you at a bad time?" Larry asked.
"Not at all. What's up?"
"I did a little homework for you. I've got some plans and
ideas from a woman's standpoint so you don't have to try to
figure out a way to ask Emily. I got them all drawn up, well
most of them, anyway. If you happen to come into town tomorrow, stop by and I'll give them to you," Larry answered.

"Most of them?" Justin asked.
"It's like this. I still like to go over blueprints and de-
signs, so sometimes I make copies of the ones in magazines.
Few months ago I saw Emily admiring one." He told Justin

all about copying the plan and the conversation he'd had with her that morning.

"Well, I'd sure like to take a look at what you've got. It'd be a nice start," Justin answered.

"Good! I told the others that you'd be here for the party. Patsy wanted to make a box for you, but I told her the relatives of the other residents would be jealous if we did that. It's just that in all the years we've been here, we haven't had anyone come to the parties for us, and we're excited. Oh, and just so you know, they've changed the entry combination to seven, eight, nine, zero."

Justin put the phone on speaker and removed his sticky shirt. "You're right. It could run into lots of problems if everyone who came in had a box."

"Okay, then, see you tomorrow sometime. Patsy is at the door. We're playin' dominoes at her place tonight," Larry said.

"Have fun and thank you." Justin tossed his shirt into the hamper.

"No thanks necessary. It was fun getting to put together plans again."

The phone screen went dark and Justin headed for the bathroom. The shower was so small that he could hardly turn around in it, and he bumped his head several times on the showerhead. It would take some adjusting, but maybe by the end of summer, he'd be in his own house. The tiny bathroom had taught him one important lesson—he would build a spa shower in his new place, one big enough for him and Emily.

"Holy crap!" he muttered as he went to stand in front of the fireplace to dry off. "What on earth put that thought in my mind? Maybe it's because I need to call her before I just show up at that party."

He pulled on a pair of pajama pants and a clean shirt. Then he picked up his phone, dialed her number and held his breath until she answered.

"Hello, Justin," she said.

"Evenin', Emily. I'm calling to ask if it would make you uncomfortable if I come to the Valentine's party at the center. Larry invited me, but I didn't want to just show up and make things all awkward." He paced around the sofa as he talked.

"Not at all. The group would probably love to see you again. I should tell you, though, the residents all have boxes made for cards. You don't have to bring anything, but it would tickle the Fab Five if you put one of those little school-type valentines in each of their boxes."

He sat down on the sofa. "Okay. Anything else?"

"We have finger foods, cookies, and punch afterward."

"Do I need to bring anything for that?"

"No, the center takes care of the refreshments. This is really pretty exciting. Every year that I've been there the Five haven't had any guests for the party. It'll be a huge thing for them, so don't be surprised if they introduce you as their grandson."

He could hear the humor in her voice and imagine her blue eyes twinkling. "No problem there. I don't mind a bit. Is it a dress-up affair?"

"If they know you're going to be there, it will be, but I'll try to keep the ladies from wearing tiaras and evening gowns." She laughed.

He could have listened to the tinkling sound of her laughter all night. "So I don't have to get out my tux?"

"Nope, and I won't be wearing the Crown Jewels," she said.

"Want to go somewhere for a cup of coffee when the party is over?" he asked.

"I can't. I'm the cleanup committee afterward, but thank you."

"I'll be glad to help with that, and then we could go for coffee," he said.

"I never turn down help, and I'll sure be ready for a quiet cup of coffee," she said.

"Then it's a date. Good night, Emily." He laid the phone to the side and then picked up the remote to start the movie again. Suddenly, *Hatfields & McCoys* did a fine job of holding his attention. One of the tall women on the screen even reminded him of Emily.

Chapter Twelve

Justin had a bowl of cereal and three cookies for breakfast the next morning, but he hadn't taken coffee to the cabin so he stopped by the big house. Levi and Cade were sitting at the table with papers in front of them. Justin's first thought was that Levi wanted to change the house plans one last time before the foundation was laid. He poured a mug of coffee and pulled out a chair, and then he realized they were looking at the whole ranch, not just house plans.

"Glad you finally made it," Cade said. "This is an aerial map of the Longhorn Canyon. And this one is of the Johnson ranch, which borders ours." He cut the two maps and put them together. "As you can see, Canyon Creek runs right through the Double H place like it does ours, so there's water."

"We've talked about adding his place to ours if the opportunity ever came up." Justin sipped his coffee and traced the thin line of the creek with his fingertip. "Has he made up his mind to sell?"

"He has, and he's giving us first chance before he puts it on the market. You want to live in that house?" Cade pointed to the small frame structure shown in the picture.

Justin pointed to an area at the far corner of the ranch, about a mile from the cabin as the crow flies. "No, and tell the truth, I'm not really sure that this is something we should do right now. We're short on hired hands anyway, and that place is going to take a lot of work. Every single bit of the fencing needs to be replaced."

Levi nodded. "Justin has a good point. I heard the reason he's selling is because he can't get good hired hands."

"So do we make an offer or not?" Cade asked.

"I vote no," Justin said.

"I agree. It's just too much for us to take on right now, but maybe if it doesn't sell in the next year, we can see about it," Levi said.

"Speakin' of that, two hired hands called in sick today, so I'm on the fencing crew until dark. See y'all this evening." Justin settled his hat on his head and started out the door.

"Whoa!" Retta yelled from the kitchen. "I've got a sack lunch made for each of you. Gloria and I've got to go talk to the CPA, so we'll be gone at noon."

Justin's phone rang on the way from house to pasture. When he saw that it was Emily, he answered it on the second ring.

"Hey, Emily."

"I forgot to tell you something about the party. The relatives who live close by usually come in and drop their cards into the residents' Valentine boxes earlier than that evening. If everyone tried to put them in right before or during the hour of the party, it could get really hectic. Not that you have to bring cards, but if you want to, then plan on doing so a day or two early," she said.

"If I bring them this evening, will you go have ice cream with me?" he asked.

"Yes, but don't y'all usually have supper at six?"

"What time do you get off?"

"Five thirty," she answered.

"I'll be there right before that. Just don't tell my mama that I ate ice cream for supper," he teased.

"I never tattle, except on my brothers," she said. "See you this evening then."

"Yes, ma'am, you will." He could have danced a jig if he hadn't been in a moving vehicle. Emily had agreed to go with him for ice cream that evening, and then after the party for coffee. The Sunday date would wind up being number three instead of number one, the way he figured it. He turned on the radio and sang "Honey Bee" with Blake Shelton at the top of his lungs.

The day went fast and the hired help was more than glad to quit at four thirty that afternoon. Justin reached the center with ten minutes to spare, and two boxes of cards in his hands. He punched in the numbers Larry had given him and was on his way to the long table full of decorated Valentine boxes when an orderly came through the room.

"Hey, you need some help with those?" he asked.

"No, it won't take me long," Justin answered. "But you might point me in the direction of Larry's room."

"You mean Larry of the Fab Five or Larry Deacon?"

"Of the Fab Five," Justin said.

"I'm going that way. Want me to tell him to meet you here?"

"Yes, thank you."

Justin had just finished putting a card into Emily's box when Larry rounded the corner with a big manila envelope tucked into the bib of his overalls. "Here you go. Hey, here comes Emily."

"Perfect timing," Justin said.

"Y'all goin' somewhere?" Larry's eyes twinkled.

"For ice cream," Justin said out of the side of his mouth. "Hi, Emily. Are you ready?"

"Have fun." Larry waved as he hurried down the hall.

"Don't run," Emily called after him.

He threw up a hand in a wave over his shoulder.

"What have you got there?" She glanced at the big yellow envelope.

"Larry had some papers he wanted me to look over," he answered.

"Think we might go to the Dairy Queen for a burger and a shake? I was so busy that I didn't take time for lunch, and now I'm starving," she said.

"Sure. I haven't had supper either."

"I'll meet you there. It's on my way home, so I might as well take my car."

*   *   *

Nikki was right about kill it or cure it, Emily thought. Maybe he'd do something stupid that would end it in one evening, and she wouldn't be attracted to him anymore. She needed to get this whole thing under control—one way or the other.

Justin must've taken a back-roads shortcut because he was leaning against the fender of his truck when she pulled her car into the lot. Before she could turn off the engine, he'd opened the door for her.

"Thank you," she said politely as she slid her long legs out of the car. "I can already smell the burgers cooking."

His hand went to the small of her back. "Smells pretty good, don't it."

It's not a date, she told herself. *I'm still wearing my scrubs. It's just a couple of folks going out for food. But oh, my, that woodsy cologne he's wearing smells so good.*

She decided on a bacon cheeseburger with double meat, fries, and a chocolate malt. He laid a bill on the counter before she could even get money from her purse, and said he'd have the same. The cashier gave him a receipt with their number on it and started to hand him the change.

"Keep it," he said and handed Emily a self-serve drink cup. "Booth or table."

"Booth, please." She stopped long enough to draw up root beer.

He did the same thing and followed her.

"Since this is not a date, I'll pay half," she said.

"You can buy next time." He slid into the seat across from her. "It's been a day. Some of our hired hands are out with the flu. I hope no one gets it at the center and the party gets spoiled."

"Me too. It would be a shame if some of the residents couldn't attend," she said. "Are you replacing wood with metal?"

"Basically we're tightening up what we've got. It tends to need that after a hard winter," he said.

"Bull tight." She remembered what her dad and grandpa said when they were doing the same job.

"You know a lot about fencing," he said.

Before she could answer, their number was called and Justin went to get their food. She couldn't take her eyes off his broad shoulders and the way his body tapered down to the snug-fitting jeans.

Kind of like that do you? It was definitely her mother's voice in her head.

"Oh, hush," Emily whispered.

Justin brought the tray to the table and popped a french fry into his mouth before he even removed the paper from his burger. "To answer your question. We've still got a lot of wood posts from back when my granddad had the ranch. They're in bad repair, so we're trying to replace everything with metal. It's hard work, but it'll save hours every spring when that old wood starts to rot. You ever do any fencin'?"

"A few times," she admitted. "Couldn't let my brothers show me up."

"Three brothers. Got any cousins?"

"Oh, yeah. I come from a pretty good-size family. How about you?"

"Yep. Do you get homesick?" he asked.

Sure she got homesick to see everyone, but only for a short while. Not enough to move back and have her brothers meddling in her life, or her mother trying to fix her up with every bachelor in the Texas panhandle.

"You're takin' a long time to answer," Justin said.

"I had to think about the question a while. I miss the sunsets out in the panhandle, and I miss my folks, but am I actually homesick? I'm not sure," she answered. "People who ache to go back home must not really want to leave."

"Why did you want to leave? Were you running away from or to something?" Justin asked.

"Explain that." She squeezed ketchup onto her fries.

"Were you running away from ranching in general, or were you running to a job that you wanted to do, and you thought you couldn't have both?" he asked.

She held up a finger, glad that she had a mouthful of food so she didn't have to answer right away. When she swallowed, she said, "Never thought of it like that. I knew I wanted to work with people. And someday I hope to work with kids again—that is if I ever leave the center. So maybe I was running to something. But it never dawned on me that I might have both."

"Why not? Claire is going to live on the Longhorn Canyon, and she has a quilt shop in Sunset. She loves having a dog and cats and animals around, but she has no desire to live on the ranch like Retta does. You do know that Retta takes care of all the book work and the payroll?"

"I kind of figured that out when she and your mother were talking about the taxes. For a place the size of yours, that would be a full-time job," Emily answered.

"Pretty much, but she loves to cook, so she does that, too. We have a housekeeper who comes in once a week. Retta wouldn't have time for that, too, and with the new baby coming, we might have to hire a part-time cook." Justin squirted ketchup over his pile of fries. "Did you like going to your grandma's place when you were a kid?"

"Yes, I did." It was one of those little white lies. She'd actually lived on the same huge ranch as her grandparents until she went to college. When guys knew that she was part of Big Sky Ranch, things changed—they looked at her with dollar signs in their eyes instead of love.

"Ever think of ranchin' full-time?" he asked.

"I love the day-to-day stuff on a ranch. I like hauling hay, feeding, and even pulling a calf when I need to, but I'd hate to do Retta's job. Sitting still behind a desk is not for me." She toyed with the straw in her milk shake.

"Me, either. We're all glad that Retta does that job now.

Cade took over the books right out of college, but he hated it," Justin said.

"You design houses. Ever think of doing that full-time?" she asked.

"No, ma'am. That's just a hobby. Ranchin' is what I love," he answered without hesitation.

Emily slid out of the booth. "We should be going. Thanks for supper."

He did the same and took her hand in his. "I'll walk you to your car."

She expected him to open the door, but instead, he caged her with his hands on top of her car. "I was serious when I said I think of you all the time," he drawled.

Before she could smart off, his lips were on hers and her arms were around his neck. His hands were around her back, and every kiss was hotter than the last. Finally, just when she was about to pull him inside the car, a truck pulled up and an old guy yelled, "Get a room."

"Guess that's our cue to call it a night," she said.

"One of these times, we aren't going to get interrupted," he groaned.

"Maybe this is fate's way of telling us to slow down."

"If it is, she's doin' a damn fine job of it," he said.

She slid behind the wheel and watched him make his way to his truck and drive away, wishing the whole time that he could have taken her home and walked her to the door. Then she could have pulled him inside to see where those kisses could lead.

Chapter Thirteen

When Justin made it back to the cabin that evening, he opened the envelope Larry had given him. With papers covering the coffee table, he was surprised to find a picture of a two-story house. He had envisioned a rambling ranch style until then, but the moment he laid eyes on the page from a magazine, he could envision the house set back in the pecan trees on the southwest corner of the ranch.

Larry had said that it needed to be about ten feet bigger on each side to accommodate the big closet and the huge walk-in pantry. It would also allow for a small nursery next to the first-level master bedroom, which could be turned into an office when the children were big enough to go upstairs. That would give the second-floor bedrooms a bathroom of their own and prevent future squabbling from the kids as well as provide privacy for guests.

Justin imagined the laughter of children running through the house, sliding down the banister, and begging him to read them "just one more" bedtime story. With that picture still in his mind, he got out his graph paper, sharpened a pencil, and began to work. It was almost midnight when he finally finished the rough draft for the first floor.

The next day was hectic at the ranch. Two more of his hired hands called in with the flu. By noon his energy level was dragging, and he was grateful for an hour to sit at the table with Levi, Cade, and Retta.

"You look like you've been pulled through a knothole backward. You know you can move back in here anytime. We've decided to make the guest room into the nursery, since it's closer to our bedroom," Retta said.

Justin helped himself to a healthy portion of meat loaf and then passed it on to Cade. "Thanks, but where I live isn't the problem."

"You're not getting the flu are you?" Levi asked.

"Nope, just tired from being shorthanded. And I've got that drive out to the panhandle next week to buy that breeder bull. I'm not looking forward to it one bit," he said.

Cade sent rolls and hash brown casserole around the table. "Spring break is coming up in two weeks. We can always put out the word that we need some help, and we'll have high school boys standing in line to get a week's paycheck from us."

Levi nodded in agreement. "That should get us through flu season, and we'll be right back on track. It's like this every couple of years."

"Remember when me and you got it at the same time the second year after we were out of high school?" Justin asked. "Cade didn't even come home from college because he was afraid he'd get it."

"Hey, that was my last year of school," Cade said. "I wanted to get done with it all so I could come home for good, not just vacations and summers. I sure didn't need the flu to keep me from getting finals done."

"It always hits at calving season," Levi said. "But we'll get through it."

Gloria entered the kitchen by the back door, hung up her jacket, and sat down beside Justin. "I heard you had a date with Emily last night."

"Gossip travels faster than the speed of light." Justin chuckled. "We had burgers. That doesn't qualify as a date."

"Well, what does making out in public qualify as?" Gloria asked.

"Two consenting adults sharing a good night kiss." Justin's expression went from amused to serious.

"I don't like it, son," Gloria said.

"Why, Mama?" Cade asked. "Emily seems like a responsible, kindhearted woman. She's sure a far cry from what Justin usually goes out with."

"I think under all that…" She paused and took a deep breath. "Sugar sweetness she's got an ulterior motive, like marrying up in the world."

"You think Emily is a gold digger?" Retta gasped. "Why? You didn't think that about me."

"You aren't a big girl," Justin said through clenched teeth. "Mama wants me to have a pretty blonde who barely comes to my shoulder."

"I'm not that kind of woman," Gloria argued. "It's just, I feel like there's more than she's tellin'. Call it mother's intuition."

"So why don't you invite Emily to lunch or for coffee some evening? Get to know her better. If you spent some time with her, you'd see her the way I do."

"I just might do that. Are you taking her to the panhandle with you?" Gloria asked.

"No. She'll be at work. I'm planning to leave on Monday and come back Tuesday." Justin hadn't ever seen his mother with this attitude, and he didn't like it.

Gloria shrugged and changed the subject. "I guess we're having dinner with Mavis and Skip, and those old folks on Sunday."

Retta refilled tea glasses. "They sure livened this place up for a week. Mavis and I talked about it. We decided not to all get together for Sunday dinner. We thought it would be easier on Benjy not to have quite so many folks over at their place this first time that the group from the center is there. Kind of ease into it with Benjy, even though he knows all of us and them."

Justin blocked out the rest of the conversation and thought about Sunday. Maybe it was because Emily wasn't easy that made her so attractive to him. For more than fourteen years he'd been dating or chasing women, but he'd never known anyone quite like her.

What makes her so different? This time it was his grandfather's voice in his head.

He couldn't begin to answer the question because he had no idea, but he really, really liked spending time with her.

*   *   *

Emily took the red dress she'd worn to the Valentine's party last year from the closet and hung it on the back of the bathroom door that Thursday morning. The hot shower would steam the wrinkles right out. Just before party time she'd rush into the lounge and change into it.

Cards were filled out and in the boxes. She mentally checked that job off her list.

The caterer had confirmed that she would be there ready

to set up immediately after supper had been served. Emily only had to put a few touches on the table centerpieces. Another check.

And Justin is going to be there, she reminded herself as she towel dried her hair. A third check.

She was thinking of what she might be forgetting when she knocked her dress off the hook. It landed in a mass of red at her feet and there on the back of it was a big nasty green stain.

"Dammit! I should've taken it to the cleaners." She remembered the incident the previous year. One of the little kids had left a sugar cookie with green icing on a chair and she'd sat down on it. There wasn't another red outfit in her closet, so she would have to wear another color.

She dressed in scrubs, picked up her daily tote bag along with a kit that contained her shoes, makeup, and all the other necessities for the party. The minute she was in her car, she called Nikki and put it on speaker. She told her about the problem and said, "Now what am I going to do? I have red shoes, red lipstick, and everything but a dress. I don't think all of this will look good with scrubs."

"Not to worry. We've got time to fix this," Nikki said. "We've got an hour at lunch. Let's run into that fancy new shop down on Main Street. It's not far from the center, so we can dash in and out in twenty minutes."

"Oh, right!" Emily groaned. "I'm sure they've got all kinds of cute things in size four to maybe fourteen. But something in an eighteen?"

"Never know until we look, and besides I need to find a dress too. I've been studying so hard for this nursing test, I forgot all about needing a party outfit until this morning," Nikki said.

"We can try, but I won't hold my breath. I may have to

tie a red bow in my hair and go in scrubs." Emily parked in her reserved spot. "See you inside in a few minutes."

The sun's rays were warm that morning as she went from the car to the center. A robin hopped about, looking for worms in the grass under the oak trees. But that didn't mean that spring was on the way. Not even in north central Texas, where it came earlier than it did up in the northern part of the country.

Emily didn't like change and yet the world was in a constant cycle of just that. Seasons changed. Babies were born. Old folks died. That last thought caused a catch in her chest. She didn't like thinking about her residents passing away. She'd had to endure a few funerals, and they'd been tough, but when any one of her precious Five passed on, she'd probably go to pieces.

Nikki met her at the door. "I called the new shop and they go all the way up to size twenty-four. She says she'll pull everything in red for both of us, and have it in dressing rooms ready for when we get there."

Emily stopped long enough to give her a hug. "You are the best. I owe you one."

"I will collect." Nikki pushed her medicine cart on down the hallway.

Emily's job that morning was to make all the table centerpieces for the evening party. While she worked, her thoughts kept going back to the kisses that she and Justin had shared. Unlike the other guys she'd dated, he didn't know that she came from one of the biggest ranches in Texas. So that couldn't be the reason he was interested in her.

But why has he caught your attention? the voice in her head asked.

"Because he makes me happy," she muttered.

Nikki poked her head in the door. "You ready to go. It's noon."

Emily's eyes went to the clock on the wall and then to all the arrangements on the table. "How'd time go by so fast?"

"Looks to me like you were pretty busy. We've only got an hour. We'd better get goin'," Nikki answered.

Larry grabbed her by the hand as she passed the Fab Five's table in the dining room. "Is Justin coming tonight?"

"I think so," Emily said. "But right now I've got to go. My dress is ruined, and I'm going to look for another one."

Sarah leaned around Larry and said, "Buy something sexy as hell, something that will knock his eyes out."

Luck was with them—they made every green traffic light and were in the dress shop in five minutes. The owner was waiting for them and led them right back to the two dressing rooms.

Emily was grateful that the space wasn't cramped, and there was lots of cool air flowing from an overhead vent. She kicked off her shoes, threw her scrubs on a chair and stood before the three-way mirror in nothing but her panties and bra. She turned this way and then that. What would Justin's expression tell her if he saw her like this? Or worse, yet, when she removed the double-D bra and stood before him naked?

"Am I ready for that step?" she asked her reflection.

"Are you talking to me?" Nikki asked in the adjoining room.

"No, myself," Emily said, raising her voice.

She tried on the first dress and visualized Justin's eyes when he saw her in it. She took it off and tried on the other two. None of them really suited her, but the last one had the simplest lines, and it matched shoes she already had.

"I found mine. How about you?" she called out to Nikki in the next room.

"Yep, first one I tried on. You still got yours on?" Nikki asked.

"Nope, I'm ready to check out," Emily said.

"Me too. Let's pay out of this joint and go get some ice cream," Nikki suggested. "I've got some news, and I wanted to wait to share it until we were alone."

They paid for their purchases, and Emily drove to the ice cream store just down the block. They ordered sandwiches and shakes and went back to the center. "We've still got fifteen minutes. Let's eat out here. You said you have news. Got a new boyfriend?" Emily asked.

"I wish." Nikki handed a sandwich to Emily. "But this is even better than a boyfriend. If I pass my nursing test the hospital is offering me an RN position as emergency room nurse. I'll be working twenty-four hours on duty, then I'll be off for twenty-four."

"Oh, no!" Emily gasped.

"You don't think I should take it? Is it the hours?" Nikki fired off the questions. "My salary will double, so I can get a decent car and a better apartment."

"No, it's a great job. It's just that I'll miss you so much. We hired on at the same time, and I get to see you every day." Emily sighed.

"I'll miss you too, but on my days off we can still grab supper at least once a week and catch up. And just think about the doctors." Nikki's eyes twinkled with excitement. "I might find us both one to date if things go south with your cowboy."

Emily flashed on her reflection in that mirror and frowned. "I'm not so sure that things will ever go anywhere with Justin."

"Yeah, right. What happens when you kiss him?" Nikki poked her on the arm. "He makes your toes curl up more than any other man ever has. When he comes around, you're all flustered, and nothing or no one has ever flustered you like he does. So things are going somewhere, darlin'." She dragged out the last word like a true cowboy would. "Take him to bed, and see if he's any good."

"Good Lord, woman!" Emily gasped, but her palms went clammy at the thought of seeing Justin naked. Heat started on the inside of her body and worked its way out, settling into two spots of high color in her cheeks.

"Aww, I made you blush, so I must've hit a nerve." Nikki stuck straws in the two chocolate milk shakes. "That don't hardly ever happen. I've never seen you so red. You really need ice cream to cool you down. Stop runnin' from Justin, and let him catch you. If you don't like what you see when he peels out of them tight-fittin' jeans, then I'll rustle us up a couple of young doctors."

Emily put her hands on her hot cheeks. "You are terrible. You're just sayin' this stuff because you didn't want to see me cry about you leavin'."

"Nope, I meant every word," Nikki said.

"Sure you did," she said. "Do I get to be your maid of honor when you marry your sexy doctor?"

"Of course, and I don't care if he's sexy or not. I just want him to be rich," Nikki declared.

"Not me. I want to be in love, like Claire and Levi are and like Cade and Retta."

Nikki shook her head slowly. "Haven't you heard? It's just as easy to fall in love with a rich man as a poor one."

"What if fate puts your soul mate in your pathway, and he's a poor old farmer barely makin' it?" Emily asked.

"Then I'll change my mind," Nikki said. "After all it is a woman's prerogative."

*   *   *

Everything was ready for the party to begin. All that was left was for Emily and Nikki to rush into the bathroom and get dressed. Ten minutes didn't give them time to do much with makeup, but Emily reapplied her lipstick. Then she shook her hair free of the ponytail and slipped into her dress.

"I like that one better than the one you wore last year, and would you look at this." Nikki pulled Emily's shoes from the tote bag. "They match. It was meant to be, just like you and Justin. You look like a model. Justin is going to drool all over his shirt."

"Oh, yeah!" Emily said sarcastically. "And every guy's eyeballs are going to bug out when they see you in that getup."

Nikki wore a cute little red jumpsuit that she paired with silver high-heeled shoes. For the first time, Emily wished that she were a small girl, like Nikki—and Allison.

"Thank you, dawlin'." Nikki bowed. "Now I've got to get on out of here. I haven't had time to put my cards in the boxes yet. So I'll see you out there."

The moment Emily entered the room she gave it a quick scan to see if she could locate Justin, and she found him sitting at a table with the Five. Stepping back into the shadows, she stared as long as she wanted. The old folks were beaming because they had a guest. And he looked as if he was having a good time.

She stepped out of the shadows and stopped at each table to say a few words to the residents. Long before she reached Justin's table, she could feel his eyes on her. Suddenly, it was very warm in the room, but at least the heat didn't settle in her cheeks and melt her makeup.

"This is the best party ever," Bess said when Emily arrived.

"Pull up a chair," Otis said.

"I don't have time. In three minutes I have to start the program," she said.

"Well, before you have to leave, let me tell you that you sure do look pretty tonight." Justin's gaze caught hers and held for several seconds.

"Thank you." She'd never been flustered behind the microphone, but that evening her hands shook as she walked toward it.

"Welcome, everyone," she said.

No one paid a bit of attention. Few even looked her way.

"Welcome!" she said a second time after she remembered to flip the switch to turn on the microphone.

The room went quiet, and Justin winked.

"We want to thank all you relatives and friends who've come to help us celebrate Valentine's Day this evening. We'll have some music and refreshments in a few minutes but first we have a couple here in the center who's been married seventy years. They're going to tell us their story, so let's give a big round of applause to April and Leonard Wilson."

The clapping went on from the time the elderly couple left their group until they made it to the microphone, holding hands the whole way. Emily took a seat over to the side and tried to focus on them, but it was difficult when she wanted to stare at Justin. He looked downright sexy in those tight jeans and that black shirt with its pearl snaps. He was a good person to be spending his evening at a senior citizens' party, especially when he could be at the Rusty Spur dancing with all the ladies.

With an effort, Emily turned her attention back to the

couple at the microphone. Leonard was one of those tall, lanky men who always wore black dress slacks and white shirts buttoned all the way to the top. April had blue eyes set in a bed of wrinkles and short gray hair cut in a bob right below her chin.

Will I look like that when I've been married seventy years? Emily wondered. *Do I want marriage and kids, or can I be content with what I have right now in a career and these sweet old folks to take care of?*

"I'm not sure how to start this story, so I'll just begin." Leonard kept his wife's hand in his. "I was in the second grade in a little tiny school just across the Red River into Oklahoma when I fell in love with April. She was in the first grade and she had the biggest bluest eyes I'd ever seen. But after that one school year, her family moved to Texas and I didn't see her again until we were sixteen. I was friends with a boy who was dating her best friend, and he invited me to go to a birthday party with him. She was there, and I proposed to her before the night was over."

April stepped up to the microphone. "We were dancing on the grass in our bare feet that evening, and I said yes, but that we'd have to wait until we were grown-ups. So Leonard would borrow his dad's old truck and come see me on Sunday afternoons. At the end of that year, he graduated from high school and joined the air force, and he wanted me to marry him before he went off to his first duty station."

Leonard kissed her on the top of the head. "She'd promised her parents she would finish high school. So I went through basic, and I qualified for flight school. I went into training and wrote to her every night for the next year."

April patted him on the shoulder. "We got married in 1949 when I finished school, but he was still in training. We had a tiny apartment, and I went to work at the base store as a clerk. We thought we'd done died and gone to heaven. Leonard was going to make a career of the military and someday we were going to have children."

He smiled and said, "Everything was going pretty good. We had two children and then Vietnam happened, and my plane was shot down in enemy territory. I spent two years as a POW."

Emily dabbed a tear from her eye. She was a strong woman, but she wasn't sure she'd survive something like that. Thank God, Justin was a rancher and not a soldier.

April shook her head slowly from side to side. "I never believed for a minute that he was dead. My heart would have known if he wasn't alive. One day I was outside hanging up clothes, and a big black military-looking car drove up. For a minute there, my positive attitude took a nosedive, but my Leonard got out of the car and limped toward me."

Leonard draped an arm around her shoulders. "She dropped the clothespins and froze. She didn't rush to meet me like I'd imagined. I had to go all the way to her before she'd believe she wasn't seeing things."

"That's right." April smiled up at him. "And that was the end of his military. When he got his health back, he got a job in Dallas flying for an airline, and we had four more children. Many of them live in this area, so we chose this retirement home so we could spend our last days close to them."

Emily wondered if she and whoever she married would be in a retirement home, close to their children when they were near ninety? Or would they still be living on a ranch somewhere?

A ranch? Her mother's voice popped into her head. *Well, that's a surprise. What ranch might that be?*

"I don't know," she whispered softly.

"We've had a wonderful life," Leonard was saying when her attention went to what he was saying. "And now if Miz Emily will put on the song I asked for, I'd like to start this party off by dancing with my beautiful bride. The rest of y'all can join in if you'd like, or if you want the refreshment table is now open."

Leonard took April by the hand and then turned back to the microphone. "One more thing. This song is the way I feel about my life. The hardships made us stronger and made us appreciate the good times even more. I love you more today, April Wilson, than I did in that little bitty apartment, which by the way, was even smaller than the one we have here at Oakview. Y'all listen to the words to this song because I'm sure it was written especially for me this night."

There were a few chuckles, and tissue boxes passed from table to table as the first piano notes for "The Older I Get," by Alan Jackson, started playing. The song was half done when Justin stood to his feet and crossed the floor. He held out his hand to Emily.

"May I have this dance, please, ma'am?" he asked.

She put her hand in his, and he led her to the middle of the floor. Everyone clapped for both couples. The present and the future right there on the floor—or at least that's the way Emily saw it.

"Like it says," Justin whispered into her hair. "It's those folks you love, not the money and stuff that makes you rich."

"And that's supposed to mean?" she asked.

"You think about it," he said.

The next song on the list was a request from Otis, and Justin didn't let go of her but kept dancing to the beat of "Storms Never Last" by Jessi Colter and Waylon Jennings.

"This is my song to the beautiful lady in red tonight," Justin said.

"Oh, yeah, why's that?" she asked.

"You make the sun want to shine, like it says," he said.

When the song ended, he led her to the refreshment table. He brought her hand to his lips and kissed it. "Is there any way I can help you out with the food?"

She shot a look over his shoulder to the Five. "You're the first guest they've had at this thing in the five years I've been here. It's more important that you spend the time with them."

"Then I'll be around to help with cleanup afterward." He went to the table where he held out a hand to Sarah for the next dance. After that, he had a turn with Bess and Patsy. Then he got a plate of food and sat with them while he ate.

"He's a good man," Nikki whispered as she joined Emily behind the refreshment table. "Those ladies are almost swooning."

"It would be easy to fall for him," Emily said out of the side of her mouth.

"You almost fell down?" Otis frowned.

"No, she was talking about that time when she slipped and sent papers flying everywhere." Nikki quickly covered for her.

"I'm glad." Otis smiled. "You and Justin looked real good out there on the dance floor." He leaned across the table and lowered his voice. "I think he likes you."

"Oh, really?" Emily raised a dark eyebrow.

"Yep, and I think you like him too. But that's your business, not mine. You do what your heart tells you and never look back or have regrets, because when you follow your heart, it's the right thing to do. Now please put two of them brownies on my plate. I'll take one to Sarah. She really likes them and she already ate hers."

Emily did what he asked and then used the remote to turn the music down, since everyone had settled down to eat and visit with their families. In another hour there'd be nothing but cleanup, and then the folks would take their boxes of cards to their own apartments, where they'd read through their Valentines numerous times for the next few days.

She made the rounds one more time, telling the visitors how much she appreciated their support. When she reached the table where Justin was still sitting with the Five, she pulled up a chair and joined them.

"It's a big success," Larry said. "Best one ever."

Sarah nudged him on the shoulder. "You're a lucky dog that Justin was here to dance with me this year."

"My hip has gotten worse since last year. Don't think I could keep up with a sexy fox like you," Larry teased.

"Your hip was fine when we were at the ranch, and you wanted to ride bulls," Patsy said. "So don't give us any of that crap. I oughta make you dance with me for lyin'."

Larry cut his eyes around at her. "You're too short to dance with me. You better get Otis out there. I'd be in the therapy room a month if I had to bend far enough to dance with you or Bess."

Bess threw up both hands. "Hey, leave me out of this fight."

"So are you going to stay up all night and read through your cards a dozen times?" Emily asked, changing the subject.

"I am," Otis said. "I'm going to take a big plate of them leftover cookies and some of them pigs in a blanket to my room. I'm going to eat until I feel like a stuffed turkey and read through every one of them. I've always loved Valentine cards even when I was a little boy. I kept them until they were frayed and ugly and cried when Mama made me throw them away."

"I still got a few hidden away that my wife gave me through the years. It's one of the few things I kept when I sold my business," Larry said. "I'll read all my cards to her tonight. I hope there really are holes in the floor of heaven, and she can hear every word I say."

"That's so sweet," Sarah said. "Makes me wish I'd married. Times like this, I wish that I'd had a family, but..."

"But what?" Patsy asked.

"But my soldier didn't come home, and I'd given my heart to him. Just wasn't ever able to get it back to give to another man," Sarah answered. "But this ain't a night to be melancholy. I'm ready to take all my Valentines to my room. Thank you for a beautiful party, Emily, and for the dance, Justin. I felt like a young woman again."

"I can't believe you said *ain't*." Patsy giggled.

"Y'all old rednecks has rubbed off on me." Sarah laughed. "I bet I got more cards than any of you."

"How much?" Larry's eyes twinkled.

"Five bucks," Sarah answered. "And I'll even let an impartial party count for us. Y'all meet me in my room in five minutes. And don't you dare stuff your box with those extras you have in your room." She shook her finger under Larry's nose.

"I'll watch him," Bess said.

"And I'll keep an eye on Sarah for you, Larry, so she don't slip in a few extras," Otis said. "I'm ready. Are y'all?"

"Yep, but I got to get a hug from Justin first," Sarah said. "Boy, you can't ever know how much it means to us to have family here tonight."

When he stood up, she hugged him tightly, then she stepped back. "Now you'll have to bend down to hug these two."

"No sacrifice at all." Justin gave each of them a hug, and then shook hands with Otis and Larry. "I've had a great time this evening."

"Will you come back next year?" Otis asked.

"If y'all invite me, I sure will," Justin answered.

"That was so sweet," Emily said after the Five had picked up their boxes and taken them down the hallway toward their rooms.

"What?" Justin asked.

"The way you became their family tonight," she said.

"Everyone needs a family. I'm glad they let me into theirs," he said. "Is it cleanup time?"

"It won't take long." Emily nodded. "I just put what few leftovers there are in containers and wad up the rest of the stuff in the tablecloth and toss it."

"Then we have time for one more dance?" He held out a hand.

She let him pull her up. "My feet hurt. Mind if I kick off these high heels?"

"Not one bit. You can pretend you're dancing on green grass in your bare feet," he said.

Emily had no idea what was next up on the playlist she'd gotten from the residents for the evening's music. But when "A Picture of Me Without You" started playing, Justin pulled her tighter into his arms.

"Great choice to close out the evening," he said.

She laid her head on his shoulder. "I'm surprised that you know all these old tunes."

"My grandpa was a huge country music fan. He kept it going on the radio from daylight to bedtime. I've heard the songs that were played tonight my whole life. How about you?"

"Same story, different part of Texas."

She wished the music would've gone on until morning, but in less than four minutes it was over. Justin planted a kiss on her forehead, and then took a step back. "Let's get this place in order. Where's the dust mop. I'll take care of the floor while you do the table business."

"The morning maintenance crew will take care of the floor. We just have to do the tables and be sure everyone picked up their cards. Looks like they did. Even Nikki's is gone, so I guess she's left for the night."

"There's a box left on the table, and it's got your name on it."

"I wish we'd had one for each guest. It doesn't seem fair that I've got a whole box of cards and you don't have even one," she said.

"Dancing with you means more than six boxes of cards," he said.

They finished the job quickly and she said, "I have to get my things. Meet you back here in five?"

"I'll be the one in the cowboy boots sitting in that chair." He pointed to the one still by the door.

"Grab my valentines," she said.

"Will do." He nodded.

She shoved everything into her tote bag and found him holding the box and her shoes in his lap when she returned. "Guess you'd better put these on, right?"

She felt like Cinderella when he knelt in front of her and slipped them on her feet.

"Now, where do you want to go for coffee?"

"The ice cream store makes good coffee," she suggested.

He rose to his feet and took her hand. "Then that's

where we'll go. Tonight was special. I enjoyed all of it, but especially spending time with you."

"Well, you sure made the Fab Five's night—and mine," she said as they made their way across the parking lot to his truck.

He opened the door for her and leaned in once she was inside. He traced her jaw with his forefinger, and then his mouth covered hers in a long, lingering kiss.

Emily was glad she was sitting because her knees trembled. She just hoped that they would recover enough to walk in the high heels from the truck to the store.

"And I'll need one more of those when I bring you back for your car," he said. "Just to see if I like your kisses better with or without the taste of coffee."

Every hormone in Emily's body hummed. This was either the start of something wonderful or else she was going to get her heart broken, but like Nikki said, she either had to kill it or cure it to get any peace.

Chapter Fourteen

Emily toted her bag and the box up the stairs to her apartment, and tossed them on the table. She touched her lips to see if they were truly as hot as they felt, but they were actually cool. Melting onto the sofa, she closed her eyes and relived the dances, the kisses, and the way his eyes had drawn her to him all evening and then the way he held her hand on the table at the ice cream shop. She took a quick shower, made sure her new dress didn't have any stains before she hung it up, dressed in pajama pants and a baggy nightshirt, and crawled up in the middle of her bed with her box of cards. Just like when she was a little girl, she removed the lid, closed her eyes, and picked out a card.

The first one was from Otis and had a picture of Betty Boop and a little bag of three sweetheart candies attached to it. The second one was from Nikki and had the same picture on it, but Nikki had taped a miniature chocolate bar to the back. The very next one she picked up had a heart-shaped lollipop stuck to it. She picked it up and held it to her chest before she read it. The message on the front said BE MINE. She flipped it over to find a drawing of a heart on the back and *J+E* written inside it.

She slipped her feet into the same high heels she'd worn to the party, grabbed her purse, and drove to the Longhorn Canyon ranch. Otis had said to listen to her heart.

It didn't hit her that she was doing a totally stupid thing until she'd gone down the bumpy lane to the cabin and parked behind his truck. She was wearing faded pajama pants, a baggy shirt with none other than Betty Boop on the front, and absolutely no bra or panties.

But he gave me the lollipop, she reasoned.

She opened the car door and glanced up into the rearview mirror. Her damp hair hung limp and she'd washed off every bit of her makeup. She shut the door, thought about what she was doing and where she was.

This isn't me. I take the bull by the horns and spit in his eye, she told herself.

It was something that a teenager would do, not a grown woman. Maybe it was the ranch. Which one of the Five had said that they felt like the old people in the movie *Cocoon*? Perhaps there was a strange energy on the place that made everyone feel younger.

She opened the car door and gingerly made her way across the yard. With a long, deep breath, she hurried to the porch and knocked before she could talk herself out of it.

No one answered, so she knocked again.

That time she could hear movement, so she waited,

shivering as the cold wind let her know she should have at least worn a jacket.

"Emily?" His wet hair indicated he'd just gotten out of the shower.

"I..." Her teeth chattered.

"For goodness' sake, come on in," he said.

Her breast brushed against his bare chest as she slipped past him. Even through the nightshirt, it made every part of her body tingle. She went straight to the fireplace and warmed her hands. "I shouldn't have come out here un-invited. I'll get warm and..." She turned to find him not three feet behind, his arms open in invitation.

"You are welcome here and the door is never locked. Don't knock, darlin', just come right on in," he said.

She walked into his arms, suddenly self-conscious about her breasts under that thin nightshirt. "Thank you, but..."

"I'm glad you're here." He took her hand and led her to the sofa, where he pulled her down onto his lap. Without saying a word, his eyes closed and he leaned in to kiss her.

"Thank you," she muttered when they both came up for air, panting as if they'd run a marathon.

"For?"

"The lollipop." She kicked off her high-heeled shoes.

"You're welcome."

She stood up and turned to face him. "I may regret this tomorrow but my heart says it's the right thing to do. I've never done something this impulsive in my life, Justin. I want you to know that."

Taking him by the hand, she led him toward the bed. "Turn out the lights."

"No," he said. "I want to see your beautiful body, Emily. All of it."

"But…" She wasn't a virgin, but she'd never had sex in a well-lit room. Darkness covered a multitude of things, including her body.

He slowly pulled her shirt up over her head and ran his hands down her sides. "So soft."

Then he removed her pajama pants and held her out at arm's length. "You are gorgeous, Emily Baker."

His eyes said that he meant it, and she truly felt as if she was the prettiest woman on the earth in that moment.

*   *   *

Had he known that a simple card with a red lollipop on it would create this kind of thank-you, he'd have given her the biggest box of candy he could find. That thought caused him to realize what was about to happen, and he wasn't sure the timing was right. This wasn't a one-night stand. This was Emily, the woman he'd fantasized about living with in his new house, the lady who might be the one. What if he broke her heart or if she broke his?

She cupped his face in her hands and brought his mouth to hers again. Then as if she could read his mind, she said, "No strings attached. We'll just see where this goes, right?"

He nodded and peeled off his shirt. "I feel like this is my first time."

"Please tell me you haven't used that line a hundred times," she whispered as she wiggled free of his hands and slid his pajama pants down over his hips. "Oh, my! You are ready."

"I have been ever since you got here," he said. "And, honey, that is not a pickup line." His naked body pressed against hers as he walked her backward the rest of the way to the bed. Her legs buckled on the last step and she fell backward, dragging him down on top of her when she did. Without stopping the steaming hot kisses, they shifted positions until they shared a pillow. Then he was on top of her, feeling all that glorious body underneath him. With one hand she reached down and guided him into her, and they began to rock together as his hands roamed her body. Her soft breasts pressed against his chest. The rhythm quickened and she groaned when he slowed things to a crawl. She brought his lips to hers in a series of hard, passionate kisses.

"Please, Justin, now," she begged.

He stepped the pace up again, and they both hit the top at the same time. Then he rolled them to one side, keeping her in his arms. Her head on his shoulder, his face buried in her still damp hair, he realized this wasn't just a game of chasing a lady who was playing hard to get. It could lead into something special.

"Wow!" he said.

"Amazing." She slung a leg over him and closed her eyes.

He pulled the edge of the quilt over them and cuddled up close to her so it would cover both of them. They slept until after midnight, when a movement awoke him and he opened his eyes to see her getting dressed. He raised up on an elbow and watched her movements. Graceful. Fluid. Brown hair streaming down her naked back. She whipped around to smile at him and he wished that she didn't have those pajama pants on so he could see her completely naked one more time.

"You going to respect me tomorrow?" Her blue eyes bored into his.

"Of course. You going to respect me?"

"I'm the one who knocked on your door, Justin. You only did what I wanted." She pulled her shirt on over her head.

"It's what I've wanted for days, so you don't get to carry that burden alone. Give me a minute to get dressed and I'll walk you to your car."

"No." She held up a hand. "I parked close to the porch. No need for you..."

He slung his long legs off the bed and walked naked to the door to open it for her. "Now I know what making love means. It's a helluva lot different than having sex."

"Me too." She nodded.

"I'll see you Sunday."

"I'll call you long before then." He kissed her on the tip of her nose. "This might lead to a pretty fantastic relationship if you are willing."

She blew him a kiss and he closed the door behind her.

*   *   *

Emily laid her head on the steering wheel of the car when she was inside and had started the engine. What in the hell had she just done? And all over one red lollipop. If he'd given her one of those fancy, red, lace-covered hearts full of chocolates, she might have dropped down on one knee and proposed to him.

She finally got a grip and drove home. But her insane, impulsive stunt troubled her as she made her way up the steps to her apartment. Her phone pinged as she unlocked her door, and she dragged it out of her purse to find nothing but a link to a song. She hit PLAY as she headed to the shower.

Chris Stapleton sang "Tennessee Whiskey" as she adjusted the water for the second time that night and imagined Justin singing it to her as his hands roamed over her naked body.

She got out of the shower, dried off, put on a clean nightshirt, and started to throw the one she'd worn to the ranch in the hamper. Instead, she buried her nose in it to inhale his scent—something woodsy, clean, and with just a hint of Stetson cologne.

She picked up the phone and sent back a heart emoji.

She slept fitfully, waking several times to find that she was hugging nothing but a pillow instead of Justin. Every time she awoke, she gave herself a lecture about how she'd never do something that crazy again. Thank God, she was on the pill because neither of them had even thought of protection.

Her alarm went off and she slapped the snooze button. At seven she finally got out of bed and groaned when she saw her reflection. She had one hour to make that person staring back at her look presentable, and the job looked damn near impossible.

Nikki met her at the door when she got to work, exactly on time. "Did you party after the party? You look like you've got a hangover. You need my famous remedy?"

Emily went straight to the break room to get her first cup of the morning. "No hangover, but I could use a cup of coffee. Didn't sleep well."

Nikki followed right behind her. "Dreamin' about dancin' some more with that handsome hunk of a cowboy?"

"Oh, yeah!" Emily said. "That's exactly what I was dreaming about."

Nikki poured two cups of coffee and handed one to Emily when she had put her things into her locker. "Did you finally wake up and smell the roses?"

Yes, and they smell like my sleep shirt, which I've hung on the back of a chair because I want to smell Justin's aftershave on it one more time? Emily chose to ignore the question.

"The dining room is buzzing and will be for days. They're all talking about the party and how it was the best ever." Nikki sat down at the table. "You goin' to grab a plate this morning or did you already eat—maybe you had breakfast with Justin?"

"I didn't." It was the truth, but now she wished that she had spent the night and had breakfast with him. "And I am hungry so maybe I'll make myself a scrambled egg sandwich."

"I'm having the full breakfast," Nikki said. "You might as well get a plate and eat with me. You don't have bingo until nine o'clock."

Emily's phone pinged and she slid it out of her hip pocket. She tried not to smile when she saw the text from Justin, but it was impossible. A picture of at least a dozen heart-shaped red lollipops arranged in a vase like a bouquet appeared on the screen.

She hurriedly typed: *In your dreams!*

A smiley face emoji wearing sunglasses appeared immediately.

"Justin?" Nikki asked from across the table.

"Maybe." Emily shoved the phone back into her pocket.

"We've been friends five years. You've dated and been in a relationship, but I've never seen your eyes get all twinkly like they do when you think of him."

"It's all so new and wonderful. I don't want to talk about it for fear I might jinx it," Emily said. "Let's go get some breakfast."

"Well, at least you aren't saying *never* anymore." Nikki rinsed her cup and put it in the drain board.

"No, I'm not." Emily did the same with her cup.

"Good. I'd just love to have a sexy cowboy look at me like he does you," Nikki said.

Oh, honey, if you only knew how much further this has gone than just looks. And how he made me feel when he saw me naked with the lights on, Emily thought.

*   *   *

Justin kept busy the rest of the day, so he didn't have time to send more texts, but he hummed the tune to "Tennessee Whiskey" while he worked. He'd finished replacing a couple of rotten beams in an old barn that afternoon and had gone to the tack room to clean up when he found an old jacket that had belonged to his grandfather. He took it off the hook and slipped it on. Grandpa Maguire had been a big man, as tall as Cade and even broader in the shoulders, so it fell off his shoulders a bit and was too long in the sleeves. Justin sat down on a wooden bench and wrapped it tightly around his chest.

"Okay, Grandpa, talk to me. Remember when you got sick, and we all knew it was your last days. You told me to wear your hat when I had a problem and you'd still talk to me. But when you died, Granny buried that old hat with you so all I've got is this coat. This mornin' I need to hear your advice."

He sat there for another five minutes and then said, "Okay, I'll lay it out for you. There's this woman, Emily Baker, and I like her a lot. She's funny, and independent as hell and the kindest woman I've ever known. And she's beautiful."

"Then what's the problem?" Skip startled him when he sat down beside him.

"Where did you come from?" Justin asked.

"The house. Thought I'd see how you was comin' along with that beam, and if you needed help with it this afternoon, but you got the job done. You're wearin' your grandpa's coat and talkin' to him, right?"

"Yep, but he's not talking to me."

"Reckon I could do that if you want me to," Skip said.

Justin explained as much as he knew about Emily leaving the ranch where she grew up and why, and told Skip everything else that he could think of—except the lollipop story. "Do you think I'm crazy? I've only known her a few weeks, and I've been outrunning women who want to settle down for years, so why this one."

"Nope, I don't think you're crazy. I'm going to give you the same advice your grandpa would if he was alive. It's something simple but sometimes it's hard to do, and that's just to follow your heart," Skip said. "Now I reckon you'd better hang up that coat so we can go have some chili. Retta made a big pot full and it smelled pretty good when I came through the house."

They walked back to the house together without either of them saying another word. The smell of chili hit Justin's nose the minute he and Skip came through the back door. Cade had already dipped up a bowlful and was at the table. Levi and Claire were next in line at the stove, and Retta was sitting beside Cade.

"Hey, did you get the barn repaired?" Levi asked.

"Did you see that the contractor already has the blocks up for our foundation?" Claire asked. "It's going to be beautiful."

"What did you think of the Valentine party last night? We haven't talked all day," Retta said.

Justin filled a bowl and took it to the table. "Barn is finished. The contractor told me that the walls will be up by next weekend if it doesn't rain and you'll be able to move in by early summer. Party went fine. Next year y'all have to go with me. Some of those residents had six or seven guests. Our old folks were so excited that I was there and pretended I was their relative."

"Details," Claire demanded as she tucked a strand of blond hair into her ponytail.

"Okay." Justin grinned. "I spliced in a piece of wood about three feet long out in the barn, then I used two pieces of metal to hold it—"

"Not that!" Claire butted in before he could go on. "Details about what is happening today with our house. I know it'll be finished in the summer, weather permitting, but how long until it's in the dry."

"I'm more interested in the party. And Emily. Did she get all dressed up?" Retta asked. "It's been less than a week, but I miss her being in and out of the house."

Justin laid his spoon down. "I already told you it was really nice. Emily wore a pretty red dress. I danced with all the ladies that came to the ranch, and with Emily. I helped her do a little cleanup and then walked her to the car. I came home. I expect she did the same," he said.

"What she wants to know is if you kissed her good night, and if you thought she was gorgeous." Cade chuckled.

"Yes, she was stunning, but a cowboy don't kiss and tell." To him she was just as sexy in her pajama pants and the faded nightshirt as she'd been in her red party dress. And they'd done a helluva lot more than share a good night kiss.

Justin focused on his supper and was glad that the conversation went back to Claire and Levi's house, rather than about Emily. When he finished eating, he carried his bowl to the dishwasher. "My house plans are callin' my name. I thought maybe in the morning before I come to work I'd go over to the place I'm plannin' to build and see how many trees will have to come out. I hate to get rid of any of those big pecan trees."

"No problem," Levi said. "Maybe you could check out the biggest barn in that area and see if it's going to need any work. I thought we'd put this year's small hay bales in it, but it needs to be in good shape."

"Will do." He put on his jacket and slipped out the back door. When he reached the cabin he checked his phone, but there were no texts or messages from Emily. He put in a comedy movie, but that didn't hold his attention. He was on his way to take the DVD out of the player and put in another one when his phone pinged. He fished it out of the carrier on his belt and read a text from Emily: *Have chocolate syrup. Bring ice cream. Will leave the porch light on.*

And then it gave her address.

He shoved the phone back in the carrier and sent a text back: *What flavor?*

Immediately an answer popped up: *Any kind*

He stopped at the grocery store and bought a half gallon each of vanilla, mint chocolate chip, and pecans and praline. Chocolate syrup would be good on any of those. When he passed the fruit aisle, he picked up four bananas, just in case they decided on banana splits. Then he added whipped cream and a bottle of maraschino cherries.

He plugged her address into the GPS and the mechanical lady guided him right to the porch light at the bottom of an outside staircase that led up the side of a double-car garage. Carrying his bag of groceries, he took the steps two at a time and knocked on the door with the toe of his boot.

*   *   *

The clock had moved at a snail's pace the past half hour while Emily waited. The chocolate ice cream topping was sitting on the table in her tiny kitchen. The bedroom door was closed so she wouldn't be tempted. Her sofa was only made for two people, and there was barely room for one end table. No coffee table or recliner. A picture of the beach hung above the sofa.

When she heard him coming up the steps, she started toward the door, but she made herself wait until he knocked. Her heart raced. Her pulse thumped in her ears. She took a deep breath and counted to ten before she opened the door. He planted a kiss on her forehead as he walked past and then unloaded the bags onto the kitchen table.

"I thought we'd have banana splits."

"That's a lot of ice cream for two people," she said.

She got out an ice cream scoop and two bowls. "That sounds delicious."

"It does to me, too. I love ice cream even more than cold beer."

Justin's shoulders were wide and his biceps huge, but they seemed even bigger in her small apartment. His presence filled the whole living room/kitchen area and spread warmth throughout her whole body. When she closed her eyes she could almost feel him cuddled up next to her in the bed at the cabin. When she opened them, she could imagine him sitting next to her on the sofa, bodies pressed together. The room got so warm that she flipped a switch to turn on the ceiling fan.

"Wow! I love pecans and pralines with chocolate topping. I bet bananas will make it even better." She opened the boxes and looked across the table at him. "One, two, or three?"

He removed his denim jacket and tossed it on the sofa. "I want a dip of each kind. I'll get the bananas ready."

She picked up the two bowls, put them back in the cabinet, and got down two larger ones. "And you brought whipped cream and cherries."

"Got to do it up right the first time I'm invited to your house." He winked.

"It's hardly a house."

Justin arranged the long slices of bananas and slid the bowls to her. "Is it a home?"

Emily dipped out a rounded mound of each flavor of ice cream. "It's had to do for one for the past five years."

"Is it where your heart is?" He drizzled the chocolate syrup she handed to him over his ice cream, then added whipped cream and a cherry on top of each.

"Never thought about it, but if I moved I wouldn't miss it so much, so I guess not." She worked on her creation. One scoop of vanilla and one of pecans and pralines. Then she followed his example, only she put two cherries on each.

"Are we eating here at the table?" he asked.

"Yes. We need to talk." She put the rest of the ice cream in the freezer of her apartment-size refrigerator. "I miss a huge walk-in freezer and refrigerator."

Justin chuckled as he dipped into his ice cream. "So you do get homesick for something about the ranch?"

"Sure, I do. The kitchen for one. I like to cook, so someday I'll have a place with the walk-ins. And I miss my grandmother's sassiness but not her bossiness when it comes to my biological clock. This is better than Dairy Queen."

"So, you should be havin' babies?"

"According to my grandma, I'm about to cross over the

bridge to infertility. It'll be burned behind me. In her era, thirty was the end of the time for having children. She had six by then, all girls except the baby of the family, who was a boy," Emily said between bites.

"Retta's in big trouble then. She wants at least three or four kids, and her era is about gone, since she's already thirty," Justin said. "You said we need to talk. Is it about last night?"

"That's part of it," she said.

"And the other part?"

"Justin, there's undeniable chemistry between us, but why start something we can't finish," she answered.

"Why won't we finish?"

"You are sitting in my world. I've visited yours. They are as far apart as…"

Justin stuck his spoon in his ice cream and leaned forward toward her. "Are you saying that neither of us knows how to compromise? I'm not asking you to marry me, Emily. I'm asking you if we could date, although I'm not real good at that."

She swallowed hard. "Don't give me that line, cowboy."

He crossed his heart with a forefinger. "It's the truth, darlin'. I've had lots of one-night stands, but the last official date I was on was for the senior prom in high school. I'm no good at this relationship stuff, and besides, Cade's situation kinda broke me from suckin' eggs, as Skip says."

"I thought he and Retta were the perfect couple."

"They are." Justin ate a few more bites. "But before Retta, there was Julie. They grew up together, went to college together, got engaged, lived together, and then she planned this huge wedding. And I mean gigantic." He stopped to eat some more. "Don't want this to melt."

Questions went through Emily's mind, like did Retta know about Julie? Was she a first wife or did she die? Emily ate a few more bites but she could hardly wait for Justin to finish, so he'd tell her the rest of the story. He finally pushed back his empty bowl.

"Julie wasn't brave enough to tell Cade that she hated ranchin', and that she didn't love him enough to live on the Longhorn Canyon. So she kept hoping, right up to the last minute, that she could change his mind. She wanted him to move to the city and work in a bank, using his business degree," Justin explained.

"And?" Emily asked.

"She gave me a note the morning of their supposed wedding day. I thought it was a love note, since they weren't supposed to see each other. I took it to him and he went to pieces. The wedding was off. It was embarrassing as hell for the family, and I thought Cade would never get over it. He might not have, if Retta hadn't come into his life. We all owe her big-time for putting the light back in his eyes," Justin said.

"And that broke you from sucking eggs, how?" she asked.

"I saw how much pain he was in. I vowed to never let myself get in that position."

She toyed with the last bite of ice cream. "You've changed your mind?"

He took his bowl to the kitchen and rinsed it, looked around for a dishwasher but didn't find one. So he left it in the sink. "No, you and my grandpa did."

"You talked to your grandpa about me?" She almost dropped her spoon.

"Kinda." He sat down on the small sofa. "He died when I was a little boy." He went on to tell her about the hat and the coat.

"What if I'm your Julie?" Emily whispered. "What if we follow this yellow brick road and it ends up making both of us miserable?"

"If this relationship goes past a few dates are you going to insist I leave the ranch?"

"I would never do that. It's what you love," she said without hesitation.

"I would never ask you to leave your job at the center or if you decide to work with children again, either. It's what you love," he said, seriously. "That's called compromise. Julie wasn't willing for it, so you can't be her."

"Seems crazy to be talkin' like this when..." She paused.

He patted the area of the sofa beside him. "When we haven't even had a real date?"

She sat down and he took her hand in his.

"But then I don't usually go to bed with someone until I've been out with him three or four months."

"And I'm the opposite," he admitted.

"Well." She laid her head on his shoulder. "They say opposites attract."

He brought her hand to his lips. "Ever wonder why that happens?"

A shiver that had nothing to do with the cold ice cream in her stomach danced down her backbone. Every single time he touched her, she reacted that way. Did he feel the same thing? Was this what happened when two people were true soul mates?

"Because God has a sense of humor," she finally answered.

Justin was silent for several minutes and then nodded. "I should be going. First thing tomorrow morning I want to go inspect the place where I'm hoping to put my new house. Want to go with me?"

"Love to," she said. "What time should I be at the cabin?"

"Seven thirty," he said.

"That's pretty early."

"You could go home with me tonight. I'd bring you right home after we look at the land and a barn to see if it needs any repairs," he said.

"I'll get my toothbrush and a nightshirt."

He tipped up her chin and kissed her. "Just a toothbrush will do fine."

Chapter Fifteen

Emily awoke to the chirping of a bird instead of to the sound of the neighbor's car doors slamming as they either left for work or came home after a graveyard shift. For a split second she thought she was dreaming again when she smelled the combination of cinnamon and coffee. But her eyes were open and her mind was going in circles.

She grabbed the sheet, pulled it around her body, and sat up so fast that it made her dizzy.

"Good mornin', gorgeous," Justin said as he brought a tray with coffee and cinnamon toast to the bed.

"Mornin'," she said. "Is this place for real? I'd forgotten how quiet it is back here."

He sat down beside her on the edge of the bed and picked up a piece of toast. "That's why I'm building my house in a spot like this. It's located about a mile west of here as the crow flies. There is a pecan orchard between where I'll set the house and the fence that marks the border of the ranch.

Only time it'll be noisy is when the harvesters come in to get the nuts. I can't wait for you to see it."

Rather than taking a bite, he held the toast to her mouth. "A queen should be fed from the hands of her lover. She should never get her hands dirty."

"But what if the queen wants to plant flowers or put in a garden, or maybe even put on a pair of gloves and haul hay? Or pull a calf or help build a barn? Can she get her hands dirty then?" she asked.

"Are you for real? Would you do those things?" he asked.

"I love ranchin', just not all the paperwork of a big operation. We talked about this before. Remember? I want to know how many times you've done this?"

"What? Had sex with a gorgeous woman? Fed her breakfast in bed?"

"All of the above," she answered.

"Lost count on the first one. Never on the second. You are the first, Emily, and words can't describe last night. I feel like I've known you for years, not weeks," he said.

"Is that your best pickup line?" She sipped the coffee and set it back down.

He picked it up. "No, I've got much better ones, but that's comin' from the heart, not the lips." He leaned in for the first kiss of the morning.

His tongue tickled her upper lips. She opened slightly to allow him entrance and enjoyed the taste of cinnamon and coffee blended together. Who'd have ever thought that those two flavors could be so erotic? Someone should make a mouthwash that tasted like that. Her hands went around his neck. The sheet fell to her waist, but she didn't care. She didn't want him to ever stop kissing her. His rough hands skimmed her sides from her breasts to her waist and then down to her hips. Every nerve ending begged for more just like they had the night before when he'd done the same thing.

"We're supposed to be somewhere this morning, aren't we?" She panted as she pulled away, knowing that five more minutes of making out was going to put them in the bed for the rest of the morning. She shivered, thinking of how embarrassing it would be if Cade and Levi came looking for Justin, and found them all tangled up in the sheets.

He nuzzled the inside of her neck. "Yes. No. Maybe. It can wait."

"And if your family comes to see if maybe you're sick because you've never been late to work?" She tugged the covers back up over her breasts.

He picked up her hand and began a string of kisses from her wrist, up her arm and to that soft spot on her neck again. "I'll put a DO NOT DISTURB sign on the door."

"You going to make an honest woman of me if my daddy comes lookin' for me?" she asked.

He stopped suddenly and chuckled. "Does your dad have a shotgun?"

"More than one." She wrapped the sheet around her body and headed toward the bathroom. "I'll be ready to go in ten minutes."

"Want me to wash your back?"

"There's not room in that tiny shower for that."

He wiggled his dark eyebrows. "Is there room in your shower?"

"Nope."

"Guess we'll have to see about skinny-dippin' in the big bathtub in the bunkhouse tomorrow then." He grabbed the end of the sheet and tugged as she went by.

The sheet fell away. She stood there, wearing nothing but

a puzzled look. "Tomorrow? We have a date for church and dinner, right? What's that got to do with the bunkhouse?"

"One week after y'all left, remember?"

"Oh!" she exclaimed. "I forgot about that. I thought the church date was replacing that drinkin' thing."

"Are you backing out on a bet?"

"I'd never do that. Do you really think we should do that on Sunday? Seems kind of sacrilegious, don't it?"

"Nothing says we can't settle the bet tonight." Justin slung his long legs over the side of the bed and stood up—stark naked and with that dreamy look in his eyes.

She almost turned around and took him back to bed. They were consenting adults, so she shouldn't care who knew they'd spent the night together.

"Tonight it is, then. I'll bring the fried chicken." She crossed the room and shut the bathroom door behind her.

*   *   *

Justin waited until he couldn't hear the water running in the shower anymore before he stepped into the bathroom. "Move over, darlin'. While you get dried off and dressed, I can get a shower."

She took a step toward the vanity to give him access. He took the opportunity to tip up her chin with his knuckles and kiss her.

"I love wet kisses," he whispered in her ear.

He stepped into the shower, adjusted the water so that it was cooler, and hoped that helped with the instant arousal he got from simply looking at all those luscious curves. He sang at the top of his lungs.

The bathroom door was open when he slung the shower curtain to the side. Her back was to him, and she was pulling

a knit shirt down over her body. Even that simple movement was sexy. He slipped his arms around her waist and
hummed a country tune as he swayed with her.

She flipped around, the shirt barely covering a lacy bra.
Her fingertips combed through the soft hair on his chest as
they made their way up to his neck.

"I'm tempted," she said, softly.

"Me too." He dropped the towel. "Let's give in to what
our hearts want."

"Can't." She kissed him on the cheek. "I'm already
dressed."

"I know how to take care of that little problem."

"I don't have a single doubt that you do." She stepped
away and jerked her shirt the rest of the way down. "But too
much of a good thing gets old after a while."

"That's one old sayin' that I don't believe." He chuckled.

When he'd dressed, he slung open the door and Beau
rushed inside. The dog tucked his nose into Emily's hand and
wagged his tail. She dropped to her knees and rubbed his
ears. Then she kissed him on the top of his head and asked if
he'd like to go for a ride with them.

"Beau is a sweetheart. And so are Gussie and Hopalong." Her voice got high and pitchy, like she was talking
to a baby.

Justin could have sworn the dog was smiling up at her.
He remembered his grandpa saying—you can't fool dogs or
kids. If either one shied away from a person it was best to
beware of them.

"Okay, sweetie pie," Emily crooned to the dog. "We've
got to go but you can go with us and tell Justin what you
think of his house site." She straightened up and headed out
the door.

He ushered her toward his truck with a hand slung

around her shoulders. The minute that Justin opened the door for her, Beau hopped inside.

"Daddy takes our old ranch dog in the truck with him all the time," she said.

"Your ranch dog? I thought your grandmother was the one who owned the ranch."

"She does, but we've got a dog," she answered.

A mile down a path even rougher than the one back to the cabin, he stopped and pointed at a grove of pecan trees. "Right there. I just have to figure out how many trees I need to remove to get my house set back in there."

"You'll want a yard, right?" she asked.

"With a fence around it." He nodded. "What do you think of a split rail?"

"It's a shame to cut down pecan trees. What if you set your house in front of them, and then planted a couple of fast-growing shade trees on the sides right outside the fence?" she asked. "Let's go walk around and pretend we're inside the house." She opened the door and barely made it out before Beau did. He took off after a squirrel, chasing it up a tree. Justin had to hurry to catch up to her as she made her way down the rutted pathway toward the bare pecan trees.

"What if you turned the house around so that the front was looking at the trees? It would be like a park," she asked.

"A park?" he asked.

"It looks like a beautiful park to me. I see a wide porch on the house with the summer breezes flowing across it. You're sitting in a rocking chair with a glass of sweet tea or lemonade in your hand as you watch children play tag or chase around the trees." The soft tone in her voice and the dreamy look in her eyes said she was looking into the future.

Justin wondered if she was sitting in the rocking chair right beside him on that porch in the vision that made her light blue eyes look like that.

*   *   *

Back in her apartment Emily packed a small case with what she'd need for Sunday morning. There was no way she was driving home after proving that she could drink Justin under the table. She'd finished taking everything she needed out of the bedroom when someone rapped on the door. Expecting it to be Justin, she slung it open to find Nikki on the other side.

"Hey, want to go get some pizza and catch a movie?" Nikki's eyes went to the bags and the dress draped over the top of them. "Oh, you're about to leave. No problem. We'll do it later. Tomorrow afternoon?"

"Got that date to settle the debt tomorrow," Emily answered.

Nikki slapped her forehead with the back of her hand. "That's right. I forgot. Well, I'll catch you next weekend."

"Hello, Nikki," Justin said from the bottom of the steps.

"Well, hello." She grinned.

"Maybe you could help me out here." He climbed the stairs and stepped past her into the apartment. He nodded toward Emily with a mischievous look on his face. "We're about to settle an argument about who can hold their liquor the best. You know anything about Emily's tolerance?"

Nikki giggled. "Let's just say you better get ready to lose this battle. What's the stakes?"

"The joy of being the winner," Emily answered.

"Well, I'll get out of here and let the party begin." Nikki threw a sly wink at Emily.

"See you Monday morning." Emily blushed.

"If you need my famous hangover remedy just give me a call." Nikki turned around to leave and then looked back. "I mean that for you, Justin. She won't need it."

Justin waved at her and sniffed the air. "I smell fried chicken. I can't believe you cooked. I figured we'd pick up a bucket on the way to the cabin."

"Did you bring good liquor?" she asked.

He nodded. "Jack Daniel's, Patron—the best."

"Then I bring good food. You take the basket right there with our picnic in it, and I'll get my suitcase and Sunday dress. I'm not driving home after consuming that much alcohol."

"Yes, ma'am," he said. "So do you want to do this in the cabin instead of the bunkhouse?"

She shook her head. "Nope. When you pass out cold, I'm having a long, hot bath in that huge tub. I never did get one when we were there with the Five."

"And if you pass out cold before I do?" he asked.

"Honey, there ain't that much alcohol in the liquor store," she bragged. "I'm Irish, remember. We have booze running in our veins instead of blood. And I'm a big girl to boot."

"Baker is Irish?" he asked. "Well, darlin', the Maguires are Irish too. And Mama was a Finn, which is also Irish, so we may need to stop by the liquor store on the way out of town and buy enough to fill up that big bathtub."

"We could go skinny-dippin' and use straws." She locked the door behind her.

His laughter echoed out across the dark night. Emily could imagine it reaching all the way to the stars surrounding a sliver of a moon.

"I feel like a kid who found the liquor cabinet unlocked." She put her things in the backseat of the truck.

"Did you ever do that?" He settled into his seat and started driving toward the ranch.

"Oh, yeah," she said. "The twins were fourteen, and I was fifteen. We didn't want Mama to find out that we'd been drinking, so we just sampled each bottle."

"Which was your favorite?"

"Jack Daniel's," she said without hesitation.

"Your least?"

"Christian Brothers brandy. That crap tasted like paint thinner smells." She shivered. "We decided that its name was deceptive."

He laughed again. "It's not so bad if you mix it with something, but rest assured, darlin', I didn't buy a bottle for tonight. I got tequila, Jack Daniel's, a bottle of wine and one of rum, plus the stuff to make whatever mixed drinks you might like."

"I never mix wine and whiskey. Gives me a headache the next morning for sure," she said.

"That's called a hangover," he told her.

"No, darlin', that's a headache. A hangover is something more drastic that requires Nikki's famous cure, which is really bad. If I ever had to use it, I'd probably never drink again," Emily said.

A few minutes later he parked the truck behind the bunkhouse and turned to look at her. With nothing more than the moonlight, she could see enough of his expression to know that he appreciated what he saw. He'd never mentioned that she was a big girl, that she had a sprinkling of freckles across her nose, or that she should do something with her hair, like put highlights in it—unlike her last boyfriend. He just kept telling her that she was beautiful and he loved her curves.

"You have the most gorgeous eyes," he said.

She opened the car door. "They're blue like yours."

"No, darlin', yours are the color of a summer sky. Mine are dull compared to that. And you're supposed to wait for me to be the gentleman."

Gussie rubbed around her legs the moment she stepped out, and Emily stooped down to pick her up. "This isn't a date, and d-ar-lin'." She dragged out the word to several syllables. "I appreciate being treated like a lady, but I do know how to open doors."

"Why is it not a date?" He followed her to the back door of the bunkhouse.

"Because we're not going in the front door, which means you don't want anyone to know we're here," she said.

"Honey, we can do this at the ranch house in front of Cade and Retta if you want to. I'm not ashamed of being seen with you. Matter of fact, I'll stand up in church tomorrow morning and confess that we've been sleeping together." He entered the house behind her.

"Sweet Lord!" She gasped.

More than a dozen candles were lit, throwing just enough light to make the room sexy. A vase of red roses was centered on the coffee table, and petals led from there to the bedroom, where more candles burned. She followed the trail all the way to the bedroom, and then into the bathroom, where she reached down and picked up a few to feel the velvety softness.

"This is pretty sexy," she said.

His presence behind her stirred the heat inside her to a full-fledged blaze. He slipped one arm around her waist, gently pushed her hair away from her ear, and whispered, "Not as sexy as you are. Shall we go skinny-dippin' before we start drinkin'?"

She glanced at the tub. Bath oil and salts were laid out

on the seat of a ladder-back chair with two big fluffy white towels draped over the back. "Yes, please. But let's bring the bottle of tequila and the shot glasses. We can start while we're in the tub."

"You start the water while I'm gone." He whipped around and disappeared before she could blink.

Emily got the water to just the right temperature and dumped in both the oil and the salts, then she stripped out of her clothing, tossed it all at the bed in the other room, and got into the tub. When he returned, he was naked and carrying a bottle and two shot glasses. He pulled the chair up to the tub and set it all down before he joined her.

Her legs, almost as long as his, were stretched toward one end of the tub and his toward the other. He reached out over the edge of the tub and filled two shot glasses. She took one from him when he handed it over and threw it back in one gulp.

"First one always brings the most fire," she said.

"Yep," he agreed and refilled both shot glasses.

She downed that one and held out the empty toward him. While he poured, his foot edged its way up the curve of her hip, stopping at the indention of her waist and then moving up her ribs.

Well, two could damn sure play this game. She moved her foot up his inner leg and watched his eyes the whole time. When she reached the top, he gasped.

"Water too warm?" she teased. "I could add some cold."

"I was thinking more of adding ice," he admitted.

"Let's play a game. Whoever loses gets a shot. The winner gets a pass," she said.

He shook his head. "That's not fair. The rules were to see who could hold their liquor better."

"Okay, then, we'll leave the shots out of it. Here's the

game. You can use one finger and only one to touch me anywhere above the neck for one minute. And I can't say a word. Then it'll be my turn," she said.

"You played this before?"

"Nope, but I read it in a romance book one time. I never wanted to play it until now." She glanced up at the clock on the wall above the toilet. "Time starts now."

He moved forward just slightly and traced her jawline with a touch so soft that it made her insides go all mushy within fifteen seconds. Then he moved to her lips and spent the rest of his minute making love to her mouth with his index finger.

"My turn," she whispered when the time was up.

She started at the nape of his neck and brought her finger around to the soft spot under his ear, where she made lazy circles. "I'm already willing to lose this game. I want you, Emily, and I'll forfeit the drinkin' game for a night with you in bed, or hell, on the floor or right here in this tub. I've never had sex under water. Have you?"

"No, but I'm willin' to give it a try." She inched forward until she could wrap her legs around him. "After this we'll have to try bed sex to see which is better."

"On a twin bed and then on the queen-size, just so we know the difference in the three," he agreed.

Chapter Sixteen

Justin sat beside Emily again that Sunday morning. He couldn't begin to keep his mind on the preacher's sermon but instead thought about the water, the queen bed, and the twin bed sex of the night before. He personally liked the queen bed best because that was where they'd fallen asleep in each other's arms.

Grandpa always said anything worth having was damn sure worth fighting for, but Justin hadn't had to do much battling for Emily. A few roses, some tequila, and a red lollipop were all it took, and yet, it wasn't like he'd just sweet-talked a woman into going home with him from a Saturday night honky-tonk. This was far different and a lot more serious. With the other women, he had been ready to see them go the next morning—not so with Emily.

Justin took her hand in his and rested it on his knee. Larry patted him on the back from the pew right behind him, so evidently he'd seen the gesture and agreed. Pretty soon, Otis did the same, so those buzzing whispers probably meant that Larry was spreading the news.

When the benediction had been given and the last amen uttered, Emily slipped her hand free so she could hug each of the Fab Five. They acted as if they hadn't seen her in weeks rather than just two days.

"Are you coming to Mavis and Skip's with us for Sunday dinner?" Patsy asked. "We brought a cheesecake for dessert. The cook in the kitchen let us make it ourselves. It's Sarah's recipe for pecan caramel."

"No, we're going to the ranch for Italian. Retta made lasagna. But your cheesecake sounds delicious. Do you share the recipe?" Justin answered for Emily.

Sarah batted her gray eyelashes. "Honey, I'd share anything with you."

Patsy air slapped her on the arm. "Stop it. He's taken."

"Oh, really?" Emily's eyebrows shot up.

"Yep, this tall brunette that works at the center has hog-tied him." Otis threw his hand over his mouth, but the giggles escaped through his fingers.

"You laugh like a little girl," Larry said. "But then you have a voice for a guy."

"Well, you sound like an elephant far—" Otis caught himself and looked up at the ceiling. "Forgive me, Lord, I forgot where I was. Anyway, Larry, you sound like that when you laugh."

"See y'all later. We've got to go." Justin ushered Emily out a side door and headed straight for his truck. "So tell me about this brunette that's got me in her sights. Do you know her? Otis said she works at the center."

"Have no idea who he's talkin' about," she answered. "Maybe he got the places of employment mixed up and she works at the Rusty Spur or a local brothel."

"She's not that kind of woman." Justin opened the door for her and then jogged around the truck to get in out of the wind, which had picked up in the last few minutes.

"Oh, so you are seeing someone else? I have competition?" Emily asked.

He leaned across the console and gave her a quick kiss. "Darlin', you'll never have to worry about competition in my world."

"Don't tell me that's not a pickup line."

"Yep, it is, but this time it's true." He turned the radio on and found the classic country station that he liked. George Strait was singing "Check Yes or No." The lyrics talked about a little girl passing a note to a little boy at school, telling him to check the yes box if he wanted to be her friend.

"So what would you check?" Justin asked when the song ended.

"It says that they were in the third grade. Darlin', you wouldn't have chased me on the school ground when we were that age. I was the biggest kid in the class, and boys didn't chase me," she said.

"I would have," he declared.

*   *   *

Emily figured that he really believed that, but he hadn't known her in the third grade. Back then she had teeth she still had to grow into, and she really was the biggest child in class. The boys barely came up to her shoulder. From the pictures she'd seen on the mantel of the ranch house, Justin had been one of those cute little boys that the girls chased.

They were silent for the first several minutes of the drive, but it wasn't the kind of quiet that needs to be filled with words. Sitting beside him in church and riding home in his truck felt right.

Home! the voice in her head yelled.

I mean the ranch, she argued. *Three nights of sex does not make a place home. If it did, then my last boyfriend's apartment would be home,* she thought. Then Cade's ex-fiancée not ever wanting to live on the ranch came to mind. The woman must not have loved Cade nearly as much as she should have. What was that girl's name? Emily's brow drew down in a frown as she tried to pull the name from her memory.

"Julie!" she finally blurted out when she remembered.

"What?" Justin whipped around to give her a puzzled look.

"I couldn't think of her name, and when it came to me, I said it out loud," she answered honestly.

"I've done that before with people's names or even places I couldn't think of. Why were you thinking about Julie?"

"I wonder why she couldn't compromise. She could have had her job in the city, couldn't she? It can't be a rule that the women have to live on the ranch, because Claire doesn't. Or is that just because she isn't a Maguire? Hey, did your mother like Julie?"

Justin's head bobbed up and down in a nod. "Mama loved Julie and was almost as devastated as Cade when all that happened."

They drove along in silence for a few minutes. Emily's thoughts circled back around to the word *home*. As frustrating as her family could be at times, she missed them and was glad that she'd get to see everyone before long. But where was home these days?

"What do you want to do after we eat?"

She was glad that he changed the subject. "Take a walk? Maybe go back over to the place where you're going to build your house. Do you have any plans yet?"

"I've been looking at a few. It's a fairly decent day. We could take a quilt with us," he said.

"And pretend we're in your house." She pointed as he parked the truck. "There's Gussie on the porch, waiting for us. Sarah talks about her all the time. I wish the residents were allowed to have small pets."

"Sarah, and all the rest, can come visit anytime they want," Justin said as he leaned across the seat and kissed her. "It's pretty damn hard to keep my mind on church when you're right there beside me."

"Amen." She looked over her shoulder to see Gloria in the doorway. It reminded her of the few dates she'd had in high school. If she was five minutes late for curfew her mother would be waiting with that same unhappy expression on her face.

"We should get inside so we can help Retta." She gave him a sweet kiss and then opened the truck door.

"I guess so, but I'd rather stay right here and make out all afternoon," he said.

"Man can not live on sex and kisses alone. He must have food," she teased.

"I'd sure be willin' to give up food and see if that's the truth." He grinned.

They got out at the same time, but he hurried around the truck to take her hand in his. When they were inside the house, Emily picked a bibbed apron off one of the hooks in the utility room and flipped it over her head. Justin tied the strings around her waist and brushed a sweet kiss on her neck.

"I'd like to talk to you." Gloria's eyes shifted to Justin. "In the living room, please."

"Sure thing, Mama. Is it about the trip I'm taking?"

"Thought I might go with you, to keep you company," Gloria said.

"I don't think so," Vernon disagreed right behind her. "We've made plans to drive to Wichita Falls for a couple of days for that big Cattlemen's dinner."

Justin followed his parents into the living room, leaving Emily in the kitchen.

"What can I do to help?" Emily asked.

"Set the table," Retta answered. "You remember where everything is?"

"Sure do." Her eyes went to Claire. "I thought you and Levi would be at Mavis and Skip's for dinner."

"We were invited, but Levi thought it would be better for Benjy if we weren't there today." She put ice into glasses for the sweet tea.

"So that he'd talk more to the Fab Five?" Emily set a stack of plates on the cabinet and opened the cutlery drawer to get out what they needed.

"You got it," Claire answered. "So what's happening between you and Justin? Everyone at church was asking if y'all are a couple."

"I'm not sure what we are. We've only known each other a couple of weeks. Well, three if you count from the first time I came out here," she answered.

Retta patted her on the back. "I remember not knowing where I stood with Cade, but at the end of five weeks, I loved him too much that I couldn't leave."

"What did you do?" Emily asked.

"I left, made it to the end of the lane, and then turned around and came. He proposed, but we waited until fall to get married," Retta answered.

Emily shifted her focus to Claire. "And you?"

"I was the damsel in distress, and Levi rescued me. Lost control of my vehicle on slick roads and took refuge in the old cabin where Justin lives now. He found me and my niece and the rest is history. He asked me to marry him on Christmas."

"Retta, you lived on a ranch, right? But not you, Claire?" Emily asked.

"Yes." Retta pulled two pans of lasagna from the oven. "I was raised on one and couldn't wait to get away from it. I went to college and worked in Dallas. Loved it. But then my father got sick. I came home to take care of him and planned to go back to my banking job. Fate had different plans. I needed a temporary job to pay the medical bills in between selling off the farm and going to the new bank. I landed here and fell in love with Cade."

Claire took the makings for a green salad from the refrigerator. "Same story. Little different ending. I'm not a rancher. I love the animals, but getting my hands dirty isn't for me. I like my quilting business just fine. This way I get the best of both worlds." She lowered her voice to a whisper. "And I get to sleep with that sexy cowboy out there every night. I don't care if he comes home with bullshit on his boots, just so long as he leaves them in the utility room."

"Now be honest with us. Do you like Justin?" Retta asked.

"I like him a lot," Emily admitted. "He's the sweetest, kindest man I've ever met, but we haven't known each other long enough—" She paused.

Claire butted in before she could go on. "I'll pass on something Levi told me when I said we hadn't known each other very long. If you add up those hours that you were with Justin on the ranch with the Fab Five, and think about a date a week lasting maybe four hours at the most, then you've known him a lot longer than the calendar says you have."

Emily picked up the plates. "Never thought of it that way."

"Thought of what?" Justin asked as he took the plates from her hands. "Let me help you."

"We were thinking that fate has a way of messing up all your plans and rearranging them for you," Claire answered.

Emily could have hugged her. Girlfriends took care of each other, whether they'd just become friends or if they'd been friends for years, like she and Nikki were. Which reminded her, she should have already called Nikki. Maybe tomorrow night they'd go to the pizza place and eat on the buffet.

As if on cue, her phone pinged. The text from Nikki said: *Having a tough day. Meet me for ice cream at two?*

Without hesitation, she answered: *Yes*

Then she turned around to face Justin. "I have to leave right after lunch. Nikki needs me."

"Who's Nikki?" Claire asked.

"My best friend for the past five years. She and I started at the center at the same time. She was an aide at the time, working nights and going to school in the day. She got her LPN and switched to days and has been studying at night for her RN. She's taking the test for that soon and will be going to the hospital emergency room when she passes it. And that's too much information but..." Emily shrugged and caught Justin's eye.

His expression said he was disappointed. "Can you come back after you talk to her?"

"I don't know. If we get out the ice cream, it could take all night," Emily answered.

"I sure understand that." Claire nodded.

"I don't," Justin said. "Explain it to me."

"When girlfriends have a problem, they talk it to death, then revive it and talk about it some more. Guys don't understand," Retta said. "They hold everything in because they're tough. But girls have to get it out even if it means hashing it over a hundred times."

Claire looked up at him. "But when it's a big, big problem that no amount of talk, tears, or cussin' can get them through, then they get out a quart of ice cream and two spoons. No bowls. They eat right out of the carton."

"And that helps?" Justin turned to focus on Emily.

"Every time." She nodded.

"Will you send me a text if you get out the ice cream?" he asked.

She nodded.

"Cade and Levi, dinner will be on the table in five minutes," Retta called out.

"On the way," Cade yelled back.

Emily slipped the phone into the pocket of her denim skirt before she finished folding the napkins and putting them at each plate. After grace was said, Justin leaned over to whisper, "I've been meaning to tell you all week. I'll be gone Monday and Tuesday. I've got to go pick up a new breeder bull. Don't suppose you can get off work and go with me?"

"I'd love to, but I can't. I've already asked for a day off to go home to my family reunion," she said. "You'll call me, right?"

"You can count on it," he said.

"Mavis was so excited about the company today," Levi said as he passed the steaming hot yeast rolls to Emily. "She and the ladies have been texting and calling all week, planning the day. And Skip couldn't wait to talk to Larry about a new sheep pen and to Otis about some kind of special food for Benjy's livestock."

"What about Benjy? Is he excited?" Cade asked.

"It's the craziest thing," Claire said. "He couldn't wait to get out of church and take them home. I think the ladies remind him of his grandmother who died last fall. Maybe since he was around older people his whole life, he relates to them better than other folks."

"Makes sense to me." Justin took two rolls and passed the basket on to Emily.

The simple touch of his fingertips on hers reminded her of the previous night. Bathtub, twin bed, and then queen bed sex. She liked the latter better because she liked falling asleep in Justin's arms. And waking up to stare her fill of him the next morning until he finally opened his eyes.

It had to be real, didn't it, for her to feel like that? And yet there was a lingering doubt deep inside her that made her wary to even begin to put her trust in something that was less than a month old.

*   *   *

Justin parked and turned to face her, taking in the cute little freckles across her nose.

"Did I tell you that you look beautiful today?" he asked.

They were sitting in front of the store where Emily was to meet Nikki. She'd dressed in a denim skirt and a sweater the same color as her gorgeous blue eyes. It made him think of her body covered in a pale blue sheet the night before. She'd gone to sleep before he had, so he'd propped up on an elbow and memorized each detail, from the way her thick dark lashes lay on her high cheekbones, to her full bow-shaped mouth, down to that single little freckle right between her full breasts that begged to be kissed.

"Yes, but I don't mind hearing it again." She smiled.

"And there is Nikki driving up, so I'd better go now. I'm sorry about this afternoon."

"We'll do it another day." Justin cupped her cheeks in his hands and kissed her.

"One more of those and this truck is going to combust," she said.

"It'd be worth it. Text me later, or call?"

"I will," she said as she got out of the truck and followed Nikki into the store.

He watched through the window until Nikki stood up and literally melted into Emily's open arms. From the way her shoulders shook, there was little doubt that she was sobbing, so he resigned himself to the fact that it probably was going to be an all-night affair.

Justin hadn't planned to stop at Mavis and Skip's place, but thinking of an afternoon alone in the cabin or listening to another lecture from his mother wasn't something he wanted to do or hear. So he pulled into the driveway and Skip motioned to him to join him, Otis, and Larry on the porch before he even got out of the truck.

"Thought you had a date today with Emily," Larry called out.

Justin made his way to the porch and sat down on the top step. "I did but her friend Nikki is having a crisis. Y'all havin' a good time here?"

"Oh, man." Otis's tone left no doubts.

"I'm real glad that we get to go to real church on Sunday. But as much as we love a good home-cooked meal, we're insistin' that we take these folks out to eat every other week," Larry said.

"Won't happen." Skip grinned. "Benjy's not comfortable eatin' out that often, and me and Mavis love havin' Sunday company."

Mavis poked her head out the door. "I thought I heard a vehicle pull up. Come on in here and get a cup of coffee and some cheesecake. It's the best you'll ever put in your mouth."

"You haven't told us about the date yet," Skip said.

"Sorry guys." Justin straightened up. "I've got this really big sweet tooth, and cheesecake is one of my favorite desserts."

He followed Mavis into the kitchen, where the ladies were gathered around the table. Patsy patted the empty chair beside hers. "Come right on over here, you sexy thing, and sit beside me."

He'd barely settled into the chair when Mavis put a huge chunk of cheesecake and a mug of steaming hot coffee in front of him. She took her chair at the head of the table and said, "Now tell us about the date. We've been dyin' to hear. Is she the one?"

"Have no idea if she's the one, since we've known each other less than a month. But I was disappointed that we didn't get to spend the whole day together." He put a fork full of the cheesecake into his mouth.

"That's good. I hope she wasn't happy about it either. Drat that Nikki for spoilin' it," Sarah said.

"How'd you know about that?" Justin asked.

"Claire called me," Mavis said.

Patsy laid a hand on his shoulder. "I've got some advice for you. Emily is independent and strong willed. Don't push her or she'll set her heels."

"If you think she's the one, you got to let her think it's her idea," Bess said. "It takes a real good man to chase a woman until she catches him."

Justin chuckled. "I appreciate all the words of wisdom, ladies. I like Emily a lot, but—"

Patsy put her finger over his mouth. "There are no buts in real love. Either she is or she ain't the one. Y'all can have a good time together, shake hands when it's over, and go on your separate ways. Or you can figure out that you're meant for each other and have a future together. You just got to spend time with each other to figure it all out."

"Y'all ever think about putting in a counseling business?" he asked.

"Hell, no! We ain't no good at relationships. Ain't none of us ever been married, so how would we know anything about that?" Sarah said.

"But we do know Emily. She's like a daughter to us," Bess said.

"Or a granddaughter." Patsy nodded. "Now us old meddlin' hens are done with bossin' you around. Claire said y'all were kissin' at the ranch. That as far as it's gone?"

"A cowboy does not kiss and tell." Justin came close to blushing. "But I do thank you for the advice and the cheesecake."

Chapter Seventeen

"Don't cry." Emily choked up at Nikki's sobs. "Did someone die?"

"No, and I passed the test, and now I'm a full-fledged RN, and I can give my notice at the center, and I'm going to miss you." Nikki backed away from Emily and sat down in the booth. She pulled a dozen napkins from the dispenser and wiped her eyes. "It's that son of a bitch I've been dating."

"Whoa!" Emily gasped. "You didn't tell me about a boyfriend."

"I didn't want to jinx it." Nikki folded her arms on the table and hid her face. "Every time I tell you about a boyfriend, it jinxes it and we break up. It's not your fault, and besides I knew you wouldn't like him."

Emily patted Nikki on the head and shoulders. "Why wouldn't I like him?"

"He's a cow—cow—" Nikki hiccupped. "Boy."

"But you like cowboys," Emily said, soothingly.

"I did, but I'm never dating one again. You've got my word. And you shouldn't date Justin ever again, either." Nikki straightened up and blew her nose into another fistful of napkins.

Emily gathered up the soggy napkins and took them to the trash. "This isn't about me today. It's about you. What happened between you and the cowboy, anyway?" She returned and pulled more out to hand to Nikki, who still had tears streaming down her face.

Emily's phone rang. She started to ignore it but Nikki nodded and pointed.

"Answer it and I'll try to stop this cryin'. My sides hurt from it," she said.

"Hello, Hudson. Is this important? I'm in the middle of something," she said.

"I'm just callin' to say if you don't come for the family gatherin' in two weeks that me and Tag are comin' to Bowie for a whole week, and we're crashin' in your apartment. You want that?" he asked.

"I'll be there. I promise." She sighed.

Her two brothers in her small apartment would be like putting two grown grizzly bears in a two-hole outhouse. They'd tear it down and there'd be nothing left but a stinky mess.

"Pinky swear?" Hudson asked.

"Absolutely," Emily sighed.

"Well, you don't have to get excited or anything. It's just the whole family who wants to see you," Hudson said, sarcastically. "You could bring a boyfriend to make Granny happy. She's not gettin' any younger you know."

"I'm not havin' this conversation today," Emily said.

"I'll see you in two weeks. Give Mama and Granny a hug for me."

"Remember what I said. We'll be there if you aren't here," Hudson told her.

She hit the END button and turned back to Nikki. "Family!"

"I know. The other *F* word." Nikki tried to smile, but it didn't work.

"You didn't answer me," Emily said. "Why did you break up with your cowboy? You've always been drawn to boots, a swagger, and a big belt buckle."

Nikki's lower lip quivered. "He was married! His wife came to see me and she's huge pregnant. He told me he was divorced."

"Where's this sumbitch from?" Emily patted her purse where her cute little .38 special had a home in a zippered side pocket. "Me and Cora will take care of him. I've got two shovels in the garage, or we can just leave his sorry carcass out in a mesquite thicket for the coyotes."

"I'm glad I don't have a concealed weapon carry license or we might have had to use those shovels," Nikki said. "I'm even glad you weren't close enough for me to borrow your sweet little Cora because that poor baby wouldn't have a father. Why'd you name that gun Cora anyway?"

Emily smiled. "I had an old great-aunt named Cora. She could shoot the eye out of a rattlesnake at fifty yards with her old Colt .45. She never missed, and she didn't take shit off nobody." Emily giggled. "But enough about my gun. You look like hell. Have you even eaten today?"

Nikki dabbed at her swollen eyes. "I've cried ever since his wife left. That poor baby havin' a sorry, cheatin' daddy for a role model. I hope she kicks him out, and he can't find anyone to take him in. He should have to sleep on the street in a cardboard box for treating her like that."

"How about the way he treated you?" Emily asked.

"For that, I hope he can't find a cardboard box," Nikki declared.

"Did you pack a bag for tomorrow?" Emily asked.

Another nod. "Can I stay at your place tonight? I'm afraid he'll come around and try to explain. I don't want to see him."

"Of course you can, and we're goin' home right now. I'll fix you something to eat, and we'll watch movies until our eyes won't stay open."

"And we'll eat a quart of ice cream right out of the carton?" Nikki asked.

"Rocky road with extra chocolate syrup. Now let's go buy a cup of coffee so we won't feel guilty about taking up the booth for the past half hour." Emily headed toward the counter.

Nikki grabbed her purse and followed. The lady behind the counter gave them two empty cups, pointed toward the coffee machine beside the soft drink fountain, and made change for the bill that Emily handed her.

"I need high octane," Nikki said as she filled her cup from the dark roast container.

"Me too." Emily came in right behind her. "Now let's go home and make omelets, then we'll have ice cream, and if that don't do the trick, I've got some Jack Daniel's in the freezer."

"Freezer?" Nikki asked.

"That's right. Whiskey don't freeze and it's better ice cold," Emily answered.

*   *   *

It was well past midnight when Nikki finally fell asleep curled up on the sofa. Emily yawned, stretched, and worked the kinks out of her neck before she turned off the movie they'd been watching. She picked up the dirty dishes and glasses and put them in the kitchen sink and then tiptoed into her bedroom.

She didn't remember to check her messages until she had slipped beneath the covers. Raising up on an elbow, she didn't even pick the phone up from the nightstand. There were three messages: one from Tag reminding her of the same thing that Hudson had earlier; one from her mother sending a guilt trip because Emily hadn't called like she usually did on Sunday; and the last one was from Justin, which simply said: *Sweet dreams.* She ignored the first two and sent a sleeping smiley face emoji back to him.

She was rudely awakened at six o'clock by the ring tone she'd assigned to her mother. It was either answer it or Anne would bug her all day with texts while she was at work.

"Good mornin', Mama," she said.

"Did I wake you?" Anne asked. "I was afraid something was wrong since you didn't call for our usual Sunday afternoon chat yesterday."

"Nothing is wrong." Emily yawned.

"I'm pouring my second cup of coffee. Want to do Face-Time or just talk?"

"Talk is fine. I'm barely awake and look like hell." Emily had avoided letting her mother see her picture for a couple of weeks, afraid that Anne would see something that would make her ask more questions than Emily wanted to answer.

"So what's happened this week?" Anne asked.

Well, I had lots of sex and went on a date with a cowboy.

"Nothing much, but my friend, Nikki. You remember her, don't you? She came home with me last year for a weekend," Emily answered.

"Of course I remember Nikki. If Hudson hadn't been dating Courtney, I believe he would have made a play for her. On that note, I have bad news. Courtney broke up with your brother, and he's devastated. I'm glad you're coming home in a few days. Seeing you might cheer him up. Now what about Nikki?" Anne asked.

Emily started with when Nikki called her—but left out where she was at that time, and went into great detail with the story, ending with that it was time to wake Nikki up so they could get ready for work.

"The poor darlin', but she shouldn't judge all cowboys by that rotten apple. You should bring her home with you. Who knows? Maybe she'll be the one for Hudson after all," Anne said.

"Can't. She's starting a new job at the hospital since she passed her RN test and she can't take off." Emily crossed her fingers.

"Too bad." Anne sighed. "It pains me to see him like this, but at least I get to see him."

Guilt trip on the way. Pack your bags.

"Love you, Mama. See you in a few days."

"Almost two weeks is not a few days," Anne said. "You and I are getting our hair and nails done on Saturday, and don't argue with me."

Can we stop by a lingerie shop so I can buy something sexy to wear for Justin when I get back to Bowie?

"Wouldn't dream of it, Mama. Looking forward to it. Give my brothers and Daddy a hug for me," Emily said.

"I will, but you can save mine until you get here," Anne said.

The called ended, and Emily tossed the phone over on the other side of the bed.

The aroma of coffee and bacon preceded Nikki into the room. She set a tray bearing two mugs of coffee and half a dozen biscuits stuffed with bacon on the edge of the bed.

"Everything looks better this morning."

"You didn't have to do this. We could have grabbed something on the way to work." Emily smiled and sipped the coffee.

"You gave up your time with Justin to get me through a rough night. Biscuits and bacon is the least I can do," Nikki said.

*   *   *

On Monday morning Justin stopped by the center on his way out of town to see Emily one more time. The recreation room was empty so he headed on down to Larry's room, only to find that he wasn't there. He met Nikki as he was headed up the hallway.

"You lookin' for Larry or Emily?" she asked.

"Emily," he answered.

"She's in a meeting with the big bosses. Unless it's an emergency, I can't disturb her. They even turn off their phones and put a sign on the door. I'm not sure you can get into heaven if you even knock." Nikki smiled.

That was disappointing, but he got back on the road and sent her a text: *Missing you.*

An hour passed and he was on the other side of Wichita Falls before his phone pinged with a return text that simply said: *Me too. Sorry I missed you.*

It was midafternoon when he pulled his cattle trailer onto the ranch where the new bull was located. Driving up to the long, rambling house, he thought of the place he was planning. Emily had loved the location and even made suggestions. He was still zoned out in his own thoughts when someone startled him by tapping on the window. He quickly hit the button to roll it down.

"Hello, I'm Justin Maguire," he said.

"I'm Maverick Callahan. I work here on the ranch. I reckon you're here to see about buying Old Glory?" The man wasn't as tall as Justin, but he looked like he could uproot a tree with those huge arms. "We been expectin' you. My brother, Paxton, has got the bull in the corral. If you don't mind I'll ride with you, then I'll guide you back to the right place."

"Hop right in," Justin said.

"So you're from Bowie, Texas? I went through that area once. I liked the rolling hills and trees. Reminded me more of Ireland than this area. Follow the path right there." Maverick pointed.

"You been to Ireland?" Justin asked.

"Last year. Me and my brother took our Mam back to visit her relatives. Picked up a bit of the accent while we were there, but when we got back home, it all disappeared," Maverick said.

"Mam? Your mother?"

"No, Mam is what the Irish call their grandmother. She lives up around Pampa. We go see her every chance we get. Now turn right and keep on the trail. In about five miles you'll see the barn."

Justin followed the directions. "How'd your Mam get to Texas from Ireland?"

"She fell in love with a rancher that went over to Ireland to buy some fancy cattle," Maverick explained. "Right there's the barn. Pull your trailer alongside that fence. You can unhook it until tomorrow mornin' when you load Old Glory up and take him home—unless you change your mind about buyin' him. Miz Opal says that you're to stay in the ranch house tonight. They've got everything all ready for you, and the family will be comin' to supper."

"I'd planned to stay in a hotel until morning, or else take the bull home tonight." If he got the animal loaded he could easily be home by bedtime, and maybe even ask Emily to wait for him at the cabin.

"Can't do that. It's goin' to storm real bad here in a couple of hours. Take a look at those black clouds comin' from the southwest."

Justin removed his hat and turned around to find a dark sky out there on the horizon. "Guess in this flat land, y'all can see the storm comin', but what's the weather got to do with a bull?"

Maverick shook his head slowly from side to side. "Old Glory has one fault. He's afraid of storms. He'd kick his way out of that trailer if you drove him through thunder and lightning. He'll do fine if he can hug up to a barn or if he's inside a stall, but he'd be a handful in a trailer."

"Hey, are you Justin Maguire? I'm Paxton, Maverick's younger brother." He put his hand on a fence post and jumped over it.

Justin shook hands with him. "Pleased to meet you."

"Likewise. We got Old Glory inside the barn in a stall. Come on in here and look at him."

Justin followed the brothers inside. The bull looked even better than the pictures and descriptions that they'd gotten at the ranch. "Fertility tested?" he asked.

"Miz Opal's got the papers for that and everything else at the house. She'll go over them with you this evening. Some of the family would've met you but they're all tied up today.

Bein' a rancher, you know how that goes," Maverick told him.

Justin reached between the rails to pet the bull. "I sure do. Never enough hands to get everything done. The old boy seems gentle."

"Hasn't got a bit of that wild bull in him to pass on down to the offspring. He's a big old pet, but he'll bring new blood to your herd," Paxton said. "I reckon you'd better let Maverick take you on up to the house now. Marie, the cook, will show you to your room. You'll have an hour to get changed, if you want to before suppertime. They usually meet about five in the den for drinks and a visit before supper is served."

There didn't seem to be a way that Justin could get out of staying on the Big Sky Ranch that night, so he gave up even trying to come up with an excuse.

Chapter Eighteen

The house was bigger than the one at Longhorn Canyon but wasn't laid out a whole lot different. A huge living area opened off a foyer. Open doors on the other end probably led into a dining room and kitchen, but Marie took him to the end of a long hallway with doors opening on either side into bedrooms that looked unused.

"Miz Opal says you are to use this room." Marie tucked a strand of red hair back into a ponytail. "Have a little rest. The family will be home soon. If you are still sleeping, I'll knock on the door a little after five and wake you."

"Thank you," Justin said.

"Oh, I almost forgot. Miz Opal says to tell you that she's sorry the family couldn't be here. A neighbor died and they're at a funeral," Marie said.

"I understand," Justin said.

Marie shut the door behind her, and he dropped his suit-case on the floor. Thank goodness he'd brought a decent shirt and a pair of freshly ironed jeans. Hopefully, the family didn't get dressed up beyond that for supper.

He checked his messages and found one from Emily that was only a picture of a heart-shaped lollipop. He replied with one of a cupid shooting an arrow before he took a quick shower. He had half an hour before he was supposed to be in the den for drinks, so he stretched out on the bed and pulled a quilt up over his naked body. He only meant to close his eyes for a few minutes, but he fell into a deep sleep and dreamed about Emily. She'd taken the job as counselor for the girls, and she'd slipped away to meet him in the tack room for a bout of hot sex. They were curled up in each other's arms when someone knocked on the door.

He didn't give a damn about who was there. The door was locked, and they still had time to cuddle before she had to go back to the bunkhouse.

"Mr. Justin, are you awake?" Marie's voice brought him out of the dream and to full attention.

"Yes, ma'am." He raised his voice. "I'll be there in five minutes."

He hurriedly jerked on his clothes, ran a comb through his hair, and followed the buzz of conversation to the den. Smaller and much cozier than the huge living room he'd gotten a glance at earlier, it was filled with people. The guys all had beers, but the three ladies were drinking wine.

An older lady looped her arm in his and said, "Hello, I'm Opal Bennington. Come and meet everyone." Almost as tall as Justin, she had clear blue eyes and gray hair that she tied back in a ponytail at the nape of her neck. She took a few steps and stopped in front of a red-haired woman with the same crystal clear blue eyes that reminded him so much of Emily's.

"This is my daughter, Anne, and her husband, Frank."

Frank stuck out a hand. "Welcome to the Big Sky. What'd you think of Old Glory?"

"Thank you. It's a pleasure to meet you. Old Glory looks like a fantastic bull to me."

"I'll show you all the papers later." Opal pulled Justin away and took him to the other side of the room. "These three are my grandsons: Matthew, Taggart, and Hudson. Tag and Hudson are twins but not identical in looks or actions."

Justin shook hands with all three of them and then it hit him. This was Emily's family! She was from the Big Sky Ranch! He looked over Tag's shoulder and saw a family picture of all four kids sitting on the fireplace mantel.

"So you're from out around Bowie," Tag said. "Our sister lives in that town. She works at a senior citizens' place, so I doubt that y'all ever crossed paths."

"What's her name?" Justin asked.

"Emily Baker," Hudson said.

He avoided the question. "I thought this was the Bennington Ranch."

"We've always run a Rocking B brand," Opal said. "But the owners have changed down through the ages."

"It was a big joke when we got married." Frank chuckled. "It started out in the Barrett family, then went to the Blackburn, and to the Bennington, and everyone told Anne she had to marry a man with a *B* initial."

"But you don't have to worry about that now, since I'm a Baker and I'll be takin' over someday in the far, far future," Matthew said.

Justin's eyes kept darting back to that family picture. There was no doubt that the girl was his Emily, but he just couldn't believe that she'd never mentioned she was from the wealthiest ranch in Texas. All three brothers were about the same height as Justin. They all had the same blue eyes, and it wasn't difficult to see that they shared DNA with Emily. Tag and Hudson were the twins she'd talked about—evidently fraternal, because like Miz Opal had said, they sure weren't identical.

Anne, Emily's mother, moved across the room to stand beside him. "That was taken the year that Hudson and Tag graduated from high school. We really should have a new one made. We're having a family reunion in a few weeks. Maybe we'll make time for one while Emily is home."

"She's beautiful," Justin whispered.

"I always thought so. Where's my manners? What can I get you to drink?"

"Beer is fine," he answered.

"Hey, if we was to make a trip over to Bowie to see our sister, do you think it'd be all right for us to come out to your place and say hi to Old Glory? I've raised him from a calf so I'm going to miss him," Hudson said.

"Sure thing. Come anytime. You can even stay at the ranch," Justin answered.

"We'd stay with Emily, but thanks for the offer. Let's ride our cycles out there, Hud, and surprise our sister," Tag said and then turned his attention back to Justin. "You got a good place to do some dancin' and drinkin'?"

"Yep, it's called the Rusty Spur." Justin managed a smile, but it felt unnatural.

"You're from the Longhorn Canyon, right?" Hudson asked.

"That's right," Justin said.

That Tag and Hudson were brothers was obvious, but no one would ever mistake them for each other. Justin wondered if their dispositions were as different as their looks.

"Emily took her senior residents out to a ranch somewhere near Bowie for a week. I guess they about ran her ragged while they were there. She said that keeping up with them was worse than herding cats." Anne laughed. "We sure do miss her. Not just because she was a good ranch hand but also because she's so much fun to be around."

"I'm sure you do." Justin chose his words carefully. "While y'all are in Bowie, I'll be glad to show you around."

"I just want to see the Rusty Spur." Tag chuckled. "That and get some of Emily's fried chicken. Nobody here can make it like she can."

I can believe that. Justin remembered eating chicken and drinking Jack while they were skinny-dipping in the bathtub.

When he was back in his room that evening, he started to call her, but this wasn't something that they should discuss on the phone. He couldn't even make himself reply to her text telling him that Nikki was staying at her place for another night.

*   *   *

The next morning right after breakfast he loaded up Old Glory and didn't even make a coffee stop. He glanced over at the senior center as he passed it, but the clouds were gathering for the second day. The bull needed to be in the barn before the first clap of thunder rattled the stock trailer.

After he'd unloaded his things in the house, he grabbed a leftover biscuit and stuffed it full of ham. He was on the way out the door when his parents pulled their truck up beside his.

"Bull delivered in good condition?" Vernon called out as he got out of his vehicle.

Justin nodded.

"Seen Emily yet?" his mother asked.

He shook his head.

"You look like you could chew up nails." She hurried over to his side.

"I don't want to talk about it right now," he said.

"Did you and Emily break up?" She looked so happy.

"Ever heard of Big Sky Ranch?" he asked.

Vernon leaned against the fender of Justin's truck. "Of course we have. That's where you got the new bull."

"It's just the biggest damn ranch in Texas. It's probably bigger than some third world countries and the folks who own it are richer than Midas. What's that got to do with Emily or why you're in such a pissy mood?" Gloria asked.

"So you've heard of Anne Bennington Baker?" he asked.

"Of course," Gloria answered. "I still don't know what you're getting at."

"Tell me one more time why you are so set against me dating Emily?"

"I think she's a gold digger. She's not your type at all, and if things get serious, I'm going to insist on a prenup. Then she'll drop you like a hot potato. Your heart will be broken like Cade's was with Julie."

"Gloria!" Vernon raised his voice slightly. "Son, you need to be sure before you continue to really date her. Your mother might be right, even if she shouldn't call Emily that name. I understand the girl does have some education."

"She's got a social services degree," Justin said. "And her mother is Anne Baker of Big Sky Ranch. I don't think she'd be marryin' me for my money." He got into his truck and drove away, leaving Gloria with her mouth hanging open.

"Dammit!" He slapped the steering wheel and checked the time. It was more than three more hours before Emily got off work. He headed for the tack room and started cleaning it to pass the time.

Chapter Nineteen

Emily was disappointed that Justin didn't call on Monday night. Tuesday was one of those days when minutes took hours to pass. She was playing bingo with the residents when Otis tugged on the tail of her scrub top and whispered, "You want me to take over calling the numbers?"

"I'm sorry. I was wool-gathering." She picked up the next ball in the popper. "I-forty-seven."

Patsy was the first of the Fab Five to gather around her when the games ended. "Are you all right? You look a little pale."

Sarah draped an arm around Emily's shoulders. "Is it Justin?"

"I have no idea. Haven't heard from him in a couple of days. He had a business trip." Emily gathered up all the equipment and put it away. "I've got another hour. Anyone got any ideas?"

"Strip poker?" Larry nudged her arm with an elbow.

"I don't think so." She smiled.

"I'm the bomb!" Larry strutted around the room like a rooster with his hands tucked into the bib of his overalls. "I made her smile."

"Yes, you are. Now get on out of here and let me get things ready for tomorrow." She shooed them away.

"We get to go to the county livestock show this weekend," Otis said. "You going with Justin?"

"I don't know," she said.

"I hope so," Bess said. "We like pretending that you and Justin are our grandkids."

"Hey." Nikki poked her head in the door. "Did y'all know that there's still some sugar cookies up in the dining room?"

"I'm on my way." Bess led the Five out of the room.

"Now, tell me what's going on." Nikki hiked a hip on one of the tables. "You look like you're about to blow up."

"Justin didn't call last night. No texts today. He was fine Sunday but..." She shrugged.

"Do you think he's upset because I stole you away from him on Sunday?"

One shoulder raised slightly. "Don't think so. He seemed fine when we parted and was fine up until..." Her phone rang and she dug it out of her purse. "It's Mama."

Nikki headed for the door. "See you later."

"Hello," Emily answered the phone.

"We sold Old Glory. Some cowboy from out around where you live bought him. Ever heard of the Longhorn Canyon Ranch?" Like always, Anne went right into what she had to say. "His name is Justin Maguire, and he's a real nice guy. He hit it off with your brothers and even said he'd show them around if they wanted to come visit you."

Emily sat down in a chair with a thud. "Is that right?"

"Anyway, the twins are going to surprise you, but I know

how much you hate to be caught off guard, so I'm tattling. Oh, and Justin said there was a livestock show this week if they wanted to come help out with it while you're at work," Anne said.

"They're coming today!" Emily's voice went all high and squeaky.

"Should be there by suppertime and they'll want fried chicken so you might want to stop on the way home. Maybe they'll introduce you to Justin," Anne said.

Holy smokin' hell! Now what am I going to do? Justin knows all about me and we won't even have a private moment to talk.

"I can't believe they're comin'. How long are they planning to stay?"

"Until Sunday. They all had the best time and they want to help Justin with the kids' livestock show. They don't miss much about their high school days, but showing cattle is one of them," Anne said. "Now go practice your surprised face in the mirror."

"Oh, I'll be stunned," Emily said. "I'll try to call you later. What motel are they booked into?"

"They're not. They're stayin' with you. They brought sleeping bags on the back of their cycles. Don't worry. They'll take the floor in the living room. Bye now," Anne said.

Emily laid her phone down and grabbed her head with both hands. Just when things were going well, this had to happen.

*　　　*　　　*

Justin arrived at the center at exactly five o'clock and parked right beside Emily's Mustang. Most of the reason he was angry was because she hadn't trusted him enough to tell him about her family, and that was probably because she thought he'd see dollar signs when he looked at her. He figured a one-fourth interest in Big Sky would literally be millions.

He kept an eye on the rearview mirror and saw her the moment she came outside. That's when he got out of the truck, opened the passenger door, and waited.

"I guess we need to talk," she said.

"I think so." He nodded.

He waited until she was inside and then he rounded the back side of the truck and took his place behind the wheel. "Why didn't you tell me?"

"Why didn't you tell me the bull you were buying was from Big Sky?"

He turned so he could look right at her. "It never dawned on me. You talked about your grandparents' place and I figured it was maybe kind of like ours. You didn't trust me, did you? You thought I'd see dollar signs instead of what a wonderful person you are."

"Don't tell me what I think or don't think," she shot back.

"Trust is the basis of any relationship," he told her.

Emily's eyes narrowed. "Tell that to your mother. She thinks I'm out to fleece you. Or maybe you're just a mama's boy and—"

"Whoa!" Justin held up a palm. "I love my mother, but she doesn't run my life or tell me what to do. Especially not with my girlfriend."

"So am I your girlfriend?" Emily asked.

"I don't know what we are to each other. Why didn't you tell me?"

Emily stared straight ahead for a long time before she turned her gaze on him. "I dated two boys in high school. Both of them saw those dollar signs you mentioned. Then I got into a relationship in college and told him. Same thing when he found out about Big Sky. The next time I got serious about a guy, I didn't tell him. He's the one who tried to change me, and I found out later that he'd found out about the ranch. I liked you from the beginning but..." She got out of the truck. "I think this is a pretty damn stupid thing for us to fight about. Call me when you cool down."

He rolled down the window and called out to her. "Your brothers are coming."

She whipped around. "Now that's a legitimate thing to argue about. I may never forgive you for inviting them."

* * *

Emily found two motorcycles parked at the bottom of the staircase leading up to her apartment. If they wanted fried chicken then they could take their big surprising asses right down to the KFC, or else eat bologna sandwiches. She was still steaming when she opened the door to find no one in the apartment.

"Good, they've gotten a cab and gone to a hotel," she muttered as she threw her coat on the sofa, dropped her tote bag beside it, and flopped down on her bed. Everything had happened so fast that her head was still spinning. What the hell difference did it make anyway where she grew up? A ranch was a ranch. Big, small, or somewhere in between. Who cared about all that?

"Surprise!!!" Her door opened and the tiny apartment was suddenly filled with two big cowboys.

She simply had to remember to lock the door from now on. She sat up and met them in the bedroom doorway, where they tried to hug her at the same time. "Surprise, nothing. You left your motorcycles in plain sight."

"We couldn't get in so we found a shade tree around back and waited for you." Tag laughed. "But you'll forgive us because we met this amazin' guy and we're goin' to introduce ya'll."

"Justin Maguire, right?"

"Mama called, didn't she?" Hudson plopped down on the sofa.

"Yep." Emily nodded.

Tag removed his hat and tossed it across the room. "Don't let her ruin it. He's this great guy and—"

Emily held up a hand. "And I've been sleeping with him. Surprise!"

Chapter Twenty

Justin didn't want to be at the fair barn that Wednesday morning, but he had no choice. The Maguires had always been involved with the board of directors, and it was his duty to be on hand the days before the livestock show. He and other ranchers always volunteered to set up the pens, make sure each one had a layer of straw in the bottom, and check on the sound system and the electricity. It was amazing how much juice hair dryers, heat lamps, and clippers could pull in a week.

He'd sent Emily a text that morning, reminding her that he'd be coming by on Friday morning to get Otis and Larry. She'd fired one back saying that she'd already cleared it with the administration and they would be ready.

Buddy clamped a hand on his shoulder and startled him.

"I hear that you and Emma are gettin' to be quite the item," Buddy said.

"It's Emily, and I don't know about that," Justin answered. "What's your job today?"

"Some of these panels for the pens look awful. I brought my portable sprayer and lots of paint. Got me a section roped off out in the pasture behind this place where I'm going to give every one of them a face-lift," Buddy said. "What about you?"

"When you get enough panels painted, I'll set up the show pen first and then work from there," Justin said. "The FFA boys will be here this evening to help out. And Emily's brothers are here to help. There they are now." He waved them over and introduced them to Buddy.

Buddy sat down on the bottom step of the bleachers by the area where the show pen would be. "I can see that y'all are Emily's brothers. You all have the same eyes."

"When we were about four and she was five, folks thought we were triplets," Tag said. "I could live in this area. I like the trees."

"What I like best is that Mama ain't fussin' at us all the time." Hudson chuckled.

The mention of a meddling mother made Justin think of his mama. He hadn't seen Gloria since the night before. He hadn't even gone by the house that morning on his way to the fair barns. He felt a little guilty about the way things were left—both with her and with Emily. It hadn't mattered in the beginning where she came from and it didn't now. She could have been raised in a tent on the banks of the Red River for all he cared. What she wanted to do with the rest of her life was the issue. And Emily was right—she hadn't lied to him, any more than he'd lied to the Baker family about knowing her.

"Well, there's that. We're the babies, so there ain't never goin' to be a girl good enough for us, at least not according to Mama." Tag removed his cowboy hat and resettled it on his head. "Why didn't you tell us you knew our sister, Justin?"

"You only asked once and the conversation went another way," he said. "What'd she tell you?"

"You don't even want to know because we don't believe her," Hudson said. "I guess y'all had a fight about her not tellin' you that she's from Big Sky?"

"You mean Big Sky Ranch?" Buddy's eyes bugged out. "Y'all are those Bakers?"

"Yep, but we'd sure like to get away from all that," Tag said. "Maybe get us a little spread of our own and just be two old cowboys."

"I know where there's one for sale." Buddy grinned. "Right next door to the Longhorn Canyon. It went on the market this past week. You should look at it."

Tag turned toward Justin. "How big is it?"

"About a thousand acres. Lots of good pasture. Needs some clearing in a few places where the mesquite got a hold. Fences are in bad repair."

Talk about awkward, Justin thought. If he and Emily didn't make up, if her brothers lived right next door, if he had to know she was that close—not one scene wouldn't be awkward.

"Wouldn't hurt to just look at it, since you're here already. Well, them panels ain't goin' to paint themselves. Soon as they get dry, I'll get the boys to bring them in for the show ring." Buddy got to his feet.

"I can help you." Hudson followed him outside.

"I guess it's me and you. I see a bunch of straw that needs to be scattered in the show pen," Tag said. "You and Emily goin' to make up? I called Mama, and, man, is she one happy woman about y'all dating."

"I hope so." Justin wished he had the same blessing from his mother.

* * *

Emily gave Nikki a ride to work that morning and bitched nonstop about Justin and her brothers the whole way. Nikki had been nodding and adding a sympathetic word here and there, but her expression changed instantly when Emily pulled into a space right beside an unfamiliar truck.

"There's that no-good sleazy cheatin' sumbitch. Parked right beside us, and he's getting out," Nikki whispered.

"Got to confront the bastard sometime. Want me to come with you?" Emily asked.

"I'll take care of it," Nikki said.

"Get your mad on and go get him," Emily encouraged. "Want Cora for backup?"

"I'd be too tempted to shoot him before he even said a word," Nikki answered as she got out of the car and marched right up to her tall, dark, and jerksome former boyfriend.

To be sure Nikki wasn't in over her head, Emily stood in the corner of the dining room and peered out the mini-blinds. Nikki must've been counting off all his sins because she held up one finger, talked a while and then another one popped up. By the time she finished she was shaking her fist at him.

His expression said that he didn't like what she was saying but couldn't deny it. Finally, he turned around and got into his truck, and Nikki stormed into the center.

"Well?" Emily asked.

"I feel twenty pounds lighter. I owe you one." Nikki crossed the room and wrapped Emily up in a hug.

"You've already paid that debt in full by listening to me moan and groan about Justin and my brothers the whole way to work this morning. Men! Why do they have to frustrate us so much?" Emily asked.

"You think there's hope you'll make up?" Nikki asked. "This won't be your first fight if things get really serious. You'll have lots more, but the first one—it's like your first kiss. You always remember it."

"I don't know how to make up. In every other relationship I've been in, the fight ended it." She sighed.

"Oh, honey, the makeup sex is wonderful. Give it a try this time." Nikki headed toward the nurses' station for the morning briefing.

When Emily reached the activities room she found several residents already gathered around the tables.

"Good mornin', Emily." They all waved.

She went straight to the cabinets and got out several boxes of dominoes. She remembered playing the game called Shoot the Moon with her granny and her parents, and was suddenly homesick. Tag had said he'd called her mother and that Anne was over the moon that she knew Justin. She wondered if he'd told her that she'd shocked both of her younger brothers by telling them that she'd already slept with the cowboy.

She was carrying the last box to an empty table when her phone pinged. She set it down and fished the phone from her purse. The text was from her mama: *Thinkin' of you.* She sent one back: *Great minds and all that.* A smiley face wearing round glasses came back. Before she could return the phone to her purse, another text came through. When she saw that it was from Justin, the world got a whole lot brighter. It said: *We need to talk.* She wrote back: *Inventory at work. Working till midnight.* One came back that said: *We can talk while you work.*

"Bad news?" Bess asked.

"Good and bad. I was thinking of my mama earlier, and she sent a text. The bad is that I have to work on inventory, so I'll be here late," she answered.

"Need some help?" Sarah asked.

"Thanks, but it's something I have to do," Emily answered.

"You got to count every single card in the decks and all the bits of glitter?" Larry asked.

"Not quite that bad, but it'll take a while. While you're playing, be thinking about the decorations we'll start making next week to put up for Easter." She changed the subject. "After inventory I'll order all the supplies. It'll take a few weeks to get them here."

That set off a whole buzz of conversation. When a new group came in to play dominoes, they were quickly let in on the Easter idea, and several residents started making lists of possibilities.

A picture of the red heart-shaped lollipop flashed through Emily's mind. Would Justin bring her a gold egg? That was the absolute best one to find in an Easter egg hunt when she was a little girl. Or would everything be finished after they talked tonight?

*   *   *

Justin couldn't wait to get away from the fair barn that evening. Tag and Hudson invited him to go to the Rusty Spur with them, but he had no desire to join them. He and Emily needed to get this thing resolved—one way or the other. He hit the cabin in a run, kicked off his boots, and was headed for the shower when Cade burst inside without knocking.

"I need help." His brother was breathless.

"Is Retta all right? Is it the baby?" Justin shoved his feet back into his boots. Cade shook his head. "Claire's in the emergency room over in Bowie. Don't know until the test results come back if she's got appendicitis or if it's the flu, but Levi is with her. We've got two heifers in the barn about to calve. They're first-time mamas and need to be watched tonight."

"Little early for calving. That shouldn't get under way for another month," Justin said.

"These are a couple in among the dozen we bought from the neighbor last week. He didn't have records on them," Cade said. "And I forgot to tell you, Retta is running a fever. If it goes up another degree her doctor said to take her to the hospital for a test to be sure it's not affecting the baby and get her tested for the flu."

"Good lord! Why didn't you lead with that? Retta is more important than a bunch of cows. Where's Dad?"

"He and Mama went to dinner with some friends," Cade said. "She's been an old bear all day. I've got to get back if you can take care of this."

"Why didn't you call rather than leave her?"

"Your phone must need chargin'. It kept goin' to voice mail."

"Get out of here." Justin clamped a hand on his shoulder. "Call me if you have to take her to the hospital and keep me updated."

The minute he got to the barn, he checked on the two heifers and plugged his phone into an electrical outlet to charge it. Then he took a deep breath and called Emily.

"I'm so sorry but we've got a problem out here at the ranch." He went on to tell her what was going on with everyone.

"Does Retta need my help, or should I go to the hospital and sit with Claire?" she asked.

"Probably not on either issue in case it's the flu. You don't want to get sick, especially when you work with all those old folks every day," he answered. "You could come out here and keep me company."

"I'll bring burgers and malts—no onions, right?" she said. "We've got to talk or I won't be able to sleep. I've got another hour here and then I'll be there. Besides I don't want to go home to my brothers," she told him.

"They're at the Rusty Spur," he said.

"Then I might not go home at all. The only thing worse than them sober is them tipsy." She sighed.

The call ended without her saying good-bye. He checked the heifers once more. It was better to let them deliver with no help, if possible, but he was on hand if they needed him. Both were contracting, but they were still standing, so it could be a few more hours. He grabbed a blanket from the tack room and took it to an empty stall. When it was smoothed out, he went back and got two throw pillows from the futon and tossed them in the stall, too. It wouldn't be the first night he'd spent in the barn.

For the next hour he rehearsed what he'd say to Emily a dozen times, but nothing seemed right. He'd have to wing it, based on what she said, and that scared him.

"Don't look very comfortable." Gloria stepped out of the shadows.

"That's the life of a rancher. I thought you and Dad were out."

She came up to the stall gate. "Your dad isn't feelin' well, so we came home early. He's probably got this stomach flu that's goin' around. He's sleepin' right now in the trailer," Gloria said. "I want to apologize for the way I've been behaving and the things I've said."

"Why were you acting like that?" Justin stood up and propped a boot on one of the railings.

"Your father asked me the same thing. I've thought about it, and although it's not an excuse, it's a reason. Cade's married. Levi, although he's not my biological son, he feels like it, and he's married, all within a few months. It wasn't hard on me because I still had you. There's an old saying that goes like this: A daughter is a daughter all of her life, but a son is only a son until he takes a wife. Retta and Claire don't have mamas to go home to, so I get to step in. Emily does, so I'll be left out, and dammit, Justin, you're my baby."

"I'm a grown man," Justin said.

"I wanted another child, a girl, but it didn't happen for us, so you'll always be my baby no matter how old you are. But I realize I've been a complete bitch. If things get serious between you and Emily, then I'll never even be friends with her if I don't take a step back and change."

"Apology accepted," Justin said. "I guess you were right after all that she wasn't telling me everything. Who would've guessed she grew up on Big Sky?"

Gloria shook her head. "She probably knows more than I ever will about the outside business. I understand y'all've had an argument. Is it your fault or hers?"

"Both," Emily said as she stepped into the light, carrying a brown paper bag. "I didn't trust Justin enough to tell him about Big Sky. He got angry when he was thrown right in the middle of my family. And, Gloria, I'm sure there's a helluva lot you could teach me about ranchin'."

"Thank you, Emily. I owe you an apology too. I was way out of line several times."

"Accepted," Emily said.

"On that note, I'm going to the trailer. I'm glad we've cleared the air," Gloria said.

"Me too," Justin and Emily said at the same time.

*   *   *

"I'm still mad at you. If you were going to invite my brothers to come here, you could have at least offered to let them stay in one of the bunkhouses. Do you know what it's like to get up to a living room floor filled with snoring cowboys?"

"Yep, I do." He grinned. "But your brothers had the idea of surprising you already. They wanted to see more of their big sis."

"The cabin is bigger than my apartment." She marched into the stall and sat down. Then she removed everything from the brown bag and laid it out on separate sides of the blanket. "Dinner is served."

"I see we're sitting at different tables," he quipped as he eased down.

"Until we settle this thing, we are." She unwrapped her burger and took a bite and waited, but he didn't say anything. "Okay, then, I'll talk first. This is about a stupid thing to argue about. I just learned a long time ago to keep my affiliation with Big Sky a secret."

"But there were dozens of times you could have told me, especially after you left the ranch. Hadn't you figured out by then that you could trust me?" he asked.

"Yes, but I was waiting for the right time. Why didn't you tell me you were going to Big Sky for the bull? I would have told you then for sure," she said.

"It was quite a shock when your grandmother introduced me to your brothers, and when I saw that family picture on the mantel." He picked up his burger and removed the wrapper.

"I'm sorry," she said.

"Me too."

"I missed you these past couple of days." She squeezed a packet of ketchup over her fries.

Before he could answer, his phone rang. He hopped up and ran over to the place where it was being recharged.

"Hello, Levi. What's the news?"

He listened for a minute and then said, "Great. See you in the morning."

"Good news?" she asked when he returned.

"Claire has food poisoning, and the doctor said that's probably what Retta has too. I'm glad I didn't eat breakfast with all of them this morning because that's what must have made them sick." Justin sat back down in his spot. "And I promise next time your brothers are in town, I'll talk them into staying at the ranch while they're here. They probably don't love sleeping on your floor all that much either. But they're talking of buying the ranch right next door to us, so hopefully they'll have their own place soon enough."

"Holy hell! That's not a solution. It's making things worse. They'll be all up in my business for sure." She sighed.

"So tomorrow night, can I take you somewhere for supper?"

"How about the cabin?"

He bit into the burger. "I'll grill steaks."

"I'll bring dessert and wine."

"Sounds like a plan. What kind of dessert?" he asked.

She wiggled her eyebrows. "Are we really okay, Justin, and are we really going to get into a relationship?"

"Yes, Emily. I'm ready for that. Now can I ask for a special dessert?"

"Okay," she said cautiously.

"I'd like to order those red high heels you wore to the Valentine's party, a white towel around your body—at the waist would be fine—and a smile. Think you could get that ready?"

"Only if you promise to have two helpings of dessert."

"I was thinking of three helpings." He winked as he moved across the blanket to sit close to her.

Emily pushed her food away and cupped Justin's cheeks in her hands. "I'm miserable when we argue."

"Me too." He covered her hands with his and moved in for a hard kiss.

Chapter Twenty-One

And where are you going?" Tag asked Emily on Thursday night when she picked up her tote bag and started out of the apartment. "You haven't made us fried chicken yet, and we'd planned to stay in tonight with you. Next two nights are taken up with the livestock show, and we're leaving bright and early Sunday morning."

"I've got a date. If I'm not home by midnight, y'all can fight over which one gets to sleep in my bed. And there's a KFC in town if you want chicken." She waved as she walked out the door.

She could smell the steaks cooking as soon as she stepped out of her car. The grill was on the porch, but Justin was nowhere around. She tied the belt to her long black coat tighter around her waist and gingerly picked her way from vehicle to cabin in her red high heels. She rapped on the door and then opened it to find a blaze in the fireplace, candles lit on the table, and the bed turned down. Justin came out of the bathroom wearing nothing but a pair of loose-fitting pajama pants.

"Steaks are warming in the oven and everything else is ready." His eyes scanned her from high heels to the top of her head.

She untied the belt and removed the coat letting it puddle up at her feet. His eyes popped out and a grin covered his face. She was wearing nothing but a bath towel that she'd fastened with a broach and the shoes he'd asked for.

"I thought we might have dessert first." She unpinned the broach and the towel fell away. The absence of inhibitions felt wonderful, and the way Justin's eyes went all dreamy said he liked her just the way she was.

"Wonderful idea." He covered the distance in a couple of long strides and wrapped his arms around her. "Maybe we'll even have two helpings of dessert first. God, I've missed you so much."

His lips found hers as he walked her backward toward the bed. When they were close, she kicked off her shoes, and then slid his pants down over his hips. "Oh, my! You did miss me." She stretched out on the bed.

"I'll show you just how much." He stretched out beside her.

It was almost ten when they finally got around to eating supper. The steaks might not have been as juicy as they were three hours before, but after the appetite they'd worked up, Justin and Emily had no problem eating them. Nor did they have a problem falling asleep in each other's arms sometime around midnight.

Sunrays shone in through the window when Emily awoke to find Justin coming toward her with a cup of coffee and a box of breakfast pastries. She sat up in bed and pulled the sheet up over her breasts. He leaned in for a kiss and she turned her head to the side.

"A few sips of coffee first. Morning breath," she said.

He kissed her on the cheek and handed her the mug. "Hurry. I've wanted to kiss you for half an hour but I didn't want to wake you. Are you going to wear that towel and those shoes to work?"

She took a couple of sips of coffee and pulled his face to hers for the first kiss of the day. "My tote bag with my scrubs is in the car."

"I'll get it," he drawled but he didn't make a move to leave the bed.

When they absolutely had no time left if she was going to get to work on time, she got a quick shower and dressed, and he followed her to the center in his truck. When they got out of their vehicles, he tucked her hand into his, and just that simple touch created a whole array of sparks.

To take her mind off the mind-blowing sex of the night before, she asked, "Just exactly where is the Montague County fairground?"

"Just outside Nocona." He opened the door for her. When they were halfway down the hall toward the activities room, he pulled her into an empty room and kissed her half a dozen times.

"What time will the Fab Five be home?" she asked breathlessly as she leaned in for more.

"It'll be after supper, but there's food vendors set up in the fairbarn kitchen, so don't worry about them going hungry." He strung kisses from under her chin to her lips.

If they didn't stop making out right then, she was

going to be late for work—something that had never happened in the five years she'd worked at the center. She pulled away and pulled a tissue from a box. "You better wipe the lipstick off or Otis and Larry will tease you all day."

"I don't mind tellin' them how I got these pretty red smears on my lips." He chuckled but wiped them away. "Tonight and tomorrow night will be hectic at the fair barn, but I'll pick you up for church Sunday morning. Okay?"

She nodded. "And then we'll go back to my place for dinner. I'll cook, and we can spend the afternoon together. But I'll see you tomorrow night at the premium show. Derek has plans with his family that night, so I'll have to chauffer them back to the center."

"It'll be a long night for us." He groaned. "But once it's over and we get things cleaned up, it's done for another year."

"Then I guess waiting for you at the cabin—" she said.

He butted in before she could finish. "Will give me something to look forward to all evening. It might be very late."

"Wake me when you get there." One more quick kiss, and she went back out into the hallway.

"Today is the day!" Sarah called out from only a few feet away. "We're goin' to wait in the lobby. Come with us."

Emily checked the time on her phone. "I've got maybe five minutes."

Otis was almost prancing as he led the parade down the hallway. "Any minute now Justin is going—"

Larry pointed. "There he is, right behind Emily. Was you lookin' for us, Justin?"

"Yes, I was. I thought maybe Derek could follow me to the fair barn." Justin slid a sly wink at Emily.

"And there's Derek, pulling the van around to the front," Patsy said.

Otis pumped his fist in the air. "I hope they've got homemade chili in the kitchen. We used to get the best chili when I helped judge."

"I think I heard there was going to be Indian tacos and chili both. If we leave now, you might have time to give the kids some last-minute pointers on how to show their animals," Justin said.

"Have fun," Emily told them and blew kisses as they left.

Justin grabbed one in the air and pretended to put it in his pocket. Emily quickly looked around to see if anyone else had seen it, and there was Nikki with a smile that covered her whole face.

"I saw that," she singsonged. "You look like you've been makin' out, so?"

"We'll talk about it later. I've got five minutes to get everything out for scrapbook day," she said.

"Yes, we will. Like tonight over the Friday night pizza buffet. My treat for getting me through the week, and I won't take no for an answer," Nikki said.

"Wasn't about to say no. Meet you there at six? If my brothers weren't at the livestock show, I'd introduce you."

"Five thirty. We don't have to change clothes. Too bad about your brothers. I remember Hudson was pretty damn fine-lookin' and Tag was too sexy for words," Nikki answered.

*　　　*　　　*

"Good lord!" Emily exclaimed when she turned her phone on after work and found dozens of messages and one missed call from her grandmother, Opal.

She checked the time: 5:10. That meant she had fifteen minutes before she had to make the five-minute drive to the pizza place. She'd look over the messages later, and being on a tight schedule would give her an excuse to only talk to her granny a few minutes. She was surprised when Opal answered on the first ring.

"Where are you, and why are you not answering your phone? I could be lyin' in a ditch dying of massive wounds," Opal fussed at her.

"I was at work. Mama has the center's number for emergencies. I turned off my phone because it was pinging every five minutes with text messages, and that was interfering with my job," she explained.

"You should be here on the ranch. That's your job, Emily. I've let you spread your wings, but your mama is goin' to want to retire before too many years. You need to be learnin' all the fine points of runnin' this place," Opal told her.

"Granny, I've told you a dozen times, just get the papers ready for me to sign over my share to my brothers. They know everything there is to know about ranchin'. I don't want it." Emily leaned her head back and wished she wasn't having this conversation.

"Listen to me." Opal's tone nearly put frost on the phone. "Matthew told us last night he won't ask for a prenup. Good God Almighty! Do you realize what that could do to this empire that we've built here on Big Sky Ranch?"

"Why would he refuse to do that?" Emily's temples started to ache.

"He says that he loves her too much to ask, and it would ruin the trust between them," Opal answered. "He might listen to you, so you've got to come home and talk to him."

"Can we talk about it next weekend when I come home for the family gathering?"

"If that's the best you can do." Opal sighed. "But one weekend won't do the job. You need a few days."

"I'll see what I can do," Emily said.

"That's good," Opal said. "Love you, girl."

"Love you more," she replied and the call ended.

Emily shoved the phone into her purse and drove straight to the pizza place where Nikki had already claimed a booth. She made a beeline toward it, plopped down, and laid her head on the table.

"What happened last night?" Nikki asked.

"You were right. The makeup sex was amazing."

Nikki grinned. "I told you so. Girl, you're knee-deep in quicksand and sinkin' fast."

"I know and I'm scared," Emily said.

"Don't be. Just dive right in and see where it goes. That's what I intend to do. I gave my two-week notice today. My last day is March eighth," Nikki said.

Tears welled up in Emily's eyes and spilled down over her cheeks. "I'm going to miss you so much."

Nikki handed her a paper napkin. "I'll miss you too, but this means I get to do more than just pass out meds. On one of the evenings I'm off each week, we'll have pizza or Chinese buffet and catch up. Agreed?"

Emily dried her eyes and nodded. "Absolutely. Now my story." Between bites, she told Nikki everything she could remember, including the phone call she'd gotten that evening.

"Would you sign a prenup if things went that far with Justin?" Nikki asked.

"I'd insist on one. It's just good sense when a piece of property the size of the Longhorn Canyon or the Big Sky ranches comes into the picture," Emily answered.

"Did Retta or Claire sign one?"

Emily shrugged. "I have no idea, and I sure wouldn't ask, but it's entirely too soon to even think about that."

*   *   *

The sight of the little red Mustang parked beside the cabin put a smile on Justin's face and a little spring in his step on the way inside. He let himself in as quietly as possible and used his phone as a flashlight. Making his way to the bathroom, he noticed a white towel and the red shoes sitting on the coffee table.

After a quick shower, he dried off and was on his way to bed when Emily sat up in bed and rubbed her eyes. "Justin, is that you?"

"Yes, darlin'." He slipped beneath the covers and wrapped her up in his arms.

"Tired?" She yawned.

"Exhausted." He kissed her on the cheek.

"Me too. Just hold me tonight. We'll make wild, passionate love in the morning."

"You got it, darlin'," he said and was instantly asleep.

The sun was shining brightly through the kitchen window when he opened his eyes the next morning. Emily was in the kitchen. She wore a pair of Minnie Mouse pajama pants and a T-shirt that testified to the fact that she wasn't wearing a bra. Just looking at her making coffee aroused him.

She turned around and smiled. "Good mornin'. I think I remember you getting into bed with me. My brothers are having a fit for me to come home and cook at least one meal for them, so I'm going there pretty soon. I haven't spent much time with them, so I owe them a couple of hours this morning." She crossed the room and sat cross-legged in the middle of the bed.

He sat up and kissed her on the forehead. "You look worried. What's the matter?"

She told him about the problem at the Big Sky Ranch with the prenup. "That's probably more information than you need. If she really loves him, I don't see what the big deal is with signing a prenup."

"I can understand where Matthew is coming from. I'd never ask a woman I loved to sign one," Justin said. "That's like saying, 'I love you but I don't trust you.' Neither Cade nor Levi asked Retta or Claire to do that."

"We'll have to agree to disagree on that." Emily left the bed and went to the kitchen where she poured two mugs of coffee. "What do you want for breakfast? Cinnamon toast and bacon all right?"

"I want to talk some more first." Justin took one of the cups from her hand. "Where is all this with us going, Emily? I'd never ask you to quit your job or to do anything that would change you. I think you're perfect just the way you are. You can be whatever you want to be, work at whatever you want, or not work at all if sometime in the future you want to be a stay-at-home mama."

"So you want children?" she asked.

"I do." He nodded. "Lots of them. I'd like five or six, but would settle for at least two. I grew up with a sibling, but Levi didn't. In a sense, we were all like brothers, but he's always said that he missed not having a brother or a sister of his very own."

"If you wanted all that why haven't you been searching for 'the one'?" She made air quotes around the last two words.

Another nod and then he took a sip of coffee. "I wasn't

ready until now. And I'm tellin' you, when I settle down, I won't need a prenup—but I'll want children. What about you?"

She waited for a full minute before she spoke. "I would want a prenup, not for my protection but for yours. And I love children. I'd like to even work with them again someday."

He took the coffee cup from her and set it on a bedside table beside his. "We don't have to figure out our lives all the way to the day we meet our Maker at the Pearly Gates. I just need to know if we have some kind of future, because I'm beginning to do a hell of a lot more than just like you, Emily. I want to tell folks that we're dating, that we're in a relationship and—"

She leaned toward him, and kissed him. "You can stand on the rooftops and tell everyone that you want to. I'll tell my family when I go home for the reunion."

*   *   *

A month before, Emily would have declared a person insane if they said she'd be in a committed relationship in the next four weeks. But there they were, talking about the future, and even kids. She wanted to pinch herself to see if it was real.

Justin walked her to the door after she'd showered and got dressed. They shared a long good-bye kiss and she drove to her apartment. Her brothers were in the kitchen when she arrived. Hudson was frying bacon. Tag was making biscuits.

"We need to talk," Hudson said.

"About?"

"It's one thing if we don't know a person you're sleeping

with. It's another if we do and like him. What if he's just using you, sis?" Tag asked.

"In other words, we're worried about you. We want you to be happy but we want assurances that you're bein' treated right," Hudson added.

"I'm a big girl. I can take care of myself. Justin and I are in a relationship and I don't want it jinxed by a couple of brothers who butt in where they don't belong. Now move over and I'll fry the eggs," she said.

Chapter Twenty-Two

It had been a relatively quiet week after the livestock show until Thursday afternoon at quitting time. Emily had spent most every night at the cabin, and she sure wasn't looking forward to the long drive to Tulia the next morning.

Sarah must've been lurking around the corner when Emily told Derek that she was going to be gone the rest of the week. Emily had planned on just letting them find out that she was gone from Derek the next morning when they all showed up in the activities room to start working on St. Patrick's Day decorations for the center.

Then Larry called Justin, and Emily had no idea what was said there. It didn't matter, because whatever it was, it affected Patsy horribly. At fifteen minutes until five, she was on her way to the dining room and stopped by Emily's room.

"Tell me it's not true," Patsy said with tears in her eyes.

"What?"

"That you're leaving us to go back to West Texas, and you're never coming back. What did Justin do to hurt your feelings? I've got a good mind to go out there and give him a piece of my mind." Patsy had begun to pace around one of the long tables.

"Justin didn't do anything. I was going home to see my folks anyway, so I decided to make it a four-day weekend," Emily said soothingly. Just ten more minutes, but she couldn't leave when Patsy was so upset.

"Is Justin going with you?"

"No, he is not," Emily answered.

"Why?"

"Because I didn't invite him. And a few days of us being away from each other will be good for both of us. Besides with the cattle sale and the reunion, my folks can always use my help."

Patsy grabbed her chest and sank to the floor. Her eyes rolled back in her head and she twitched a few times. Otis came running from the hallway and yelled for someone to call 911. "Patsy's had a heart attack. My wife acted just like that when she died."

Larry appeared out of nowhere, phone in hand, and pressed the numbers. "Send an ambulance to Oakview Retirement Center. We've got a resident down with a heart attack."

Emily ran to get the on-duty nurse but was told that she'd had an emergency call from the hospital saying that her son had been in an accident. She'd left a few minutes before. Nikki yelled from the other end of the hallway to just call 911.

Before Emily could get back to the room, the ambulance was already there and the paramedics were loading Patsy up on a gurney. She opened her eyes, took a few breaths, and held out her hand. "Go with me, Emily. Bess will be crazy. I need you."

Emily took the small hand in hers and nodded. "Of course. I couldn't let you go alone."

"I'll drive the four of us out to the hospital," Otis said.

"Don't worry, sister," Bess called out. "I'll be there in a few minutes. Don't you dare die. I can't live without you."

Emily's eyes misted over as she crawled up into the ambulance. It was a tight fit with her and the paramedic both sitting on the narrow bench beside Patsy, but it was only a five-minute drive. The waiting room was full when they wheeled Patsy straight back through the doors into the emergency area. Watching them take Patsy away, with no one to hold her hand or stay with her, was one of the hardest things that Emily ever had to do. Bess was right behind her, wringing her hands. Sarah had an arm thrown around her shoulders. Otis and Larry had taken seats over against the wall.

To Emily's surprise, Justin came dashing through the doors no more than five minutes after they arrived. "What are you doing here?"

"I'm so sorry," Justin said as he wrapped her up in a hug.

She closed her eyes and listened to the steady beat of his heart. When she opened them, she caught a glimpse of Otis elbowing Larry, and Bess smiling. That was her first clue that something was definitely wrong.

"Thank you, but how did you find out that Patsy..." Her dark brows drew down over her blue eyes.

"Larry called me. He said she might die," he said.

"And you beat the ambulance here, all the way from the ranch?"

"Cade and I were already in town." Justin tucked a strand of hair behind her ear. "We were less than a mile away, so we dropped everything and came right on. Cade is parking the truck. Is she going to be all right? Was it really a heart attack? What did the nurse at the center say?"

"I don't know. The nurse at the center had an emergency…" Emily started.

Before she could finish, the doors flew open and everyone in the Patsy party stood up. Linda Smith, the nurse from the center, stopped in the middle of the floor and said, "I wish I had whoever pranked me by the hair. I'd strangle them until they turned blue and then slap them for being that color. My son is fine and so is all the rest of my family. And Patsy is most likely having a panic attack. They're running some tests, but the doctor doesn't think it's a heart attack."

"What caused the panic?" Justin asked.

"Praise the lord," Sarah said.

"Can I see her?" Bess asked.

Emily took Justin by the arm and led him away from the crowd. "She doesn't want me to go to Tulia without you. She thinks that I'm never coming back," Emily whispered.

"Then I'll go with you. Tag already invited me," Justin said.

"No. I need to go alone. We need a little breathing space to be sure this is all real, and I've got things to get settled at home," she said.

"Such as?" he asked.

"This isn't the time or place to talk about it. Just trust me, Justin. I need to go alone," she said.

"Why? I thought we were good," he said.

She could read disappointment in his face. "We are more than good. It's not you, darlin'. It's me. There's stuff going on at home, and remember what they say about absence making the heart grow fonder," she said as she brushed a kiss across his lips.

"I'm afraid of that other saying: out of sight, out of mind," he said.

"Never," she told him.

"Promise?" He headed outside.

"Absolutely."

"I thought Justin would stay longer," Bess said.

Nikki pushed through the doors at the same time Justin was leaving. "I came as quick as I could after I gave out the evening meds. Since Linda wasn't there I had to take up the slack. Is Patsy going to be okay?"

Emily gave her the latest news. "And someone prank called Linda. Her son is fine and so is the rest of her family."

"What can I do?" Nikki asked.

Emily slumped down in a chair and motioned for Nikki to sit beside her. "We're waiting on the tests to get done. She thought Justin and I were fighting because he wasn't going with me, and that I wouldn't ever come back."

"Tell me neither one is true."

"We aren't fighting, but I think he's disappointed that I didn't want him to go with me, and I'll be back on Monday."

Nikki nodded and started to comment when a tall lady in scrubs pushed a wheelchair bearing Patsy through the doors and out into the waiting room. "She's ready to go. The doctor says that it was just a mild panic attack. Is there someone here to take her back to the center, or do we need to take her in the ambulance?"

Otis raised his hand. "I'll take her."

"Did you tell Justin that he can go with you?" Patsy asked.

"No, I didn't. I've got family stuff to do, so I'm going to be busy," Emily answered.

Patsy grabbed her chest with both hands. Her head fell

backward and she rolled her eyes back into her head. Emily started toward her, but Nikki laid a hand on her arm.

"Stop it, sister!" Bess slapped Patsy on the arm. "It won't work a second time, and Justin's already gone home."

Patsy got out of the wheelchair and grabbed Bess's hand. "It was a fine performance though, wasn't it? We should all be actors. Now as the curtain draws, we'll take a bow. Please hold your applause until we're all holding hands."

The other three joined them while Nikki, the nurse, and Emily all watched in speechless silence.

"I didn't know that the retirement center had dementia residents. Were they ever actors?" the nurse asked.

"Not to my knowledge," Nikki answered. "Come on, Emily, I'll drive you back to the center to get your car."

"Can us girls go with y'all?" Sarah asked.

Emily pointed at all of them. "No, and if you were children instead of grown adults I'd ground you for a month. I'm tellin' the supervisor tomorrow morning."

"Tattletale," Larry muttered.

"Does that mean we can't go to church next Sunday?" Bess asked.

"No, but you better not pull a stunt like this again. You need to go to church and spend the whole hour repenting for your sins." Emily spun around and was on the way out the door when she heard the five of them giving themselves a round of applause.

Emily made it to the car and had the seat belt fastened before she and Nikki burst out in laughter. "That's even worse than anything they did at the ranch."

Nikki handed Emily a leftover napkin from the pizza place. "Are you really going to tattle on them?"

"No." Emily wiped her eyes. "And promise me that you

won't either. Causing such a panic in the center and making prank calls could get them evicted."

"I've laughed so hard and I can't breathe. You really aren't going to tell on them?"

"That's just a warning," Emily said between more giggles as she wiped the black smudges from her cheeks. "I swear to God, raising them is worse than children could ever be."

"Only difference is when you get kids grown up, they've got years and years to live. When this bunch is raised, you'll be attending funerals," Nikki told her.

Emily shivered. "I can't think about that."

"And when they're all gone, you'll have empty nest syndrome, because there'll never be another group like them at the center." Nikki parked beside Emily's car. "I'll pick up some Subway sandwiches. You go on home and get started packing."

"Thank you." Emily looked around the parking lot. "I wonder where they are."

"Probably stopped for ice cream." Nikki grinned. "You didn't give them a curfew."

"I'll have to remember that," Emily said as Nikki got out of the car.

Just to be sure, she drove by the ice cream store, where she could see all five of them through the window. And a cute little waitress was handing out sundaes.

"I may be ready to give up my job and go to ranchin' by the time they're all . . ." Emily couldn't make herself say or even think the word.

She tried to think about what she'd need that week as she drove the rest of the way home. She stopped long enough to tell her landlady that she'd be gone so the old gal wouldn't worry. Then she took the stairs two at a time to her apartment. She unlocked the door and shoved it open, went straight to her bedroom and pulled her suitcases from the shelf in the closet.

"Hey, I found your sunglasses in my car. Thought you might need them on the trip," Nikki yelled without knocking. "And you dropped something."

Emily peeked around the door to see her holding out an envelope. "What is it?"

"Don't know. It was on your floor. Has your name on it. Think we should call in the bomb squad. After what the Five did tonight, I wouldn't be surprised if they brewed up some kind of powder to make you sick so you couldn't leave."

Emily took it from her outstretched hand, and holding it out away from her face, ripped into the envelope to find one red, heart-shaped lollipop. She sat down with a thud in the middle of the floor and put her hands over her eyes.

"What is it?" Nikki plopped down beside her.

"I know it's from Justin, even though there's no note. It must've been propped against my door, and I kicked it inside," she said.

"Are you cryin'?" Nikki asked.

"A little."

Nikki slung an arm around her shoulders. "That is just the sweetest thing ever."

Emily raised her head and swiped the tears away with the back of her hand. "Don't I know it."

Chapter Twenty-Three

When the packing was done, Emily decided that she couldn't sleep anyway so she might as well drive partway that night. She could stop out near Vernon for the night, and make it to the ranch before lunch the next day. Nikki hadn't argued but gave her a hug and made her promise to text or call every day to keep her caught up on the news.

It was after ten when she reached the Vernon city limits sign, but she wasn't sleepy. There was no need to pay for a hotel room when she wasn't sleepy, she decided. Between the country music songs on the radio that kept reminding her of Justin and those two red suckers on her dresser at home, her every thought was on Justin. She hoped she hadn't hurt his feelings too badly when she refused to let him go with her.

"We've got a request for several Josh Turner songs," the radio DJ said. "So let's make it five for Josh right now, starting with 'Your Man.'"

Emily began to tap to the music with the steel guitar lead-in. Josh Turner's voice reminded her of Justin's, with that deep drawl. A shiver crawled down her spine as she remembered his whisper when he told her that she was the most beautiful woman he'd ever known. She imagined Justin singing each of the next three songs to her as the miles melted behind her.

"And we'll end the Josh five top requests with 'Soulmate,'" the DJ said.

Emily had never heard the song, and even though it was sung by a guy, she applied the same words to what she wanted, as a woman, when she committed her heart to a future with a man.

It was after midnight when she turned down the lane to the Big Sky Ranch. She passed the original ranch house on the right and kept driving down the lane for another mile before she parked outside the yard fence. The house was dark, but she still had a key. She left all her baggage in the car and slipped inside. Using her phone as a flashlight, she made her way across the familiar living room and down the hallway to her old bedroom.

She touched a small lamp on the bedside table one time. It gave off just enough light for her to dig around in a dresser drawer for something to sleep in. She kicked off her shoes and removed her scrubs. Pulling a nightshirt over her head, she crawled into the bed and closed her eyes.

She slept poorly the rest of the night, and at five o'clock she awoke in a sweat after dreaming about Justin making love to her in the cabin. She didn't even try to go back to sleep but got up, found a pair of jeans in her closet and a western shirt, and got dressed.

She was sitting at the kitchen table with a cup of coffee in her hand when her mother came wandering in. Anne stopped in the middle of the floor and blinked a dozen times.

"Am I seeing things?"

Emily pushed her chair back and went to hug her mother. "Mornin', Mama. Coffee is ready. What're we makin' for breakfast? And where are my lazy brothers?"

Anne Baker was as tall as Emily but slim as a model. Her red hair was pulled up in a ponytail and her blue eyes sparkled just looking at her daughter. No one would ever guess that she was past fifty years old.

"They'll be here when they smell bacon." Anne hugged Emily again. "Let's don't even start it, so we can have some time to talk first."

Emily took a deep breath and let it out slowly. "That might take so long that they'll starve."

"Not in one day." Anne took her by the hand and led her back to the table. "Start at the beginning and catch me up, but give me time to pour a cup."

For the first time ever, Emily wanted to tell her mother everything in her heart, but she wasn't sure where to start, or how to word what she couldn't even understand herself. "You want me to start with 'in the beginning God made dirt'?"

"I'm all ears," Anne said. "You can go back before that if you need to."

"I'm in love with Justin Maguire. It sounds crazy. We've only known each other a few weeks, but..." Emily went on to tell her mother the whole story.

"I like that cowboy. We all do, but I wouldn't tell your father that you've already been sleeping with him." Anne smiled. "And don't worry about his mother. She'll come around and learn to love you as much as he does."

"But he hasn't said that he loves me," Emily said.

"He will, and darlin', I'm awful glad you trusted me enough to talk to me about this," Anne said.

"I'm afraid he's terribly disappointed that I didn't want him to come with me, and now I wish I had brought him."

"Never too late to ask him," Anne said.

"Not after I said I needed some time to think about us. I had lots of that on the drive, and I'm sure that I love him." She shook her head. "But I already miss him, and it hasn't even been a day."

"There's a difference in loving someone and being in love with someone. I kind of see it in Darcy. She loves Matthew, but I'm not sure she's in love with him. That's why we want the prenup so badly."

"I'm in love with Justin," Emily said softly.

"Then tell him," Anne said.

"Hey, you got a hug for your daddy?" Frank grinned as he opened up his arms.

Emily hurried across the room. Taller than her by six inches, her father was a big man with wide shoulders and a bit of a belly that hung out over his belt buckle these days. But in the wedding picture of him and her mother on the mantel in the living room, he'd been quite the handsome young cowboy.

"Why didn't you tell us you were comin' early?" Frank asked.

"I wanted to surprise you. Got a job for me today?"

"I could use another hand on a tractor. This time of year, we got lots of plowin' to do," he said.

"I'd rather fence, but I'll gladly drive a tractor. It does have a radio, right? Or do I need to take my MP3 player?"

"It's got a radio," Frank said. "And welcome home, baby girl."

Home?

That was in a little cabin on the backside of the Longhorn Canyon with Justin Maguire, and she intended to tell him as much as soon as she got back there.

*   *   *

Justin tossed and turned both Thursday night and Friday night. On Saturday morning he was up at five o'clock and made a pot of coffee. He'd never believed in love at first sight, or even love that happened in a short time. That was something that built over time, maybe a year or two, not in a month. But the simple truth was that he was in love with Emily.

Levi knocked on his door but came right in without waiting for an invitation. "Got coffee made?"

"In the pot." Justin pointed. "What are you doin' out here this early?"

"Cade's sending me to Happy, Texas, to pick up a load of heifers. About a dozen from a ranch that's sellin' out and has some really fancy stock. Anyway, if you don't have anything real pressin', I wondered if you'd want to go with me. Tulia is on the way."

"I wanted to go with her but..."

His phone rang and he grabbed it, hoping it was Emily. "Hello."

"Justin, this is Anne Baker. I'd like to surprise my daughter tonight. I know it's a lot to ask, but could you come out here and join us for our reunion? She misses you, but she won't call and ask," Anne said.

"What time?" Justin asked.

"We put the food on the table at noon," she said.

"I'll be there. Might be a little late but don't give up on me." He ended the call and turned to Levi. "Give me time to get my bag packed."

"You know I never would have picked that girl for you," Levi said as he watched Justin toss clothes into a suitcase.

"Why?"

"I figured you'd fall for someone as wild as us, and then spend a lifetime tamin' her down." Levi grinned. "Or maybe spend a lifetime lettin' her tame you down."

A vision of Emily naked in the bed right over there—he glanced that way—filled his mind. There were different kinds of wild, and no one could ever say that what he and Emily had in that bed wasn't better than anything he'd experienced with a bar bunny he'd sweet-talked into coming home with him from the Rusty Spur.

Chapter Twenty-Four

Justin called Cade to let him know what was going on before he got into Levi's truck, fastened his seat belt, and threw the seat back to a reclining position. The last thing he remembered was Levi whistling as he drove away from the ranch. When he awoke, the radio was playing something by Conway Twitty and Levi was singing right along.

"Well, good mornin', sleepin' beauty," Levi teased. "I haven't heard this song since we were kids. Grandpa Callahan used to play it on an old vinyl record for Granny."

"What's the title?" Justin asked.

Levi thought for a minute before he answered. "I think it's 'Your Love Had Taken Me That High.' That's right. It's right there in the lyrics."

Justin brought the seat up, took out his phone and found the song, and then he captured the link and sent it to Emily. He was about to go back to sleep when his phone rang. Hoping that it was Emily, he answered on the first ring.

"This is Anne again. How close are you? Tag says to tell you that you can stay here at the ranch."

"Thank you." Justin had just figured he'd have dinner and ride back to the Longhorn Canyon with Levi. "I caught a ride with Levi and we're halfway there. He can pick me up on his way back from Happy. Does Emily know I'm coming?"

"No, it can be a surprise. I need to see her face when you arrive."

"Why?" Justin asked.

"Trust me, son. When you are a parent someday, you'll know why," Anne said. "Y'all drive safe and bring Levi with you. Tag and Hudson have talked so much about all of you that we feel like we know your family. Especially after y'all talked them into staying for church and invited them to Sunday dinner before they left. We'll be glad to have him."

"Thank you," Justin said.

"I heard most of that," Levi said, "but I'm going to drop you and then get right on up to Happy to load those cows. I'd like to be home before dark."

*   *   *

Emily would have just as soon slept late on Saturday morning rather than go to the beauty shop with her mother and grandmother. But there she was, yawning, in the backseat of her granny's car on her way into Tulia when she remembered that she'd turned off her phone the night before.

Nikki had sent two messages, both telling her to call Patsy, who was freaking out because she wanted to talk to Emily and couldn't get a hold of her. The second was a link from Justin. She hit it and immediately the car was filled with an old Conway song.

"Where'd you find that old goodie?" Opal looked up in the rear view mirror. "I've still got a vinyl with that on it. Your grandpa would play it for me when we had an argument."

"Justin sent it to me," Emily answered, honestly.

"Now, I've never been one to meddle," Opal started.

"Hmmph," Anne snorted.

Opal shot a dirty look across the console. "I was about to say, except when I thought you were making a mistake. But, honey, you can kick any mesquite bush in the whole state of Texas and a cowboy will come ridin' out. Why do you have to pick one so far away when there's enough here in your part of the state to choose from? We'd have to put one of them take-a-number machines on the porch post if you let out the news you were ready to come home and settle down."

"Did you talk to your brother?" Anne asked.

"Yep, and he's not budging, but I think y'all are forgetting something. This ranch legally belongs to you and Daddy. Check with a lawyer, but the way I'm thinkin' the only thing she could get if she divorced him was half of his assets," Emily said.

"Hummph." Opal snorted. "That would be a lot. He's probably got a fortune in savings."

"That's his choice, Granny, but I'm pretty sure Big Sky is secure. I also talked to Tag and Hudson. They're looking at a little starter ranch right next door to the Longhorn Canyon. Is that going to create a family problem?"

"They've talked to their father, and his opinion is that it might settle them down to be totally responsible for their own little place. They'll always have a home if they fall flat on their faces. Besides you'll be close by to keep an eye on them," Anne said.

"Oh, no!" Emily's voice went all high and squeaky as she parked the vehicle in front of the beauty shop. "I'm not going to babysit them or settle their arguments."

Opal opened the passenger door. "Maybe if they move out there, you'll come home and find a local cowboy just to get away from them."

"I love you, Granny, but ninety-nine percent of those cowboys who'd take a number would only be interested in getting their hands on Big Sky, and you know it. Y'all go on in. I'm going to call Patsy and see what's going on at the center. I'll join you in a few minutes." Emily found Patsy's number in her contacts and hit the CALL button.

"Hello, is this Emily?" Patsy answered on the first ring.

"Yes, it's me. Nikki said you've been trying to call me. Is everything all right?" Emily asked.

"We're all fine. No more panic attacks and we're sorry we scared you so bad, but it's like this, we're old and we'd like to see a grandchild or two before we kick the bucket," she said. "So we kinda took things in our own hands and we're sorry."

"Grandchild?" Emily gasped.

"Honey, we done prayed and asked God to make you and Justin wake up and smell the wedding cake. Y'all are the nearest thing we've ever had to kids, so we've decided that we're going to be grandparents, but we ain't got many years left, and we'd like to at least be a part of the first child's life," Patsy said. "I'm putting this on speaker now because we got some big, big news to tell you."

"Hi, Emily," the rest of the Five singsonged.

"Okay, just so none of us get to tell it all, we got it worked out five ways, but I get to go first," Otis said. "You remember seeing that big old two-story house right across the street from the church over in Sunset?"

"Just barely. It had a wraparound porch, right? With a little white picket fence?" Emily answered with a question. Surely they weren't planning on buying that place for her and Justin. He'd never go for a place in town, not even a place as small as Sunset. Larry knew he was designing his own house, so why would they even consider such a thing.

"Well, we made some calls, and it's for sale," Larry said. "We almost broke the rules because it's just barely inside the Montague County line. We went and looked at it on Wednesday. It's an old house but it's been well maintained and it's even got a lift chair to go up and down the stairs."

Why would she and Justin need a lift chair? It'd be years before either of them was too old to climb to the second floor.

"My turn," Bess said. "There's five bedrooms and a bathroom on the second floor and the downstairs is real nice with an office space and a bathroom off the foyer. And it's got the cutest yellow daisy wallpaper in the kitchen. I'm going to get Claire to make us some eyelet lace curtains for that room."

"Now me," Sarah butted in. "The price was a little higher than Larry thought, but we decided not to haggle about it, since we all loved it so much. We each chipped in one-fifth, and we'll do the same for groceries and utility bills."

Emily finally understood what they were saying. "Are y'all pulling another prank on me?"

"This is me, Patsy. I knew you'd say that so I saved my part until last. We're not kiddin'. When we came here, it was because we were lonely. Bess wasn't fit to live with on a twenty-four-seven basis, and I needed some people around me if I was to put up with her smart mouth."

"That's a crock. It was my idea so I didn't have to watch

you grow old and make a fool out of yourself with all the men in our town," Bess argued.

"Hush, it's my turn," Patsy said. "We've formed us a family of our own with you bein' the child we never had. Now that we've had a taste of that little church and the ranch, we want to bust out of this place and just the five of us live in our own house. Us ladies will do the cookin' until we get too old, then we'll hire it done. Between the lot of us we've got more money than we'll spend between now and the day we die."

Tears welled up in Emily's eyes. The five were leaving and Nikki was going. Life would never be the same at the center.

"We're even seein' a lawyer about that after we get settled in our new house," Otis said. "We've decided to be cremated, and all our ashes mixed up together and buried somewhere on the Longhorn Canyon Ranch."

Big teardrops made their way down Emily's cheeks and dripped onto her shirt. "When are you doing all this?" she managed to get out without sobbing.

"We done bought the place. Since we're payin' cash, we get to move in anytime we want. But we got to get us some furniture, so we told the supervisor here that we'd vacate the center on the fifteenth," Patsy said.

"And we're havin' a party soon as we get settled. You and Justin are goin' to be the guests of honor," Sarah said.

"But—" Emily started.

"No buts. It's a done deal."

"But what if things don't work out between us. We're just now starting to figure out how we feel," Emily spit out.

"Listen to your heart," Larry said. "Signin' off now. Can't wait to see you Monday. We'll take you to see the house."

"And one more thing. I bought an SUV, too, so we could

all be more comfortable, since I'll be the chauffer for all these old folks." Otis laughed.

"Bye now," they all said, and the call was over before Emily could say another word.

"I'm not bein' nosy," Opal said. "Don't look at me like that, Anne. She's cryin', so it had to be bad news. Was that Justin? There's tissues on the seat beside you. We can't go into the beauty shop with you cryin' like that. The biggest gossips in the panhandle come here so they can find out the latest news. By mornin' you'll have come home because you've been jilted, and you are pregnant with twins."

"You've been reading too many romance books, Mama," Anne said.

Emily removed a makeup mirror from her purse and fixed her face as best she could. Her grandmother might have been reading too many steamy romance books, but she was telling the truth about Tresa and the beauty shop. It was the best place in the area to hear all the latest rumors.

"That's much better. Now tell us what's goin' on." Opal parked in the last available spot in front of Tresa's Hair and Nails.

"It's not about Justin. I've told you about my favorites at the center. Well, they've decided to buy a place of their own and move out. And my best friend, Nikki, has given her notice, and she's going to work at the hospital. I hate change," Emily said.

"Don't we all."

Emily checked her reflection one more time and then sent a text to Justin: *I wish you'd come out here with me. I need you.*

*   *   *

Justin got the text from Emily while he was changing into clean clothes in the bathroom of a service station. Half an hour later Levi was driving onto the Big Sky Ranch. Justin called Anne, and she talked him through the rest of the way to the sale barn where, judging by all the noise, the party had already started. He could hear a country music band in the background, the buzz of dozens of conversations going on, and babies crying in the background.

"Call me in the next hour and let me know whether to swing back by and get you," Levi said.

"Let's hope I get to wave you on."

Anne met him at the door. "I'm glad to see you."

Justin took a deep breath. "Lead the way, please, ma'am."

Locating Emily among all the people wasn't difficult. She was that gorgeous, curvy woman on the dance floor with her brother Matthew. Most folks were wearing jeans, but not his Emily. She wore cowboy boots and a form-fitting blue dress the color of her eyes. And she was listening intently to whatever her partner had to say.

Justin didn't feel brave as he crossed the dance floor to tap the guy on the shoulder, but dammit, he was in love with her and it was high time that she knew. Emily turned to see Justin weaving his way around the folks on the floor. She took a step back from Matthew.

Her gaze met his as he got closer and closer. The band kept playing and people kept dancing and talking, but the whole world disappeared and everything was stone cold quiet. The only thing Justin heard was the sound of her boots on the wooden dance floor as she came toward him.

"Hello, cowboy," she said.

"May I have this dance?" he asked.

She looped her arms around his neck. He removed his

hat and held it at the small of her back. He didn't even hear what the band was playing but knew deep in his heart that he was in love with this woman.

He drew back just far enough to look deeply into her eyes. "You said you wanted to talk."

"I love you, Justin, and I'm in love with you too. I fought it. I ran from it, but I'm admitting it right now."

"I love you and I'm in love with you too. Anything else we need to talk about?" He twirled her around and then brought her back to his arms.

"Yes," she said breathlessly. "The Fab Five are leaving the center. So is Nikki. It'll be awfully lonely without them. What if I wanted to quit working there and help out on the ranch—maybe help with the kids this summer? And if the senior citizens' week became an annual thing, I could help with that. I can drive a tractor or string barbed wire, deliver calves or whatever needs to be done, but please don't make me spend time doing book work..." she said.

He stopped dancing and tipped up her chin. "You can work away from the ranch like Claire or work on the ranch with me. Whatever you want, darlin', is fine with me, but I'd be one happy cowboy to have you beside me every single day."

She didn't care if the entire family was watching, or what they would say. She met his lips halfway. The kiss was so full of promise that it almost brought tears to her eyes. When it ended, he ran his knuckles down her jawbone.

"I'm in love with you, Emily. I want to come home at night to find you there, to wake up each morning with you in my arms. I want to spend the rest of my life with you, but you can call the shots on the speed that we go," he whispered.

"This song is dedicated to Justin Maguire and Emily Baker from her two brothers Hudson and Taggart," the lead singer said.

She expected some sappy song about falling in love, but the female singer took the microphone and nodded toward the band, and started singing Shania Twain's "Any Man of Mine."

Justin threw back his head and laughed. Instead of dancing with her, he crossed his arms over his chest and stood still. If that's the way he wanted to play it, then she'd give the whole damn family a show. She sang with the lyrics as she touched his cheek with a finger, and when it talked about shimmy and shakin', she did just that.

The whole crowd applauded when the song ended.

"And this next one is for the couple from Emily's brother Matthew." The male singer took the microphone.

Justin recognized the song immediately when the music lead-in to "Your Man" by Josh Turner started. He grabbed Emily's hand, spun her out, and brought her back to his chest. "Darlin', I mean every word of this song, especially that part about us not getting in a hurry."

"Thank you," she said as he swung her out again, keeping her hand in his as the two of them did some fancy dance steps. The rest of the dancers backed up and gave them the whole floor.

The next time he brought her to his chest, he said, "You're a helluva good dancer."

"So are you, and I can see all my girl cousins salivating."

He gave her a quick, sweet kiss, and said, "I don't see another woman in this whole place."

"And now one more," the female singer said, moving back up to the microphone. "This is from Miz Opal and Miz Anne to Justin and Emily."

Emily blushed when the steel guitar player hit the first few chords to "Rockin' Years," but she wouldn't let either her mother or grandmother get ahead of her. She led Justin up on the bandstand and took the microphone from the singer, picking up on cue and in perfect pitch. When it was time for Ricky Van Shelton's part she handed it off to Justin, who didn't miss a bit when he harmonized with her.

When the song ended, she took a bow, and said, "I want to introduce y'all to my boyfriend, Justin Maguire."

Justin settled his hat on his head, picked up her hand, and brought it to his lips, before he turned to the crowd. "Please to meet y'all. Now I want to dance some more with this stunning girlfriend of mine."

Chapter Twenty-Five

Justin opened the door to the cabin and scooped Emily up in his arms like a new bride that Sunday afternoon. He waltzed across the floor with her and sat down on the sofa with her in his lap.

"Have I told you today that I love you?" he asked.

"Ten times, but I kind of like to hear it."

"I love you, Emily. And I've got something that I really want you to look at."

Her eyes went to the bed. "You mean other than that?"

He grinned and pointed to the coffee table.

"What's this?" She slid off his lap. "It's your new...oh, my gosh." She picked up a page from a magazine showing a two-story house. "Where did you get this?"

"Larry gave it to me." He pointed at one part of the blue-prints. "This is your big pantry. This is the closet for nothing but your shoes. And this is a bathroom with a garden tub so we can go skinny-dippin'. When it's all finished, will you move in with me?"

"Do we have to wait that long?" she asked.

Justin's heart almost jumped right out of his chest. He hadn't even let himself hope that she'd be willing to live with him that soon.

"All I've got to offer until the house is built is this cabin, but the door is always open to you, darlin'. So do you approve of the plans? Do you want to make changes?"

"They're perfect. It's my dream house. Don't change a single thing. I can't wait to live in it." She stood up and led him toward the bed but then stopped midway and pointed toward the kitchen table. "Why's that lollipop stuck inside the empty beer bottle?"

"To remind me every day that you are the special one," he answered. "Every single step of this journey we're on together is on your time, darlin'. But just so you know, I'm ready for you to move in with me right now, and I'm ready for one of them lifetime commitment relationships," Justin said.

She pushed him backward on the bed. "I'll tell my landlady that I'll be moving out at the end of the month."

He pulled her down beside him, gave her one of those long kisses that almost fogged the windows, and whispered, "I love you, Emily."

"I love you, Justin. Is the door locked?"

"You bet it is," he said.

Keep reading for a peek at the next book
in the Longhorn Canyon series
Cowboy Rebel

Coming in Spring 2019

Chapter One

The woman at the end of the bar looked like she'd been around the block, and Tag Baker sure wasn't interested in buying her a drink. But as luck would have it, the cowboy next to him took to the dance floor with a tall redhead, and the woman moved to sit down right beside him.

"Anyone ever tell you that you got pretty eyes?" she asked.

"Couple of times, ma'am." He nodded.

She motioned the bartender over by holding up her glass. "Bartender, refill me and give this cowboy a shot of whatever he's drinkin' and put it on my tab."

"Thank you." Tag tipped his cowboy hat toward her. Up close, she looked even rougher than she had from a distance.

The bartender set a double shot of tequila in front of the woman and gave Tag a healthy two fingers of whiskey. "Anything else, Miz Scarlett?"

"Not right now." Her smile showed red lipstick on her

front tooth that matched the stain on the rim of her glass. She nudged Tag with an elbow. "Haven't seen you in here before."

"Been here lots of times, ma'am. Usually come in on Saturday nights though, not Fridays." A cowboy should be nice to whoever bought him a drink, right?

He'd raised his glass to his mouth when a big, burly man burst into the bar, came right at him with his hands knotted into fists the size of Christmas hams, and started yelling.

"I knew I'd find you here," the guy growled.

"And what business is it of yours where I go?" Tag asked.

"I'm not talkin' to you, so turn around and shut up. I'm talkin' to my woman. When she gets mad at me, she always comes here. Come on, Scarlett, we're goin' home." He grabbed her by the arm and tugged.

She slid off the stool, shook off his hand, and got nose to nose with him. "I'm not going anywhere with you. If you want a woman, go get Ramona."

"I told you that was a mistake. I broke up with her weeks ago, so don't give me that old shit." His voice got louder with every word.

He drew back his hand as if to slap her, but instead grabbed a hand full of her hair and jerked her to his chest. "I said you're coming home. I made a mistake, but so did you."

A bouncer who looked like a strutting little rooster hurried across the room, got between them and demanded that the guy leave. Tag could see from the fire in the bigger man's eyes that he wasn't going anywhere. It wasn't one bit of Tag's business, but then the juke box began to blast out Tim McGraw's old song, "Live Like You Were Dying." Since that had been Tag's motto for more than a decade, he figured it was a sign. The woman might not be a lady, but she had bought him a drink. He threw back the rest of his whiskey and stepped right in the middle of the argument, fully meaning to help the bouncer out a little.

"Miz Scarlett here says she's not going home with you," Tag said. "It'd be wise if you just scooted on out of here."

The big fellow put his hands on Tag's chest and pushed. Tag grabbed for anything that would keep him from falling and got a hand full of a shirt. The bouncer fell into the woman and they all crashed together. Before Tag could get out of the pile of arms and legs, Scarlett kicked the man in the knee about a half a dozen times. He went down like a big oak tree, landing to the side of Tag.

"You bitch." He growled as he popped up to a sitting position and grabbed a beer bottle from a nearby table. "You know that's my bum knee." He drew back the bottle to hit her with it.

She ducked, and it slammed into Tag's chiseled jaw. Tag had always considered himself a lover, not a fighter, but there was something about blood flowing that brought out the anger. Then he saw that his best cowboy hat was now ruined with splatter. He popped up on his feet, but the bouncer had brought out an equalizer in the form of a Taser, and the big man was already jerking around on the floor.

"You've killed my husband. He's got a bad heart," Scarlett screamed. "I'll sue the whole damn lot of you. Call an ambulance. He's got to go to the hospital."

Tag could see that the bartender was already on the phone. He picked up his hat, settled it on his head, and slipped out of the bar before anyone could rope him into testifying or giving his story.

"Glad I didn't drive my motorcycle tonight," he grumbled as he got into a black truck with two bumper stickers on the back fender. One said, ONCE A REBEL, ALWAYS A

REBEL. The other was the title of McGraw's country song, LIVE LIKE YOU WERE DYING.

He removed his plaid shirt and held pressure on the cut with one hand while he started the truck engine with the other. The hospital emergency room was the first place he'd checked out when he moved to Montague County the previous month. That information was pretty damned important when he lived by what was written on those two bumper stickers.

He wasn't too concerned when the blood seeped through his fingertips and dripped onto his snowy white T-shirt. They'd stitch him up or hopefully throw some super glue and bandages on it, and it would heal up without too much of a scar.

The only parking place he could find was all the way across the lot. By the time he walked across the pavement in the heat, he was getting more than a little woozy. The walls of the empty emergency room did a couple of wavy spins when he passed through the double doors. A nurse looked up from the desk and yelled something, but it sounded like it was coming through a barrel full of water.

Then suddenly someone shoved him into a wheelchair and wheeled him into a cubicle, helped him up onto a narrow bed, and flashed a bright light above his head. He expected to see his whole life flash before his eyes any minute, but instead Nikki Grady, his sister's best friend, took the shirt from his hand.

"Want me to call Emily?" she asked.

"Hell, no! Call Hud. His number is on the speed dial on my phone. It's in my hip pocket," he muttered.

"What happened?" she asked. "Looks like you were the only one at a knife fight without a knife. Was the lady worth it?"

"Beer bottle, and she wasn't a lady." Tag tried to grin but it hurt like hell. "Just glue me up. Give it a kiss to help it heal and call Hud to come get me."

"Honey, with this much blood loss and the fact that I'm lookin' at your jaw bone, it's goin' to take more than glue and a kiss," Nikki said.

*　　*　　*

Taggart, or Tag as the family called him, was one of those men who turned every woman's eye when he walked into a place—even an emergency room in a hospital. The nurses, old and young alike, were buzzing about him before Nikki even got him into the cubicle. With that chiseled face, those piercing blue eyes, a cowboy swagger and a smile that would make a religious woman want to drink whiskey and two-step, it's a wonder he hadn't already put one of those "take a number and wait" machines on the front porch post of his house.

"The doctor is on his way. He just finished stitchin' up a patient with a knife wound. From the looks of you, I thought you might have been in on that fight." Nikki applied pressure to the wound with a wad of gauze.

"What have we got here? I'm Dr. Richards." The white coated guy introduced himself as he gently lifted the edge of the gauze. "Knife?"

"Beer bottle," Tag said.

"Well, the first thing we're going to have to do is shave off that scruff. Deaden it up and then shave off the area around it, Nikki. I'll take care of the kid with a bean up his nose and be right back," Dr. Richards said.

"Yes, sir." Nikki nodded.

The doctor had been instrumental in getting Nikki her

first job as a registered nurse, and she really admired him. An older man with a white rim around an otherwise bald head covered in freckles, he was the best when it came to stitches. Tag was a lucky cowboy that Dr. Richards was on call. It could have been an intern doing the embroidery on his face, and it would be such a shame to leave a scar on something that sexy.

"You still going to go out with me even though I'm clean shaven and got a scar?" Tag asked Nikki as she prepared to shave part of his face.

"If I don't work, I don't eat, and I'm real fond of cheeseburgers," she answered.

"What's that supposed to mean?" He winced when she picked up a needle to start the deadening.

"That I don't have time to take a number and wait in line behind all those other women wanting to get a chance at taming you," she answered.

He wrapped his hand around her wrist before she started. "I'd move you to the front of the line, darlin'."

"Well, ain't that sweet." She patted his hand and ignored the heat between them. "But honey, you're way too fast for this little country girl. Now, be still and let me get you ready for Dr. Richards."

Without blinking, he focused on her face as she sank the needle into several places to deaden the two-inch cut. Whispers of other conversations penetrated the curtains on either side of Tag's cubicle, but heavy silence filled the space as Nikki put in the last shot.

"That all," he finally asked, his piercing blue eyes never leaving her face.

"Except for cleaning up around it," she answered. "And you were a good boy. I'll tell Dr. Richards to give you a lollipop before you leave."

"It ain't my first rodeo," he said. "Did you call Hud?"

"Not yet," she said.

"Then don't."

"With the amount of blood you've lost plus the shot Doc will probably give you for pain, you'll need a driver or you won't be released," she said. "So it's Hud or Emily. Take your choice."

"You're a hard woman, Nikki," he said.

"And you're a hard-headed man," she shot back as she carefully shaved the scruff from his face.

"We ready to fix this cowboy up?" Dr. Richards threw back a curtain. "What'd the other guy look like?"

"Not a scratch on him, but he was limpin'. His woman tried to kick his kneecap out the door," Tag answered as Nikki picked up his phone to call Hud.

Dr. Richards chuckled. "And I bet you were defendin' her in some way."

Tag grimaced when he tried to smile. "Just helpin' out the bouncer a little. Seemed like the thing to do since she bought me a drink."

"Good job there, Nikki. Now it's my turn," Dr. Richards said. "We could try glue and strips but as deep as this is, stitches will do a better job. I'll expect you back in my office in a week for a checkup. Might take them out then or might wait another few days. Depends on how well you're healing."

"Yes, sir," Tag answered.

"It's up to you whether you shave your face clean when you get home, but if you don't, you're going to look a little like a mangy dog."

"Looked worse before," Tag drawled. "And probably will again."

Another nurse in pink scrubs poked her head between the

curtains. "Sue Ann just arrived. You do better with her than any of us, Nikki. Would you mind?"

"Go on," Dr. Richards said. "I've got this."

Once they made their way into the hall, Rosemary laid one hand over her heart and fanned her face with the other one. "Lord have mercy. That cowboy could melt my panties with those blue eyes."

"Sue Ann strung out or drunk?" Nikki ignored what Rosemary said.

"Maybe both. Did I hear you turn that man down when he asked you for a date? Are you bat-crap crazy?" Rosemary said.

"You are married and have four kids," Nikki said.

"And I'm on a diet, too, but that don't mean I can't stare in the window at the candy store." Rosemary laughed. "Oh, there's another good-lookin' cowboy out in the waiting room who says he's here for Tag. Want me to let him come on back?"

"I'll get him if you'll keep Sue Ann pacified for another minute." Nikki made a quick right turn.

Tag's twin brother, Hudson, stood up when he saw her. "How bad is it this time?"

She motioned for him to follow her. "Stitches on his jaw. The cut was deep. Doc's takin' care of him right now."

From the first time she met the brothers, Nikki had had no trouble seeing that they shared DNA. The cleft in Tag's chin was more pronounced, and he wore his hair longer than Hud did, but those crystal-clear blue eyes were the same. Even with their similarities, there were enough differences that she could hardly believe that they were twins. However, the joke was pretty true that it took two personalities to make one when it came to twins. Tag was the wild and crazy twin. Hud was the more grounded brother with a funny streak and a big heart.

"Right here." Nikki eased the curtain back to Tag's cubicle.

"What'd you do now?" Hud asked.

"Had a little run-in with a beer bottle," Tag answered.

Nikki hurried away to take care of Sue Ann, their regular weekend patient in the Bowie emergency room. Some folks were happy drunks, but not Sue Ann. When she had too much liquor or snorted too much white stuff up her nose, she became the poster child for hypochondria.

"Oh, Nikki, darlin'," Sue Ann slurred her words. "Just take me on into surgery and take out my stomach. It's got an alien in it that's trying to eat its way out through my belly button."

"I need a list of all your medicine, whatever you've taken in the way of alcohol or drugs in the past twelve hours—no, make that twenty-four hours—before we can do that, honey." Nikki pulled a pen from the pocket of her scrubs and was ready to write before she realized she didn't have her tablet. "You think about what you've had, Sue Ann. Things are hectic here tonight. I'll be right back."

"All done," Dr. Richards said as Nikki slipped inside Tag's cubicle to get her tablet. "You see to it that you call my office tomorrow and make an appointment for next Friday so I can check this. If you start running a fever, call me. I think Nikki did a good job of cleaning it up, but one never knows when it comes to bar floors and beer bottles."

"I'm riding a bull on Friday night at a rodeo," Tag said.

"We'll see about that." Doc turned to Hud. "See to it your brother behaves this week."

"That's an impossible job." Hud grinned.

"Then I'll admit him for a week. We've got restraints that

we can use to keep him in the bed, and the nurses will love taking care of his catheter." Doc winked at Hud.

"I'll be good," Tag growled. "But I don't have to like it."

"Nope, you don't," Doc said and turned his attention to Nikki. "You need me with Sue Ann or can you take care of it, Nikki?"

"I'll call if I need you." She picked up her tablet. When she reached Sue Ann's cubicle, the woman was sitting up in the bed. She was as pale as the sheet she tucked around her thin body. One hand was over her mouth and the other was pointing toward the bathroom. Nikki dropped her tablet on the table and barely got a disposable bag to Sue Ann in time.

When she finished, Sue Ann handed it to Nikki and said, "I had a little drop of tequila at the Rusty Spur tonight."

"How big of a drop?" Nikki picked up her tablet and stylus pen. "Tell me the truth. If we have to do surgery, it'll make a difference in how much anesthetic we give you. You wouldn't want to wake up before we got done, would you?"

"Five shots. No, six, and then maybe four," she lowered her voice to a whisper, "of those pills."

"What pills?" Nikki asked.

"The ones I bought from that cowboy who was dancin' with the pretty girl. That damned alien got in my stomach. They told me it was just the worm in the bottle of tequila when I drank it with a little lime and salt, but I know better. It looked like a baby alien, and I just swallowed it whole. Then my stomach started to burn and hurt. I saw that cowboy passing some pills to a lady, so I knew ... " She shrugged.

Nikki had thought she'd seen and heard everything when she worked at the nursing home in town, but this would be a story she'd have to share with her best friend, Emily. "Okay, then several shots of tequila and four pills of some kind. I think we can kill the alien and fix you right up without surgery."

Sue Ann fell back on the bed with a sigh. "I don't know about that. Don't you need to do one of them TSA things?"

Nikki bit back the giggle. "You mean an MRI?"

"That, too. Do all the tests you need to. I want this thing out of me." Sue Ann put a hand on her stomach.

"I'll talk to the doctor and be right back. Are you still taking..." Nikki read off a whole page of prescription drugs. "You do realize that you're not supposed to drink with about half of these or take unprescribed pain meds with them?"

"I know my body better than you do," Sue Ann declared. "My grandma drank every day of her life and she lived to be ninety-eight."

"Yes, ma'am," Nikki said. "I'll go talk to the doctor and be right back."

She stepped out of the cubicle, tablet in hand this time, and stopped so fast that her rubber-soled shoes squeaked on the tile floor. One more step and she would have collided with Tag.

"It's just not my night." He smiled down at her. "I get in trouble for taking up for a woman, and now one almost falls into my arms, but doesn't."

"It might be a sign that you need to peel those stickers off your truck and begin to reform a little," Nikki told him.

"Never." Tag grinned.

About the Author

Carolyn Brown is a *New York Times*, *USA Today, Wall Street Journal* and *Publisher's Weekly* best-selling romance author and RITA® Finalist who has sold more than four million books. She presently writes both women's fiction and cowboy romance. She has also written historical single title, historical series, contemporary single title, and contemporary series. She lives in southern Oklahoma with her husband, a former English teacher who is the author of nine mystery novels. They have three children and enough grandchildren to keep them young. For a complete listing of her books (series in order) and to sign up for her newsletter, check out her website at www.carolynbrownbooks.com or catch her on Facebook/CarolynBrownBooks.

Second Chance Cowboy

A Crossroads Ranch Novel

A.J. Pine

The night Ava Ellis let Jack Everett go, her heart was breaking. She was young and scared—and secretly pregnant with Jack's baby. Now, ten years later, the sexy cowboy is back and Ava finally has an opportunity to right the wrongs of the past. But how will he feel about the son he's never known? Could this be their second chance—or their final heartbreak?

FOREVER

New York Boston

PRAISE FOR A.J. PINE

"A fabulous storyteller who will keep you turning pages and wishing for just one more chapter at the end."
    —Carolyn Brown, *New York Times* best-selling author

"Cross my heart, this sexy, sweet romance gives a cowboy-at-heart lawyer a second chance at first love and readers a fantastic ride."
    —Jennifer Ryan, *New York Times* best-selling author, on *Second Chance Cowboy*

"This is a strong read with a heartwarming message and inspiring characters."
    —RT Book Reviews on *Second Chance Cowboy*

Second
Chance
Cowboy

ACKNOWLEDGMENTS

Thank you, first and foremost, to you—the reader. To those of you who followed me from my romantic comedies to my foray into the wonderful world of cowboys, I'm so grateful for your continued support. And welcome, new readers. I've got two more sexy stories coming your way for Luke and Walker!

A huge thanks to my fabulous editor, Madeleine, for your excellent guidance on Jack and Ava's story. Can't wait to work on Luke next.

Thank you, Courtney, for finding the Everett brothers a great home.

To my wonderful critique partners and friends—Lia Riley, Chanel Cleeton, Jennifer Blackwood, Megan Erickson, and Natalie Blitt—I love you all to pieces. Your friendship and support are everything—as are our daily conversations that usually leave me laughing until I'm crying.

Jennifer Ryan, I cannot thank you enough not only for reading and giving Jack and Ava your stamp of approval but for being a fabulous friend and mentor. You are truly the best.

Thank you, S and C, for being the best fans even though you're not old enough to read my books yet. I love you to infinity.

PROLOGUE

Ten Years Ago

Ava snaked her fingers through Jack's and squeezed.

"Come on," she said. "It's going to be fun."

His head fell back against the seat as he put the truck in park. Parties weren't his thing, especially here. He'd only been at Los Olivos High School for five months, so celebrating graduation as the odd man out wasn't exactly top on his list.

But it was top on Ava's list, and there was nothing he wouldn't do for the girl who'd made those months bearable.

No. That wasn't fair. Time with Ava was more than bearable. It was everything that got him out of bed in the morning and kept him from cutting class when he would have been fine taking the GED, even if it meant losing his baseball scholarship. It's how he endured not being able to play his senior year. And it was the reason that maybe— after college and getting some distance from this place— he'd be able to come back and see it differently.

"I love you," she said softly, her pale cheeks turning pink as she leaned across the center console and kissed the corner of his mouth.

He blew out a breath and skimmed his fingers through her thick, auburn waves.

"And I know you're leaving soon for summer training, but I think we should tell my parents about us. Unless—I mean if this *is* only a senior year thing."

He tugged her closer, his palm cradling the back of her neck as he brushed his lips over hers. "You're it for me, Red," he whispered against her. "But I thought they were still getting over you and Golden Boy breaking up."

She groaned. "I know you know Derek's name."

The corner of his mouth quirked into a crooked grin. "Doesn't mean I have to say it."

"You wanted to wait, remember?" she reminded him. "Because my dad is way overprotective."

Jack laughed, the sound bitter, and his smile faded. "And thinks I'm gonna be like *my* father. I got it then, and I get it now."

It didn't matter that Los Olivos was an hour away from Oak Bluff, Jack's hometown. News traveled fast when three new students transferred into a school second semester. And a drunk almost killing his oldest son was the best sort of gossip for a small California wine country town.

It wasn't as if he didn't have the same fears. The apple usually didn't fall too far from the tree.

He hadn't planned on anything more in Los Olivos than biding his time and getting the hell out of town when summer came.

He hadn't planned on *her*. So when he'd suggested they keep the relationship quiet—that he didn't want to make waves in her seemingly perfect life—she hadn't argued.

She cupped his cheeks in her palms and tilted his forehead to hers. "He doesn't *know* you. Plus I'm not good at secrets. Or lying. As soon as he sees how amazing you are, he'll know there's nothing to worry about."

He closed his eyes as she kissed him. Maybe this could

be him now, the guy a girl brought home to her parents instead of the one people whispered about when they thought he couldn't hear.

"I love you, too," he finally said. "In case you didn't know."

He felt her lips part into a smile against his.

"Oh, I know," she teased. "But I like to hear you say it."

Both of them startled at the sound of the passenger side window rattling.

"Party's out back!" someone yelled as another graduate drummed against the glass again.

Ava giggled. "One hour," she said. "If it sucks after an hour, then we leave. Promise."

He pressed a soft kiss against her neck and she shivered.

"Anything for you, Red."

He leaned across her and opened her door. Then he hopped out of his own and met her at the passenger side.

Maybe this was what it had been like for his parents before it all went to hell—when his mom was alive and his dad sober. He couldn't remember anymore. The past five years couldn't be erased, but maybe whatever the future held could cushion the blow.

Ava swayed when her feet hit the ground outside the truck, and Jack caught her by the elbow.

"Hey there," he said. "You okay?"

She forced a smile even as her stomach roiled.

"Yeah," she said. "I'm fine. It's just so hot out tonight." Thankfully, that was the truth—even if it wasn't *her* truth. "I need to splash some cool water on my face. That's all. Head out to the bonfire, and I'll be right back."

He hesitated, but she needed to get inside—quick.

"Go." She nudged his shoulder. "I'll meet you out back."

"I'll come with you," he said insistently, and she could see the worry in those blue eyes.

"Ava!"

They both turned to where a group of girls were coming up the street toward Jack's truck, her friend Rachel heading up the pack.

"Ohmygod," Rachel said in one breath. "Please tell me you know where the bathroom is and that you can get me there safely."

Saved by the drunk friend.

"See?" Ava said to Jack, grabbing Rachel's hand. "I'm not alone. See you in five minutes."

He ran a hand through his overgrown blond waves, then kissed her on the cheek.

"Five minutes," he relented. "You're sure you're okay?"

She nodded, afraid if she opened her mouth again her lie would be exposed. Instead she and Rachel ran for the front door of the house up the drive.

Once in the bathroom, she dropped to her knees in front of the toilet and emptied her stomach.

"Damn," Rachel said. "I thought *we* prepartied too much."

But Ava hadn't had one drink that night. And this was the fourth time this had happened in the span of a week.

She grabbed a wad of toilet paper and wiped her mouth, then flushed and turned toward the sink.

"Yeah," she said absently. "Too much prepartying." She cupped cold water in her palms and drank, then thankfully found a tube of toothpaste in the medicine cabinet. "I'll see you out there."

She slipped out of the bathroom and into the small hallway off the foyer, heart hammering in her chest.

She pressed a palm against her flat belly. She would

have to take a test to confirm, but she was already over a week late. It looked like she had something to tell Jack before they broke the news to her parents that they were dating.

"There you are," a voice crooned from the end of the hall.

Ava rolled her eyes. "Not now, Derek," she said, attempting to push past him as he came nearer. Instead he backed her into the corner where the wall met the doorframe to the guest bedroom.

"Not funny," she said, trying to slip out from where his arm palmed the wall above her shoulder.

"I miss you," he said, his breath tinged with the scent of liquor.

"You're drunk. You always miss me when you're drunk."

His free hand cupped her breast and she swatted it away. "What the hell do you think you're doing?"

But he wasn't deterred. This time he pressed the length of his body against hers. "Come on, babe. I know how much you like taking in strays, but enough is enough. Two years, and you never gave it up for me, but you give it up for that trash from Oak Bluff?"

He ground against her pelvis, pressed his fingers hard against the base of her throat. He was too close for her to knee him in the balls—too big to push away.

"Stop it, Derek."

Golden Boy. Right. Nothing could be further from the truth.

She pushed her palms into his chest, but he wouldn't budge. It only made his weight against her feel heavier, his fingertips on her skin pressing harder.

Over his shoulder she saw Rachel step out of the bathroom. The girl caught Ava's eye and grinned, then pressed her fingers to her lips in a promise to keep quiet as she started backing away. After all, Ava and Derek Wilkes had been the couple most likely to—well—*everything* just before the holidays. Until she wouldn't give him what he wanted for Christmas. To Rachel this probably looked like reconciliation.

"Rach—" she started, but Derek shut her up by pressing his lips to hers.

This wasn't happening. Except it was. So she bit down on his lip.

"Shit!" he growled, backing away and swiping the back of his hand across his mouth, his skin smeared with blood. "You little—"

He reached for her again, but his hand never made contact. In a blur, someone slammed Derek up against the adjacent wall.

"She said *stop*, asshole."

Jack was seething, something dark and dangerous in his eyes.

"Thanks for breaking her in for me," Derek said with a sneer. "But I think I can take it from here."

Jack slammed him against the wall again.

Derek laughed.

Ava yelped, and Jack's eyes met hers.

"I'm okay," she said. "Let's just go."

But then his gaze dipped to her collarbone. She ran her fingers over the skin, wincing when she felt the beginnings of bruises.

That was all it took for Jack to lose his focus—and for Derek to throw the first punch.

Ava watched in slow motion as Jack's head snapped to the side and blood trickled from the corner of his mouth.

And then before she knew it, Derek's head crashed into the wall as Jack's fist collided with his face again and again until blood poured from Derek's nose and a group of guys Ava hadn't seen arrive were pulling Jack from his limp human punching bag.

She hadn't even known she was screaming until the commotion settled and one of the guys let go of Jack to keep Derek—now unconscious—from crashing to the floor.

Jack stared down at his bloodied knuckles, then up at her, his eyes wide with horror.

"I'm *him*," he said softly—like he hadn't meant anyone else to hear but himself—as sirens wailed in the distance.

CHAPTER ONE

Jack glanced down at his rumpled shirt, then ran a hand through his perpetually overgrown hair. Despite a sleepless night, he had somehow made the five-plus hour drive from San Diego to the outskirts of San Luis Obispo County— and the blip on the map that was Oak Bluff—without killing himself. A shit night of sleep was the norm. Spending the entire morning on the 101 with only the two cups of coffee he'd bought on his way out of town and thoughts he'd rather not have the time to *think*? That was another story. A man alone with his thoughts for too long was a danger- ous combination. It was one of the reasons he rarely came home. Another one of those reasons was about to make his way six feet underground.

His vision blurred, and he shook his head, swerving to avoid a blown-out tire in the middle of the road right before the entrance to the cemetery. The coffee wasn't exactly do- ing its job.

He let out a bitter laugh as his truck rolled to a stop on the narrow lane along the gravesites. "Would you have appreciated the irony?" he asked aloud. His voice was deep and hoarse after the hours of silence, hands white- knuckled on the steering wheel of his now-parked truck.

"Me kicking the goddamn bucket the day I come to see you laid to rest?"

No one answered, of course. He glanced at the cattleman hat on the passenger seat, still not sure why he'd kept it all these years in San Diego, or why he'd felt the need to bring it with him for the drive back. As soon as he made sure Luke and Walker—and even his aunt Jenna—were taken care of, he had another life to get back to.

Because *home* wasn't here anymore. Hadn't been for years. He wasn't sure any place fit that definition these days, but it sure as hell wasn't the small, ranching town of Oak Bluff. Boxed in amongst vineyards and only miles from the ocean, tourists who wanted a quaint, off-the-beaten-path segue from wine country kept the place on the map. But Jack hadn't taken *that* segue in a decade. Until now.

He hopped out of his truck and grabbed his suit jacket from its hanger in the back of the cab and the fresh bouquet of flowers from the floor. In the distance he could see the distinct figures of his younger brothers, his aunt, and a fourth body—most likely some funeral officiant—standing at the grave.

That was it. The four of them and a stranger to preside over the burial of a man he wasn't sure deserved even that much. Yet here he was.

As he approached, his aunt Jenna was the first to look up. Not even ten years his senior, she'd always felt more like a sister, and a pang of unexpected longing for the family he'd left behind socked him square in the gut. It had been over a year since he'd seen her—since he'd seen any of them. God, she looked more like his mother now than ever, her short blond hair having grown to her shoulders since the last time they'd met. At thirty-six, Jenna, the baby sister, had now seen more years than his mother ever would.

He stopped at the grave next to his father's and knelt down, laying the small arrangement of white and purple orchids on the grass in front of the headstone that read CLARE OWENS-EVERETT, BELOVED WIFE, MOTHER, SISTER, AND DAUGHTER.

"Hey, Ma," he said softly. "Still miss you. Brought you your favorite."

"Has it really been fifteen years?"

He heard Jenna behind him, the lilt of her Texas twang that never left, much like his mother's—but he lingered several more seconds with the orchids and his memories. He silently wished for his mom to send him some sort of sign that she was at peace. Had she known what happened to her husband after he lost her? What he'd become and what he'd done to her boys?

"I tried," he said under his breath, not wanting Jenna to hear. "I tried to fix him. But he didn't want to be fixed."

He stood then, towering over the woman who'd taken them in when she was barely done being a kid herself.

"You're huge," she said as he pulled her into a hug. "Were you always this tall?" He laughed, and she pushed far enough away to rest her palms on his lapels. "Look at you, Jack. Christ on a cracker, you're all grown up. You bring home any of your fancy lawyer friends for your aunt? Maybe on the other side of thirty, though."

She winked at him. Still the same Jenna.

"Not this trip," he mused. "Maybe next time."

She hooked her arm through his and pulled him the last several feet to their destination, where his father's casket sat suspended over the rectangular hole in the ground.

"Nice suit," Walker sneered. Jack could barely see his

brother's eyes under the brim of his hat, but he knew they were narrowed.

"Aren't you supposed to remove your hat to show respect for the dead?" he countered.

Jack thought he heard his youngest brother growl.

"Is that what that getup is?" Walker asked, taking a step closer. Jack was sure he smelled liquor on his brother's breath and decided to let any sort of comment about drinking before noon slide. He'd give him a free pass for today. "A sign of *respect*?" Walker continued. "Since when do you respect the man who almost killed you? And since when do you have a say? This ain't your home anymore, pretty boy."

Jenna gasped.

The funeral officiant cleared his throat.

Luke, taking his role as middle brother literally, stepped between the other two men, removing his own hat and holding it against his chest.

"All right, boys. Let's save this twisted pissing contest until later and shove our dicks back in our pants. Shall we?"

Jack caught sight of the laceration across Luke's cheek, the few stitches holding it together. "What the hell is that?" he asked.

"Here we go," Walker said, turning away. He'd either lost interest in pushing Jack's buttons or was happy to let the attention fall on Luke.

"Tried my first bull," Luke said with an easy grin. "He didn't like me much."

"You're riding bulls now? I thought this rodeo stuff was a hobby. When the hell are you gonna take life seriously?"

Luke's ever-present smile fell. "You mean like running the ranch *you* left? Hell, I know you send money, Jack. Helping in your own way. But I take life plenty seriously when I need to. When there isn't need, I think I'm entitled to a little fun."

Jack spun to Jenna, who had conveniently backed away from the conversation. "You knew about this?"

She shrugged. "Y'all are big, grown men now. You can make your own decisions." Then she laughed. "Though I hate to see him mess up that pretty face of his."

Luke threw his hat back on his head. "If it's any consolation, Jenna, the ladies do *not* complain."

His aunt shook her head and squeezed her eyes shut. "Sometimes I think it was easier when you were teenagers."

Jack gritted his teeth and fisted his hands at his sides. It didn't matter how long he'd been gone. After their mother died, their father had been far from a model parent. Jack had practically raised his brothers himself through their teen years, but he wasn't going to lecture Luke, not now. Instead all he muttered was "It's dangerous."

Luke threw an arm over his big brother's shoulder. "It's *fun*, asshole. Thought by now you'd have figured out what that word meant."

Again, the sound of a throat clearing interrupted their reunion, and all four of them looked up to find the funeral officiant, a small man with a gray comb-over in a suit one size too big, fidgeting as he stood at the head of the grave.

"Sorry, folks," he said. "But I have another service in an hour. I don't want to rush you, but—"

"Good," Walker said, joining the fray again. "Let's get this over with."

The officiant swallowed. "Does anyone have something they'd like to say about Mr. Everett before interment?"

Jack's stomach twisted. He wouldn't speak ill of the dead, but he sure as hell wouldn't say anything of import for the man who only knew how to speak with the back of his hand. He remembered standing here for his mom's burial, the space crowded with family and friends—their local pastor leading the small ceremony. Jack had been thirteen, Luke twelve, and Walker ten. They'd watched the cancer *and* treatment ravage her body for a year. That was all they'd had from diagnosis until the end. When they'd lowered her into the ground, tears had streamed down both his brothers' cheeks, but Jack decided then and there he had to be strong—for his brothers and his father. It hadn't taken him long to realize he'd failed at the latter, but as for Luke and Walker, he was still trying, even if they ended up hating him for it.

"If no one says anything," Jack finally said, "does that mean it's over?"

The man raised his shoulders. "I work for the funeral home, so this is not a religious ceremony," he said. "Usually the way it works is a family member or friend reads something. Or—or gives *me* something to read. If you have something prepared—"

Jack shook his head and looked at his brothers, who both studied their boots.

"Well, then..." The officiant wrung his hands. "If no one has any words..."

"I do!" Jenna said, a little too loudly for the small gathering. "I mean, someone should say something, and if y'all don't want to, that's okay. But—but someone *should*."

She strode up to the head of the grave, and the man stepped aside. In her floral dress and cardigan, she really did look like their mother. Jack was so used to Jenna in a tank top and denim shorts—rain boots up to her knees as she stepped inside her chicken coop or chased rabbits from her garden. If this was a new look for her, it would take some getting used to.

She squared her shoulders, and the Everett boys all gave her their attention.

"Hi," she said. "Um, yeah. Okay." She took in a long breath and blew it out. "Jackson Everett Senior was my brother-in-law and the love of my big sister's life. When we moved here from Houston, I was a scrappy seven-year-old who knew nothing more about love other than crying when our baby chick died. We lost our daddy when I was too young to remember him, and though I loved our mama— like I said, I was all about the chickens when we came here."

She swiped at a tear under her eye, and Jack thought he should go to her, hold her hand or something. But the thought of standing there while she paid her respects to a man he'd lost all faith in years ago only made him clench his teeth harder, so he dug his heels into the soft ground and decided to stay put.

"When Clare, my sister, came home from her first day at her new high school, she told me she had met the boy she was going to marry, and when Clare Owens said something, it was the truth. Always. When she and Jackson were only eighteen and got pregnant with you, Jack?" Her eyes glistened when she looked at him. "Well, he practically married her on the spot. His dreams were always your mama and Crossroads Ranch. You boys were his legacy—the second generation of Everetts on that piece of land." She took a breath, the tremor in it audible amidst the silence. "They built the place up with the little savings they both had, filled the house with boys born to be ranchers, but—" Another pause as Jenna seemed to relive the loss of her sister—their mother.

Jack noticed Walker was holding his hat at his side now. Bitter as he was toward Jack Senior, his baby brother would never disrespect his mother, no matter how many years she'd been gone.

Jenna choked on a sob. "He broke when he lost Clare. We *all* did. I know that. But something in your daddy broke real deep. And I'm so sorry I didn't know—" A hiccupping breath stole her words. "I'm so sorry—"

Jack was at her side now, his arm around his aunt. No way in hell was he going to let her fall down the rabbit hole of guilt. He'd spent enough time there to know it wouldn't do her an ounce of good.

"Jenna, don't," he said as he led her from the grave. "You didn't know," he added. "No one knew."

He'd made sure of that. Because despite the verbal attacks—and the physical ones—Jack Senior was all he'd thought they had. He'd cut his boys off from any other family. Jack had always believed he could wait it out until he was eighteen. Because what was the alternative? Report his father and risk him and his brothers getting separated in the foster system?

Instead Luke and Walker had almost lost him completely.

She wrapped her arms around him and buried her head in his chest.

"I'm sorry," she said again.

All he could do was whisper "shhh." She might have been eight years his senior, but she felt like a child in his arms, clinging to him to keep steady.

He knew her tears weren't for his father. And as much as Jenna missed her sister, the choking sobs weren't for her, either. They were for what Jackson Everett Sr. had hidden from everyone for five years—until that 911 call and the last words his father ever spoke in his presence:

Help. I think I killed my boy.

* * *

Ava Ellis stood in the open doorway of the empty bedroom—empty but for the countless portraits lining the floor—the ones filled with still lifes of fruit or images of the dog in various states of play—and the easel in the corner, the one holding the blank canvas waiting for another attempt at the one thing she still hadn't captured. She could make a million and one excuses not to walk in there.

I should really catch up on laundry.

I haven't put in enough hours at the vineyard this week.

It's almost noon. I should start prepping dinner.

It's Saturday. It would make more sense to try again on Monday.

Ah, yes. That last excuse was her favorite. Everything seemed possible on a Monday—until Monday actually came around and the week got away from her again.

The sun peeked through the curtains, dappled light and shadow cutting across the blank canvas—the silhouette of the olive tree outside the window.

"Don't tease me, tree," she warned before huffing out a breath and reaching behind her neck to tie her auburn mane into a loose bun. "I'm just—*preparing*." She laughed quietly. "Preparing and talking to a tree."

She'd been intending to paint it since she'd moved into the house several years ago. The hulking yet beautiful tree had been what drew her to the property in the first place, a reminder of something she'd lost and was still trying to find.

She pulled the small case of charcoals from the back pocket of her jeans.

"It's only drawing," she said to no one in particular as she crossed the threshold into the room. She certainly wasn't still talking to a tree, trying to trick it into acquiescence. "We're not ready to paint, yet." *We're*. Shit. She *was* still talking to the tree. "Fine," she added. "If we're going to be spending the weekend together, I guess we both better get used to the talking. I don't do quiet."

Yet here she was, in her quaint split-level, alone in what many would consider blissful silence compared to the whirlwind that was her life, and she was ready to go mad.

She opened the case and set it on the table beside the easel, eyeing the different widths of the charcoal sticks before settling on a short, stubby one that fit comfortably between her thumb and fingers. She rolled it there for a minute, getting the feel for it as it smudged the ridges of her skin. And then, as if it was the most natural thing to do, she drew a leaf. One, simple, perfect, lonely leaf. It barely took a minute—barely took any space up on what now felt like a colossal piece of canvas.

"Shit," she said. "It's too goddamn quiet."

She dropped the charcoal onto the table, not bothering to fit it back into the case. What would be the point? She was coming back. Eventually. Another day or two meant nothing in the grand scheme of years—except that now she actually had a deadline. If she wanted to apply for late admission to Cal Poly's art program, she needed to produce a piece of meaningful art. Soon. *Still Life of Labrador Catching a Frisbee* wasn't exactly meaningful.

She *would* succeed. Just—not today.

Famous last words.

Barely touching the six steps to the lower level, she grabbed her sunglasses off the kitchen table, raced toward the back door and out to the shed. It was the weekend, after all, and the grass wasn't going to cut itself. And hell, she needed *noise*.

With the mower on, maybe she could ignore the stupid,

taunting tree. Maybe she could forget walking past the room with a wistful glance for the past six years, always aware of what lay beyond the curtained window. And maybe, if she kept at it, straight through to the front yard, she could convince herself that a tree—a freaking *tree*—had not been getting the best of her for each of those six years.

She yanked the starter on the mower, smelled the familiar odor of gasoline, and then there it was—noise.

But it didn't matter if she wouldn't admit it out loud, not when her own inner monologue refused to shut up.

The first place she'd seen him had been under an olive tree more than ten years ago, across the street from Los Olivos High School. She couldn't hear what he was saying but knew by the way the other two boys listened to him so intently that it must have been important. There was no mistaking that they were brothers; each boasted a similar mop of golden, California waves. But he was the oldest, patriarchal in his care for the younger ones. She could see it in the way he tousled the youngest one's hair even though the boy responded by slapping his big brother's hand away, in how he gave the other that all-knowing single nod of the head. All this while he balanced easily on his left leg, keeping his weight off the right, the one wrapped in plaster from the knee down.

That was where she'd first laid eyes on Jack Everett, and it was where, six months later, she'd broken both their hearts.

She pushed the mower across the lawn, her jaw clenched and heart seeming to constrict with each beat. Breaking up hadn't been her intent when she'd asked him to meet her there one late summer night, even after what had happened at the graduation party. She'd had other news to tell him.

But instead she'd told the boy she loved with all her heart that she didn't love him at all. Ava had *freed* him under that very same tree—and then she'd gone and bought a house with its doppelgänger looming in the backyard. She'd thought if she could paint it—draw it at least—that would mean she was over it. Over him finding happiness in a life that didn't include her. But she hadn't been able to finish a single attempt. Today's leaf was the furthest she'd gotten in months.

Ava knew the truth of that tree, why she'd wanted to be so close to it. Whether or not she'd ever gotten over her first love didn't matter when she couldn't forgive herself for what she'd done. *That* was why she was an artist who couldn't create anything more than a replica of fruit or the dog. It was the real reason she needed the tree. Because why let guilt eat you from the inside out when it could stare at you every day?

"Good question," she said aloud, over the roar of the mower. The tree didn't answer. Not that it ever did.

Then she bumped straight into said tree.

"Damn it!" She yelled as the handle jammed into her ribs. She turned the mower off and growled at the ugly beast of a plant. "Enough," she said, a small weight lifting with the word. *"Enough,"* she repeated, and her next breath came even easier. "I don't need your approval," she snapped at the tree, and for the first time she actually believed it.

There was plenty of meaning in her life. Maybe not the dog catching a Frisbee, but there was so much inspiration to draw from. She'd pick a new subject to paint, complete her application, and turn it in by the end of the month. *It's time to stand on my own two feet*, she thought. She'd given up her independence for her son, and she wouldn't trade the experience for what she'd thought was her carefully constructed life plan. But she didn't want to rely on her parents anymore for financial stability. She didn't want a job at the family vineyard. She wanted a career. A passion. Something just for her. And nothing—not even a tree—was going to get in the way of that.

CHAPTER TWO

Jack stood for several long seconds outside the modest two-story house, the living quarters of what was commercially known as Crossroads Ranch. The rich wood of the shingled siding had paled in some areas, so that now patches of weathered tan mottled against the dark brown looked like fading bruises. The wraparound porch was still intact, but he could tell on first glance it needed to be refinished and stained. He'd add that to his to-do list. He was sure that after they'd gone through Jack Senior's things there'd be repairs here and there to make, but he also knew Luke and Walker had kept an eye on the ranch, so he wasn't worried about having to stay too long. He'd need to check the stables and the herd, meet with the accountant to ensure they could continue paying the hired hands. All this, of course, following today's visit from his father's estate attorney.

It wasn't as if he'd forgotten the place and all the work it took to run it. That was why he sent money each month to help keep the place afloat—to make sure the mortgage got paid. Luke and Walker were plenty capable. They'd proved that well enough. But the money only did so much to ease the guilt of his absence—not from the ranch but from his brothers' lives. Now that Jack Senior was gone, he could be the positive physical presence he hadn't been all those years ago. At least until he up and left again.

"You gonna take a damn picture?" Walker asked as he strode past him and up the porch steps.

Luke approached next. "That's *asshole* speak for 'Come on in and grab a beer,'" he said with a grin.

"When you're ready," Jenna added, standing next to him now. "And maybe when you need a break, you can drive me home. Walker picked me up but..."

She trailed off, only confirming what he'd suspected when he'd smelled the liquor on his brother's breath. Walker would be in no shape to drive anyone anywhere in the immediate future.

"He's been pissed at me for a lot of years, hasn't he?" he asked. "I left. I own that."

But his brothers had understood. Hadn't they? He'd *had* to go. After what he'd done to Derek Wilkes, he was lucky the guy's family hadn't pressed charges. He'd only meant to be gone through college. But plans had changed, thanks to the fiery redhead he'd never quite forgotten.

Jenna lifted a hand to his shoulder, giving him a gentle squeeze. "Did you ever think that maybe it's not *you* he's pissed at?"

She didn't wait for him to answer but instead followed her other two nephews into the house.

He squinted at what used to be his home, trying to see what it had been prior to fifteen years ago, but the well of his memory came up dry. He knew there had been happiness behind those doors. There had been a family. But he couldn't picture it. The only thing he saw in his mind's eye now was Walker getting backhanded across the face—or a dazed Jack Senior at the top of the stairs, staring down at his oldest son's broken form. Losing their mother would have been enough to reshape their history. But instead it had been so much worse.

"You must be Jack Junior."

The voice came from behind him, which meant the man couldn't see him grit his teeth. He'd never truly escape the connection to his father, not when he was his namesake. And that one little thread that kept them bound also kept that tiny voice in his head questioning how alike they were other than a shared name. The loss of Jack's mother had sent Jack Senior over the edge. What would it take for him to do the same?

Jack spun to face the man.

"Mr. Miranda, I assume," Jack said, and held out his hand.

The guy didn't seem much older than he was, maybe early thirties. He wore a plaid shirt with the sleeves rolled to his elbows and dark jeans, and it finally hit Jack that although this man was a stranger to him, it was *he* who was the odd man out on the front lawn of his own childhood home.

"Please," he said as he shook Jack's hand. "Call me Thomas. And damn if you don't look just like him—or like I bet he looked before the drinking." Thomas ran a hand through his wavy, dark hair. "Damn it. That was out of line. I apologize."

Jack loosened his tie, feeling overdressed and misplaced. He shook his head. "No apology necessary, not when it's the truth."

Thomas gave him a nervous smile. "I don't normally do this on the weekends," he said. "But your aunt told me this was the only day she could be certain you'd all be in the same place at the same time. Do you mind if I come in?"

"Not at all," Jack said as he moved toward the porch steps.

Thomas followed closely behind, and the two of them—both strangers to this place now—entered a house Jack hadn't stepped foot in for ten years. Now it was simply a reminder of a father who'd lost himself in his grief and taken it out on his boys—of a past he'd been trying to outrun for a decade. Before today, he thought he'd gotten past what this place could do to him.

Now he wasn't so sure anymore.

"Grapes?" Walker asked, tipping back his third bottle of beer since they'd all sat down at the wooden table in the kitchen. It hadn't been there growing up, and Jack wondered what would have possessed Jack Senior to buy new furniture when all he'd ever seemed to spend his money on was whiskey. "He left us grapes?"

"A small vineyard," Thomas clarified. "He left you three equal shares in the ranch—which he mortgaged to buy the vineyard."

Walker scoffed, slamming his empty bottle down in front of him. "So—*grapes.*" His cheeks were flushed and his eyes a steely gray as he pushed back from the table and headed to the fridge, undoubtedly for another beer.

Yeah, after six hours in the car this morning, Jack knew he'd be driving his aunt the hour ride back to Los Olivos.

"We can sell it, though, right?" Luke asked. "I mean, Walker and I have enough on our hands working the ranch, and we don't know shit about wine."

Walker nodded as he opened the fridge. "Bet our big brother knows plenty, though. All those fancy restaurants he goes to on the bay in San Diego."

Christ. Was that really what they thought of him? It wasn't as if he'd fallen off the face of the earth in the past decade. He'd come back to Jenna's for at least half the Christmases he'd been gone, but it hadn't been easy, not when he knew Ava Ellis lived nearby and wanted nothing to do with him.

A weight pressed firm on his chest.

He hadn't run from *her*.

Shit. He had a goddamn useless piece of land to worry about. He couldn't afford to let his mind wander down that destructive path.

"Look, asshole," Jack said to Walker. "It's not like Oak Bluff is the ends of the earth. We may have our tiny pocket of cattle land here, but shit. You've experienced a restaurant once or twice before. We *are* smack-dab in the middle of wine country."

Walker opened his mouth to lob a comeback at him, but Jack ignored his brother and turned to Thomas. "Can we?" he asked. "Can we just turn around and sell it?"

Thomas blew out a breath. "That's where things get tricky."

Walker was back at the table now with the rest of his six-pack—and he wasn't offering to share.

"The vineyard's not thriving," Thomas continued. "Your neighbor—the one your father bought it from—let it go once he decided to sell. And, well, Jack Senior wasn't exactly in the best shape to get it going himself."

"How long's he had this thing?" Walker asked, popping the top off another bottle.

"Six months," Thomas said. "I know it's hard to believe, but he had his moments of lucidity. He knew he was sick and needed to get his affairs in order. I can assure you he couldn't have bought the vineyard without being sober, and the same goes for his will. I helped him finalize everything and—he knew what he was doing, boys."

Luke shook his head like he was trying to wrap his brain around it all. "Six months?" he asked. "Six months and he never said shit about it to us?"

Jack narrowed his eyes. "When would he have said something?" He knew his brothers had been keeping the ranch running, that Jack Senior was drunk and incoherent for most of his waking hours, but he hadn't suspected much in the way of interaction between his father and his brothers.

Luke blew out a breath. "We weren't going to say anything because we knew it'd piss you off, but c'mon, Jack. Jenna got us through the years we needed looking after when we were still minors, but after a while an hour drive twice a day gets to be too much. The days got longer. Jack Senior got sicker. It seemed like the right thing to do, moving back and all."

The right thing to do?

"Is this some sort of joke?" Jack pressed the heels of his hands into his eyes. "It didn't cross your mind to tell me you've been living with the man who lost his right to even speak to you before you turned eighteen?" He gritted his teeth and looked from brother, to brother, to aunt. "How long?" he asked. His pulse raced, and he recognized the feeling—the anticipation of the back of his father's hand or a fist to the ribs. The fight or flight as the wind was about to get knocked out of him. "How damned *long* have you been back?"

Tears pooled in Jenna's eyes as she waited for one of her nephews to answer. It was Walker who finally did.

"Two years," he said softly, for once with no hint of anger or resentment in his voice.

Two years? Christ.

"So you all flat-out lied to me about what's been going on around here?"

Luke shrugged. "You didn't ask, and we figured it wasn't something you'd want to know. Judging by your reaction, I'd say we were right."

Jack's jaw tightened, and he could feel his pulse throbbing in his neck.

"It's their *home*," Jenna added. "Their livelihood and their home. I never would have let them talk me into it if I thought they were in any danger, but look at them, Jack. Look at your brothers. They are strong, smart, grown men who knew what they were doing when they decided to come home." She opened her mouth to continue but must have thought better of it and said nothing more.

He knew what would have come next: that it was his home, too.

But it wasn't. Not anymore, no matter how much he missed the open land with nothing looking down on him but the sky above.

There had been physical distance between him and his brothers when he left, but it hadn't registered until now how far he'd really gone—how great the divide was between him and his only family.

"I'm going out for a ride," he said, pushing back from the table and standing, relieved that he'd changed into jeans and a thermal before beginning their little meeting. "Check out the herd—the grapes too. Leave whatever needs to be signed, Mr. Miranda. I'll drop it by your office later this week."

Thomas stood to shake his hand, and in seconds Jack was out the door and headed toward the stables. Just because he no longer lived on the ranch didn't mean he'd forgotten how to ride.

The horse whinnied when he threw open the stall door, but when her eyes met his, she steadied as if she'd been reacquainted with a long-lost friend. She made no protest as he saddled and readied her to leave.

"Hey, girl," he said, running a hand along her silky, caramel-colored coat. "Hey there, Cleo." And without another thought, he led her out of the stable, mounted the saddle, and took off for the hills.

They rode past the herd, which did little more than glance in his direction as he sped by until nothing but green pasture rolled out ahead of him, stopping only where he could see the hint of grapevines—rows and rows of them.

He steeled himself against the memory of a vintner's daughter, his last good memory of home—and also one of his most painful.

He breathed deep as he tapped his boots against the horse's flanks, urging her faster and farther toward the oak trees in the distance, welcoming the burn of the leather reins against the flesh of his palms.

This, he thought, *is the only part of the ranch that feels like home.*

CHAPTER THREE

Jack woke to the sound of a buzz saw in the kitchen. At least, that's what the noise *felt* like after however many shots he'd thrown back the night before. But when he managed to open one eye and peel his half-naked body from the leather couch, he realized—thank God—that what he'd heard was coffee beans grinding.

"You look like shit," Walker said as he leaned against the counter. Jack couldn't tell if that was his brother's norm or if he did it for balance. He guessed it was a little of both.

"You seen a mirror lately?" Jack asked. "What the hell was in that bottle last night, by the way?"

Shot glasses still lined the table. He vaguely remembered getting back from his ride and Jenna sitting him and his brothers down at the table with a takeout pizza and a direct order that they bond. Apparently bonding meant getting shitfaced and not remembering when or how he'd ended up on the couch.

"Where's Jenna?" he asked.

Walker squinted as if he was searching for the answer, but after a few seconds he shrugged. "She took your truck. Said something about buying feed for her chickens, which she'd planned on doing when she thought she was going to be home yesterday. Said you could run her home once you were awake and could see straight."

His brother leaned his forearms on the counter and dropped his head to rest as well.

"Because even the morning after *you* don't. That right?" How long would he be able to chalk Walker's drinking up to age and immaturity? He was twenty-five already. As much as he feared for his own hereditary instincts, it scared him more to see it in one of his brothers. But Walker wasn't one to talk, nor to listen or give a shit about what his big brother feared. The only way to get through to him was to use his own language.

Walker's head rose lazily, but there was serious intent in his steely gaze. The coffee finished brewing, and he poured himself a cup. "There's no sugar," he said.

"I'll take it black." Jack stumbled toward the kitchen wearing nothing but his jeans from last night. He scratched the back of his head, felt his hair standing out at strange angles as he opened the cabinet that still held the mugs. "Jesus," he said, pulling out the one with a collage of the three brothers when they were kids. *Before.* He remembered his father, in a drunken outburst, backhanding the mug off the counter. "The handle had broken off," he said, more to himself than to his brother. "Exploded into a bunch of pieces. I was there. I saw it."

But even as he inspected the mug, he knew he wasn't looking at a replica. He ran his finger over the handle, felt the slight ridges where the separated ceramic had been glued back together. But to look at it—you'd never know. Unless you knew.

"He fixed some of the things he broke," Walker said. And Jack heard in his brother's voice what neither of them would even think about saying. Because damn if the three of them weren't still just as broken as they had been when they were removed from their father's care and sent to live with Jenna.

"Who's hungry?"

Their aunt's question sing-songed through the front door as she burst into the house—all smiles and sunshine, a welcome interruption to wherever the conversation was veering between him and Walker. He never knew how she did it. Even when she'd been barely twenty-five, without parents of her own, and found herself the legal ward of three teenage boys, she'd rarely faltered.

The two men turned toward her, and Jack was sure he smelled...bacon.

Walker, suddenly steady on his feet after one sip of coffee, strode in her direction. "Bring on the grease," he said, and she held out a bag that was soaked through with it.

"There's a farmer's market midway between my place and yours. Turns out this guy—new to the area. He's opening a little diner out that direction soon, and he just so happens to be looking for an egg supplier."

Walker tore open the bag and pulled out one of three wrapped sandwiches. He moaned as his teeth sank into the first bite. "Damn. I love a good buttermilk biscuit," he said, his mouth full of food. "What the hell is a diner owner doing at a farmer's market?" he asked. "Not that I'm complaining," he added, pointing at her with what was left of his nearly demolished sandwich.

She shrugged. "He likes to buy fresh ingredients from the locals." She playfully batted her lashes. "Like me," she continued. "And he's trying to advertise his new place. So he rents a booth and sells samples of his upcoming menu."

Jack poured his coffee, only realizing after the fact that

he wished he'd switched mugs. He slid into a chair at the kitchen table and unwrapped his own sandwich.

"I don't remember this," he said, knocking on the table-top. "If Jack Senior had to mortgage the property for that damned vineyard, what the hell was he doing buying furniture?"

Jenna grinned and bounced her hip against Walker's. "*He* made it."

Walker coughed and looked away as Jack's eyes met his.

"You *made* the table?" Jack laughed, and Jenna narrowed her eyes at him. "Wait. You're serious?" Jack had never seen his younger brother show interest in anything besides women or booze. The weight that had been pressing on his chest since he'd entered the town limits got heavier. Apparently he'd missed more than he'd realized.

Walker's eyes remained focused on his sandwich as he shrugged. "I did an apprenticeship with one of the Callahan brothers. Ain't made anything worth its salt other than that table, though."

"It's good." Jack ran his hand along the wood grain. "Real good."

"Yeah, whatever," Walker said, filling his mouth with food again, effectively ending that little tidbit of brotherly bonding. And since he wasn't here to push, Jack let it slide.

"Where's Luke?" Jack asked, realizing they were one short. Then he finally tore into his biscuit and let out his own moan. "Christ, this is good."

Jenna rolled her eyes. "Luke's out riding bareback like a maniac, I assume for some rodeo coming up. And you're welcome, by the way."

Both men grunted out a *thanks* while they continued to eat. Jenna poured herself some coffee and then opened the fridge.

"Shit. Y'all don't even have milk. Tell me you know your way through a supermarket, Jackson, because I'm not sure this refrigerator ever gets fully stocked if I'm not stopping by with groceries."

She took a sip of her black coffee and grimaced. "Hell, Walker. I bet a spoon would stand up in this sludge."

Walker grunted. "Keeps the hair on my chest."

She set her mug down on the table and blew out a breath. "Yeah, well, I don't need or *want* any hair on mine, so I'll pass. I had a cup at the market, anyway. With a new friend. I don't really need a second."

Jack's eyes darted up to meet hers. "With the egg guy?"

She shrugged. "Maybe." Her cheeks flamed.

Both men stood in unison, their chairs skidding across the wood floor.

"What's this asshole's name?" Walker asked.

"What do you know about him other than he's opening some diner? Did you get the name of it? He's not coming to your place to pick up the eggs, is he?"

She burst out laughing. "Is that a euphemism? *Picking up eggs?*"

Jack crossed his arms and Walker popped the rest of his breakfast in his mouth, staring her down as he chewed.

"You," she said, pointing at Walker. "I appreciate the attempt at big-brotherly protection, but I got more than a decade on you. So, simmer down, cowboy."

Walker scowled.

Jack cleared his throat.

"And *you*," she said, turning her gaze to her oldest nephew. "Put on a damn shirt if you want me to take you seriously."

He glanced down at his bare torso and shrugged. "I can still big brother you without a shirt."

She scoffed. "I was already reading Judy Blume by the time you were born."

Walker's brows rose. "The sex one? Go, Jenna."

Now she groaned. "God. No, Walker. I was *eight*. And how do you even know about *Forever*?"

He shrugged. "There was this girl in high school I wanted to make out with. She wanted to read me Judy Blume. We compromised."

Jenna shook her head. "You're impossible. And I was talking about *Superfudge*."

"Is *that* a euphemism?" he added.

She backhanded him on the shoulder. "I don't even know what that would mean!" she cried.

Jack tried to bite back his laughter, but it was useless. Plus, this felt *good*, he and Walker giving Jenna shit about dating like they used to do when they were in high school. Their situation had never been a normal one, but they'd found their rhythm back then, and it felt like maybe they were finding it again now.

Jenna swiped the third sandwich from the table and then held up her hands in defeat. "I'm going to go check on Luke. Bring him his breakfast before you two animals devour it."

She spun on her heel and headed back toward the door.

"What's his name?" Jack called after her.

"Or do we call him *Egg Man*?" Walker added.

Using her free hand, she answered them with one finger.

"*Egg Man* it is!" Walker shouted before the screen door slammed behind her.

Jack lifted his coffee mug from the table and held it out toward his brother. "Well done," he said.

Walker gave him a sly grin and held up his own mug. "You're still an asshole."

Jack leaned back against the counter. "And you're still a dick." He sipped his coffee.

"They let you say shit like that in your fancy lawyer office?"

He laughed. "Is that what you think San Diego is? Look around you, brother. You grew up in the middle of *wine* country. You're one-third owner of a vineyard. You're so goddamn fancy, I'm finally feeling underdressed without a shirt."

"Screw you," Walker said, eyes peering over the top of his mug.

"Screw you right back." And with that he strode back to the couch to retrieve his shirt. He threw it over his head and then padded toward the front door where he hoped his boots were, found them, and pulled them on. "I'm gonna grab my shit from the truck, shower, and take Jenna home. You can spend the rest of your morning wrapping your head around 'fancy' because we're gonna have to keep that vineyard."

Regardless of how much he'd had to drink the night before, he hadn't forgotten the simple math of the whole situation. The mortgage Jack Senior took out on the ranch was more than he guessed their piece of wine country was worth—at least not while it wasn't thriving. If they could get it up and running, then maybe they could turn a profit—or at the very least break even.

He'd stay long enough to see that his brothers were headed in the right direction. And maybe he'd check in on Egg Man as well. Not that Jenna needed looking after, but still. He felt like he should take care of her—of all of them—while he was here. It wouldn't make up for the years he'd been gone, but it would count for something. Wouldn't it? Luke and this rodeo bullshit. Walker and the furniture making—and drinking. Visits to Jenna's throughout the years had been tense, but he guessed now they'd all been on their best behaviors, not wanting to rock the boat. But there was no pretense now. He'd come back to more than he'd expected and had lost more than he'd anticipated being gone so long. He'd bridge the gap between him and his brothers. Jenna as well. He had to.

Jack hefted his bag out of the truck's cab and rolled his head along his shoulders. He wouldn't survive another night on that couch, but he wasn't sure how well he'd sleep in his old room, either. No. He *was* sure. Because he was a shitty sleeper no matter where he was. Unless, apparently, multiple shots of tequila were involved, and he knew better than to make that a habit. Despite the name they shared, he wasn't his father…yet.

That's what he'd been telling himself for ten years. Soon, he might even believe it.

"You were never planning on going home yesterday, were you?" Jack glanced toward Jenna in the passenger seat.

She shrugged. "I knew y'all would need to reconnect, but I also knew you wouldn't do it without a little push. So…I pushed."

He shook his head as he pulled onto her narrow street. "You think you know me that well, huh?" But she was right. That was his way—jumping right into the fray when it came to his brothers. But then he'd taught himself to pull back as well, to maintain just enough distance so it wouldn't hurt too much to leave.

"You've been pretty quiet this whole ride," she added. "Figured you needed some time to think. But we're almost home, and I got some things to say. So I'm gonna say them, okay?"

He kept his eyes on the road now and simply nodded.

He'd been grateful for the silence. The least he could do was let her say her piece.

"I've never once in all these years told you what to do. Hell, I barely knew you anymore when you came to stay with me, and then I only had you under my roof for the better part of a year before you took off for college."

"Mmm-hmm," he said, jaw tight. He wasn't sure what was coming, but her tone told him it wasn't anything he wanted to hear.

"And I'm proud of you. Real proud. Your brothers are, too."

He let out a breath. "I think you're mistaking pride for resentment."

She crossed her arms and angled herself to face him. He still maintained eye contact with the road ahead of him, but he could feel her gaze now, boring into him.

"Now what on earth ever gave you the idea those boys..." She shook her head. "I guess they're grown men now, aren't they? Jack, how can you think they did *anything* but look up to you, especially after what you did for them? What you've *done* for them."

"Don't," he said, his voice firm. "Jenna—don't. I'm not a martyr. I was a dumbass kid who thought...Shit. I don't know what the hell I thought." But he always knew that as long as he was on the receiving end of his father's fist— or sometimes boot—his brothers weren't. All it had taken was one time. A thirteen-year-old Walker trying to pull what he'd thought was an empty bottle from what he'd also thought was a sleeping Jack Senior's hand. But passed out drunk was worse than asleep, because when he woke with a start—dazed and disoriented—Jack Senior backhanded his youngest son across the cheek so hard it knocked him to the ground.

Afterward, Walker locked himself in his room for two days. Even missed school. Jack Senior had miraculously stayed clean for a full week after that, promising it was the last time anything of the sort would happen. Of course it wasn't. Jack and his brothers had gotten used to those kinds of promises—and them not sticking.

Walker was never the same after that. None of them were. But of the three of them, he had been the one who was still a kid—who'd still had that spark of hope. And just like that it was extinguished.

Jack pulled into Jenna's drive and was grateful for the timing, hoping it would end this conversation, or at least send it in another direction. The truck rolled to a stop, but she made no move to open her door. Instead she kept her gaze fixed on him.

"What are you still runnin' from, Jack? You can be a lawyer anywhere. If you just love San Diego to pieces and can't bear leaving, tell me. I'll believe you. Otherwise, when's it gonna be time to come home?"

He felt the muscle in his jaw tick, ran his fingers through his overgrown hair. He'd always thought the time would be now, when Jack Senior was gone and he could finally start over. But he'd built a life in San Diego—one safe from the memories that he could only keep at bay with physical distance. And now he had a chance to get even farther—as far from here as he could go without leaving the country.

"Stay 'til the vineyard's up and running," she added. "See this thing through, and *then* go back to San Diego."

Although they'd stopped, he gripped the steering wheel with both hands. "It's not that simple. You know it isn't. It could take months. Years, even, depending on what rudimentary knowledge of farming we have from... what? Living with our aunt for a few months?"

"Years," she corrected him, blowing out a breath that sounded like exasperation. "Luke and Walker were with me for years. And *yes*. I know it's not that simple, but if you get someone out there who knows grapes, you'll figure it out. You always do."

He could sense there was more coming, but she trailed off and turned toward the car door.

Now? She was getting out now that she'd baited him with that tone? Well, he wasn't biting.

She sat there, hand on the lever and facing the window, but she still didn't move.

"Fine," he growled. "I'll bite. What about getting someone out there who knows grapes?"

She shrugged and glanced at him over her shoulder. "You don't think I missed you sneaking out after curfew back then. Did you?" She laughed. "Look, I know things were a mess when you left. But this isn't one of your whirlwind visits where you're in and out in forty-eight hours. Do we still have to pretend the Ellis girl doesn't exist?"

There it was, the real reason for his silence. Yesterday he'd driven from San Diego to the ranch in a daze. Call it lack of sleep or lack of connection after being gone for so long, but he'd been able to keep his emotional distance on that drive. Yet one night with his brothers and Jenna had flipped a switch, and now he was here. Walking distance from the Ellis place and their vineyard…and what he'd done to prove that he wasn't good for her.

"You knew about her," he said. Not a question but a realization. Jenna had tiptoed around him in those early months after he'd left the ranch in an ambulance, the last time he'd been there before yesterday. He'd come home from the hospital—to Jenna's home, in an unfamiliar town—with a broken tibia, two fractured ribs, and no desire to *talk about his feelings* despite the few visits they'd forced on him with the hospital psychologist. Somewhere, deep down, he'd known it was for his own good, but all he'd wanted to do back then was forget.

And then there was Ava Ellis, the girl who'd chipped away at his foundation until she finally broke through. Shit. He could see her now talking to the assistant in the school office, those long, cinnamon waves framing her snow-white, freckled skin.

"I'm going to trig, too," she'd said, lingering as he waited for his schedule. Nothing like starting a new high school six months before graduation. "I could walk you there."

He remembered glancing down at the plaster that had peeked out from his jeans.

"I can walk fine," he'd said like an asshole. But to be fair, he'd felt entitled to a little bit of asshole at the time. He'd paid his dues.

"Right," she'd said, brows raised. "I can see that. Just thought you might want to know the way." Then she'd stalked out the office door, her head held high—and had waited for him a few paces down the hall.

That was all he'd needed—her not taking his bullshit—for him to realize maybe he didn't want to dish it out. At least not to her.

"Of course I *knew*," Jenna said, bringing him back to the present. Finally she opened her door and hopped out of the truck.

He followed her, grabbing her bag from the pickup's bed and hoisting out the sack of chicken feed as well. He set the second on the ground.

"Why didn't you say anything?" he asked. "About me sneaking out? Ignoring any semblance of a curfew you tried to impose? About any of the shit I pulled? I couldn't have made things easy for you."

Jenna turned to him and reached for her bag, and he handed it over.

"Your mama and me, we lost our daddy when I barely knew my ABCs. I lost her when I was just learning how to be a grown-up and then our own mama a few years later. I might have been twenty-five when you boys came to me, but I was an orphan. I *needed* all of you as much as you needed me. And if sneaking out 'til all hours of the night with the Ellis girl made you happy, then it made *me* happy, too." She reached a hand for his cheek, and Jack realized how long it had been since he'd felt this surge of affection for anyone. "I didn't have a clue how to be a parent, but I hope I did right by you boys." A tear escaped down her cheek, and she laughed. "I need to stop saying 'boys.' You're almost thirty, for crying out loud."

He bent his head and kissed the top of hers. "Not for another eighteen months," he reminded her. "And you did more than right by us, Jenna. You kept us a family. I would have—the state could have—" He broke off. "I don't know if I ever really thanked you."

She shook her head. "You did what you had to do to keep you and your brothers together."

"So did you," he added. "*Thank you* for that."

She shrugged and swiped at her damp eyes. "Then I guess we're even. Or something."

"I guess we are."

"You coming inside?" she asked.

Like a magnet, his head turned in the direction of the Ellis Vineyard, only a mile walk from where he stood. He squinted in the sunlight. After all that had happened his last week in town, he'd never forgotten that red hair—or the freckles on her shoulders and across her nose. He'd also never forgotten that his only possible reason for coming back had told him they were nothing more than a fling when he'd been foolish enough to think it was love.

"She's not there anymore," Jenna added.

He felt a sudden jolt of something that he couldn't name and turned back toward his aunt. He kept his voice even. "Did they sell the property?"

"No. But she and her mama left the area soon after Thanksgiving your first year at school. I've seen her since then—Mrs. Ellis. But not *her*."

He scrubbed a hand over his stubbled jaw. Not wanting to risk running into her, he hadn't come home for any holidays that first year. The joke was on him, he guessed. She'd left, too.

"Ava," he said. "I'm not gonna lose my shit over a name."

Those three letters tasted bittersweet on his lips. He'd gotten past that last terrible night, but he wasn't sure he'd ever gotten over it. Or her. Wasn't that the saying? *You never get over your first love?* He'd always thought she would stay close to home. She'd been accepted to Cal Poly for art. He remembered that. He remembered too much.

Where the hell had she gone?

High school felt like a lifetime ago. He wasn't that kid anymore, the one who let a beautiful girl make him believe in a future that held something better. Still, there was that jolt of something again, of knowing she wasn't there. It was like missing something he'd never had, if that was even possible.

"You never said anything before," he said. "I *have* been back."

"I can count on one hand how many times."

He narrowed his eyes at her.

"And," she added, "you never asked."

He scratched at the back of his neck and let out a breath. "I wasn't asking now. So why say something after all these years?"

Jenna crossed her arms. "Because you never looked wistful like that before, staring down the road and all. This is what I mean," she said, waving a hand in front of his face. "Maybe you still need some closure. Maybe if you found her and talked about that night..."

"Stop," he said, cutting her off. She flinched. He hadn't meant for the word to sound so harsh, but enough was enough. "That relationship wrecked me, okay? Is that what you want to hear? I was a goddamn mess to start, and then I went and put a kid in the hospital. I don't blame her for ending things, but it doesn't mean I took it well. Especially after—"

"After all the terrible stuff you had to deal with for years," she interrupted. "You made a mistake, Jack. A big one. But that one night doesn't define you."

It did for the one person who'd seen past the rumors only for him to prove them true.

This was only a fling, Jack. It was always going to end.

Jesus, that was ten years ago. Enough already.

"I gotta head back. We have a shitload of work to do in the house before I figure out this vineyard thing. Will we see you later this week?"

She sighed but smiled at him. "As soon as my car's all fixed up. Had a little fender bender last week. That's why Luke picked me up."

"What the hell? You never said—" He started checking her over for signs of injury, but she waved him off.

He used to call to check in once a week. Then the calls

moved to once a month. And soon, distance made this part of his life seem a million miles away instead of only a few hundred. Now the guilt hit him in small, unexpected waves every time he realized something he'd missed.

"I'm *fine*," she insisted.

She was. He believed her. But who was around on a regular basis to make sure?

"The egg man—he a good guy?" he asked.

She blushed a little and smiled. "Yeah. Yeah, I think he is. But maybe I need to ask him out *before* he buys my eggs. Avoid any conflict of interest."

Jack laughed. "Is *that* a euphemism?"

She rolled her eyes and reached for the bag of feed before he could hand it to her. Then she started backing up the drive. "Welcome home, Jack." She turned and headed toward the house.

"Jenna?" he said.

She stopped, but kept her back to him as if she could tell she didn't want to hear what was coming next.

"They're making me a partner," he said. "My firm...in their New York office."

She spun on her heel, and he braced himself for an earful. But Jenna's gaze was soft, gentle even.

"Congratulations, Jack."

And then she made her way to the front door.

He watched to make sure she got in okay. It didn't matter that she was older, that she'd lived on her own before he and his brothers came or had continued to do so after they'd all left. He was going to start making up for the years he'd been away. For however long he had, he'd be the brother— or nephew—he should have been...even if he was picking up and leaving again.

CHAPTER FOUR

Mowing the lawn hadn't taken enough time. Ava was back inside now, not daring to enter the painting room again, and she just couldn't take it. Even when she wasn't torturing herself trying to re-create that stupid tree, the house was *too* quiet, and damn it, she was used to noise. She should have at least kept the dog home instead of sending him along for the sleepover at her parents' house. That would have been a decent distraction. But she'd thought complete and utter solitude would somehow spark her long-dormant creative juices.

She'd thought wrong.

So it was settled. She wouldn't wait for the noise to come to her. *She* would head to *it*.

She pulled out her phone and rattled off a text to her parents.

Know you guys are out till after lunch. Heading over to check stock in the tasting room.
    See you this afternoon.

It was Sunday, and her parents had one of their weekend employees working the tasting room. She could stop by, check on the gift shop, busy herself with something other than her empty, quiet home.

She hopped into her cherry red Jeep Renegade and practically peeled out of the driveway—a woman on a mission. It was only a thirty-minute ride to the Ellis Vineyard and she'd made it there in twenty-seven, only to swerve off the narrow road as she approached the entrance. A white pickup truck idled on the wrong side of the road, blocking her turn.

"Shit!" she yelled, throwing the car into park once she came to a stop in the grass. She was grateful she was in the car alone, knowing she'd never hear the end of letting profanity slip in certain company—again.

She hopped out of the car and stalked toward the driver's side of the truck, ready to give whoever was in there a piece of her mind. But he was out and heading toward her before she had time to think of what to say. And then she lost her words altogether as the dust cleared and she saw Jack Everett striding in her direction.

Her stomach dropped, and she wondered if she was falling. She stumbled back a couple of steps until she was able to brace herself against the hood of the Jeep, but she *was* still standing.

"Ava?" he said, taking a step forward, those stormy blue eyes laced with concern. "Shit. Are you okay? I didn't think—"

She held up a hand, halting him from moving any closer.

"I'm fine," she said, though she was anything but. Physically speaking, she didn't have a scratch. But her heart—she thought she could actually hear it beating, it was thundering so loud. "I just need a minute," she added. But for what? There was no way one minute was sufficient to accomplish anything, let alone ten years of *everything* flooding back at once.

Her chest ached being this close. She remembered walking him to class on his first day at Los Olivos High, how he was so broody and intent on keeping his distance—how gorgeous he was anyway and that she'd wanted to do anything to make him smile. Once he had, she was a goner.

Now he stood there in that untucked flannel shirt and faded jeans with his arms crossed, silent and stoic and as devastatingly gorgeous as she remembered. His blond hair was just enough on the long side that he was probably due for a trim, but God it looked good on him, especially with that golden scruff along his jaw. He wore the past decade well, and she'd missed all of it.

"Ava," he said again, and this time he closed the distance between them, stopping when his boot came toe to toe with her sandal. "Are you *okay*?"

Okay? How was there anything okay about seeing Jack again after the way things had ended? He'd left thinking she was afraid of him—and she'd *let* him—when nothing could have been further from the truth. But the alternative would have been forcing him to stay in a place that was poison to him.

The tenderness in his words tore at her, but that voice belonged to a man now. A man she didn't know. Gone was the boy who'd stolen her heart—and broke it *twice* without ever knowing. She wondered what he saw when he looked at her, if she stirred as much in him after all these years as he did in her.

Time was supposed to heal. Wasn't it? Make the past easier to bear. But when she looked at Jack, all she could think was how much she'd give to turn back the clock and try things differently. Then, maybe, she'd deserve the warmth she heard in that voice—the hint of affection.

She cleared her throat and stood straight. "I'm *fine*," she lied. "Did you just get back from England or something?"

His brows pulled together.

"Driving on the other side of the road?" she added, the dizzying effect he had on her diminishing as she turned her thoughts to the here and now.

The corner of his mouth teased at a grin, and with that gesture the dizziness returned. But she could not, *would* not, fall under his spell. Too much had happened since they'd last seen each other to let herself get carried away by feelings she'd long since buried. Besides, she'd already put her foot down. This was the year she got her life back on track—the year she finally let herself pursue the dreams she'd put aside for a decade. A chance encounter with Jack Everett—who hadn't as much as sent her an email in all that time—wasn't going to change things.

Okay, it might change *one* thing. The truth always did that.

"No," he said, drawing out the word. "I was driving Jenna home, and she said you'd moved away." He shook his head. "I don't even remember deciding to drive by." He ran a hand through that overgrown hair and squinted toward the sun. She watched as fine lines crinkled at the corners of his eyes, lines that hadn't been there the last time she saw him. "I just got back in town," he said. "My father died."

He said it so matter-of-factly it took a few seconds to register, and when it did, instinct took over, and she stepped forward, wrapping her arms around him.

"Oh, Jack. I'm—I'm sorry."

She didn't know if those were the right words or if hugging him was anywhere near appropriate, but that's what you said and did when someone died. And this was Jack Everett. *Jack Everett.* In her arms. As the warmth of his skin seeped into hers, a part of her she'd tucked away for ten long years began rising to the surface.

He said nothing at first, simply stood there as she hugged him, breathing in the scent of fresh soap, the outdoors, and something so inherently *Jack* she swore she'd know it was him with her eyes closed.

Then his arms enveloped her. She could feel his hesitation, though, the way he didn't squeeze too tight, didn't breathe too deep.

"I was just going to check up on some things in the tasting room," she said, reluctantly pulling away.

She still had a few hours before everyone returned. It would be time enough to ease into this reunion—to tell him what she'd planned on telling him when he came home after finishing his degree. Except as far as she knew, he never did return. At least, he'd never contacted her if he had. Not that she blamed him.

"Come inside for a drink?" She laughed nervously. "If wine isn't your thing, we have a fridge in the office. I'm sure there's soda or bottled water. Or something."

She wasn't sure if she'd ever expected to see Jack Everett again, not after he hadn't come home—and she'd sought him out in Los Angeles only to find that he'd definitively moved on before she'd ever had a chance to see him. But now that he was here, nearly forcing her off the road, she felt the desperate need to get him to stay. Maybe his father's death wasn't the right time to shake up his world even more, but she'd always promised herself that if he came back—if *he* chose for their paths to cross again—she'd tell him all the things she couldn't say when they were teens and she knew that no matter how he felt about her, he'd needed to get as far away from here as he could.

He shoved his hands in his pockets. "I'll follow you in" was all he said before heading back to his truck.

Had there been a ring on his left hand? She hadn't thought to look until it was too late. Or was she avoiding what she didn't want to confirm? She guessed they'd get to that soon.

Oh God. Jack Everett was really here, and he hadn't bolted at the first sight of her.

She rounded the bumper until she was at the driver's side again, and then somehow she made it back behind the wheel, navigating through the property and to the winery while she tried to process how the hell to tell him—*everything*.

The drive down the winding path behind Ava's Jeep was hardly enough for Jack to get his shit together. She wasn't supposed to be here, and he sure as hell wasn't supposed to force her off the road.

She wrecked me.

It had been minutes since he'd uttered the phrase to Jenna, and now here he was going to have a drink with Ava Ellis. He was out of his mind. But then again, the him she'd destroyed had been an eighteen-year-old mess who had one foot out the door the whole time they were together. Except he'd always planned on coming back after college...for her.

This was only a fling.

It was always going to end.

All it had taken was a few words for his plans to change.

He heard the door of her Jeep slam and realized he was still sitting in his truck despite the fact he'd already parked. He pulled the key from the ignition and stepped out of the vehicle to see her leaning against her bumper, arms crossed as she watched him exit. She offered him a nervous smile but before he could consider reciprocating, they were interrupted.

Tires crackled over gravel, and both their gazes shifted to a sedan rolling toward them.

"Looks like you got new customers," he said.

Her eyes flashed toward his, and despite the sun's glare, he could see a desperation he hadn't been expecting—not that anything about this meeting had been expected. But just as quickly, she schooled her features and held out her arms as a young boy barreled out of the car and headed straight for her.

"Mom!"

The boy threw himself at her so quickly, clinging to her, that Jack didn't even get a chance to see his face, just the auburn waves—exactly like his mother's—where Ava now buried her face, peppering his head with soft kisses as she did.

"Mom?" he heard himself ask as something inside him clicked into place and then sank.

"Owen!" she cried, falling against the back of her car, unable to contain her laughter. "You're getting too big for me to hold you like this," she added as he slid down her torso so he was standing on his own two feet.

"Grandpa got your text, and he asked if I wanted to go to the park and practice pitching or if I wanted to surprise you instead."

She ruffled his hair and as he took a step back, Jack could make out the color of the boy's eyes. Not green like his mother's, but blue.

A chocolate Lab bounded out of the car after the boy, stopping only to give him and Ava sloppy kisses as the two of them roared with laughter.

Not green like his mother's.

Did he have his father's eyes?
Owen.

"My mother's maiden name was Owens," he said, his voice sounding rough and far away.

She bit her lip. "I know."

"Margaret, take Owen inside."

An older man and woman approached, and Jack recognized Margaret and Bradford Ellis, Ava's parents. Mr. Ellis narrowed his eyes at Jack.

"Come on, honey," her mother said, motioning to Owen. "You and Scully come in with me while Grandpa talks to Mom for a second."

The boy—Owen—backed up and glanced at Jack.

"Who are you?" he asked, with the unreserved curiosity only acceptable from a child.

Ava's father patted his grandson on the shoulder. "No one, son. Follow your grandma. She'll get you and Scully something to eat."

"But I thought the rule was no dogs in the wine shop."

Mr. Ellis let out an uneasy laugh. "We're bending the rules, only for today."

Owen pumped his fist in the air. "Yes! Come on, boy!" He kissed Ava quick on the cheek and scampered off after his grandma, Labrador in tow. As soon as they were safe behind doors, Bradford Ellis dropped his painted-on grin and turned, teeth gritted, toward Jack.

"Dad, don't—" Ava started, but Jack knew the look of a man with an agenda. Just like he'd done time and time again with his own father, he stood his ground and braced himself for whatever came next.

"I know who you are," he said. Her father was a tall man, still well built, but Jack had at least an inch or two on him. "I knew it the second I saw that piece-of-shit truck."

Jack's jaw clenched as he thought about the accounts he'd set up in Luke and Walker's names, about how much more this new position in New York would help get them back on their feet after Jack Senior mortgaged the property. Every goddamn cent he made—other than what he needed to live—was put away for his family. But he wasn't going to dignify Bradford Ellis with an excuse for the vehicle he drove. Instead he stood there, impassive, as the man lit into him. As the unmistakable reality of who the boy was sank in, and as it registered that Ava's father had called Jack *no one.*

"Nice to see you, Mr. Ellis," he said, fighting to keep his voice even.

"You put the Wilkes boy in the hospital," the other man said in a low, warning tone.

"For assaulting your daughter," Jack retaliated, though he knew it was a shit excuse. He'd pulled Derek off of Ava without issue. He could have left it at that. But when he saw those bruises...

"Ava didn't press charges," Mr. Ellis snapped.

"Dad!" Ava cried. A look passed between father and daughter that Jack didn't understand. "Stop. Please."

"Ava," the older man said, addressing his daughter but still facing Jack. "You told us it wasn't him. You said he wasn't the father, and we took you at your word."

"It's complicated," she said, her voice starting to shake. "I told you what you wanted to hear—what would make it easier for everyone."

Jack couldn't move. He was frozen where he stood. So he just listened to this warped version of his past play out.

"*We* raised that boy with you. We helped feed him and clothe him. You put off school and took a job at the vineyard, *our* family's business, and have never wanted for anything. We're Owen's family, Ava. Not him. If he thinks he can show up after ten years—after what he did—and be a part of your life—a part of Owen's life—without our say?"

"Dad, I said *stop*." She cut him off.

Jack turned at the sound of Ava's voice. Mr. Ellis did as well.

She faced Jack with pleading eyes. Jack glanced back toward the winery, to where *his son* had disappeared behind closed doors.

His *son.*

"Christ, Ava."

She covered her mouth, and her green eyes glistened.

He pressed the heels of his hands into his own eyes. Then he stared at her for several long beats. He thought about the baseball scholarship he'd almost lost because of his broken leg senior year. Then, without warning, he thought of loss in a whole new way. But there wasn't time to process.

"He plays ball," he said. "He has *my* goddamn eyes, my mother's *goddamn* name, and he plays ball?"

"I'm so sorry. I'm *so* sorry," she repeated, the tears pooling now.

He slammed his palm against the side of the truck bed, and Ava yelped.

"Hey!" her father yelled, taking a step toward Jack and then lowering his voice. "That's my daughter. And *my* grandson in there," he said, pointing toward the winery. "I will do anything I need to do to protect them, even if it means calling the cops on you right now. No one forgot what you did, Everett. Or who your daddy is. I don't care what happened between you and my daughter in the past. Because there is no future for you here. You're not good for either of them."

Jack felt the sting in his palm and started backing toward the driver's side of the truck.

"Was," he said, and he watched the other man's brows furrow. "You know who my daddy *was*," he amended. "He died earlier this week."

Ava let out a quiet sob that mingled with his name.

"I shouldn't have come," he said, his voice tight with strain, his hands balling into fists. He fought to maintain control, to keep from scaring her again. But his anger was justified. He knew that much.

He shook his head and spoke softly. "Hell, Ava."

Bradford Ellis took another step in Jack's direction as he pulled open his truck's door.

"Please, Dad. Stop. Please." Ava pressed her hands to her father's chest and urged him back again. But he kept speaking over her shoulder.

"You're trespassing, Everett. I suggest you head on out, now."

Jack didn't wait to see if she'd turn around again. He was in the truck, engine roaring to life, before he lost it completely.

He had a *son*.

In the span of ten years—and ten minutes—Ava Ellis had wrecked him not once, but twice.

And here he was, doing what he did best—leaving.

CHAPTER FIVE

Ava had been in a fog ever since Jack Everett had sped off the Ellis property yesterday. The proof was in the coffee. She couldn't even stomach a cup, and she didn't normally acknowledge the morning until she'd had at least one, if not two. Her mug rested full and steaming in front of her, but all she could do was stare at it. Owen sat across from her at their round, wooden breakfast table, shoveling Cheerios into his mouth like they were his last meal.

"Hey there, slugger. Slow down. The bus isn't coming for—" She glanced at the clock above the stove. "Shit!" she yelled, sliding her chair back from the table with such momentum that she knocked the full mug over.

Owen jumped up, bowl of cereal and spoon in his hands as he protected his precious cargo. *"Mom,"* he scolded in that sweet boy voice of his, but he was giggling. "You swore *and* almost gave me *coffee-Os.*"

Both their heads turned toward the front of the house as the slow hiss of a school bus stopping sounded outside.

"Shit," Owen said under his breath and swallowed his last bite.

"Language!" Ava yelled. "Quick. Grab your backpack. And your baseball bag. Are your cleats in the bag? I'll grab your lunch from the fridge. And—shoes! Put your shoes on. Did you brush your teeth? Doesn't matter. You'll do it before bed tonight. Twice."

The two of them scrambled through the kitchen and into the living room, Ava snagging her son's lunch on the way while he frantically tied his shoes and stuffed his cleats in his baseball bag. She stuck her head out the door and waved at the bus driver, who tapped at his wrist as if she didn't know they were running late.

"Lunch!" she called, and Owen looked up just in time to catch the paper sack and drop it into his backpack. "Grandma's gonna pick you up and take you to practice, and I'll be there by the time it's over." He had a bag on each shoulder and was halfway through the screen door.

"Love you!" She strode toward him and planted a kiss on his tousled mop of hair.

"Love you!" he echoed as he bounded off the porch, across the yard, and up the steps onto the bus.

"Thank you!" she cried, waving to the driver. "Sorry!"

Then she stepped back inside and fell against the door, closing it with her butt and letting out a labored breath. That's when she heard the off-tempo, staccato drips against the kitchen's tile floor—along with what sounded like a tongue lapping the spilled liquid.

Shit.

"Scully!" she yelled, sprinting the few feet into the kitchen, stopping short at the scene before her. Her lovely Kona blend blanketed the kitchen table, puddles forming under the edges where the coffee had run off and onto the floor. Their Lab stood, paws in puddles, slurping up the spilled coffee. "Scully, *get!*" His head shot up, his wide eyes meeting hers. She pointed toward the doggie door that led out to their fenced backyard. *"Out!"* The dog obeyed, traipsing caramel-colored paw prints across the tile as he went.

She surveyed the damage, which was still significant, and decided that catching him after only a few sips—along with the milk and sugar she used to dilute the liquid—had probably kept him clear of any caffeine-related danger, but she'd call the vet to make sure. First, though, she had to clear her head, which meant processing what had put her in this fog to begin with.

She'd satisfied Owen yesterday afternoon, explaining away her reddened eyes as having been surprised and excited to see an old friend she'd missed for a long time.

Owen understood the concept of a happy cry and didn't think much of her lie of omission, but Ava knew that's what had kept her up all night and this morning settled into an aching knot in her gut.

She had lied to Jack, and now her son had *seen* his father, and she had lied to him, too.

Then again, she'd been lying for ten years. Hadn't she? Owen hadn't really grasped the concept of *father* until he was in preschool. And when he'd asked if he had one, she'd simply told him *yes*, that she loved his dad very much, but he'd had to move away before Owen was born.

But damn it, there was a right way and a wrong way to do this, and getting surprised by Jack like that—and then by Owen, too—wasn't the *right* way.

She grabbed the paper towels from the counter and set to work cleaning up her mess. Well, the one that could be easily absorbed with a roll of Bounty Select-A-Size. That other, bigger mess—the one she planned on tending to as soon as she de-coffeed her kitchen—was another story.

Fifteen minutes later, Scully's paws were clean and he was back inside. The vet had assured her he hadn't consumed enough caffeine for her to worry. Now she sat in her Jeep, smelling like she'd just come off a ten-hour shift at Starbucks. Smelling like coffee was the least of her concerns, though. She pulled her phone from her purse and set an alarm for 3:00 p.m. so she didn't lose track of time this afternoon like she had this morning. It would be one thing for Owen to miss the bus—she could have driven him the fifteen-minute ride to school, the only consequence his disappointment at missing out on the extra time with his friends. But forgetting him at practice? It wasn't as if anything like that had ever happened before, but then the events of yesterday afternoon had never happened before, either.

She did a final check in the rearview mirror, decided she looked about as frazzled as she felt, and thought *To hell with it* as she backed away from her house, headed on the hour drive to Oak Bluff.

Ava's tires crackled over the gravel driveway in front of the Crossroads Cattle Ranch. The knot in her stomach tightened not only at the thought of seeing Jack again but at what it must be like for him to be here after all this time. He hadn't talked much about his parents when they'd met. He didn't need to. The gossip preceded his arrival. And once they'd become close, the most he'd done was confirm that his mother had died years before and that his father's drinking and abuse was the result.

She thought about her own father's behavior yesterday afternoon. She'd hated him for it in the moment, but realized she had what Jack never did—parents who'd do anything to protect her.

Tears pricked at her eyes as she rolled to a stop behind the white pickup that had caused her to swerve off the road less than twenty-four hours before, but she swallowed them back. She had no right. *He* was the one who'd had the rug pulled out from under him, not her.

She reached for her key, ready to pull it from the ignition, and found that it and the rest of the keys on the ring already lay in her lap. Huh. So she'd turned the car off. Must be that brain fog again.

She yelped when someone rapped their knuckles against the driver's side window. She turned, heart in her throat, to find Luke Everett grinning at her. He might have aged a decade, but she'd never forget that devil of a smile.

He stepped back to let her open her door and she climbed out, albeit on wobbly knees. There was no turning back now, not that she would. She owed Jack an explanation at the very least. At the most—well, she owed him ten years she couldn't give back.

"Red," Luke said, invoking the nickname Jack had given her when they were teens. He took his hat off and squinted at her. "Well, you sure as shit look the same as you did in high school. Lemme guess. You heard about dear old Dad and came to pay your respects?"

Luke *had* changed. He must have hit a growth spurt sometime after Jack left, because the boy she remembered had been a head shorter than his big brother and lanky as the day was long. The man who stood before her was exactly that: a *man.* Tall and broad with corded muscles lining his exposed forearms. And a nasty gash across his cheek.

Ava made an attempt to smooth out the wrinkles in her peasant skirt, then remembered the wrinkles were meant to be there and forced her fidgeting hands to stay still.

"Are you—okay?" she asked, pointing at her own cheek.

He winked. "You should see the bull," he said, then laughed. "Not a scratch on him."

She bit her lip. "Jack told me about your dad," she said but then paused. She knew *sorry* wasn't exactly the right word but also knew that she didn't wish death on anyone, no matter how awful a person was.

"I know," Luke said, as if he was reading her thoughts. "What do you say about a man who knocked his kids around and drank himself to death? I don't think they make a greeting card for that."

He offered her a warm smile, which put her more at ease. She still wanted to throw up from nerves—but to a lesser degree.

"Wait a second," Luke added. "Jack *told* you? I didn't know you two were still in touch."

"No." She swallowed, her level of nervousness climbing the chart again. "I mean, yes. We spoke yesterday. Did he—did he not say anything about running into me?"

He ran a hand through his blond hair and dropped his hat back on his head.

"Well, shit," he said. "That explains him going on a bender with Walker for a second night in a row. He came home yesterday afternoon, did some work in Dad's office, and then helped Walker finish off a bottle of whiskey. I thought he'd still be sleeping it off, but he took off for the vineyard thirty minutes ago." He gave her a nod. "You did some number on him back in the day, Red. Guess you still have that magic touch."

She blinked a few times as realization set in. He hadn't told his brothers about Owen.

"Vineyard?" she asked. "I thought this was a ranch."

"It is. But apparently Jack Senior bought a vineyard without letting any of us know. Just off the property. So big brother thinks it's on him to figure out what to do with it." He shrugged. "If you ask me—which he hasn't yet—he ought to sell it right back to the first buyer he can find so we can try to get the deed on the house back, though I doubt we'd break even. I've got some money saved up, though. Maybe we can dig this place out of debt. Then Walker and I can get back to ranchin', and Jack can get back to lawyerin' and pretending this place doesn't exist."

She heard a bitterness in his tone that didn't quite mesh with Luke's playful disposition. But he painted that smile back on quick enough that she almost second-guessed herself. *Almost.*

"You said he's at the vineyard now?" she asked, already feeling like she was overstepping her welcome yet doubting she'd be welcome at her next destination at all.

Luke nodded. "If you back out of the drive and head west, take the second right onto the main street, Oak Bluff Way. It's a mile from there, right through town." He looked her up and down, taking in her top, skirt, and sandals. "It's a nice walk through the ranch property, too—if you're dressed for it." He winked at her again.

That must have been what Jack had done, seeing as his truck was still here.

"Thanks," she said. Her heart twisted as she realized how much Owen would like his uncle if he ever got to meet him. "I'm good with driving." She held out her hand, not sure what the proper parting gesture was between two people who shared a short past—and maybe, she hoped, some semblance of a future. Between Jack and his son. She and Jack were the past, right? They were different people now. Plus, she had a college application to complete, a long-awaited education to begin the following semester, and *he* had a life in San Diego. They'd both been moving in different directions since the day they'd said good-bye, and it seemed they were still on two different paths that weren't meant to intersect.

Look at what he'd done—college, law school, joining a successful practice. She'd followed his career from afar. Even if she'd chickened out trying to contact him, she knew he'd done well, and part of her found satisfaction in that. Pushing him to leave *had* been the right decision at least in that respect.

Luke took a step toward her and dipped his head to kiss her on the cheek, snapping her out of her reverie. "You look good, Red."

A sudden warmth spread through her. At least one member of the Everett family was happy to see her.

"You too," she said. "Say hello to Walker for me."

He laughed. "Now he *is* sleeping it off. But will do when he rejoins the land of the living."

She smiled and stepped back toward her car, opening the door. "Thanks," she said.

Ever the gentleman, Luke gave her a quick tip of his cowboy hat. "My pleasure. And if he's pissed at someone interrupting his alone time, be sure and tell him I sent ya."

She laughed at that and settled herself back into the car. But as she slammed the door and pulled slowly back onto the street, the ease of being in Luke's presence gave way to the sinking feeling she'd had since she'd watched Jack lay eyes on his son for the first time. She'd explain as best she could, and that would be that. That was why she'd made the drive today, to get everything out in the open. Owen was what mattered now, and if Jack decided he wanted to be a part of his son's life, they'd figure out what that meant for them. They could make their version of a family work for Owen's sake.

Even if Jack never forgave her.

CHAPTER SIX

The breeze cooled Jack's skin, and he was grateful for it. It was seventy degrees at best, but the cloudless sky made the sun feel much stronger. It didn't help that he'd left his hat in the truck—or that he still felt like he'd been hit by a freight train. Whether that was because of the booze or his encounter with Ava the day before was still in question, though he guessed it was probably both.

He walked the rows of grapevines slowly, his steps measured and his head pounding. The whiskey had helped his inability to process what had happened at the Ellis Vineyard, but it wasn't doing shit for his capacity to remain upright. Maybe he should have waited the ten minutes it would have taken him to make a pot of coffee, but after two nights in that house, the walls were closing in on him. He needed out.

He ran his hand along the leaves. Here and there he found a clump of grapes, most of them wilted.

"How the hell are we gonna breathe new life into *this*?" he asked out loud.

"With a hell of a lot of blood, sweat, and possibly tears?"

He stopped mid-step and tilted his head toward the sun, allowing himself one long breath before he spun to face her.

Her red waves rested on her shoulders, radiant in the sun, and his breath caught in his throat despite his anger. Because he *was* angry—and so many other things he couldn't yet name. Whatever he was feeling, though, Ava Ellis was responsible, and he sure as shit didn't like anyone having that kind of power over him.

"What the hell are you doing here, Ava?" It wasn't as if he didn't know the answer or that their meeting again was inevitable, but he hadn't counted on *inevitable* being *this second*, and he wasn't sure he was ready for whatever came next. And despite the lightness he felt at her nearness, he wouldn't let the sliver of happiness he'd felt at seeing her yesterday override the betrayal he felt now.

She took a step toward him, and he did nothing to encourage her. He did his best to remain impassive even as his head throbbed in time with his pulse.

"I just want a chance to explain," she said, her voice soft and tentative. "I don't expect you to forgive me, but I do need you to understand *why*."

He crossed his arms over his chest. "Really?" he asked. "Because I spent the whole ride back here yesterday trying to answer that same question. And when I couldn't, I drank myself into a stupor." He pinched the bridge of his nose and squeezed his eyes shut for a second, trying to keep the pounding at bay. But it was useless. "I took off from this place so I could leave that shit behind. So I wouldn't become *him*. I'm back two damned days, and I'm already acting more like Jack Senior than I did when I lived here."

Bitterness and blame dripped from each word, and he knew she wasn't responsible for all of it. He had free will, made his own decisions. But that didn't change the fact that he couldn't figure out how to process what had happened since his return without simply numbing himself to it.

A tear slipped down her cheek, and she was close enough that if he wanted to, he could swipe it away. But he wasn't relinquishing any more control.

"That," she said, the one syllable word breaking as she spoke. "That's *why*. You needed to *go*."

He shook his head. "Without knowing?"

"Yes." Another tear fell. "Would you have gone otherwise?"

He ran a hand through his hair, tugging at the too-long strands. "Christ, Ava. That wasn't your decision to make. I should have had a goddamn choice, but you didn't give me one." The volume of his voice rose, and he could feel the beat of his own pulse in his neck.

She wiped away her tears, but they were falling faster now, and another one simply took the former's place. "I was *eighteen*," she said, her voice rising to a level to meet his. "And scared. I was so scared, Jack. I was going to tell you at the party. And then—well, I couldn't. I called you to meet me the next night so I could. But once you got there and told me about Walker...that, after what happened with Derek, I couldn't do it."

He'd started to pace, but the mention of his brother's name stopped him cold. "Walker? How the hell does he have anything to do with this?"

She wiped her eyes again and then wrapped her arms around her shoulders. As she did, he felt the slight shift in temperature, as if the ocean breeze had made its way ten miles inland.

"Do you...remember what happened?" she asked, and he could tell she was proceeding with caution. "Do you remember what you said to me?"

He was the one stepping closer now because this cryptic bullshit was going nowhere, and he wanted to make sure she heard him crystal clear.

"I remember plenty," he said, jaw tight. He swallowed back the ache he felt as he neared her. "I remember you walking away. I remember calling you every damn day before I left and you not answering." He shook his head and opened his mouth to say something else but stopped when his eyes met hers, their brilliant green now clouded and reddened by tears.

"Jack," she said, and his name was a plea.

She didn't want to say whatever came next. He could sense that with every fiber of his being. But she had to. Whatever it was, he knew she had to.

"What?" he asked, his voice strained.

She moved in, close enough that he could smell her morning coffee and the sweet citrus scent of her skin.

"Walker's fifteenth birthday was the next day," she said, the words followed by a soft, hiccupping breath.

The weight that had been threatening to crush his chest dropped to his stomach, and he had to keep himself from staggering. Ava must have noticed, because she made a move to reach for him but pulled her hand back almost as quickly.

He clasped his hands behind his head and tilted his head toward the sky. That's when he felt the first drop of rain—and with it, the undeniable anguish of the memory.

He dipped his head so they were eye to eye, shoved his hands under his arms to keep himself from hitting something because there was nothing to hit other than the damn vines.

"Jack Senior sent him that pint bottle of whiskey," he said, his voice rough and almost unrecognizable as his own.

"And he drank the whole goddamn thing before he'd even made it back from the mailbox."

She nodded but didn't speak. So he went on even though he didn't want to—knowing that he *had* to. To understand everything that happened in the aftermath of the party, he had to relive it because he'd apparently blocked it all out— tucked all of those memories somewhere safe where they couldn't knock him on his ass again. Yet here he was. "There wasn't even a card," he added. "Just a note telling his *fifteen*-year-old son that if he ever needed to forget, the bottle would do the trick."

"I know," she said, not stopping herself as she reached for him now, resting her palm against his chest. Heat spread through him, and he didn't—*couldn't*—push her away. "I remember."

He shook his head. "Did I tell you what it was he wanted to forget, though? How two years wasn't enough for my brother to get past his father backhanding him across the face so hard it fractured a goddamn bone in his cheek? And just like I did, he protected Jack Senior. Told the ER doc it was one of the horses."

Walker's birthday *gift* and his first experience with liquor had all happened the day after the party.

"Deputy Wilkes sent me home after taking my statement. I still don't get why he didn't press charges after what I'd done to his son. And then Walker..."

Everything was falling into place. Every part of that weekend played out like the worst of his nightmares come true. And that's exactly what it had been.

Her hand fisted his shirt and the other flew to his cheek. The rain fell freely now, and he watched as the water obscured her tears. He was powerless against her touch, powerless against the memory. Because he knew what came next—the part he hadn't given a second thought. But he knew it meant everything now.

"I told you right then and there that I didn't want kids."

She nodded slowly, hand still on his cheek.

"After what I'd done to Derek and the way Jack Senior kept his hooks in us even when we weren't under his roof, I said I'd never take the chance I'd turn into him. That I'd never become a father if I could help it. I said that to you while you were pregnant with our child."

She covered her mouth with her hand, nodding once more.

"We're one hundred percent them," he said, the truth of it setting in. "My parents. They got pregnant with me when they were teens, and look how the hell it all turned out."

"You had to go," she said. "I brought you there to tell you about Owen, but I knew—after the party and Walker I knew I couldn't. I couldn't force you to stay in a place that brought you so much pain. Because even though you were off the ranch, it wasn't over. So I had to say whatever I could to make sure you'd go." She paused, letting the rain pelt her skin, and he watched it run in rivulets down her cheeks. "You always said you'd come back—and a part of me believed that even after what I'd said, you would, that I'd get the chance to tell you when you were ready." She shook her head, pressing her lips together to stifle what he guessed was a full-on sob. "But you never did. Not until now."

He backed away. "I felt like a goddamn monster, Ava. And you telling me to go...I swore that's what you thought of me, too."

She sucked in a sharp breath. "I'm sorry. I didn't know what else to do. We were so young, and suddenly I had to deal with what Derek tried to do, what you did to him, and the fact that I was pregnant. It was too much."

"What about when Owen was a year old? Two? Jesus, Ava, I get why you didn't tell me that night, but ten years?"

"You were engaged!" she cried.

His eyes widened. "What the hell are you talking about?" He wasn't denying it, but how in God's name did she know?

"I *went* to UCLA," she said, bitterness dripping off her words. "When you didn't come back for me, I went after *you*." She laughed, but her smile didn't reach her eyes. "I found out you were a clerk at a local law firm, and I went to see you. To tell you everything." She blew out a long breath. "I sat there in that office while the receptionist went on and on about how much the partners loved you, that you were exactly like your fiancée—putting work and school above everything else." Her hands fisted at her sides. "I left, Jack. I left as soon as she went down the hall to find you." Now she crossed her arms over her soaked torso, and that warmth he'd seen in her eyes turned to something he recognized all too well—resentment.

"Ava—"

But this time she was the one to shake her head. "You—you were getting married after I'd spent years changing diapers at four in the morning...joining the preschool PTO because yes, there was one...buying two extra car seats because the only way to be included in the carpool clique was to have all of the necessary equipment!"

She was yelling now, and he wasn't sure if it was from the rain or because she was pissed.

He closed the distance between them. "*You're* angry?" he asked, incredulous.

She groaned through gritted teeth. "Yeah! *I'm* angry!"

He was the one laughing now, the sound just as bitter as

hers. "So, what? Am I supposed to apologize for not keeping you up to date on *my* life? Or for not being there for a kid I never knew about?"

Her chest was heaving. "Yes!" she cried. "Yes! I know it doesn't make sense and I'm being completely irrational, but there you go. I want you to apologize for finding happiness without me even though that's what I wanted for you. Because I never found it without you!"

He held his left hand in the air, brandishing it at her. "There's no ring, Ava! No goddamn ring. And no happiness. Just the same messed-up guy you sent packing ten years ago."

Even with the rain, he could hear her breath catch in her throat.

"You're...divorced?"

He pressed the heels of his hands into his rain-drenched eyes. Then he looked at her. "No," he said, his voice calmer now. "I didn't marry her."

She stood there, mouth hanging open, but she said nothing.

"You had your reasons for pushing me away...and I had mine for not being able to truly move on."

"Closure," she said quietly, but he could still hear her over the rain.

Maybe that's what she was hoping for, too. Because none of it had felt right back then. He'd messed up. Big-time. But he'd also known that what had happened between them was more than a fling. He'd *known* she was lying to him, which was why he called her every day before he left for baseball training—and at least once a week the first month he'd been gone. But she'd always sent him right to voice mail. He might have loved her, but he wasn't an idiot, and his pride could only take so much. He'd finally let himself believe she'd stopped loving him, and that was when he'd stopped calling.

What else could he have done when she'd locked him out of her life so completely?

"I want to hear you say it," he said finally.

"What?" she asked.

"I want to hear you say that you loved me when you made it clear that you didn't." He tried to tell himself that her coming to find him didn't matter, that what she said now wouldn't change how he felt. It couldn't. But maybe it would heal the wound that had refused to close up for ten long years.

They were near soaked at this point, but neither seemed to care. The only thing that mattered was what she said next.

She didn't hesitate to answer.

"I loved you, Jack. I loved you *every* day we were together, and I'm pretty sure I'd fall for the man you've become if I had the chance to." He reached for her but stopped himself. "I love our *son,*" she continued, "and I'm so sorry I deprived you of the chance at that kind of love, that Owen never knew—"

Before he knew what he was doing, his mouth was on hers, his hands cupping her cheeks, skin slick with rain and tears. She kissed him back, and despite the chill in the air he felt heat beneath his palms. Ten years of loss and ache and longing for something he hadn't known still existed poured from his lips. Her tongue plunged into his mouth, and he knew whatever it was he was giving to her he received in turn.

This was Ava—*Ava Ellis*. He'd kissed these lips hundreds of times, yet everything about them was foreign to him now. The girl he knew didn't exist anymore. The person he held in his arms was all woman. He slid his hands down her sides, following her curves until they rested on her hips. He might not know her like he had a decade ago, but his heart sped up just the same at the mere memory of how she used to make him feel.

Hopeful.

Whole.

Loved.

She stumbled backward, but he caught her with a hand on the small of her back. His fingertips pressed firm against her soaked shirt, and he felt the heat of her skin against his. He kissed her harder, searching for the connection he knew was buried deep. Ava's hands splayed against his chest, his heart thundering against her palm. He felt it—their past and present colliding in the clattering of teeth as her pelvis rocked against his. He was hard in an instant, yet in that same moment knew it didn't matter. That this was wrong. All of it. No matter how right his mouth felt on hers.

He pressed his hands to her shoulders and pushed her from him, freeing himself from the momentary spell as the pieces of their chance meeting yesterday fell back into place.

The tips of her fingers brushed her kiss-swollen bottom lip, and he ignored the urge to say *To hell with it* and suck it between his teeth.

"I'm not welcome in your life!" he called over what was quickly becoming a downpour. "Or did you miss that exchange between me and your father?"

He knew there was more to his hesitation than that, that if this went any further he'd have to deal with the real issue. Without warning, he'd become what he'd sworn he never wanted to be—a father.

He started to back away.

"I told them you weren't the father," she said. "And they chose to believe it because it was easier for them—and easier for me." She shook her head. "I was so scared if they knew—if my father knew—he'd find a way to make Deputy Wilkes change his mind—or worse."

"Worse?" His head was swimming.

The police had questioned everyone at the party, but there'd been no arrests, not even for the alcohol. It was like the whole thing got swept under the rug, and he'd never understood why.

He'd deserved a night or two in jail, if not more. Instead they'd hauled him into the station, taken his statement, and for reasons he couldn't fathom, sent him home.

He'd always known that once news of his home life in Oak Bluff traveled to Los Olivos, people would look at him and his brothers differently. And it had happened almost the minute they'd arrived. Kids from the other side of the tracks, so to speak. Sons of an abusive drunk with one brother, after one messed-up night, already showing signs of following in his father's footsteps. Why the hell wouldn't her parents suspect the same from him? Wasn't that why he and Ava had kept their relationship a secret? Wasn't it exactly what he'd feared himself?

"They took my statement, too," she said. "I told them about what Derek did and agreed not to press charges against *him* as long as he sought treatment—and as long as no charges were pressed against you. If after all of that my father found out you were Owen's dad? He was tight with the deputy. I wouldn't have put it past him to try and threaten jail time to make you sign away your legal rights to your own son."

The cops had let him off with a warning and one

stipulation—that he send paperwork proving he was seeing a counselor to deal with whatever had led to him pummeling Derek that night.

"So you're the reason I didn't go to jail. And why I spent my entire freshman year seeing a campus psychologist." Maybe he'd been forced to seek help, but it was help he'd needed. He'd just been too young and too damned stubborn to admit it.

He slicked his rain-soaked hair off his face. It was too much—all of it. Too damned much.

"Maybe I overstepped, but it was the only thing I could think to do for you that you might not do for yourself. I still believe my father was wrong about you then, and I'm willing to bet he's wrong about you now. You had *one* bad night after years of hell that I can't even imagine. But I never for one second thought you were a monster." Her teeth chattered as she spoke. "I don't expect anything from you that you don't want to give, Jack. But you're welcome in Owen's life. If that's what you want."

That was the thing. All he'd ever wanted was to leave. She'd gotten that part right. If he took her up on her offer, he ran the risk of wanting to stay, and he wasn't sure what the hell to do with that.

"Let me drive you home," she added. "And then I'll leave you to think about—about everything."

She was soaked, visibly shaking, and her eyes were bloodshot from the salt of her tears. She was in no shape to drive. And him? Well, he'd been better. But he'd been steady behind the wheel on no sleep. He could be steady for the mile drive back home.

Steady. It was what Jack Everett did, and despite everything, he'd do it for Ava now.

"Give me the keys," he said, and she didn't even question him as she reached into some hidden pocket in her skirt and handed them over.

He nodded, and they both strode in the direction of the closest road, where she had parked on the shoulder. He unlocked the Jeep with the key fob and pulled her door open, instinctively grabbing her arm when her foot slid in the grass. Once inside himself, he started the car, turned on the heat full blast, and drove.

Neither of them spoke a word, but it didn't matter. The past ten years filled the space between them. And even though they'd escaped the downpour, Jack couldn't help but feel like he was drowning.

CHAPTER SEVEN

Ava stood on a rug in the front foyer of Jack Everett's childhood home, her skirt turning it from a place to brush off your shoes to a squishy, spongy swamp.

"Wait here," Jack said, stepping around her and disappearing toward the kitchen.

She attempted to shrug, but it felt like a shiver, so she waited. What else was she going to do?

"Who the hell are you?"

Her eyes widened as she followed the sound of the voice to the top of the stairs in front of her.

The man staring down at her wore nothing but a pair of low-slung jeans. He scratched at his abdomen and then at the back of his head, his dirty-blond hair sleep tousled. His almost-beard made her do a double take, since she was sure the last time she'd seen him he hadn't even been able to grow facial hair.

"Walker?" she asked, knowing it had to be him, since she'd already seen Jack and Luke. She was no math expert, but the odds were pretty much in her favor that either it *was* the youngest of the three brothers, or the Everett boys multiplied in the rain.

He narrowed his eyes and made his way down the stairs

until he was standing in front of her, arms crossed. He looked her up and down as she stood there in her ever-growing puddle, and his eyes finally glinted with recognition.

"Ava-freaking-Ellis," he said. "And here I thought Jack Senior's passing would go unnoticed by the rest of the world. Guess it brought someone out of the woodwork. Just wasn't thinking it would be you."

She swallowed hard, then rubbed her hands on her arms, trying to fight against the shiver of cold and realization.

Neither Walker nor Luke had any clue what she'd kept from their brother.

Jack reappeared with a towel and what looked like clothing stacked on top of it. He offered the pile to her, though he was still drenched himself.

"There's a bathroom off the living room, across from the kitchen. I'll throw your clothes in the dryer after you change. Can't let you drive home like that."

While it was a sweet gesture, his voice was flat, and she knew it was just Jack being Jack—performing his obligatory duty for someone else in need. It was what made her fall for him in the first place—the way he took care of his brothers, even in the early weeks when they'd first met and he'd been in a cast. Her insides felt like they were caving in as the memories also brought her back to their first kiss—and Jack wincing when she'd pressed her palm against his torso. She'd never forget the bruises over his ribs, a terrifying kaleidoscope of purple, blue, black, and yellow. But that had been the type of pain that would heal. What lay beneath was something she'd never truly be able to understand.

"Thanks," she said, grateful for anything other than the cold clothes stuck to her body. She grabbed the offering and headed toward her destination. As she did, she heard Walker mumble something about a bigger bathroom upstairs—and Jack responding with an emphatic *No*.

She didn't know the full details of Jack's last night in this house as a kid, but his father knocking him down those same stairs where she'd been reacquainted with the youngest Everett brother was all the information she needed to understand. Once inside the bathroom, with the door shut and locked behind her, she let out a long, shaky breath.

Of course he never came back—not for her. Not for anyone. And she didn't blame him, either.

She steadied herself, swallowing back the memories, and peeled off her wet clothes. The towel provided welcome warmth, but when she pulled the gray T-shirt over her head, she startled at Jack's scent, at the nearness of him, and her thoughts zoomed in on that rain-soaked kiss.

There'd barely been enough time for her body to react when it happened. She'd been wrapped too tight in the emotion of it all, but now something long ignored, long dormant, suddenly woke. Her nipples peaked against the thin cotton of his shirt, and she knew it had little to do with body temperature.

She'd kissed Jack Everett the boy years ago. Fallen for him. Made love to him. And though there'd been other men since, she'd never ached for their touch like she did for his now. Funny how the heart and body could reconnect, even after all this time.

I loved you every *day we were together, and I'm pretty sure I'd fall for the man you've become if I had the chance to.*

Chance or no chance, it didn't matter. She knew it the day she'd shown him to his first class at Los Olivos High, the second he stepped out of that truck yesterday—and again when she found him at the vineyard this morning.

But there was more at stake this time around. Her future, for one. She'd put her life on hold to raise Owen, and there were no regrets there. But she was getting back on track now. All that stood between her and art school was one stupid painting that she *would* produce. But her son—*their* son—was still the most important person in her life.

Owen came first. Before she even thought about protecting her own heart, she had to protect his.

She emerged in the too-long T-shirt and shorts she'd had to creatively fold and roll at the waist to keep them from falling down. Jack stood at the kitchen counter in a fresh T-shirt and jeans himself, his feet bare, a steaming mug of coffee in his hand. He tilted his head toward a second mug on the kitchen table.

"I hope black is okay. We're out of everything." He forced a small smile, and she tried not to read too much into it. She'd dropped a bomb on him, and not in the way she'd hoped to do it. He'd need time to adjust, and she'd give him the space.

"Black is fine," she lied. "My clothes—I should run them to my car." Her eyes dropped to the towel-wrapped bundle in her arms, and he quickly set his coffee down and moved toward her.

"No," he said, taking the clothes from her. "I said I'd take care of that."

"Thank you." She ran a hand through her wet hair, trying to finger comb the tangles and keep herself from fidgeting in the presence of this strange yet familiar man who'd just kissed her until her lips were swollen.

He walked through the kitchen to what must be the laundry room, calling over his shoulder. "Everything here dryer safe?"

She laughed absently as she followed him, pausing in the open doorway. "I'm a single mom. I don't have time for clothes that *aren't* dryer safe."

A thick silence filled the air after that, punctuated moments later by the forceful slam of the dryer door. His back was still to her, and she swore under her breath.

"I'm sorry," she said softly. "That came out wrong. I mean, it's a mom joke, single or not. Shit. I don't know how to be me around you, Jack. I don't know how to do this." Not that she knew what *this* was. Was the coffee a peace offering or another obligatory gesture while she waited for her clothes to dry? Could he not even stand to be in the same room with her, or did a tiny part of him want her here?

He started the dryer and turned to face her, arms crossed and expression, as always, unreadable. Damn him for being able to hide like that when she wore her emotions like an obnoxious holiday sweater—screaming at you whether you wanted to see them or not.

"Yeah, well," he said. "I don't know how to be angry with you while a part of me still wants you, so I guess that makes two of us."

She exhaled. She'd spent all these years mired in guilt for not telling him, then resentment for thinking he'd found the life she'd always hoped he would—without her and Owen. Now she was wearing his clothes, and he *wasn't* wearing a ring, and what the hell did all of it mean?

She had no freaking clue. Still, she took a leap of faith with one tiny step over the threshold so they were now in the same room.

"So—you don't *hate* me?" she asked in complete earnest. Because right now that's all she needed to hear, that there was something salvageable between them, no matter how small.

He dropped his arms and pressed his hands against the dryer behind him, his gaze boring into hers.

"Shit, Ava. No. I don't hate you. I may not like how things went down, but that doesn't mean I don't get it—that I don't claim some of the responsibility. I've spent so goddamn long reminding myself what you did to me. I'm only now realizing what I did to you, and I need some time to wrap my head around that. Around all of this."

"I can live with that." She shivered.

"You're still cold," he said. A pile of folded towels sat atop the dryer in a basket, and he pulled one from the bottom and draped it over her shoulders. As soon as she felt the heat she understood why.

"You gave me the warmest one," she said, suppressing a smile. She wasn't going to let this silly bit of chivalry get to her.

Except it was already getting to her.

He tugged the cozy terry cloth around her, and she stumbled forward into his chest. She moved to step back, to pull at the tether that still seemed to bind them, but he kept each end of the towel firm in his grip—which kept *her* firm against *him*.

She swallowed and then took a chance, pressing her palms against his chest.

She felt his heartbeat, so strong and sure, and she wanted that sureness to be about her—about them. But they were strangers now. They had to proceed with caution.

For several seconds they just stood there, their mouths close enough so that warm breath mingled between them, but their lips didn't dare meet. Her heart rose in her throat as her pulse thrummed in her ears.

There was something in that moment before a kiss, in the anticipation of it. An exquisite ache. A rare hope. The promise of amazing—or of unimaginable heartbreak. Ava felt all of those things in Jack Everett's arms, and for this one moment she threw logic out the window and welcomed every single possibility if it meant his lips on hers again.

"I'm so goddamn angry." His voice rumbled in his chest, and she could feel the vibration of it against her palms.

"I know," she said, and she also knew that anger went deeper than what had happened between him and her.

"I spent so many years hung up on a warped version of the past. Now here you are—showing me what I've missed—and I don't know what to do with all of it. I just need a few minutes where I don't have to think about what comes next."

His breath was ragged. She could feel that same need—feel it building up until she thought she'd burst.

"No thinking," she agreed. She could do with forgetting, just for a few minutes, what it was that had gotten them to this moment.

And just like that, the towel dropped to the floor. His hands cupped her cheeks, and hers slid around his neck. As their lips met, still hungry yet more cautious than before, everything else fell away. Gone were the past ten years— her heartache, her regret, and her longing for something she wasn't sure she'd ever find.

All that mattered was this moment—Jack's hands on her skin, the electricity building between them as his tongue slipped past her parted lips and she tasted a sliver of re-demption. Restoration. Release.

His hands slid down her neck and then her sides, and a new kind of shiver ran through her as they rested on her hips, his fingertips kneading her over her shirt.

She unclasped her own hands from his neck and grabbed his wrist, moving his palm beneath the fabric of his T-shirt that she wore and onto her bare skin.

"Jesus, Red," he growled.

And there it was, the nickname he'd given her finally rolling off his own lips.

"I thought only Luke remembered what you used to call me," she said.

He shook his head and leaned back. "Didn't seem right before."

Does it seem right now? She wasn't going to ask.

"Stop thinking," she whispered. "We agreed. No thinking. Just for right now."

She guided his hand higher until the tips of his fingers brushed her taut nipple, and he hissed. She hoped this meant he'd listened to her request because her ability to speak, let alone think, no longer existed. She answered his touch by kissing him harder, deeper, begging him for more.

His thumb and forefinger pinched her tightened peak, and she drew in a sharp breath. Their bodies vibrated against the thrum of the dryer, and every one of her nerve endings was on heightened alert. She'd never been so sensitive to another man's touch, and it was this realization—this momentary weakness of logical freaking *thought*, that had her gasping and pulling away this time.

His blue eyes were a tempest of emotion, confirmation that this had gone too far.

"I'm sorry," he said. "I thought—"

"I told you not to think. I *wanted* you not to think." She shook her head. "But as much as I want to, I can't turn off my own voice of reason. The thing is, there's a little boy caught in the middle of this, and he has no clue about any of it. It's not fair to him, Jack." She had to force herself not to wince at his stricken expression—and not to fall apart when she saw his walls go back up, hiding any part of him he'd let slip through. "And it's not fair to us," she added.

He nodded.

"I'd like you to meet him," she said. "If you want to. I won't tell him who you are. Not until you're ready for him to know." She swallowed hard at the next thought. "And if you decide you don't want him to know—then we'll cross that bridge when the time comes. But I won't get his hopes up when there's the chance of them being shattered."

Jack's brows pulled together. "How would you—"

He didn't finish the question, but she'd guessed what he was asking. She'd spent the whole night before working it out, how she could let her son meet his father without any pressure of what came next.

"I told him you were a friend I hadn't seen in a long time. Once I tell him you played baseball all through high school and college, you'll automatically be his friend, too."

His lip gave a slight twitch, and although he didn't smile, she knew a part of him wanted to.

"He's a pitcher?" Jack asked.

Ava smiled. "He's really good. A natural. My dad gives him some pointers every now and then, but that part of Owen is all you." She glanced down at her attire and then lifted her shoulders. "I should go. I'm gonna write down my number. You can call me if you want to trade our clothes back—and if you want to see Owen again."

He stood there, jaw tight, his expression stoic.

She stepped toward him, leaning close to place a soft kiss on his cheek.

His shoulders relaxed.

"Thank you for hearing me out," she told him. "And for maybe, in some small way, understanding."

He nodded. "You're welcome. And Red?"

"Yeah?"

"I'm sorry you did all this alone."

She swallowed hard and started to back away toward the kitchen but paused as another idea struck that was either brilliant or foolish or both.

"The vineyard's beautiful," she said. "If you decide to keep it, I could help you get it up and running." She gave him a nervous smile. "Strictly business, of course. Though I wouldn't charge you much."

He pressed his lips together, not quite a grin but not a frown either.

"I'll consider your offer," he said, and she decided not to ask which one.

That night she lay in bed, exhausted but unable to fall asleep. At a quarter past eleven, her cell phone vibrated on her nightstand. She assumed it was a text, but when the vibrating continued, she remembered that she'd turned her ringer off after Owen had fallen asleep. She grabbed the phone quickly and accepted the call even though she didn't recognize the number.

"Hello?" she said in a half whisper, tiptoeing to her door and closing it so she didn't wake her son.

"You were sleeping. Shit. I shouldn't have called so late. Sorry if I—"

"Jack?"

"Yeah."

"I wasn't asleep."

"Oh."

"And—I'm glad you called."

He was silent for a few beats, so she waited, giving him his space.

"Red?"

"Yeah?"

"He's my son."

"Yeah," she said again, her voice breaking softly as she crawled back into bed. He'd said it with such conviction she wasn't sure what to make of it. But that didn't matter. He knew about Owen and acknowledged him, and that was already more than she could have hoped for after all this time.

"Of course I want to meet him. I never for a second should have made you think I didn't."

"It's okay." She swiped at a tear, then rolled her eyes at herself. Hadn't she cried enough for one day? But this was a happy tear. A hopeful one. She kind of liked it for a change.

"No," he said. "It's not okay. I was an asshole for letting you leave today without saying anything, but it's been a hell of a two days."

She laughed at this, and God it felt good to smile. The weight hadn't lifted from her chest, but it was suddenly a lot lighter. "I think you've earned a free pass or a get-out-of-jail-free card. Or something."

A deep, soft laugh sounded in her ear, and it only made her smile broaden.

"Jack Everett, did you just laugh?"

She heard the sound again.

"I think maybe I did," he said.

She opened her mouth to say more but then bit her tongue. She liked being the reason he laughed, but knowing it was enough. She wasn't going to break the spell by gloating.

"What about tomorrow after school?" he asked.

She grinned. "He gets out early. Noon, I think. Teacher in-service day or something like that. Are you free for a late lunch?"

"How about this great little barbeque place in town, BBQ on the Bluff? I hear they buy local, and from what Luke and Walker tell me, Crossroads Ranch has some of the best beef in the area."

She laughed again. "Did you make a joke?"

"I think maybe I did."

"We'd love to meet you for lunch," she told him. "And as far as Owen knows, you're my good friend Jack who I haven't seen in years."

He cleared his throat. "So, one o'clock?"

She let out a long breath and nodded, then remembered he couldn't see her. "Yeah. One o'clock. We'll see you then."

"Red?"

"Yeah?"

"I'm glad I called, too."

And then he was gone.

After the adrenaline wore off, her head sank against her pillow. She barely had time to double-check that her alarm was set before she drifted off into her first restful night of sleep in years.

She dreamed of kissing a boy under an olive tree—and what it would have been like if he'd stayed.

CHAPTER EIGHT

Jack's brothers both sat at the kitchen table, a spread of sandwich fixings laid out before them. The last of what was left in the fridge, he guessed. Both had risen early to do some work in the barn while Jack tended to paperwork regarding the mortgage and the inevitable sale of the vineyard. Walker must have had a tame evening because he was awake and alert as early as Luke had been. This had set Jack somewhat at ease for the morning. Maybe he wouldn't have to worry so much about his youngest brother once he went back to San Diego. And since he had the two of them together—sober—he figured this was as good a time as any to tell them.

"I'm meeting Ava for lunch."

The two of them barely looked up, let alone acknowledged, he'd said anything at all. He got it. After a morning of manual labor, nothing stood between a man and his next meal.

"She's bringing her nine-year-old son," he added. Luke offered a nod, and Walker grunted something that probably meant *I don't give a shit*. So Jack decided to go in for the kill. "His name is Owen. And he's mine. Which means you two assholes are uncles. Congratulations."

Walker coughed on a piece of roast beef he'd just shoved

in his mouth. Luke stopped mid mustard spread. Jack crossed his arms and raised his brows. Silence rang out for a beat. Then another. And one more after that.

Finally Walker swallowed. "You got a kid?" he said.

"It appears that I do."

"Did you know?" Luke asked.

Jack ran a hand through his shower-damp hair, hoping the gesture would mask his erratic heartbeat. His first reaction to the news had been fight or flight, and he'd chosen flight. Now—now he was going to meet this portion of his past head-on. He still didn't think he had what it took to be a father, let alone a good one, but he owed it to the boy—to *Owen*—to see.

"No," he told them. "And before you start talking shit about Ava for keeping this from me, know that the whole situation is complicated as hell."

Walker finished piecing together his sandwich and took a savage bite. "You know how you keep things *un*complicated, big brother?" he asked without giving two shits that half his snarling mouth was full of food. "Cover your dick, or keep it in your prepubescent pants."

Luke snorted.

Jack ground his teeth. Some things were funny as hell, but his past with Ava—how Owen came to be—sure as shit wasn't. "Everything's a joke to you, asshole," he said. "Christ, we were eighteen. We used protection. It didn't work. I didn't know until two days ago. End of story."

"Didn't know what?"

Jack pivoted to see Jenna standing in the doorway, tote bags in each hand with what looked like groceries.

She wasn't kidding. His brothers would probably starve without her help.

He strode to where she stood and relieved her of half

the bags, welcoming the diversion even though he knew it would be short-lived.

"That we're uncles," Luke said, standing to peek at what she'd brought them. "Eggs," he added. "I like eggs."

Jenna deposited her bags on the counter and spun to face Jack, who was ready and waiting for her reaction.

"Why are they uncles?" she asked, and his brows pulled together. Jenna backhanded him on the shoulder. "Why are they uncles, Jack?"

He could hear the hysteria building, which was not a good sign considering Jenna didn't get hysterical. She didn't get *anything*, really. They'd gone from walking on eggshells around Jack Senior to someone who rarely let them see her angry at all.

He put a hand over hers, hoping the gesture and his attempt at a soothing tone would reassure her. "Ava," he said. "Ava Ellis. We were—well, we—that spring—"

"Let me spell it out for you," Walker interrupted. "He knocked up the Ellis girl and then skipped town for a decade."

Jenna gasped, and Jack whirled on his brother, who was standing now as well. He grabbed Walker's collar, fisting it between his fingers.

"I didn't know, damn it!" Jack said through gritted teeth. "Christ, I didn't know. So cut me some slack or shut the hell up."

Walker's cheeks flamed with a building rage Jack hadn't seen before. He let go of his youngest brother and took a step back.

"There's a lot of shit you don't know, *Junior*."

Jack winced at the nickname. His father had first called him that when he was child not much younger than Owen. Later that name became a warning.

Watch it, Junior. You better shut the hell up, Junior. Pour my bottle down the drain one more time…Junior.

Walker threw open the fridge and found himself a beer. "Lost my appetite," he said, brushing past them all and out through the back door.

Jack pressed his palms against the counter where Walker had stood. He knew being back in this house would have its challenges, but he hadn't anticipated his brothers being one of them. They'd been allies once. He'd been their protector, and he didn't expect recognition or thank yous or anything like that. Yet he'd somehow taken for granted that they'd remember what he *had* done—assumed that being there back then, when he knew they truly needed him, would make up for being gone.

But intermittent visits, emails, and texts hadn't been enough. He didn't know his brothers anymore.

He felt a hand on his shoulder and knew the gentle gesture came from his aunt. When he turned, he saw Luke striding out the front door, sandwich in hand, and he wondered what his brother's ever-present grin hid beneath the surface.

"I didn't think it'd be this hard," he said, and she gave his shoulder a soft squeeze.

"If it was easy, everyone would do it."

"If *what* was easy?"

Jenna shrugged. "Coming home, facing your past, mending fences. Meeting your *child* for the first time?"

He let out a long, shaky breath. "I have a son," he said, the word still so foreign on his tongue. "She named him *Owen.*"

Jenna's hand flew to her mouth, stifling a gasp—or maybe a sob. Because the word—his son's name—was like an automated switch, and a tear that seemed to come from nowhere sped down her cheek.

Jenna *Owens*. It was her name, too.

He was ready to apologize for—he wasn't sure what. But he knew that whenever he opened his mouth lately, someone seemed to get upset. Before he could say anything, though, she dropped her hand to reveal a beaming smile.

"I'm a great-aunt!" she said, laughing. "Well, shit. You just aged me a half century."

Her joy was contagious, and Jack found himself smiling, too.

"We're not telling him who I am. Not yet, anyway," he said.

It took less than ten words for Jenna's expression to fall. "Of course," she said, feigning nonchalance. "Of course. You and Ava have a lot to figure out. I didn't think—" But she stopped herself, and Jack could tell she was fending off a different kind of tears.

He hugged his aunt. "I don't know how you do it," he said.

"Do what?" she asked, wiping the back of her hand under each eye. "Turn into a basket case almost every time you see me?"

He shook his head. "Your first instinct with me and Luke and Walker—when you hadn't seen us in years—was to take us in. You have this heart that's bigger than anything I've seen. You haven't even met Owen yet, and you love him already."

"Family is everything," she said. "And you feel something too, Jack. I won't let you pretend you don't."

He shoved his hands in the front pockets of his jeans. "Maybe. But I don't know how to love like that—like you do."

Jenna pressed her palm to her chest. "Oh, honey. You

were too young to remember, but I do—how your mama and daddy looked at you like you had the power to make the sun come up in the morning. I was so jealous of all the attention my big sister gave to you." She smiled wistfully. "They loved *you* like that. And I know somewhere in that protected heart of yours, you have the capacity, too. You just need to unlock it."

Jack's jaw tightened. It wasn't that he didn't appreciate what his aunt was trying to do. But the only father he remembered was some sort of funhouse mirror reflection of the man she tried to recall for him now. Where she remembered smiles, Jack saw a sneer. Terms of endearment were twisted into angry words filled with disdain and blame.

If she didn't have to work so hard taking care of you boys, she never would have gotten sick.

"That's not the man I knew," he said with such force it made her flinch. "Shit, Jenna, I didn't mean—"

"It's okay," she interrupted. "I mean, no. It's not okay to talk to me like that, but I'm going to let it slide. You've come against more than I reckon you bargained for coming back home, and I'm sure it's a lot to take in." She reached up and brushed off his shoulders and then slapped her hands against his cheeks. "You look good, nephew."

He looked down at his checked shirt and worn jeans. It was fine attire for a barbeque, but for meeting his son?

"I don't know what the hell I'm doing here. I really don't." He scrubbed a hand across his jaw. "I'm out of my goddamn element. I don't know how to talk to kids. And he could hate me the second he meets me. Not sure if you noticed, but I'm not exactly the easiest guy to be around these days." He cleared his throat. "And I shouldn't have snapped at you. I'm sorry. You're right about that much."

"I know I am, darling," she said with a grin.

"But," he added, "it doesn't help to hear what kind of man my father used to be. Because that's not the man he was in the end."

He kissed her on the cheek and backed toward the front door.

She pointed a finger at him. "It also says nothing about the man *you* are, Jack Everett."

He swallowed hard but kept moving, wishing he could believe her. But Jenna had just reminded him that his father was someone else entirely before his mother got sick. Maybe once he'd seen his son as someone who could light up the world. But then he plunged himself into complete darkness at the bottom of a bottle, blaming his own children even though they had lost their mother, too.

He was at the door now, but neither of them had broken eye contact. He thought about making his aunt flinch, about slamming his hand against his truck when he was at the Ellis Vineyard, of all the times he'd had to remind himself to rein in the anger before he simply exploded like he had with Derek Wilkes.

You're not good for either of them.

Ava's father's words ran on a continuous loop in his head.

"Actually, Jenna, it says everything."

CHAPTER NINE

O wen squirmed in the wooden booth next to her. "Mo-*om*. I'm so hungry I think I'm going to die."

Ava laughed, hoping her son couldn't see through the re-action to the nerves that lay beneath. Normally she'd give him a snack in the car—a bag of goldfish crackers or one of those squeezie applesauce pouches—but she hadn't wanted him to be full once they got to the restaurant. He needed the food to keep him from getting bored. And to keep him from being idle enough to scrutinize anything about Jack he might not want scrutinized.

"In a few minutes, bud. Promise."

But it was five minutes to one, and Jack wasn't here. *Yet.* Because of course he was coming. She hadn't spent the whole hour mentally reassuring herself only for him not to show.

Oh shit. What if he didn't show?

She'd chosen to sit with their backs to the door. Oth-erwise her eagerness to see Jack enter would get the best of her. But this only made things worse. More than once she'd attempted to casually look over her shoulder only to meet the curious eyes of several BBQ on the Bluff patrons.

"Are you two ready to order, or are you waiting on someone else?"

Ava startled as a young woman with a blond pixie bounced a pen against a pad of paper. "It's cool if you're still waiting. I've got a couple of nephews, though, probably around your little guy's age, and all they ever do is *eat*. Figured he might be hungry."

Ava smiled and turned to Owen, who gave her a pleading look.

"We *are* waiting for someone, but I guess it couldn't hurt to—"

"Lily Green, since when do they let the cook out of the kitchen?"

At the sound of Jack's voice, a warmth spread through Ava's veins like chocolate fondue, hot and sweet and delicious. She shook her head. This was *not* the place to let his smooth baritone start—*doing* things to her.

"Since I'm short two servers this afternoon," the other woman said with a grin. "And how about you tell me why I've already seen you twice in the span of four days? Luke told Tucker you'd be hightailing it out of Oak Bluff first chance you got." She turned her attention to Ava. "My husband and Jack's little brother, Luke, are good friends. Best friends, actually. But me and Luke? We butt heads like you wouldn't believe. Wonder if big brother here is as difficult as the other." She winked at Jack.

He smiled and slid into the booth across from Ava and Owen.

"Am I late?" he asked, and Ava shook her head. He glanced back at the woman with the notepad—*Lily*. And Ava couldn't help the surge of relief she'd felt when the woman said *husband*.

"Start us off with that cornbread you sent over the other night, will ya?" Jack added. "I've been craving it ever since."

Lily shoved her pen behind her ear and dropped the pad into her apron pocket. "You got it. I'll get the rest of your order when I deliver the goods."

Only after Lily was gone did Jack give Ava his full attention, and she had to remind herself to breathe when he looked right past her and let his eyes fall on Owen.

"Hey, bud," he said. "You like cornbread?"

Owen narrowed his eyes at Jack—at his father—and Ava watched as the boy studied the man. Finally, her son nodded.

"Yeah, I like it," he said, then looked back and forth between his parents. "My mom calls me that, by the way. *Bud.*"

She held her breath, and Jack cleared his throat. He was nervous, and Owen was already giving him the third degree. But then Jack crossed his arms and smiled. She wasn't sure what she was expecting, but he seemed ready to take whatever Owen had to dish out.

"What should *I* call you, then?" Jack asked him, and Owen crossed his arms as well.

"You're a friend of my mom's?"

"I am," Jack said.

"A *good* friend? Because if you were a good friend I think I would have heard of you before."

Jack let out a nervous laugh while Ava seemed to ignore her earlier directive reminding herself to breathe.

"Truth is," Jack started, "your mom and I used to be real good friends. Then I left town, and we lost touch for a while." He turned his attention to her, his blue-eyed gaze steady and intent. And Ava's heart stuttered like it had the first time she saw him in high school. "But I think I'd like for us to be friends again."

Owen tilted his head toward her so that both of their gazes were fixed on hers.

"Do you wanna be friends with him again?" Owen asked.

Ava cleared her throat. "Yeah, bud. I think I do."

Because friendship she could admit to wanting. Friendship was a start. What she wouldn't do was hope—this early on—that it would lead to more.

Owen nodded and faced Jack again. "One more question."

"I'm all ears," Jack said, his lips hinting at a grin.

"Marvel or DC?"

Jack's brows raised, and Ava bit her lip.

"And here I thought I was going to get a *hard* question," Jack said. "Because the only right answer is Marvel, and the top Avenger, of course, is the first Avenger, Captain Steve Rogers."

Owen pumped his fist in the air and shouted, "Yes! Okay, Mom. This guy's cool. I think you two should be friends again."

Ava's breathing finally steadied, but she had a rising tide of emotion. Because Jack and Owen had connected. Her son had just given his own father the seal of approval. And she—well, she'd never expected this day to happen, let alone have it be a success.

"Cornbread for all my friends!" Lily said, placing a basket on the table.

The spell was broken, but a new one took hold as Owen devoured a piece before Lily even had time to leave the table. They all watched as he sank into the booth as he swallowed—satiated for the moment.

"Did he even chew that?" Lily asked.

Owen grinned and rubbed a hand over his belly. "Whatever I did, I'm gonna do it again." He reached for piece number two, but Ava's hand landed on his wrist before he could swipe another golden square.

"Drink something, bud. You're gonna choke or make yourself sick if you don't slow down."

Jack scratched the back of his neck and squinted at Lily. "I remember my brothers saying this place had the best strawberry lemonade. You still got that?"

She shook her head, and Ava watched as Owen deflated.

"I change the menu monthly. But I've got a frozen strawberry limeade that'll knock your socks off. What do you say?"

Owen perked up again. Ava smiled and lifted her shoulders. Jack slapped a palm down on the table.

"I guess that settles it," he said. "Three strawberry limeades, and judging by this guy's appetite, I think we're ready to order."

Forty-five minutes later, Owen was working off his short ribs at the vintage Pac Man machine with a stack of quarters—courtesy of Jack. Ava was still picking at her brisket sandwich as she watched Jack take a long, slow swig of his limeade.

"You're good with him," she said softly, and the anticipation of his response made everything inside her constrict.

He set his glass down on the red and white checkerboard tablecloth, running his thumb down the cool condensation. "I'm flying by the seat of my pants, here. I'm just lucky you raised an amazing kid," he said, eyes trained on the hand still holding the glass, his voice rough. "Made today a whole lot easier."

She took a chance, bold as it was, and laid her palm over his free hand. "*We* made an amazing kid," she whispered. "That's not all me, there."

His eyes met hers, clouded with too much emotion for her to read. She guessed there was still anger—at her in particular. She owned that and would continue to do so. But pain lay beyond those blue irises, too. A pain she'd always wanted to take away, even when they were teens. But she learned too late that she hadn't possessed that kind of power. And maybe she never would.

But Owen was pure magic. She'd felt that every day for almost nine-and-a-half years. And if Jack could lasso even a thread of it, maybe he'd understand the type of joy only a child could bestow.

"You mean baseball and Marvel? That just means he's smart." Jack laughed. "I gotta be honest," he added, and Ava noticed he hadn't pulled his hand from hers yet. "I didn't think it would be a good idea to let this go beyond lunch."

She sucked in a sharp breath, soft enough, though, that maybe it went unheard. But he did hear, because his hand left the glass and covered hers, her palm sandwiched between his.

Now her breathing grew shallow for an entirely different reason. She knew this discussion was about Owen, but Jack touching her was something else. Because his thumb moved in slow, soft strokes against her skin, and her stomach flipped with each small movement, making her forget for a moment what they were even talking about.

Owen. This is about Owen. It wasn't the time for her to lose focus or get lost in thoughts of what might have been... or what could be. Owen and Cal Poly. That was all she could handle right now.

But this man who'd been so afraid of who he'd become already knocked it out of the park with their son, and she wasn't sure what should come next.

"And now?" she asked, reeling herself back in.

"Now I kinda don't want to let him out of my sight. Not yet. I mean—if it's okay with you, I'd love for you both to come by the ranch after we settle up here. I could show him around, maybe even introduce him to the two assholes who live there."

She bit her lip, hesitating. She'd already gotten more than she'd bargained for out of this day. She wanted to be near him—God, yes she did. But she didn't want to fall for someone who might not stick around. She wouldn't survive it again.

"I'm not sure that's—" she started, but he interrupted.

"As friends, of course," he said. "I'll call ahead and let everyone know the situation."

"Of course," she agreed. "And maybe," she added, knowing she needed to get the words out before she lost her nerve, "we should keep it as just friends, too. For now. While we're figuring this out." Her world was already spinning out of orbit. Anything more than friends would knock her off her axis wholly and completely. Then where would she be?

Just uttering the phrase made her chest feel hollow. There had been so much pent-up emotion in their first frenzied kiss—and in their stolen moment in the laundry room yesterday. So much that they couldn't put into words was spoken in the touching of their lips. But Owen was the first priority. Plus, she'd gotten her hopes up about inviting Jack back into her life before, and it had crushed her to see he'd moved on. Simply because he hadn't gone through with the marriage didn't mean whatever was brewing between them meant anything.

It was probably nothing more than heat. Pent-up chemistry that would dissipate with time.

Jack stirred his straw in his glass. "Of course," he said again, this time with less conviction.

"I'll do anything I can to keep from hurting him, Jack. *Anything*. You need to know how much I want you in his life, but if he finds out who you are and you leave again? That will crush him."

Because the crux of it was that she hadn't meant to hold a torch for him all these years. But the reminder of how much she'd loved him was in her son's eyes—in his very essence. Jack Everett had always been with her. After her failed attempt at reconnecting with him in L.A., she'd given up hope of ever seeing him again. If he'd ever come back to his aunt's place, he hadn't come looking for her. Now here he was, the man she always knew he'd become—and he had more power to hurt her than he ever did.

"You're right," he finally said, then slid out of the booth. He laid a couple of twenties on the check Lily had left. Ava opened her mouth to protest, but Jack simply shook his head. "Your money's no good here. Besides, you heard how she's married to Luke's buddy, Tucker. They've been struggling a bit, so I want to leave a little extra—not that it will help."

Ava slid out of the booth as well, marveling at Jack's generosity. She wasn't surprised at the man he'd become, not one little bit. But he wasn't the only one who'd missed out on these past ten years. He was a natural with Owen. He could have been back then, too, if she'd have been brave enough to have given him the choice.

"I want to help you and Owen, too. I mean—" He scratched the back of his head. "I have money. And a promotion in the works. No matter what, you and Owen won't want for anything, financially speaking." He laughed. "As long as this damn vineyard doesn't sink the ranch further into the hole."

"I take care of Owen just fine," she said, the words coming out sharper than she'd intended.

"Of course. I didn't mean..." He trailed off.

"Look. I appreciate what you're offering." But this time she was the one without words. Because how did she tell him that she wasn't looking for financial stability to come from anyone else? She'd fallen back on her parents in terms of money and an easy income since she'd graduated high school. She didn't bring Owen here to meet his father just so Jack could offer them more money in the bank.

That was why she was finally applying to school again—why she'd take every cent of financial aid she could get and repay it with an impressive graphic design job—or maybe she could restore pieces at the San Luis Obispo Museum of Art. Whatever it was, *she* was going to do it. Owen didn't need money. He needed a father. And *she* needed...Was it fair to insert herself into this scenario when she should put her son first? Because no matter how hard she tried, she couldn't stop thinking of the *what ifs*.

What if she fell for him again?

What if he stayed?

What if he left?

Finally she crossed her arms and smiled. What they *both* needed was a subject change. "Is this where you take me up on my offer to help you get it up and running?"

He sighed. "Jack Senior's lawyer doesn't think we'll get

back what he bought it for without it thriving. Keeping it until then might be the only option."

"Just tell me you need my help, and it's yours," she said. "It's not harvest season, so things are slow at the Ellis Vineyard. I manage the shop and tasting room, mostly, but it's not hard to get coverage for that if I need to. Plus, I've never taken a vacation, and I know the owners. I'll just have to ply them with extra time with their grandson."

He raised a brow. "You gonna tell them what you're doing? Who you're spending your time with?"

"I don't answer to them," she spouted, a little too defensively. Because despite being a grown woman, in a way she did. If it wasn't for her parents, raising Owen these past nine years would have been a hell of a lot more difficult. "But I also have nothing to hide. So yes, I'll tell them." Until she knew *how* Jack was going to fit into Owen's life, she wasn't sure what to tell them.

"Fair enough," he said, not pressing her to say more. So she didn't. "Then I guess all that's left is a question." He cleared his throat and cocked his head to the side. "Ava Ellis, will you help me restore a vineyard?"

She grinned. "Well, Jack Everett, I thought you'd never ask."

And just like that, the deal was done. He promised her he'd be in town for at least a month, and in turn she promised him she'd make sure Luke and Walker were well on their way to producing the maiden vintage by the time he left, if that's what he decided.

For now she'd convince herself that the compromise would be enough. After all, none of this was part of Jack's plan. She understood that.

He hadn't planned to drive by the vineyard the other day. But he did. He hadn't planned on fatherhood, yet he'd just spent the better part of an hour dissecting the friendship between Captain America and the Winter Soldier with his son.

He hadn't planned on the vineyard, but he was staying to get it off the ground. And maybe—just maybe—Oak Bluff wasn't where he saw his future.

But maybe now that things had changed ... it was.

CHAPTER TEN

D o not let Luke or Walker mess this up," Jack barked into his cell phone, and a long pause stretched out between him and his aunt. "Jenna? Did you hear me?"

What *he* heard was a soft sniffle. Christ. Maybe it wasn't his brothers he needed to worry about.

"Jenna?" he said again, drawing out her name, and she cleared her throat.

"We—we get to meet him? We get to meet Owen?"

He sighed. He should have realized this would be almost as big of a deal for them as it was for him.

"Yes," he said. "But we're going to be there in a couple of minutes, and I need your word that the three of you can handle this, that you can handle not letting him know who you are yet."

Jack glanced in his rearview mirror to see that Ava's red Jeep was still behind him. "Of course," Jenna said. "We can handle this. We won't tell Owen anything before you do."

"We can handle it, asshole!" he heard Luke yell into Jenna's phone. "She's the one getting all weepy and shit. No worries, brother. We're not going to blow your cover."

Jack let out a long breath as they were pulling up the ranch's driveway. He guessed he'd have to trust them.

Maybe it was a foolish, impulsive decision to invite Ava and Owen back, but something warred within him not to let them go home. Not yet. It had just been lunch, but it was also something entirely more. And Jack had no idea what to do with more. So instead of handling it himself, he'd pawn that responsibility off on the most dysfunctional of families—his own.

He hopped out of his truck and turned to where Ava pulled in behind him. He crossed his arms and tilted his head toward the sun, squinting.

Here went nothing.

He dropped his gaze toward his guests and was startled to see Owen mirroring his stance—arms across his chest and head raised to the sky. Something in his own chest sank. Or maybe it lifted. He couldn't tell. All he knew was that the sight of this boy—and this place—knocked him off-kilter.

"What is it?" Ava asked, striding toward him.

Jack shook his head. "Nothing. Let's—uh—go inside."

Ava shrugged, and Owen's head dropped so their eyes met.

"This is your house?" the boy asked. His eyes volleyed from the ranch, to the barn and stable, to the cows grazing in the pasture beyond the residence. "Is it a farm?"

Jack chuckled softly, grateful to Owen for breaking the ice, even if he didn't realize he was.

"This *is* my house," he said. "But I don't live here anymore. My brothers do. And it's not a farm. It's a ranch."

The three of them headed for the porch's front steps, for the door he knew would open to let Owen and Ava in—to let them past the threshold that was his life.

"What's the difference?" Owen asked, and Jack ruffled his hair, the strands thick and wavy beneath his fingers. Like his own, yet softer—and red like his mom's.

His fingers twitched. Then he pulled his hand away.

"Well," Jack said. "For starters, we don't grow anything but cattle. And farmers tend to know a lot more about the land—about growing things from the earth."

Owen nodded as they climbed the steps. "Like Mom and our family does with grapes?"

Out of the corner of his eye, Jack saw Ava smiling at them. "Yep. Growing grapes is like farming. And it so happens I have some grapes of my own to tend to, and your mom offered to help me learn how."

He pulled the screen door open and gestured for Owen and Ava to walk inside.

"She's a good teacher," Owen said, stepping into Jack's childhood home. "She taught me how to ride a bike and tie my shoes. She even taught me how to memorize the fifty states in alphabetical order—but not a whole lot of my friends think that's cool, so it's kind of our secret." He looked at his mom and then back at Jack. "I guess you're in on the secret now, too."

The boy, unassuming and unafraid, strode past Jack and his mom, his curiosity seeming to take over as he started down the hall and toward the kitchen.

"He knows how to ride a bike and tie his shoes," he said, an unexpected twinge of envy socking him in the gut.

"Yes," Ava said softly, keen understanding in her tone. "But there's still so much for him to learn." She paused for a moment, worrying her top lip between her teeth. "You just taught him the difference between a farm and a ranch. I'm guessing there's a lot more you could teach him...if you wanted to."

But there wasn't time for him to respond because as the door clicked into place behind them, he caught sight of Jenna emerging from the kitchen, her hand outstretched to shake Owen's.

What *did* he want? Jack wanted to do right by this kid who had no idea his world could be turned upside down at the drop of a hat. He wanted to do right by his brothers, his aunt, and the woman who'd sacrificed her own future to give him the one she thought he wanted.

The one *he* thought he wanted.

New York. He was moving to New York. *That* was his future—one where he could keep the ranch and vineyard financially afloat. One where he could make sure Ava and Owen never wanted for anything.

But even he knew that wasn't what it meant to be a father. *Or* a brother. New York was the logical next step in his career. But was it still the logical next step in his life?

Owen turned to them as they caught up. "Mom. This is Jenna, Jack's aunt, and she said that I can go to the stables with Jack's brother and that I can ride a horse and go see all the cows, and I know you're going to say that I've never ridden and I could get hurt, but *please* say yes. I'll be careful. *Please?*"

Jenna smiled sheepishly. "I'm sorry. I maybe should have asked you first, but I get a little excited around sweet kids like this one, and he just walked in here, introduced himself, and I couldn't help myself."

Jack understood Jenna's nervous energy, but he kept quiet, knowing this was Ava's call. He didn't have a say in what Owen did or didn't do.

Luke sauntered in from the laundry room off the back of the kitchen and tipped his cattleman hat to his guests. "Did

Jenna say I'm taking Shortstop here for a ride?" he asked with a knowing grin.

"*Shortstop?*" Owen asked, crossing his arms again as he'd done outside. "I'm taller than most of the other kids in my grade. *And* I'm a pitcher."

Luke crouched before his nephew, resting his elbows on the knees of his dirty jeans.

"A ball player, eh? Like your friend Jack." Luke raised a brow at his brother before turning his attention back to Owen. "You may be taller than the other kids," he said, sizing his nephew up. "But you sure as shit ain't taller than me." He winked. "*Shortstop.*"

Jenna playfully slapped her younger nephew on the back of the head as he stood. "Language, Luke."

Owen shrugged. "It's okay. Mom says it all the time."

Ava gasped. "I do *not*!"

Jack's eyes widened with amusement as he waited for the story to unfold.

Owen nodded. "Sometimes when you leave the window open in your painting room, I hear you when Scully and I are playing out back." He pressed his lips together and looked at the rest of them. "Painting pisses her off."

Ava's mouth hung open, and Jack tried to ignore the implication of what Owen had just revealed. The Ava he remembered had loved painting above everything else. Painting didn't make her upset. It was what she did when she was already pissed off in order to calm down.

"Owen," he said. "This is my brother Luke. There's two things you need to know about him. One, he knows horses, and there's no one better to teach you how to ride one. And two—once my brother gives you a nickname, he's not likely to call you anything else, so get used to Shortstop. Wear the name with pride."

Owen let out a breath. "Can I ride, Mom? *Please?*"

Luke took his hat off and held it against his chest. "I'll take him out on Cleo. She's our gentlest, doesn't mind being led. I'll never let her go beyond a walk."

Ava's shoulders slumped. "You promise he's safe?" she asked, squinting at the still healing wound on Luke's cheek.

The man winked again. "Don't worry. I'll save the bull riding for lesson two." Luke clasped a hand on Owen's shoulder. "What do you say, *Shortstop?*"

Owen groaned, but he was smiling as Luke led him back the way he came. Ava pressed her lips together—a wince she seemed to be forcing into a smile.

"Don't worry," Jenna said. "Luke may be a daredevil when it comes to his own safety, but Owen's in good, capable hands with him. No one knows those horses like he does."

The back door opened, and Walker ambled in from the deck.

"Nice of you to make an appearance," Jack said.

The youngest Everett brother raised the bottle of beer that was in his right hand. "Figured you wanted the family to make a good impression on the kid," he said with a mild sneer. "And I wasn't really in the mood to impress."

Jack opened his mouth to say something but Jenna put a hand on his arm.

"Don't," she said softly. "Not today."

There was enough genuine concern in her tone that Jack let it slide.

He hadn't realized Walker's drinking had become this— regular. And how often did Luke get injured with the rodeo shit? Was Jenna happy? And Christ, he had a son who already knew how to ride a bike, tie his shoes, and say the fifty states in alphabetical order.

"Jack?" Jenna said, and it sounded like it wasn't the first time she'd said his name. "Are you okay?"

He shook his head softly, bringing himself back into the moment, and realized Jenna, Ava, and Walker were all staring at him.

"I'm fine," he said, his words short and clipped. "Ava says we can get the vineyard up and running, that she can help. Once we see if we can turn a crop, we can decide whether or not to put it back on the market. So I thought we could all sit down and talk, figure out a game plan."

Jenna clapped her hands together. "Is there going to be a tasting room? A gift shop? Y'all are pretty handy, right?" She looked Jack and Walker up and down. "You could, like, build something, right?"

Walker brushed past them, set his empty bottle on the counter, and tore open the stainless steel refrigerator to retrieve another. He peeked around the corner of the door.

"I'm assuming we're going to be at this awhile. Who else wants one?"

Ava and Jenna both declined, using the fact that they'd both be behind the wheel soon as their excuse. As much as he'd love to dull them, Jack wanted to keep his senses razor sharp. Everything hinged on this damn vineyard—on getting it running so he could get his life back. Whatever that meant.

Walker shrugged. "At least no one can accuse me of not sharing." He dropped into one of the high-backed wooden chairs at the long kitchen table that Jack still couldn't believe his brother had made. Jenna and Ava took their seats as well.

"I'm going to grab the paperwork," Jack said, and made a detour to his office before returning. He sat down, opened a leather-bound binder, and ran a hand through his hair as he started skimming pages.

He shook his head. "What the hell is a *Burgundian varietal*?" he asked.

Ava's eyes brightened. "May I?" she asked, motioning for the binder.

"Please," Jack said, sliding it in her direction. "Translate."

She laughed. "We grow the same grapes," she said. "This will be easier than I thought. I mean, I know the varietals and what we can make—pinot noir, maybe. Chardonnay. But I saw the plants, and they've not been tended to properly in quite some time. The trick will be producing a viable harvest first."

"Well," Walker said, popping the top off his bottle. "You gonna be able to teach us how to do magic?"

Jack shook his head, but she held his brother's gaze.

"Yes," she said. "If you're all up to the task, then so am I." She looked at Jenna. "And your aunt is right. You should think about a tasting room, something to get customers in the door so they learn the difference between Crossroads Ranch and Crossroads Vineyard."

Jenna beamed. "Crossroads *Vineyard*. I don't know about y'all, but I love the sound of it."

Walker leaned forward, resting his elbows on the dark wood of the table. "There is a structure on the outskirts of the property. It's not complete, but I've been out to inspect it. I think that's where all the tanks and barrels and shit are supposed to go."

"Liking the sound of it isn't enough. I'm sorry, Jenna." Jack rubbed his eyes with the heels of his hands. "Shit. It'd be easier to sell it at a loss. This is going to be more than an investment of time. You know that, right?" He hadn't directed the comment at anyone in particular, but he was sure they knew he meant Walker.

"There is the life insurance payout," his brother said, and Jack nodded.

"That might scratch the surface," he added.

"And Jack Senior may have been pissing away his own savings, but I've been putting money away—my own account, not that one you set up for me. Plan was to build my own place eventually, but maybe I don't need to. Not right now."

Jack's eyes widened, and the two women looked on, watching whatever was about to unfold—unfold.

"I can't ask you—" Jack began, but Walker cut him off.

"You aren't the only asshole who gets to make decisions around here, *big brother*. If this is what's best for the financial state of the ranch, then this is where I'm putting my money. Luke can decide what the hell he wants to do, and if you want to add some of your precious lawyering cash to the heap, that's *your* decision. But I've made mine."

Jack gave his brother a slow nod. Issues aside, somewhere underneath Walker had a good head on his shoulders. And no matter their differences, his brother was still putting family first.

"I'm in," Jack said. "Adding my cash to the heap."

The corner of Walker's mouth twitched into something that almost resembled a smile.

"Who's in?"

Luke and Owen traipsed in from the mudroom.

"Are you done with your ride already?" Ava asked, and Owen shook his head.

"Luke showed me how to brush Cleo and put her saddle on and—I got thirsty."

Luke clapped his hands together. "Came back for some

lemonade, but it looks to me like I'm walking in on something pretty big."

Jenna beamed. "Jack and Walker are investing in the vineyard. Ava's going to help get us on our way to harvest, and..." She paused for a few seconds. "And I'm just so damned happy to see you three together again."

Luke raised a brow but said nothing as he headed for the fridge and emerged seconds later with a pitcher of lemonade. He poured Owen a glass, then filled four more, setting one in front of Jenna, then Ava, and then Jack. He finished off the pitcher on a final glass—his own—then raised it.

"I'm in," he said.

Walker held up his bottle. "To the damned grapes."

"Language!" Jenna yelled, but she was laughing.

Jack laughed, too, and then the rest of them said in unison—Owen too, "To the damned grapes!"

Every single one of them bore some semblance of a grin, even Walker. It was one hell of a sight, one Jack wanted to enjoy awhile longer.

He'd tell them about New York tomorrow.

CHAPTER ELEVEN

Owen drummed his hands on the passenger seat head-rest in time with the music playing on the radio. Ava didn't recognize the song, but then again, her mind kept wandering somewhere else.

Her world had been so small for so long—only her, Owen, and her parents. But in a matter of days, Owen's family had grown exponentially to include a father, two uncles, and a great-aunt, all who'd welcomed him into the fold like he'd always been one of them. She swallowed back the guilt at what all of them had missed out on these past ten years. After she'd given up hope about Jack coming home after college, she'd resigned herself to this solitary life, convinced that her son was enough. In many ways he was. But she knew now, after seeing Owen with the family he'd never known existed, that it wasn't enough for *him*.

"Did Jack really play college baseball?" he asked, forcing her back into the moment.

Ava grinned.

"Yeah," she said. "He did."

"Did you know him then? When he played?"

She shook her head. "When I met Jack, he was injured

and couldn't play. A broken leg. Once he went off to college? Well—we lost touch."

Owen bounced in his seat. "I bet it was from an epic slide into home. Or maybe he had to wrangle some cattle with Luke and Walker and he got trampled or something." She caught sight of him in the rearview mirror, his eyes bright with excitement. "I can't believe there are real cowboys right here in our county—and that you *know* them."

She forced her smile not to falter and kept her eyes trained on the road. How she wished that was Jack's story—an *epic slide into home.* She couldn't imagine what it was like for him to be in that house with those memories, a place that held far more pain than anything she'd ever endured. She'd expected today's meeting with Jack to end with lunch, and instead he'd invited her and Owen to cross a threshold of sorts. She knew Jack was strong, but to let them in like he did today? She wondered if he had any clue how strong he really was.

"You liked the Everetts, huh?" she asked.

Owen laughed. "If you promise not to tell him, I even sort of like Luke calling me *Shortstop.* It's like having a big brother or something."

Ava couldn't control the tear that escaped the corner of her eye, but she wiped it away without a sniffle, hoping Owen didn't notice. He was quiet for several long seconds, and because she didn't know what else to say, so was she.

"Do you think *he* does cool stuff like the Everetts?" Owen finally asked, and she knew what was coming. It had been a long time since anything had triggered questions like this.

"Your dad?" This time she did sniffle, because today had been amazing and wonderful and everything she'd wanted. Yet it had also been a lie. But the ball wasn't in her court anymore. It was in Jack's. She owed it to him to let things unfold on his timeline, to be sure about what role he wanted to play in his son's life before they told him.

"Yes," she answered him. "I think he does a lot of amazing things. You know he wouldn't have left if he didn't have to, right? I know it's hard to understand, bud, but he was—*is*—a good man. I'm sure of it. But sometimes, even when people care about each other, their lives go in different directions. And that's what happened with us."

The tears were impossible to hide now, so she let them flow, rummaging in her purse for a tissue as they did.

"I'm sorry, Mom," Owen said softly. "I didn't mean to make you sad."

"Never apologize for asking where you come from, sweetheart. It's okay to be curious," she said. *And it's your right to know.* She was caught between two of the most important men in her life. She knew now, though, that whatever Jack decided about Owen—being in his life or not—they *both* owed their son the whole truth, which meant the pivotal role Ava played in all of this.

"Did he know about me?" Owen asked. "I know he left before I was born, but did he know I was...you know...on the way when he did?"

The last time he'd asked about his dad was a couple of years ago, and he'd always readily accepted that he'd had to leave before he got a chance to meet his son. She'd let him come up with theories of him being a secret agent or a superhero, telling herself it was okay to indulge his imagination because it comforted him. But the one question he hadn't yet asked was the one he was asking now, and Ava didn't want to lie anymore.

"He didn't," she admitted. "Not when he left. I was too scared to tell him because I knew he needed to go. It might not make sense to you now, but if I had told him, his life would have turned out much differently. Staying here would have been very painful for him." She finally ditched the sunglasses so she could use the tissue to dry her tears. "That doesn't mean that having you in his life wouldn't have been a good thing, Owen. That's not what I'm saying. But if he had stayed? I'm afraid some bad things would have happened to him, and I loved him too much for that."

It was all the truth, as much as she could tell him without letting Jack tell his own part of the story.

They were finally on their street, approaching the safety of home. She reached her free hand toward the back seat and squeezed Owen's knee. He rested his hand on top of hers.

"So you were kind of a superhero, too, then. Right?"

"What do you mean?" she asked.

"You saved him," Owen said, matter-of-factly.

Maybe she had saved him from something bad, but she'd also robbed him of so much good, and now she couldn't decide which fate would have been worse.

"Did he love you as much as you loved him?" Owen asked, and she gave his knee another squeeze.

"Yeah, he did." And Ava had broken his heart, as Owen would believe, to *save* him.

"Do you think he'll ever come back? That he'd ever want to meet me?"

"I really do," Ava said.

She pulled into the driveway and put the car in park. Then she spun to look at her son—this beautiful, understanding boy who she knew someday would be an amazing man, just like his father.

"You're a lot like him, you know?" she said, and her boy beamed.

"That's a good thing, right?"

"It's all I could hope for," she admitted. "I'm so proud of you, Owen. And he would be, too."

He undid his seat belt and leaned forward, giving her a kiss on her tear-soaked cheek.

"I'm gonna go toss the ball with Scully out back," he said. "He's probably been so bored all day."

She nodded. "Have fun, *Shortstop*."

He laughed and bounded out of the car.

The lights were on already inside, which wasn't a shock, especially since her father's car was also in the driveway. She'd barely made it through the door before her parents appeared in the small foyer, her mom greeting her with a glass of red.

Ava smiled at the woman who was a mirror image of her own self, twenty-five years in the future. Maggie Ellis wore her long, red hair in a braid over her right shoulder, the silver strands woven throughout looking more like highlights than a sign of age.

"Thank you," Ava said, kicking off her shoes as she reached for the glass.

"It's from the new barrel of pinot noir," her mother said.

Her father opened his mouth to add to the conversation, but Ava knew once he did, the pleasantries would be over. So she held up a finger as she took a long, slow sip, then craned her head to peek through the kitchen and through the back door to make sure Owen was outside with the dog.

She sighed. "Dad—before you say anything, I've already agreed to help the Everetts get the vineyard back on its feet, so I'll be spending some time in Oak Bluff over the next few weeks."

He crossed his arms. "He lay claim to his boy yet?" Her

father spoke soft enough so that only she and her mother could hear.

"Bradford!" her mother whisper-shouted, backhanding him on the shoulder, but his sturdy frame didn't budge. The man was as strong as he was stubborn. For most of Ava's life the former had made her feel like the safest girl in the world. But she knew now she was dealing with the latter, and first impressions were hard to erase, especially when the man had made up his mind about Jack Everett a decade ago.

Ava sipped her wine again before answering, letting the liquid heat her veins and soften her reaction. "Jack and I will tell Owen when we're both ready," she simply said.

When we know whether he's going to be a regular for our son or if he's going back to San Diego where he has his own life—the one I wanted for him.

That much she kept to herself.

"And until then?" he asked.

Ava shrugged. "Until then I help him and his brothers figure out how they're going to run a ranch *and* a vineyard. Until then I let Jack and Owen get to know each other as friends so that when we do tell him the truth, there is a foundation set between them already."

"And if I forbid this?" her father asked.

"Oh, Bradford," her mom said, calmer this time as she rested a palm on her husband's forearm. "She's not a child anymore. We have to trust her and let her do this her way."

Ava polished off the rest of her wine. She was usually one to savor a new vintage, but she was too on edge to take things slowly.

She strode past her parents, kissing them both on the cheeks. "Thanks for coming over. And making dinner. I'll call Owen in to eat."

And because her son was the one person her father couldn't argue with, they sat and ate as the boy recounted his day at the ranch—of lemonade and riding a horse and his overall fascination that real cowboys lived right in the middle of wine country.

That night, after Owen had fallen asleep, Ava sat in her painting room with another glass of the pinot noir and a paintbrush in her hand. She was finally able to slow down—to enjoy not only the new vintage but her ability to do what she hadn't done in years.

Not the tree. She still couldn't make any headway with that. But she'd painted something, and something was definitely a start.

In the morning she made sure to hide the drying canvas where Owen wouldn't see the portrait of a boy with auburn waves playing catch with his dad.

This could be her ticket into art school, but it felt premature to think that way. Because if this all blew up in her face, so would the image she'd seen in her mind's eye that finally allowed her creativity to flow.

She was no hero, and neither was Jack. They were human. And they'd made mistakes. Maybe she'd protected Jack from more pain, but she'd also stolen from him the immeasurable joy she hadn't known was possible until she'd first held her son in her arms.

No. She was no savior. But now that Jack was back, maybe—just maybe—their son would save them both.

CHAPTER TWELVE

Jack pulled the navy thermal shirt over his shoulders and shook out his damp hair. The floor creaked as he padded through the living room where Walker was still passed out on the couch from the night before. Luke, he assumed, was asleep upstairs. It wasn't even dawn. As ranchers they'd always woken early, but they could usually stay in bed until at least sunrise.

Yet several years of living in the city hadn't done a thing to give Jack a restful night's sleep.

Besides, there was work to be done, and the sooner he did it, the sooner—what? Wasn't that the million-dollar question? Once he and his brothers got the vineyard in shape for a potential harvest, what the hell came next?

He didn't have much time to think about it because the second he pulled on his work boots and stepped outside, he was greeted by blinding headlights rolling up the drive. By the time his eyes adjusted, he was able to make out Ava's red Jeep.

He stood, arms crossed, waiting for her to emerge. And when she did, he was grateful both for the sliver of predawn light and the cover of darkness. Because damn she was a sight for weary eyes, and he wasn't prepared for how much he'd wanted to see her until she was right there in front of him.

He could tell himself again and again that they were going to take things slow, but the surprise of her presence blew logic out the window. All he wanted now was to be near her. To run his hands through her hair. To trace a pattern from one freckle to the next.

He licked his lips, suddenly parched.

"What are you doing up so early?" he asked as she strode toward him with two to-go cups of coffee in her hands. "You're not supposed to be here for at least two more hours."

Her long-sleeved T-shirt hugged her curves atop snug-fitting jeans. As she came closer, he could see how the green scarf around her neck brought out her eyes—eyes that narrowed at him before responding to his question.

"You were never much of a sleeper," she said, offering him one of the cups. He took it. "I was a little restless myself. Figured I'd take a chance you were up, too."

"What about Owen?" The name still felt strange on his tongue.

"He slept at my parents' house. They'll get him to the bus today," she told him, pressing her palms to the cup. Her sleeves had those holes for her thumbs, so she wore them like fingerless gloves.

He watched a shiver run through her body.

"You're cold," he said, stating the obvious. But what else could he do? He hadn't brought a jacket. It wasn't like he could pull her to him and let body heat do the trick, no matter how much he wanted to. They'd *both* agreed to step back, that there was more at stake here than their physical attraction. So despite wanting to warm her body with his own, he stood there, one hand in the pocket of his jeans, the other occupied with the coffee.

She shrugged and took a careful sip from her cup. "That's what this is for," she said, smiling. "I'll warm up once we get working."

"If Owen slept by your folks, that means they know where you are today?"

She nodded. "They know." But she didn't offer much else.

He cleared his throat. "Speaking of working... What *are* we actually doing today?"

She glanced back at her Jeep, which was now blocking his truck. Then her eyes rested on his again.

"Hop in, and I'll show you."

He shook his head. "Give me the keys."

She hummed out a laugh but pulled her keys from her pocket and pressed them against his chest. "Does the big, bad cowboy need to be in control at all times?"

Despite the chill in the air, her fingers were warm on his chest. He took the keys. "Behind the wheel? Always."

She gave him a pointed look. "Says the man whose terrible curbside manner forced me off the road as soon as he got back to town."

He ground his teeth together, steadied his breathing, and decided not to dignify her very accurate recollection with any sort of response. The truth was, he *had* lost control that day. Just seeing her house and letting the memory of their past seep into his conscious thought had thrown him off-kilter. Then everything that came after? Yeah, it was safe to say that after the events of that day, he'd been using any means necessary to stay in as much control as he could.

"Let's go," he said, then headed for the driver's side of her car. He climbed in behind the wheel and let out a long breath before depositing his coffee into the cup holder. Glancing toward the back of the vehicle, he found a copy of *Sports Illustrated* open to an article about the new pitcher who'd just been drafted by the Dodgers.

Ava's door opened and she slid in beside him.

"He's reading *Sports Illustrated*?" Jack asked, reaching for the magazine. He turned on the interior light and started skimming the article. "This new kid is really good," he continued.

"Kid?" Ava asked with a soft laugh. "Last time I checked, twenty-eight wasn't that old. And yeah, Owen's a great reader. I've tried to get him into *Harry Potter*, you know? Something we can read together. But I cannot pry the sports magazine from his little hands." She sighed wistfully. "His hands aren't so little anymore."

Jack's jaw tightened, and he shut off the light and tossed the magazine back on the seat. He didn't say anything else as he started the Jeep and reversed down the driveway.

They rolled quietly along Oak Bluff Way, where every shop and local eatery was dark except for Baker's Bluff, the town's bakery, and judging by the logo stamped on their coffee cups, a place Ava had already been before showing up in his driveway.

"You're quiet this morning," she finally said.

"It's early," he grumbled.

"You don't sleep," she reminded him.

Just because that was true, though, didn't mean he was a morning person.

"You haven't touched your coffee," she pointed out, and he opened his mouth to say something but then thought better of it. Or maybe it was simply that he wasn't sure what the hell to say.

"Are you—*always* this much of an asshole before dawn?" she asked.

When he didn't take her bait, she settled into her seat and sipped her coffee. It wasn't until he parked along the street lining the vineyard and let his head fall back against his own seat that he was able to put words to *why* he was being an asshole. Because she was right. He was.

"You're good at it," he said softly, eyes trained on the car's closed sunroof.

"At being a morning person?" She barked out a laugh. "I'm only conscious because I *couldn't* sleep last night. If you tried to wake me this early on a normal morning, I'd have turned into a dementor and sucked out your soul."

He looked at her, brows drawn together.

She groaned. "Harry Potter."

"You *really* want him to read those books," he said.

"I really do."

She smiled, and he felt an unexpected warmth rush through him.

"And I wasn't talking about being a morning person," he said. "Even though I admit I'm not." He glanced around the car, nodding toward the back seat. "I mean *this*."

Her mouth opened to say something, and her brows rose. He could tell she was still confused. Christ, that made two of them.

"You're *good*—at being his mom," he told her. He was certain of *this*. Where the confusion came in was *how* she'd done it.

Her green-eyed gaze softened on his. She lifted her hand as if she was going to reach for him but dropped it just as quickly.

"I've had almost a decade to work on it," she said, then laughed. "It's not like I held this tiny bundle in my arms at eighteen and had any sort of clue what the hell to do."

His chest ached at the thought of her going through the birth without a partner.

She kept talking, the smile on her face enough to tell him she didn't know her recollections had any effect on him. "And you've only seen a tiny snapshot of my parenting skills. You missed me bathing the kitchen floor in my morning coffee the other day when I was scrambling for Owen not to miss the bus. Or that time I forgot I was on snack duty for his baseball game last year and had to divide up three Larabars and a box of Wheat Thins among ten sweaty, hungry boys."

A smile tugged at the corner of his mouth, and she shrugged. "I don't get a lot of sit-down meals," she said. "My car stash has saved my life more than once."

He raised his brows and let his eyes trail from hers toward the other recesses of the vehicle.

She backhanded him on the shoulder. "My snacks are safely stowed in the trunk. And yes, I've got us covered for breakfast."

The realization of what she was saying damn near floored him. With all that she'd had to do on her own these past ten years—with all she did on a daily basis—she'd still thought of him this morning in a way no one else had in a long time. Possibly ever.

He pulled the keys from the ignition and laid them in her open palm.

"Thanks," he said. "For letting me take the wheel...and for the coffee."

"It was nothing," she said, her voice soft and sweet. It wasn't the voice he remembered exactly, but it was Ava.

And though he couldn't put words to it, he knew she was wrong. Whatever was happening between them, it was *something*.

Ava bit the tag off a pair of men's work gloves and handed them to Jack. After he pulled them on, she reached back into her bag of tricks to pull out a rubber-handled tool, which she effectively slapped into his palm.

"Pruning shears," she said.

"Yeah. I guessed."

The sun was finally peeking between the few scattered clouds, illuminating her face so he could connect the dots with each and every one of her freckles if he wanted. And yeah. He wanted. Despite their agreement, he reacted to her in ways that, in his own imagination, weren't stepping back at all.

"Today's lesson is on spur pruning," she said. Then she pulled off her scarf, revealing her long, slender neck. His eyes dropped to the V-neck of her top, and as they trailed back up to her face, he watched as a soft flush followed the same path all the way up to her cheeks.

Looked like he wasn't the only one with an active imagination.

She busied herself tugging on her own work gloves and grabbing a second pair of shears.

"Not cold anymore?" he teased, though he fought to keep his expression unreadable.

She cleared her throat. "Coffee did its job. Plus, the sun's up."

He nodded. "All right, *Teach*. Show me what you want me to do."

Ava took a deep breath and exhaled slowly. She lifted her hand to the opened trunk, and Jack stepped out of the way so she could lower it. They walked in silence from the road to the nearest row of vines.

"This," she said, grabbing what to Jack looked like a random branch growing upward, "is a spur. And this"—she stroked her hand across the plant's longer, thicker, horizontal stalk—"is the cordon. We'll need to take a look at both eventually, but today we're only focusing on the spurs. Because the vines have been left unattended, most likely since your father purchased the property, you've got too many buds per spur fighting for nourishment."

"Too many mouths to feed," Jack said with a slow nod, the words escaping his lips with a bitter tone he hadn't intended.

She pressed her lips together and forced a smile. "Yeah. Exactly. So, we need to cut them back. Anything more than three of these stalks growing from a spur"—she gripped the thick, wooden base from which each of the thinner branches grew—"needs to go."

"Sounds easy enough."

"It is. All you have to do is clip it right here at the base." She demonstrated and then smiled. "And that's it."

His eyes widened as he stared down the rows upon rows of plants.

She laughed. "We'll do as much as we can today, and that will help us determine how long it will take to finish the job. Once you show Luke and Walker, you guys will get it done in no time. You'll all be vintners before you know it." She dropped her gaze back to the spur she was pruning and clipped another branch. "I mean *they* will. I know you have a job to go back to."

He didn't respond because what would he say? He *did* have a job to go back to. In New York. He was supposed to come home to tie up loose ends and give himself the closure he needed here in Oak Bluff. Instead he'd found unexpected doors opened, doors he was both terrified to walk through as well as slam the hell shut.

So instead of saying anything else, he watched in silence as she deftly went to work. And then he moved from her side to the next row of plants and started on his own.

He was used to his ghosts. They'd been his company for the better part of ten years. What he wasn't prepared for was the pull from the land of the living.

His brothers.

This woman.

His *son*.

He hadn't planned on wanting anything in a place that hadn't felt like home for the majority of his life. A place that had taught him all the things he never wanted to be.

But most surprising was the ache in his gut at what saying good-bye to it would mean this time around.

CHAPTER THIRTEEN

It was nearly eleven when Ava decided to check on Jack, who was now a couple of rows down from her. The sun had melted away the clouds, and she had already stripped down to the tank beneath her long-sleeved shirt. She'd expected to find Jack had done the same—ditched the navy thermal that brought out his stormy blue eyes for a tight-fitting undershirt.

She mentally prepared herself for the sight of him, for how the cotton would cling to the taut muscles of a man she'd only known as a boy. What her brain had not counted on, however, was for him to be wearing *no* shirt at all.

She dropped her shears, and her mouth followed suit.

Look away, she willed herself, but free will didn't seem to exist at the moment.

A soft sheen of sweat glistened on his shoulder blades. His jeans hung low on his hips, and she followed his tanned skin, the muscles that moved and worked in precision, to the band of his boxer briefs that peeked out from the worn denim.

And then...she yelped. "Shit!"

She slapped at the back of her neck as Jack spun to face her, grinning.

"Shit. Shit. *Shit!*" she yelled, and his smile quickly faded as he strode toward her.

"What's wrong?" he asked, his brows creasing in concern.

Her hand was cupped to her neck, but it wasn't the pain of the sting that made her breath catch in her throat. It was Jack Everett, sweaty and shirtless and skin dusted with dirt—everything about him so far from the boy he was and instead so inherently *man.*

"A bee," she said, her voice shaky.

"Shit," he hissed, echoing her earlier sentiment. "Let me see."

He shoved the shears in his back pocket, which tugged his jeans a little lower, and she followed the line of golden hair that trailed from his belly button to whatever lay beneath the denim and cotton.

It wasn't like she was unaware of what was there or even that she hadn't seen it. But this brooding specimen before her was, himself, unknown to her. And as he pulled her hair back to investigate the wound, the strange man who was Jack Everett sent chills across her heated skin.

"The stinger's stuck. You got a tweezers in that bag of tricks back in the truck?"

She shook her head, wincing as his hand brushed against the sting.

"Sorry," he said, his voice rough as he stepped back to face her. "I'm ready for something other than a banana and a health food bar anyway," he said with a soft smile. "Let's head back, get rid of that stinger, and regroup. You're not allergic, are you?"

She shook her head again. For someone who worked most of her adult life outside, she'd been stung plenty and had needed to remove a stinger once before. Okay, so her mom had done it because it had hurt like hell. But she could handle the pain now. Hell, she'd given birth—had endured an IV, an epidural, and an eventual C-section. She could certainly manage a bee sting without her mother's help.

Jack drove again, and she willingly let him. She sat in the passenger seat and piled her hair into a messy bun, securing it with the hair-tie she wore around her wrist. The breeze from the open window both soothed her burning skin and irritated the lodged stinger, so she gritted her teeth for the short drive and appreciated, for once, that Jack was not the chatty type.

The house was empty when they returned, and Jack led her straight to the bathroom next to the guest room where he slept. He found the tweezers in the medicine cabinet and set it on the counter before washing his hands.

He was *still* shirtless.

"I got it," she said nervously. "Thanks. I'll be out in a minute."

He raised a brow. "You don't want my help removing a stinger from the back of your neck."

His words weren't a question, merely a statement outlining her stubbornness.

She went to work washing her own hands. After drying them on the towel hanging next to the medicine cabinet, she shook her head, the movement sending a shock wave of pain from the site of the sting straight through her entire body.

She hissed in a breath through clenched teeth. "I've got tweezers and a mirror," she said. "I'm all good."

Jack held his hands up in surrender and backed out through the doorway.

"Call me if you need me."

She pressed her lips into a tight smile—and closed the door.

Ava wasn't *in*flexible, but the position she was in now, butt against the counter and head craned to try to see the bee sting in the mirror, was ridiculous. When she brought the tweezers toward its target, she misjudged the distance between her hand and her neck, effectively stabbing the swollen, inflamed skin.

She swore, then groaned at her inability to take care of what should be a simple task.

A soft knock sounded on the door.

She spun to face herself in the mirror, rolling her eyes at her dirt-smudged face, at the spots of color on her cheeks that spoke not only of the jolt of pain at her miscalculation of depth but also at embarrassment.

"Can I come in now?" Jack asked when she didn't respond to his knock.

Needing his help for this didn't mean she *needed* him. She could have gone home, called one of the other baseball moms who weren't *exactly* friends. Because who had time for friends when she was running to practices, games, the school book fair, and the bake sale? She still had her girlfriends from high school, but they were only now starting to get married and have kids. While she was at double-header baseball games, they were dealing with colic and diapers and ohmygod—Ava had no one to call in a pinch for a stupid bee sting.

She huffed out a breath. "Fine," she said. Then only to herself added, *And please be wearing a shirt.*

The door clicked open, and he was, of course, still half naked. He set a glass of ice on the counter.

"Hand 'em over," he said, palm up, as he turned his attention to the tweezers.

She did. But before he brought metal to flesh, he set the instrument next to the glass and instead reached for an ice cube, bringing it to her neck where he rubbed small circles over the sting.

Her shoulders relaxed, and she let out a soft moan. "God that feels good," she admitted. She looked up to meet his reflection in the mirror. One strong hand rested on her left shoulder while the other, the one with the ice, kept up at soothing her skin.

"Helps if you take down the swelling a bit. Makes the stinger easier to grab."

"Mmm-hmm," she hummed, eyes closing as relief—and desire—spread through her. She didn't bother asking her body to shut off its response. There was no use. She'd all but forgotten about the bee sting.

"All done," Jack said.

"Huh?" she asked absently, eyes opening wide to see him shaking the tweezers into the sink, the tiny shard that was the stinger falling into the porcelain bowl next to a partially melted ice cube.

Cold water dripped down her shoulder as her gaze met his, and he gave her a self-satisfied grin. "The ice also works as an anesthetic for patients who might be a little more skittish."

She narrowed her eyes. "I am *not* skittish. And how did you become so adept at tending to bee stings, anyway?"

The hand that was on her shoulder slid down her side, coming to rest on her hip.

She swallowed.

"Walker wasn't always so standoffish," he said in a low tone. "There was a time, when he was much younger, that he let me help when he got hurt. When he actually admitted to needing my help."

She sighed and reached for his free hand, the one pressed to the counter next to hers, and gave it a soft squeeze. "*You're* good at it, Jack."

It was his turn to close his eyes, to avoid her fixed stare. But that didn't keep her from continuing.

"You raised them. As much as you thought you weren't cut out to be a father, that's exactly what you were to your brothers. They needed a father figure when yours wasn't up to the task, and you stepped in without a second thought."

His forehead fell against the top of her head, and he released a breath.

"What about what *you* need?" she asked him, and his fingertips pressed into her hip. "Who helps *you*?"

"Ava, don't—" he started, but her hand was already pulling his from the counter and to her other hip. He lifted his head, his eyes locking on hers.

She saw the heat that mirrored her own.

"I know we agreed to take things slow, to step back. But maybe we need to get this out of our systems first," she said.

She needed to get *him* out of her system once and for all.

"I'm leaving," he said softly, and her throat tightened.

"I know. Your life is in San Diego. A see-you-for-the-weekend dad is still more than anything Owen could have possibly dreamed of. And I don't have any expectations beyond right now—"

"Not San Diego," he interrupted.

Somehow, studying his gaze through the mirror's reflection gave her the illusion of safety, that whatever came next, she'd withstand it.

"What do you mean?" she asked.

She felt his chest rise and fall against her back as he tilted his head up and then back down again so his eyes met hers.

"I'm not taking a leave of absence because of the funeral and the vineyard. I'm moving. I've already packed up my apartment and shipped most of my things to New York."

"New York?" she blurted, turning to face him, and the safety of the mirror was gone. Nothing was between them other than a few centimeters of space, the air thick with the remnants of their past and a future that seemed impossible—especially where Owen was concerned.

He nodded once. "It's a promotion. I already accepted. With the ranch mortgaged, it's a chance for me to help Luke and Walker more than they've ever needed me to before, especially if the vineyard tanks. And I know you said you and Owen are fine financially—"

"We are," she blurted, though she knew in his way he was just trying to do the right thing. That part of him hadn't changed. "I'm starting my degree in the fall. Part-time, obviously. Between that, and Owen, and still working at the vineyard, my life is going to be pretty crazy, so it's not like I'm expecting whatever this is between us to be anything more than…"

Than what? Because right now it was a distraction, and she wasn't about to let Jack Everett, those eyes, and his ability to swoop in and save the day knock her off course again.

He was ready to offer Owen a secure financial future. But not a personal one.

What did she really expect—that he'd uproot his life for them once the truth was sprung on him?

Fine. Yes. Maybe a little bit. But that was about as rational as what she was doing right now—raising both of his hands to cup her breasts.

"Christ, *Red*."

She wasn't wearing a bra.

He let out a soft growl. "Jesus, Ava," he ground out, his thumbs stroking her taut nipples. "What the hell are you doing?"

She arched into his palms. "Getting *you* out of my system so I can freaking think straight. This is it," she assured not him, really, but herself. "This one time. Then we can both move on."

She spun in his arms again so she could only see him in the mirror, then clasped her hands around his neck. He dipped his head so his lips brushed against her ear.

"Are you sure this is what you want?" He peppered her jawline with achingly soft kisses. "Because I'll stop if it's not."

His voice was rough. And sexy. And stopping—for her—was not a possibility.

"It's what I need," she whispered. "What do *you* need, Jack? Tell me, and I'll give it to you."

He pinched one of her tight peaks and grazed his teeth along her neck.

Her breathing hitched.

"This," he whispered. "I need *this*."

They didn't need each *other*. Only *this*, their bodies' combined demand for release. Everything else would be clearer once whatever was brewing between them was allowed to boil over—and then simmer.

She grabbed his hands and guided them to the hem of her tank, hesitated for a second, then lifted her arms so he could pull it over her head.

Her jeans rested low on her hips, and he traced the line of the faint scar across her pelvis.

"Owen went into distress during labor," she said. "The cord was wrapped around his neck. I had to have a C-section."

His hand stopped moving, and she dropped her head and groaned. "I suppose childbirth talk kind of kills the mood, huh? Not the sexiest of subjects."

He hooked a finger under her chin, gently lifting it so his eyes could once again lock on hers. Then he shook his head. "You're the sexiest woman I have ever seen," he said. "And the strongest. There is nothing you could do to make me not want you like this. Don't you get that?"

What she got was that she wanted *him* like she wanted air. She wanted his hands on her, *in* her. His lips hot against hers and the taste of him lingering on her tongue long after they parted. She tried to give voice to all of this, but all that came out was a soft "Okay."

He spun them both so their hips were against the sink, their bodies perpendicular to the mirror so he could still watch as he bent to take one of her rosy nipples into his mouth.

She dug her fingers into his hair and cried out as his teeth nipped.

All the while she watched him watching them, and every synapse of every nerve fired off at the thrill of it.

She unbuttoned his jeans and gripped his hard length through his briefs. He repaid her with another satisfying growl.

"We should shower after all that hard work," she said, breathless from his touch—from touching *him*.

She snuck her thumb inside his waistband and swirled it over his wet tip.

"Ava," he groaned, then backed away from her to pull the shower curtain from the tub so he could turn on the water.

Wordlessly they finished undressing each other. She stared at the man before her for several long seconds—the light dusting of hair on his chest, the ridged muscles of his abdomen, the sheer solidness of his form. He was beautiful in a way that made it hard to breathe.

He pulled her over the lip of the tub into the warm spray, leaving the curtain open as he pressed himself to the tiled wall and pulled her back against him, their naked forms framed once again in the mirror.

She didn't protest.

"God, you're gorgeous," he said in her ear before he lightly bit her lobe.

She watched his hands cup her breasts, and then one traveled south, below her belly button, her scar, and finally between her legs.

Her breath caught as he parted her, teasing her entrance before one finger slipped inside.

"Jack," she cried softly, and his cock ground against the flesh of her back.

No sir. This was not the boy she'd fallen in love with. This man knew a woman's body—knew hers in a way he couldn't have when they were two inexperienced teens figuring this out together.

"You're like warm silk," he said, exiting her slowly until his slick finger reached her swollen center.

She whimpered, grabbing his wrist. "More," she squeaked. *"Please."*

He smiled wickedly at her in the mirror. Two fingers entered her this time, and she threw her head back against his chest, eyes squeezing shut so she could try to keep it the hell together.

She writhed against his erection, and he swore.

"Inside me," she said, almost unable to form the words. "Please," she begged.

"Open your eyes, Ava." He pumped his fingers inside her warmth, and her legs went completely boneless. Somehow, though, she didn't fall.

Jack wouldn't let her.

She opened her eyes, meeting his in the slowly fogging reflection of their need.

"I'm not gonna lie," he told her. "I want to make love to you. But not like this."

He exited her again, his fingers now tracing maddening circles around her clit.

"Not…like…what?" she asked, gasping between each word.

The steam won out, and she could no longer see him— see what he was doing to drive her out of her mind.

He spun her and backed her toward the tiled wall of the tub, pressing her against it and then kissing her until she nearly forgot her own name.

"Not when you're driving me so crazy I'm not sure how long I'll last inside you." He kissed her again. "Not when I won't be able to lay you out properly and give every inch of your skin, every freckle, the attention it deserves." Another kiss. "And not when I can't promise you anything beyond these next few weeks."

There it was again, that tightening in her throat that made her unable to respond with any words at all.

"I can still stop," he said, apparently reading something in her expression. "The last thing I want is for you to regret this."

She shook her head. "Don't stop," she managed to say. "Please don't stop." Because whatever came after this, she didn't care. Not now. Not when she could have him for today. For this one moment, even if it was their last.

And before he could ask her again if she was sure, she kissed him and grabbed his cock, stroking him from root to tip.

"Ava," he groaned against her lips.

And then he was kissing her cheek, her jaw, down her neck and breasts until he lowered himself to his knees where he sprinkled kisses on the inside of each of her thighs.

She sucked in a sharp breath anticipating what would come next, but nothing could prepare her for his hot breath against her folds, for the sensation of his tongue sliding along her opening and then circling her aching arousal in achingly precise strokes.

She was nothing more than a blob of freaking Jell-O, her knees buckling as he slipped two fingers back inside while his tongue worked her expertly into complete and utter madness, all while he somehow kept her from melting into a puddle onto the bathtub floor.

The orgasm came over her like a fifteen-foot wave, pulling her under until she was gasping his name—and for air.

He held her close as she shuddered against him, as she slid down the wall and into the tub in front of him, standing no longer an option.

Who the hell was she kidding? *Get him out of her system?* She'd just let him right *in* to her goddamn system.

He was leaving. She was taking control of her life and career.

This. Was not. The plan.

He brushed her wet hair from her face and pressed a soft kiss to her lips. "*That's* what I needed."

She forced herself back into the moment. "But what about...?" She stared at his rock-hard length.

"I'm fine," he started to say, but she closed her hand around his base and squeezed. "Red." She stroked him slowly.

"Stand up," she said. "Your turn."

CHAPTER FOURTEEN

He would have been satisfied with simply bringing her to climax. He could have set her up in the kitchen with something to eat for lunch and then come back for a cold shower of his own, where he'd take care of his own release.

Because shit—he needed it. He just wasn't prepared for needing *her.*

Seeming to have regained her sea legs, Ava stood and held her hand out for his. He was still kneeling, still savoring the taste of her and wondering how he'd gone his entire adult life without it.

"Ava—" he said when they were both standing, but she shook her head and splayed a hand across his chest.

"It's only this once, remember?" she insisted, but even with the water beating down on them, he detected a hint of uncertainty. Or maybe it was him. "And despite what you might think of me," she teased, "I'm not a selfish woman."

"I never said—" he started, but she kissed him, silencing him because he couldn't say no to her lips on his. "Red," he groaned as her teeth tugged on his bottom lip, but she wouldn't respond, and he knew if he didn't get the words out now, he never would. *"Ava."* She stopped and tilted her head up, her emerald eyes meeting his. "I don't want to hurt you," he said. "I already did that once, and that's not my intention here."

She nodded. "But you didn't know," she said. "And I hurt you, too."

His forehead fell to hers. She'd destroyed him—the messed-up kid he was then. But she'd been a messed-up kid, too, one who thought he wouldn't want their son, and back then...who could say he wouldn't have reacted exactly as she'd expected?

"If we know what we're getting into, then no one gets hurt," she said, then kissed the line of his jaw. "Right now, though, you need to let someone take care of *you*."

And before he could argue, her kisses traveled south, down his collarbone, his abdomen, each of his hips, until her tongue, warm and willing, swirled around his tip.

She teased him for what felt like hours—licking, tasting, stroking. Time seemed to stand still when she was near, or maybe it was that he wanted the minutes to stretch out before them. If this was his one-time-only with her, he wanted *only* to be infinite.

But without warning, the teasing was over. He gritted his teeth and dug his fingers into her hair as she swallowed him down to the base of his cock. She gripped him tight, her hand following the trail of her lips as she came back up for air. Again and again she took him into her mouth, her hand working him until he thought he might lose his mind.

The water still beat down on them, steam clouding the air, and it was as if they weren't really there. As if this wasn't exactly real. It was this realization that let him relax his shoulders, that gave her permission to take him to the edge, where he spilled over with silent release. He couldn't fully let go, but he could trust her enough to let her take the wheel—to let the smallest piece of his decade-old walls crumble here—in this fantasy world they'd created, and then piece himself back together as soon as the steam cleared.

She stood and buried her head beneath his chin, his chest heaving against her.

"You gave up control for me," she said softly. "I don't suppose that was easy to do."

She stepped back to look at him, and as much as he knew he was a dick for doing it, he shuttered his expression.

He couldn't let her see that even after climax, he still needed. He needed her close, needed her hands on him to steady the erratic beat of his heart. Needed her kiss to reassure him that this was something more than her getting him out of her system.

If she knew how far that was from how he saw things, she'd know how much control he'd truly lost, and nothing terrified him more than letting her see that.

He had no right to need these things from her, not when he was moving to the other damned side of the country.

Her smile quickly fell, and she shook her head. "You keep so much of yourself locked away," she said, then kissed the spot on his neck where he could feel his pulse thrumming against her lips. "If you're ever ready to let some of it go, I'm here for you."

She pressed her lips to his and then stepped out of the tub, wrapped herself in a towel, and exited the bathroom with her clothes in hand.

He let his head thud against the tile while the water, cooling off now, pelted him in his chest.

She was right, of course. Not that he'd say it aloud. Not that he *could.* He didn't just keep his past at bay for himself.

He did it for everyone around him. That's why San Diego was easy, why New York would be even easier.

But here? Even ten years after the fact, Ava *knew* him. He'd let his guard down for a matter of minutes, and she'd seen right through to his goddamn core.

She deserved better than that. Better than him.

When he emerged fully clothed into the kitchen, the place was a flurry of activity. Ava was carrying a tray of burgers out the back door to where he saw Luke firing up the grill. Walker stood next to the sink, slicing tomatoes on a cutting board.

Jack cleared his throat, and Walker looked up.

"What?" he said, already on the defensive.

Jack shrugged. "Nothing. I guess I didn't know you were so—domesticated."

He was used to seeing his youngest brother eating whatever he could find right from the fridge, not bothering to take the time to do anything more than open his mouth and insert food. As a teen he'd always been on the move, agitated. Jack understood. The anticipation of their father's mood was almost worse than what happened when he was in a bad one. Almost.

"I guess it's just nice to see you—relaxed," Jack added.

Walker picked up a half-empty bottle of beer and raised his brows. "Meet my brand of medication," he said before taking a sip and setting it back down. Jack normally would have worried about his brother drinking and wielding a knife, but he could tell Walker was sober. He did, however, second-guess himself as his brother pointed his knife at him. "I can take care of myself in the kitchen," he said. "But you tell anyone I know how to julienne and shit, and I'll lay you out cold."

Jack couldn't hold back the laugh. "Do you—julienne and shit?"

Walker returned to cutting, his back to him once again. "You're a dick," he said under his breath.

"And apparently you're not only Mr. HGTV but Gordon Ramsay as well," Jack said. "Who'd have guessed?"

"I need cheese!" Ava said as she came back through the kitchen. She headed straight for the fridge, grabbing a block of cheddar Jack hadn't even known they had and then opening and closing drawers until she found a knife fit for slicing it. "You still take yours medium rare?" she asked, elbowing Jack in the side but not waiting for his answer before she was out the door again.

Walker turned to face him, crossing his arms as he shook his head.

"What?" Now it was Jack's turn to play defense.

"I know I don't know my elbow from my asshole sometimes, but I'm pretty damned sure you're gonna ruin that pretty woman when you leave."

Jack crossed his own arms, a mirror to his suddenly perceptive brother. "What the hell do you mean?"

Walker strode to the fridge and retrieved another beer, twisting off the top as he spoke. "I mean I'm not blind. And if you'd open up your damn eyes, you'd see it, too." He swigged from the bottle, then wiped the back of his hand across his lips. "That girl carries a ten-year-old torch. And let's not forget the offspring. Seems like a good kid. You gonna be the father that messes that all up?"

Jack's hands balled into fists. He started forward, ready to unleash his frustration on his brother, but knew it would only leave him hollow. Instead he turned toward the front door and walked out.

Luke found him out by the stable, beating a bale of hay

on the far outside wall with the bucket of balls he'd found still tucked away in the garage.

"You still got a mean curveball," he said over Jack's shoulder.

He threw a few sliders. Then a changeup. And then several fastballs until the bucket was empty and his elbow ached. He shook his arm out and then collected the balls, gearing up for round two.

"I've stayed too long already," Jack said, tossing the ball into his glove. He could still get his hand inside it, but the fit was too small. It was the glove his father had gotten him when he'd started the new season junior year.

Jack Senior had had a rare, lucid afternoon. He'd found Jack in this very spot, fighting with his then too-small glove.

"Jackson!" he'd called as he approached, and Jack had held his breath, bracing himself for the blow. But when it didn't come, his father had simply nodded toward the glove and said, "C'mon. You won't make it through the season with that."

And they'd driven to the next town over where they had a sporting goods store—Jack behind the wheel, of course, since Jack Senior was with it enough to hand the keys over.

That was the closest his father had come to showing him affection in the years following his mother's death, so he filed it away under memories he let surface. It wasn't an apology or an end to the drinking. But it was something.

"Or maybe you haven't stayed long enough to let this place sink back into your bones."

Jack missed the hay bales and drove the ball right into the side of the stable, the wood splitting on impact.

"Shit." He shook his hand out of the glove and went to

survey the damage. As soon as he touched the point of impact, the old wood cracked clear through so he could see one of the horse's stalls.

"Looks like you'll have to hang around a bit longer to patch that up. And while you're at it, we could call one of the Callahan brothers. I was thinking we could talk to them about adding on the tasting room to the structure where we'll do all the fermenting and shit. I bet they'd fix up that wall pro bono if we gave them the contract for the tasting room."

Jack ran a hand through his hair. "I can handle a hammer and some plywood."

"Good as you can handle your pitching arm?" He grinned.

Luke was always grinning. Did nothing faze the guy?

"Look," Luke added. "You're gonna do whatever it is you need to do, and if that means getting us up and running and then heading to New York, then that's your call. But you fit here once, Jack. You could fit here again."

Jack's eyes widened. "Jenna told you?"

He crossed his arms and shook his head. "She didn't need to. I know you think you're the one who keeps tabs on us, but I can read. I check on the *San Diego Sun* every now and then. Caught the article on how your firm was making you its youngest partner—in their New York office."

"Shit," Jack hissed.

Luke laughed. "It's a good gig. Walker'n I have just been waiting for you to grow a pair and tell us."

"I was waiting for the right time," he said, not taking his brother's bait.

"Hope you're taking it because it's something you love to do, though," Luke added. "Not because you think we need the money."

"You *do* need the money," he said. "You got a mortgage to pay."

Luke shrugged. "Ranch isn't in the red yet. And do me a favor. Ease up on asking Jenna to keep your damn secrets. It's enough to ask her to pretend she's not that boy's aunt. Don't make her keep more from her family. That's not her way." He opened his mouth to say something else but didn't.

"It's my way," Jack said, finishing his brother's thought. "That's what you were going to say."

"Looks like I didn't have to." Luke turned and began to stride off.

"How can you stand it?" Jack asked.

His brother stopped and spun back to face him, overgrown blond hair in eyes that now squinted from the sun. "There was no alternative for me. No baseball scholarship—not that I wanted one, by the way." He laughed, but for once it wasn't an entirely happy sound. "I was born to work the ranch. Never wanted anything else." He turned his attention toward the pasture. "I'm happier out there on my horse or in the rodeo arena than I am anywhere else. Jenna was good to us, but when Dad couldn't take care of the place anymore, I *wanted* to come back."

"Why?"

"Not for him," Luke said. "No way. But for *her*. For what they built for us."

Jack squeezed his eyes shut and let the sun beat down on his cheeks, trying to remember what he used to love about Crossroads Ranch. Because he had loved it once. He knew that much.

When he came up blank, he dropped his gaze back to where his brother stood, but Luke was already gone.

That seemed to be the theme today.

Ava left him in the shower.

He left the house.

Luke left him here to take his frustrations out on the stable.

Leaving had been the right answer once—when he was a messed-up kid in a messed-up life he couldn't fix.

He'd sworn things would change once Jackson Everett Senior was dead and gone, but his ghost was everywhere, reminding Jack that his life was still a mess—and that he still had no damned clue how to fix it.

But he would. He'd fix the barn, fix the damn vineyard, and fix things between him and Ava. No more lapses in judgment. He wouldn't let them hurt each other again.

He shook his arm out one more time and headed back to the house. Jenna's car was parked behind Ava's now, which meant it was a goddamn party inside. He clenched his jaw and prepared himself for his aunt's third degree. But when he entered the kitchen, they were all talking. And laughing. And passing food around the table like they'd done this a hundred times before.

Jenna patted the seat next to her, and the tension in Jack's muscles relaxed slightly. He sat, kissed his aunt on the cheek, then narrowed his eyes at a scabbed-over cut on her upper lip.

She waved him off. "Nothing more than the aftermath of me trying to give a little smooch to one of my chicks. The cute little shit nipped me."

Jack let out a breath. Jenna was okay. They were all *okay*.

Ava handed him a plate covered in plastic wrap. Beneath it was a cheeseburger piled high with all the fixings and, next to it, a grilled cob of corn.

"Hope it's still warm," she said, her smile soft and conciliatory.

We're okay, he let that smile tell him.

And for the remainder of this impromptu family meal, he let himself believe what his brother had said to him. He'd fit in here once—and maybe, for the short time he'd be here, he could find a way to fit again.

CHAPTER FIFTEEN

Ava shifted in the passenger seat, trying to admire the beauty that was San Luis Obispo wine country. The rolling green of the vineyards—endless rows of grape plants leading straight to hilltops shadowed in the setting sun. Today she sat in Jack's truck, and she should have been grateful for the freedom to appreciate the view. Instead she was restless.

Jack settled a palm on her bouncing knee and she sucked in a breath.

"What's going on?" he asked, his hand flexing at her reaction before he quickly pulled it away.

Um, we've been working together for five days now, and this is the first time you've touched me since Monday's bee sting incident. But that was their deal, right? One time only. But instead of scratching an itch she'd opened the floodgates of need. Not that she could tell him that.

"Nothing," she lied. "And you really didn't have to be my chauffeur to *and* from the ranch today. That's a lot of time in the car, and I don't mind the drive."

He shrugged, both hands back on the wheel. "You've been working your ass off this week pruning those vines. Least I could do is save you some mileage on the Jeep. Plus, it's not exactly a punishment to spend a little extra time with you."

She let out a breath and tried to force her gaze out the window instead of to her left where he sat in that fitted gray tank and jeans, his *work* uniform for the warmest weather they'd had this week. And she definitely wasn't noticing how his blond hair curled above the tops of his ears—or how a few days without shaving had lined his jaw and mouth with a sexy scruff he'd never had as a teen.

Nope. She wasn't noticing any of that. And she certainly wasn't squirming in her seat because of it.

"Something's up," he said, calling her bluff.

She crossed her arms and groaned as he slowed to turn into her long driveway.

"It's *nothing*. Thanks for the ride," she said as he rolled to a stop. Then she hopped out of the vehicle before she said anything stupid.

She was almost inside the house when she heard his car door slam, effectively stopping her in her tracks.

"Ava."

Damn him for that insistence in his tone, for that deep voice that spoke her name like no one else ever had and—she was beginning to realize—like no one could. That voice could make her core tighten and her heart ache, and it was succeeding at both right now.

She turned to find him leaning against the truck's hood, all six-foot-who-knows-how-much-more feet of him, his hands in his pockets and his biceps flexing as if to say, *You know what's up, Red. And the longer you look at me, the more powerless you are against me.*

She dropped her bag at her feet and pointed at him. He wanted answers? Fine. He'd get them.

"This," she said. "You standing twenty feet away from

me. It's been like that all week. Every day out in the vine-yard you've made sure there are at least two rows between us. We've eaten lunch at BBQ on the Bluff *four* times rather than step foot together inside the ranch. And I'm pretty sure you've either been marking your territory around the vines so no rodents eat the plants, *or* you can go several hours without needing to pee because you haven't stepped foot in your own home at any time that I've been inside it since Monday afternoon when, if you don't remember, you made me orgasm until I could no longer stand." She hefted her bag from her feet and tossed it over her shoulder, trying to maintain some semblance of dignity. "Now, if you don't mind, my parents will have Owen home in about an hour, and I need to clean myself up and get dinner started. Also, Owen has spring break next week, which means he'll be home—which also means *I'll* have to be home."

He crossed his arms. "So you're not…"

"I'm not going to be able to come by Crossroads next week," she said, mustering up as much finality in her tone as she could. Because she was on borrowed time with this man. And she had an application to complete—her future depended on it. Him pulling back should have made it eas-ier for her to do the same. Instead she was losing the ability to think straight in his presence. Or maybe she'd never had it to begin with.

Besides, she said to herself, *this is probably for the best because I need to reset my damn libido so I stop reacting to you like this.*

When he didn't respond right away, she pulled open the screen door and stepped through to safety. She was in the kitchen facing the back window, already pouring a much-needed glass of wine, when she heard his work boots scuff across the tile.

"And here I thought my dramatic exit would mean you'd drive away and forget about my verbal vomit." She spun slowly to face him, holding up her glass before taking a sip.

She watched him watch her, not sure if the heat spreading through her veins was the wine or the weight of his stare. She guessed it was a little of both.

He just stood there, strong and silent as always, yet his eyes didn't waver. He never looked away.

"It's not that easy to forget," he said, his deep voice a low rumble in the quiet house.

She laughed, the sound tinged with bitterness. "No kidding. That's why they call it 'verbal vomit.' Too much comes out." She waved her free hand in the air as she took another sip. "Makes it hard to clean up."

He scratched the back of his neck, and there went those arm muscles, flexing and contracting with the slightest movement.

"I mean *you*, Ava."

She set the glass down and wrapped her arms around her midsection.

"I never forgot about you, not since the day I forced you to push me away."

She opened her mouth to say something but he shook his head. "I won't hurt you like that again," he said, the muscles in his jaw tight. "No matter what I said ten years ago, I'm going to figure out a way to do right by you and Owen—even if that means stepping back to make sure neither of you get hurt."

He still hadn't moved from the kitchen entryway, so she took a step toward him.

"You're not *him*," she insisted.

His chest rose and fell with a few quiet breaths before he

spoke. "Neither was he for a lot of years. But things change. He got pushed over the edge and never climbed back up. This shit—there's heredity to think about."

She splayed a palm against his chest, his heart thundering against it. "Maybe you need to prove that to yourself," she said. "But not to me."

She took a chance and tilted her head to where his tanned skin met the collar of his tank, kissing him softly. He sucked in a ragged breath, but he didn't push her away. She met his gaze again.

"I know you're moving across the country—and that you'll do right by me and Owen no matter where you are. Because that's *who* you are." She swallowed past the knot in her throat. "And I'll be okay if you leave again. *When* you leave again." She forced a smile. "But I have a confession. This heat between us? Monday wasn't enough to get it out of my system. So if worrying about hurting me is the only thing holding you back, don't. I'm a big girl. I can take care of myself. But if it's something else—"

She didn't get a chance to finish because his lips were on hers—rough, insistent, and exploding with need. He pivoted her around the corner so her back was against the kitchen wall, his hands roaming up her sides to cradle her face.

The kiss was deep and unrelenting, and her fingers grappled for purchase in his thick, soft hair.

"Not out of your system either?" she managed, breathless against him.

"Hell no," he growled, and he slid a palm up the front of her T-shirt to cup her breast.

She whimpered and arched against him as he pinched her tightened peak outside her bra. Heat pooled between her legs as he nipped at her lip, as he peppered kisses across her jaw and down her neck. He hiked her up onto his hips, and she wrapped her legs around him, his erection pressing against her pelvis. Her arms snaked around his neck as she held on for dear life.

She was wet. She could feel it. From just his damn kisses.

"I don't think I've ever gotten you out of my system," he admitted. "And now the woman you've become? I don't know how to stay away."

He ground against her, pushing her harder into the wall, and she cried out with need.

"Then I guess we're going to have to keep at this until we're both free and clear of—of whatever this is." Right now she didn't care. She wanted more. Whatever he was willing to give.

"Ava?" she heard faintly in the recesses of her mind. Or maybe she imagined it. "Ava?" The voice was louder this time. "The front door was open..."

"My parents and Owen!" she whisper-shouted and Jack all but dropped her to her feet.

She smoothed out her shirt but knew her face was flushed, her lips swollen.

Oh well. Here went nothing.

"Mom!" she said, rounding the corner into the living room. "You guys are early."

She could see her dad and Owen grabbing his school and baseball bags from the car. Scully, who must have been in the backyard, came barreling through the dog door and bounded toward the front entryway, as if he could sense his most favorite human in the world was about to step foot in the house.

Jack's presence was palpable behind her. She didn't have to turn to know he was there. Her parents would have seen Jack's truck in the driveway, but the look on her mother's face—jaw agape and eyes wide—told her they weren't hiding anything.

"We left practice early because Owen said he had a tummy ache."

Ava snapped straight into mommy mode and strode toward the door. "Why didn't you call?" she asked.

Her mom grabbed her wrist before she made it to the door. "Because this happened ten minutes ago. I knew you were either an hour away or already heading back, so I figured we'd wait for you. I wasn't expecting..." She trailed off.

Ava glanced back over her shoulder at Jack, who gave her mother a polite nod. "Evening, Mrs. Ellis."

Her dad was the first through the door, baseball bag over one shoulder and Owen's backpack over the other. He kissed Ava on the cheek, but his jaw tightened when he laid eyes on Jack.

"Be nice," she insisted in a whispered plea.

And then she was stooping to hug her son while fending off a very excited Labrador. She pressed her cheek to his, letting out a relieved sigh when he felt cool to the touch.

"I don't think you have a fever, bud. Can you tell me where it hurts?"

Owen shrugged. "It kind of comes and goes. I think I maybe didn't eat enough for lunch today." He wrapped his arms around her neck and squeezed tight. Not that he wasn't an affectionate boy, but something felt different.

She kissed him and finally backed away so the dog could get his fill, and in seconds Owen was on his back, laughing as Scully lavished him with slobbery, wet kisses.

Ava's dad dropped the bags in the small entryway and walked straight past Jack into the kitchen. She turned to her mom, who pulled her back to where Jack stood so Owen couldn't hear above his own giggles.

"He's missed you," she said. "You're doing a good thing—helping out with the Everett vineyard"—she smiled at Jack—"but you've missed both practices this week. Plus, you're out the door as soon as the bus comes each morning, and you barely make it back before sundown."

Ava's heart sank. It had only been five days, but her mom was right. This was the least present she'd been as a mother in all of Owen's life, and the guilt seeped into her bones.

"It's my fault," Jack said. "I took you up on your offer without realizing the sacrifice. It was never my intent to take you away from your son."

"Jack!" Owen called, springing to his feet once the dog set him free. "Mom said you read the *Sports Illustrated* article about the pitcher for the Dodgers. Do you think he'll get them back to the Series this year?"

Ava stepped back, allowing her son into their small huddle, and she watched the warm smile spread across Jack's face.

"Sure as hell doesn't hurt their chances. Does it?" he asked, giving Owen's baseball cap a friendly swat. "Might even win it this time."

"Sure as hell doesn't," Owen parroted, and at this Ava raised her brows at both boys.

"Language, you two." But she couldn't help smiling as well.

"I hear he's got a wicked curveball," Jack said.

Owen nodded. "I'm still trying to figure that one out. Maybe you could show me sometime? Mom said you were a good pitcher."

It was Jack's turn to raise a brow. *"Good?"* The corner

of his mouth quirked into a grin, and Ava wondered if he knew how gorgeous he was when he did that. "Just good?"

She laughed and backhanded him on the shoulder. "I never had the pleasure of seeing you in action. I had to take your word for it—and trust that whole scholarship situation."

Ava inwardly winced at the possible memories this would bring up, but Jack's smile never faltered.

"Sure, *Shortstop*. Sometime sounds good. But I should let you all get settled in for the night."

Owen grabbed his bag from where his grandpa had set it on the ground. "Or we could do some pitching practice while Mom makes dinner?" He glanced at his mom and grandma. "I'm feeling a little better," he said, then bit his bottom lip.

Ava's heart squeezed so tight at her son's pleading eyes—eyes so much like his father's. She wouldn't ask Jack to stay. He had to want it. He had to *want* to spend time with his son.

Jack crossed his arms and tilted his head toward the ceiling, heaving in a breath before his eyes met hers. How many times had she seen Owen do the exact same thing whenever he needed to think? It only hit her now that the gesture wasn't solely her son's. It was Jack's, too.

"I can head out when dinner's ready," he said.

Her mom patted him on the shoulder and smiled. "Or you could stay."

"If you want," Ava blurted. "No pressure. I was going to grill some chicken. Whip up a salad. Nothing fancy."

Owen watched them both expectantly. Jack tilted his head down to take in his own appearance.

"Let me just grab a clean shirt from my truck." He shifted his gaze to Owen. "I think I have a glove somewhere in the back of the cab, too. You got a handful of balls?"

Owen grinned from ear to ear.

"All right, then. How about you go on out back and get us ready while I grab my stuff and clean up real quick."

Owen shot his fist in the air and whooped as he ran through the kitchen and out the back door, Scully following at his heels. Jack headed out front to his truck, a smile still spread across his own face as well.

Ava's heart swelled. "Doesn't look like he has much of a tummy ache anymore," she said.

"He just missed his mama." Her mother gave her shoulders a squeeze. "Bradford?" she called toward the kitchen where her dad was, no doubt, sulking. "Let's leave the kids to their dinner."

Her dad emerged, his jaw set as firm as it was when he first entered the house.

"Come *on*, Dad."

He grunted. But this was not acquiescence. She knew that look. It was the one she got when she backed into the mailbox the year she got her license—the one he gave to every boy who rang their doorbell throughout her high school career—except *golden boy* Derek Wilkes. It was the look that asked, *What do you have to say for yourself?* But it was a rhetorical question. Because Bradford Ellis had the answer. He *always* had the answer.

"This is a mistake, Ava." His voice was steady. Even. The way he spoke when he knew he'd already won the argument. So she decided not to disagree.

"Then it's my mistake to make."

He let out a bitter laugh. "You're a lovesick teenager again, running around behind our backs with a boy you know isn't good enough for you."

"Dad."

He crossed his arms. "You gonna deny sneaking around with a boy who couldn't even take you on a proper date?"

Ava's eyes burned, and she could feel the heat creeping up her neck and into her cheeks. "He was in a cast for the first two months I knew him."

Her father shook his head. "You didn't answer the question. If I had nothing to worry about with you dating Jack Everett, why'd you hide it from us? Why did he *let* you?"

A throat cleared, and everyone's attention volleyed toward the front door where Jack stood with a clean T-shirt thrown over his shoulder and a baseball glove under his arm.

"Because she knew you thought the son of an abusive alcoholic might hurt her someday. And you were right."

"Jack. Don't," she said, her voice wavering. "You didn't know about Owen." She turned to her parents. "He didn't know." Not that it mattered telling them this now.

He *had* hurt her without even knowing it, broken her heart—she'd thought—beyond repair. But she'd done the same to him.

"He never raised a hand to me, Dad. He never would. Not to Owen, either."

Her father narrowed his eyes. "You're letting your infatuation with this boy blind you again. It's my job to protect you. Maybe he never laid a hand on *you*, but you saw what he did to the Wilkes boy. You saw what he's capable of. You think you can guarantee there's *no* risk of that happening again?"

"Bradford—" her mom started, but he held his hands up in surrender.

"I've said all I need to say. Even if she's right, he can still hurt her in other ways. We helped put the pieces back together the last time he left her. We'll be here to do it again. Just remember that it's not only your heart he'll break," her father said. "That boy's already taken a liking to him. What's gonna happen to Owen if he finds out the truth and then Everett leaves you both?"

"With all due respect, Mr. Ellis," Jack said, "it's up to Ava and me how to proceed with Owen from here."

Ava's mom kissed her on the cheek and then hooked her elbow with her father's, practically dragging him toward the door.

"The hell it is," he said to Jack through gritted teeth. Then her parents were gone.

Jack stood, motionless except for the pulsing muscle above his jawline.

"I'm sorry," she said, moving toward him with measured calm, as if he was an animal she might scare off and send running. "He's scared for me—for *us*. I don't condone his treatment of you, but he doesn't know how to do the protective thing without being a total asshole."

She was hoping to coax a smile from him, but she failed.

"Jack." She stood right in front of him now, close enough that she could feel the heat of his body. She could count his breaths—see how each held a slight tremor. She cupped his cheeks in her hands, and he closed his eyes. But still he said nothing.

So she did the one thing she knew she could do to make him react. She stood on her toes and kissed him.

"Ava," he finally whispered against her, the sound of his voice both an admonishment and a plea.

"He doesn't know you," she said, her lips still moving against his. "And that's on *me*. Maybe if I'd been up front from the beginning, the whole Derek incident never would have happened. At the very least I should have told them who the father was and why I pushed you to leave—" She felt the tears prick at the backs of her eyes.

He stepped back and pressed a thumb to her cheek where the first one had sprung free. "But you were too much of a mess to do that," he said. "They had to pick up the pieces because of me."

"Because of *us*," she corrected. "What happened ten years ago, that's on me, too."

"But the Derek incident *did* happen. So did Walker's birthday and me telling my pregnant girlfriend I never wanted to be a father. And then you coming to find me in L.A.?" he added. "Shit."

"They don't know about L.A.," she said.

"You dealt with that on your own—coming to tell me about Owen and then thinking I was marrying someone else? I *am* the asshole your father thinks I am."

She shook her head. "You're just someone who's still trying to put his own pieces back together. Go," she said, nodding toward the back door. "He's waiting for you."

He sighed heavily and strode past her, pulling his dirty shirt over his head before tossing on the new one. And for those few moments when his torso was bare, Ava simply stared at the beautiful man he'd become and wondered if he even wanted those pieces back in place, or if he'd already convinced himself that broken was how he'd stay.

They'd eaten outside, unable to pull Owen from his baseball glove for too long. Then he and Jack had continued practicing their curveballs until past sundown.

Now Ava looked over her shoulder to where Jack stood in the frame of Owen's bedroom door, watching her tuck their son into bed.

"You want me to sing 'Twinkle Twinkle,' little man?"

Owen squeezed his eyes shut and groaned. "I'm not a baby, Mom."

Her heart constricted in her chest. "You're right," she said. "Maybe you're getting too old for this." She kissed him on the forehead and willed herself not to lose it in front of Owen and Jack.

So he wasn't a baby anymore. So he didn't need her to sing to him. Fine. She'd be fine.

"Goodnight, bud." She stood from the side of his bed and turned toward the door where Jack waited with brows raised.

"Wait," Owen said, reaching for his mom's hand. "Maybe—just tonight. If you really want to."

Ava blew out a breath. "I *really* want to," she said, a dopey grin spreading from ear to ear. She crawled in bed beside him and softly sang the words she'd been singing since the very first time he fell asleep on her chest in the hospital almost a decade ago.

When she was done, Owen's eyes were closed, and his breaths were long and deep. So she slid quietly from the bed and turned toward the door—and Jack.

"Love you, Mom," her son said dreamily.

"Love you, bud."

"Goodnight, Jack. Thanks for the curveball help."

"Night, Shortstop," Jack said, a hesitant smile playing at his lips.

The dog lumbered in past them and hopped onto Owen's bed, stretching across the boy's feet, his paws dangling off each side.

She grabbed Jack's hand and pulled him down the hall and then the short flight of stairs until they were in the small entryway, Ava leaning against the front door.

He ran a hand through his hair, then crossed his arms as he inhaled, head tilted up.

"Ah," she said. "The thinking pose. Ya gonna let me in on what's going on in that private place of yours?"

He dropped his head so his gaze met hers. "Stay with me next week," he blurted, and her eyes widened.

"I—I can't. I told you...it's Owen's spring break, and I've been gone too much already. I can't just—"

"Both of you," he said. "Or...all three of you. I mean, Scully too. We'll work on the vineyard, and Owen and I can perfect his slider."

Her mouth opened and closed, but no words came out. It was Jack who couldn't seem to *stop* talking now.

"I'll move my shit to the bedroom upstairs so you and Owen can have the guest room. But if it will be too weird for him—for both of you, I get it. It's actually probably the worst idea I've ever had so—"

"What does this mean?" she asked warily. "If Owen gets attached to you...I don't like agreeing with my father, but he's right. It's already happening." It was for *her*, too.

"I don't know," he said. "I don't know what the hell it means other than I hate the thought of not seeing either of you next week. But you're right. It could be confusing to Owen. And you. Shit. A couple of hours ago I was ready to do what I thought was the right thing and step back—keep you both safe from getting hurt again but—"

There he went again—trying to do the right thing. The only problem was she had no idea what *right* meant for their situation.

"But Owen might not be the only one forming an attachment," she said as realization bloomed.

It was, very possibly, the *worst* idea. But this was a

chance for Owen and his dad to really connect—for Jack to see the kind of father he could be, even if from afar.

It was her chance to figure out how to reconcile these new feelings for the first boy she'd ever loved with the fact she'd soon say good-bye to him again.

But for right now, she simply kissed him.

"Is that a yes?" he whispered.

"Yes," she whispered back, her lips still on his, and then kissed him again to shut them both up because she knew. Verbal vomit was a mess that was almost impossible to clean up, and she didn't want either of them to say anything more.

Because she didn't want either of them to change their minds.

He relaxed into her, his hands gripping her hips, and she could feel him smile against her lips.

"You made his night, you know," she said.

He didn't say anything in response other than claiming her lips with his again. He didn't need to. She'd watched them both all night, the boy and the man. She'd even go out on a limb and say that Jack had enjoyed himself as much as Owen had.

It didn't matter what Jack thought he was or was not capable of because Ava had seen it right there in her own backyard.

Jack Everett was a father, and he could be a damned good one if he'd only see himself the way she saw him.

Well, now she had a week to prove it.

Except his tongue slipped past her lips, and all her bones turned to jelly. She had to stop kissing him before her brain did, too.

"You should…probably…"

But he'd taken her pause in kissing him as an opportunity to trail his lips down her neck, his stubble scratching her skin in a way that made her knees buckle. If she didn't stop him now, before he got to her breast, she'd let him take her right on the entryway rug.

"Not here," she said before it was too late.

He backed away, brows raised in question, but he was otherwise completely composed.

"How the hell do you do that?" she asked.

"Do what?"

She blew out a breath and placed her hands on her hips, even as her taut nipples were about to slice holes through her shirt. "How do you liquefy my bones and then stand there as if you weren't about to have your way with me up against my front door?"

One corner of his mouth quirked up. "You gonna catch me if I go weak in the knees?"

She swatted him on the shoulder. "That's not the point," she pouted. "As soon as you leave I'm going to have to take a really cold shower and think about doing my taxes or something."

He leaned forward like he was going to kiss her but instead let his lips brush against her ear.

"I could do your taxes," he murmured.

She groaned and slipped out from under his arm. "I just—we can't. Not here. Not yet. Owen could come down those steps at any second, and I don't want to have to explain us before I can—you know—*explain* us."

Because how could she explain to her son what she didn't understand herself?

Jack pressed his lips together and nodded slowly. Then he kissed her on the top of the head. "Your father's right. Sneaking out after curfew didn't count," he said. "Maybe ten years too late, but I'd like to make up for it."

She reminded herself that proper date or no, their lives were headed in opposite directions, with Owen the only true anchor between them. But it was no use. She was falling for this man, and if she stopped kidding herself, maybe she'd be able to admit that she'd never quite gotten back up from the first time she fell.

"I'd like that," she admitted, but she kept the rest of her thoughts to herself. Maybe the father-son bond could span the miles between one coast and another, but her heart wouldn't withstand that distance.

"Goodnight, Red." His lips brushed softly against her cheek. His warm breath tickled her neck, and goose bumps peppered her skin.

She sighed, and there was a slight tremor in her breath. She couldn't be quite sure, though, if it was due to her heightened emotional state or the fact that she was still turned on just by the nearness of him.

It was probably a combination of both.

"We'll be out there bright and early Monday morning," she said.

He nodded again. And then he was out the door.

She stayed there, peering through the window as his truck backed out of the driveway and rolled away down the street.

"I'm in big trouble," she said aloud, then marched herself upstairs and straight to her bathroom, where she turned on her shower and waited for the water to get cold enough to make her body forget how much it wanted his.

Her heart, though, that was another story.

CHAPTER SIXTEEN

I'm your buffer," Jenna said, dunking her tea bag in her mug. "You know, in case things get awkward with Ava or Owen."

"She's got a point," Luke said, smacking Jack on the back of the head as he strode toward the fridge, where he grabbed what Jack had learned was his breakfast of choice, a Red Bull and a hard-boiled egg. "You were always the socially awkward one."

Because Luke was being Luke, opting for levity over gravity, Jack let the insult slide. His younger brother's safety net was a hell of a lot safer than the way Walker dealt with things.

"Things aren't going to get *awkward*," he insisted. Then he pointed at his aunt. "You're here because you can't stay the hell away, because even though we aren't your burden to bear anymore, you can't seem to shake the mom gene." Jenna's jaw fell open, but before she could misconstrue his words, Jack stepped toward her and kissed her on the cheek. "And we love you for that," he said softly. "But I've got this under control."

He hoped. Or maybe he didn't. Having Ava and Owen here was about getting to know his son. But wasn't this also about getting to know *her* again? She wasn't his eighteen-year-old first love. She wasn't anyone he really knew anymore. But every day he was with her—every minute he was in her presence—he wanted more.

"Talk about awkward," Luke said, and then blew out a long whistle. "What the hell is that?"

Jack turned to see his youngest brother rounding the corner from the front stairway, a towel around his neck to catch the water dripping from his hair. Walker was clean shaven and wearing what looked like an equally clean black T-shirt and jeans.

Jack glanced at the clock on his smart phone, the only item indicative of the fast-paced life he'd been living just a couple of weeks ago—the one he'd been so eager to return to. True, work on a ranch was almost round the clock, but the pace of life in Oak Bluff was its own entity, a pace *he'd* been setting since he'd returned, rather than his firm and his clients setting it for him.

This morning he'd woken early to take a ride on Cleo and tend to the cattle. It was only half past eight now that they were all gearing up for vineyard work, but he hadn't counted on Walker being a part of anything before noon.

"Are you okay?" he asked his youngest brother.

Walker responded first with a glare. "'Course I'm okay," he said. "Why the hell wouldn't I be?"

Jack shrugged. "Figured you were out well past midnight again."

"Yeah," Luke said with a laugh. "I'm usually dragging your hungover ass out of bed. What's with the whole getting up on your own lately? It's like you're responsible or something."

"Screw you," Walker countered, stalking past them all and out onto the back porch.

Jenna laid a hand on Jack's shoulder.

"I know," he said. "I got this."

He followed his brother outside, where he stood against the wooden rail of the deck squinting toward the pasture. Jack hung back several feet to give Walker some space, his hands shoved in his pockets.

"You clean up like this for Ava and Owen?" Jack asked.

Walker's shoulders rose and fell, but he kept his back to his brother. "I didn't do a goddamn thing for anyone," Walker insisted.

Jack smiled anyway, since he knew his brother couldn't see him. If he pushed too hard, he was likely to spook him. So instead he simply said, "I didn't think so. But if you had?"

"I didn't."

"There's fresh coffee," Jack conceded, the only way he could think of to thank Walker. By including him in the day's plan. "We'll head out when they get here."

Walker nodded, still facing the fields. "I'll grab some in a few."

Jack took that as the closest he'd get to *thank you* and headed back inside only to find a chocolate Lab scrambling to get off a leash being held by a not-quite-strong-enough nine-year-old boy. Owen's feet were having trouble finding purchase on the wood floor, and the corner of Jack's mouth tilted into a crooked grin as he watched Scully drag the boy from the entryway toward the kitchen.

Jenna was holding the front door open for Ava, so Jack simply turned to Owen and said, "It's all right."

With that the boy unhooked the leash, and the dog came bounding toward him, barely halting before rising on his hind legs to rest his front paws on Jack's shoulders.

Jack stumbled back against the sliding glass door as

Scully gave him an affectionate greeting. The dog had shown nothing but mild interest in him before now, which was why he couldn't help but laugh—and laugh hard. Harder than he had in—well, he couldn't exactly remember.

"Someone's getting lucky tonight," he heard Luke say from his left. And then he caught sight of Ava practically sprinting toward them, her red hair wild and glowing as the sun streaming in from the front door backlit her as she moved.

"Sorry!" she called. "Shit. Sorry about the dog! He's a nervous traveler, and I think he's happy to see a familiar face and not the vet!"

"Mo-om," Owen sing-songed with laughter in his tone. "Language?"

"Shit!" Ava said again. "Down, Scully!"

The dog gave Jack one final lap against his jaw before heeding Ava's command. The second Scully relinquished his hold on him, Luke balled up a kitchen towel and lobbed it at his brother, nailing him in the chest.

"Thought you might want to dry off after that unexpected shower."

Jack nodded his thanks, and—not that he wasn't appreciative of such affection—took to wiping himself clean.

Ava's teeth were clamped together in a pained smile as Owen dropped to his knees to rub his dog's belly. "This is a lot, right?" she asked. "All three of us? I think I just realized what a handful we are."

She laughed nervously, and Jenna spoke up from behind Jack's visitors. "Sweetie, you're hanging with the Everett brothers for a week, working for no pay, and putting up with all of them? I think we know who the bigger handful is."

Luke's head tilted back as he downed his Red Bull. Then

he crushed the can on the counter and slapped his palm dramatically against his heart.

"Say what you want about Jack and Walker." He looked pointedly at his aunt. "But a guy with my devilish good looks and charm?"

Jenna pointed at her second youngest nephew. "*Not* thinking you're a handful makes you the biggest handful of them all, no matter how damn charming you claim to be."

Owen laughed. "I like it here. You guys are funny. And loud. Our house gets kind of quiet sometimes."

Jack watched Ava's expression falter before she painted a smile back on seconds later. It wasn't an insult, what Owen had said. But he saw that flicker of loss, the same one he'd felt the first time he'd seen his son. It didn't matter that he'd never thought he'd want what had been thrust upon him. Once it was there, he realized what he'd missed. And now Ava was seeing that, too.

"Quiet's good, sometimes," Jack said, and Owen shrugged.

"But loud's a helluva lot better." Luke rounded the counter, heading toward the sliding glass door. "What do you say, Shortstop? Wanna see if your dog'll give Walker the same greeting he gave Jack? I guarantee he'll react with some loud words we can all enjoy."

Jenna gave Luke's shoulder a playful push, and for a second Jack considered leaving his youngest brother in peace. But the brotherly thing to do was to give his siblings hell, so he let Luke open the back door and usher the dog outside to an unsuspecting Walker.

"What the hell?" Walker yelled as Scully pounced. Jenna ran out after them. Owen and Luke were right behind her, laughing, so Jack trusted all was well and pulled the sliding door shut.

He strode toward Ava and removed the large tote bag from her shoulder, setting it on the floor against the wall. "I'm gonna apologize ahead of time for any changes in Owen's vocabulary by the end of this week," he said, coaxing a genuine smile from her. Then he pulled her around the corner and out of view from the back door, pressing her against the closed guest bedroom door.

She sucked in a sharp breath as he dipped his head but stopped short before his lips touched hers. "Red?" he said, his voice soft.

She exhaled then, her warm breath tickling his lips. "Yeah?" she squeaked.

"Are you going to spend the whole week thinking this is all too much for me to handle?" He rested his hands on her hips, the tips of his fingers pressing into the soft skin he knew rested beneath her clothes.

He watched her throat bob as she swallowed. "Maybe," she admitted and hooked one finger into the top of his jeans.

"Maybe's not gonna work for me." Her eyes widened. "I need you to feel at home. Because handful or not—I want you here. All three of you. Okay?"

"Okay," she said, then licked her lips, and Jack was two seconds from losing it, but he wasn't going to pressure her.

"Anything that happens between you and me while you're here is your call. But I need to make something clear. Me keeping my distance isn't because I don't want you." His lips brushed hers. Not exactly a kiss, but not exactly innocent, either. "Because I can't watch you walk into a room without wanting to touch you. You're like the goddamn sun, and I'm the closest planet. Powerless against your gravity. But I am trying to do what's right for Owen—what's right for you so you don't get hurt again." This week meant everything because after this he'd have it all figured out. They'd been keeping the truth from Owen until they knew what the truth was—until Jack could tell his son what role he was going to play in his future. That was what this visit was really about, wasn't it? Owen. The truth. Everything. But that didn't change how much he wanted her. It didn't change how hard he had to fight for restraint when he was this close. "So if at any second in any of the days you're here you think that I'd rather be doing *any*thing other than feeling your lips against mine, know that you could not be more wrong."

He started to back away, but she fisted her hand in his T-shirt.

"Damn it, Jack Everett. You're going to say all that and then *not* kiss me?" she said, her breathing shallow as she whisper-shouted the words.

"Your call, Red."

Her breath hitched. "Every time you call me that, I feel like I'm eighteen again. Like we're—*us*. You know?"

"Yeah. I know."

His heart hammered beneath her fist, his chest rising and falling in deep breaths that were becoming less and less controlled. And he wasn't running from it this time—the thought of losing control.

"My call?" she asked.

He nodded, and that was all it took. She yanked his T-shirt, pulling him to her, and he let the last of his resolve crumble as her mouth demanded his.

His fingers dug into her hips as she parted her lips, encouraging him to do the same. Her tongue slipped past, mingling with his, and he could taste the hint of the morning coffee she'd probably drunk on the ride over, along with something both sweet and spicy—cinnamon. Maybe a mint.

This made him grin, the thought of her popping an Altoid or something like that. Because maybe she'd anticipated this as much as he had.

Her hand moved from his shirt, and seconds later, the door to the guest bedroom fell open, the two of them stumbling past the threshold and collapsing onto the bed he'd made for her the night before. The room also had a small couch with a pull-out bed. He'd bought new sheets for that one for Owen.

Right now, though, all Jack could think about was Ava beneath him and how long she could stay there before any of the other four people—and one rambunctious Lab—would come looking for them. He rationalized that they'd hear the back door when the chaos decided to move inside. It wasn't like either of them would let this go any further than some very heavy petting. At least not right now.

"I can't believe we weren't doing this all week long," she said, her voice breathless between each feverish kiss. She knew they were on borrowed time, too. But it was more than this day or the little snippets of time they'd have together this week.

Jack didn't know what the endgame was, but he hoped to hell that having Ava and Owen here for the next five days would give him the answers he needed—would help him figure out what was best for all of them.

He was hard. Hell, this woman did things to him. But there wasn't time for what he wanted to do to her. As if she was reading his thoughts, though, Ava tilted her pelvis, and he ground himself against her. She let out a soft cry, an even softer plea as she whispered, *"More."*

That's when the scrabble of excited paws snapped them both back into the moment, and Jack sprang to his feet as Scully came bounding through the door and dropped a baseball at his feet. The dog sat panting, tongue hanging out the side of his mouth, and tail wagging expectantly.

Ava was up and smoothing out her hair by the time Owen caught up to his dog.

"I think Scully wants to play catch with you, Ja—" But the boy stopped short when he laid eyes on the room, the one Jack hadn't officially shown Ava yet.

"Whoa," Owen said. "This is like someplace a real cowboy would live."

Relieved not to have been found dry-humping his son's mom on the guest bed, Jack laughed. He ran a hand along the knotted pine panel on the wall, one of ten that ran horizontally from doorframe to corner, stacked from floor to ceiling.

"Our father built this room for our mom," Jack said, allowing flashes of a happier time to invade his memories. "She missed her friends and family from Texas, so Jack Senior—with the help of the Callahans, some family friends who ran a contracting business—put an addition on the house that included this room. And you want to know what?"

"What?" Owen asked with an eager grin. Ava, not having heard the story before, either, said the same.

"He designed this room to look like the one our mom and Jenna loved at their grandparents' ranch back in Texas, so there'd always be a bit of home here in California."

Owen's fingers trailed Jack's across the wall and then to the queen bed, covered now with a semi-rumpled quilt.

"She made that, you know." Jenna's voice came from behind him, and Jack spun to find her standing in the doorframe. "She hated every second of it—claimed she was meant for the labor of the ranch and not for something with painstaking detail like crafting a quilt. But our nan made the one in the bedroom we always stayed in at their ranch, so Clare made sure this room had the same."

Jack ran a palm across the quilt, straightening it, and cleared his throat. "I thought this was something they bought."

Jenna shook her head. "You were probably too young to remember or too busy with baseball to notice her working on it. But that was her contribution to the room." Jenna laughed. "She probably did it to spite your daddy so he wouldn't be able to take full credit for the space. They were both so competitive. And so damn stubborn sometimes."

"Please don't, Jenna," Jack said.

Her eyes narrowed. "Please don't *what*? Remind you that they were happy? That despite the man Jackson Senior turned into, he did right by your mama and she by him? I'm not apologizing for what he did..."

Jack's hands fisted at his sides, and he tried to take a controlling breath. But control in the face of *what he did* was impossible.

"You don't get it," he snapped. "It doesn't matter what happened before she died when all I can seem to recall is what he did after. I'm happy as hell he took such great care of her when she was alive, but what about her children, Jenna? What about *his* sons?"

This was a mistake—this little trip down memory lane. Especially in front of Owen.

"Jack—"

But he wasn't waiting around to hear more.

"Enough," he said, then strode past Jenna and out of the room, calling over his shoulder, "We should get to work."

Because he wasn't about to listen to his aunt get all wistful and sentimental about his parents. Whatever Clare and Jackson Everett Senior had been before his mother died—

that was fiction. The reality was that he and his brothers lost two parents *and* a good part of their childhoods. He was wrong for even entertaining the thought that good memories could override the bad. Good memories had no place here.

Walker and Luke stood waiting in the kitchen, and Jack nodded to them and then headed toward the front door.

He needed out of this house. Fresh air would do him some good. Clear his head. Sure, he was being a dick, especially to Jenna, but she at least understood him, how he operated. He'd apologize later, and she'd give him hell for treating her like that in the first place, but she'd know he loved her and needed to let off some steam. This was their routine.

Thankfully, everyone followed him outside without so much as a *What the hell?* Not even Walker.

"We need to finish pruning by lunch," Jack said once everyone was assembled. Even the damned dog. "Then we'll eat, regroup, and check on the cover crop the previous owner planted, see if that grass needs to be tilled or torn out and replanted altogether. Bottom line is we can't have weeds. If we get this place on the path to producing a crop next year, we don't want to fall on our faces because of some damned weeds."

Ava squinted at him, the sun hitting her right in the eyes. "Sounds like you've been doing your homework. I could show you how to till—and how to recognize some sneaky weeds that disguise themselves as grass."

She smiled, but he couldn't let her get to him now that he was ready to get shit done—and get one step closer to getting the hell out. The less he had to sleep under the roof of Crossroads Ranch, the better.

"I think I got it. I passed the California Bar," he said. "A weekend of reading up on viniculture ought to do the trick."

"I see," Ava said, stalking past him toward her car. "Because certainly a weekend of reading far surpasses a lifetime of experience."

"Oh, Jack," Jenna said, shaking her head.

"Hey, Mom! Wait up!"

Owen and Scully trailed after Ava.

"What the hell did I say?" Jack asked.

"You're outta practice, brother." Luke clasped him on the shoulder. "Told ya you were the socially awkward one."

"Man, you're a prick," Walker added as he headed down the driveway and toward the stable.

Ava, Owen, and the dog were in her Jeep and backing into the street. Luke and Walker were probably taking a couple of the mares over to the vineyard. That left just Jack and Jenna.

He crossed his arms and held his aunt's gaze. He could wait her out, no matter how long she stared. They used to play this game in high school, and it always ended in Jenna groaning and throwing her hands in the air.

"What's it gonna take to get through to you, Jack?" she used to ask. "When are you gonna finally let me the hell in?"

But he wouldn't answer. Never did. Because what the hell was the point of letting *anyone* in when all he ever did was make things more complicated for everyone involved?

That's how it had felt when he and his brothers had taken over Jenna's house—or when he saw the look of horror on Ava's face after what had happened at the graduation party.

Except this wasn't then, and Jenna held her ground now. She wasn't screaming through gritted teeth. No impatient exasperation. Just cold, clean resolve.

"I got all day," she said, taking a step closer.

Jack almost flinched. Forget the fact that he was at least

a foot taller than her. The woman had a serious *Don't mess with me* vibe going on.

His jaw clenched. "I was supposed to come back for a weekend. A week tops. Now there's this vineyard, and I can't leave that to Luke and Walker to take care of on their own. Then Ava and Owen. I have a son. A *son*, Jenna. He's this incredible kid, and I'm—I'm *me*. I don't know how the hell to deal with all this."

"Ya screwed up just now," she said calmly.

He opened his mouth to respond, but she cut him off.

"I know this place gets to you, Jack. And I know you built yourself a whole new life so you wouldn't have to deal with it. But you're here now. You decided to stay for however long that might be, and you got a hell of a lot more than you bargained for, which I'm guessing you thought would include a quick graveside service, washing your hands of this place, and then hightailing it out the door again. But this shit ain't about only you anymore. Not when you're under that roof with Luke, Walker, and your son and his mother. So maybe it's time to get your shit together and *deal*."

He crossed his arms and raised a brow, waiting for a beat. "You about done?" he asked.

She pursed her lips and contemplated the question for a few seconds. "Yeah. I guess I am," she finally said.

"That your version of therapy?"

She nodded. "Maybe it is. Wouldn't hurt you to, you know, deal with your demons and all that."

He let out a bitter laugh. "I did for that whole first year of college. Stipulation of my non-arrest and all." But it seemed nothing had been enough to prepare him for coming home. "Anyway, I thought that's what I was doing coming back here—dealing with my demons. You know I'm gonna take care of them, right? He's my son. My responsibility. I don't take that lightly."

She sighed. "From across the country. Is that why you haven't told him yet? That boy deserves the truth, you know."

She was right. He knew that. But he also knew that some people weren't cut out to be fathers, and he'd always put himself in that category. A couple of good interactions with his son didn't mean he knew what the hell he was doing—didn't mean he'd be any different from the man who raised him.

"What do we actually tell him? *Hey, kid. I'm your dad. Nice to meet you, but I gotta run. It's what I do.* Or *I once beat a kid unconscious for trying to hurt your mom, Hope I don't do the same to you.*"

Jenna's features softened. She never could hold on to anger for too long. "Oh, sweetie. When are you going to let yourself off the hook for something that happened when you were a troubled kid?"

He let out a long breath, grasping at the one thing in his life that made sense—the one thing he could control. "New York is what I've worked toward ever since I left. It's my career."

She stepped forward and tapped him on the chest. "A career I haven't heard you mention once other than to tell me you're moving to the other side of the country." She laughed. "Small-town ranch boy like you? You'll hate that noisy city."

"I haven't been a small-town ranch boy for a decade," he said even as he sucked in a deep breath of Oak Bluff's crisp open air.

She patted him condescendingly on the cheek, a gesture that only Jenna could make endearing. "Aw, honey. I've lived in Los Olivos longer than I ever lived in Texas, but you will never hear me say 'I ain't been a Texan in however many years.' You can take the boy off the small-town ranch..."

He rolled his eyes and shook his head. "You want a ride to the vineyard or not?"

Her shoulders relaxed, and he knew the anger was completely gone. "Before the subject is officially changed, can I say one more thing?"

He laughed. "Could I stop you if I said no?"

She shook her head. "Make things right with Ava."

He led her to the passenger side of his truck and unlocked the door.

He'd messed up. He knew that. He had let his demons get in the way of thinking about what he said before he said it, and he'd gone and diminished her whole goddamn life's work to a quick weekend read.

Shit. How had the morning started off so well and then gone to complete and utter hell?

Oh. Right. He'd been a first-rate asshole.

"I will" was all he said, and that seemed to be enough because Jenna climbed into the truck without another word.

In a few minutes they were at the vineyard. Walker and Luke must have ridden to the far end to do the pruning there because neither they nor their horses were anywhere to be found. Jack caught sight of Owen tossing a ball and Scully fetching it, so he knew Ava wouldn't be far off.

"Hang with Owen for a minute?" he asked when they both were out of the truck.

Jenna smiled. "Of course."

Jack found Ava in the middle of a row, hair piled on top of her head in a messy bun and pruning shears in her gloved hand. She was hacking away at a branch like it was being punished. He felt bad for the poor vine since he knew it was a substitute for him.

"Hey," he said when he was close enough for her to hear.

She looked up, shears pointed up and open, like she was poised to snip off one of his limbs.

He reached for them. "Maybe put those down for a second," he said in what he hoped was a calming tone.

She narrowed her eyes but relinquished her grip on the tool he didn't want to see turned into a weapon. Jack dropped it to the ground.

"What you have been doing here this past week is amazing. And generous."

Ava shrugged. "Yeah, so?"

A small laugh escaped his lips. He couldn't help it. She was the only one who brought it out of him, and he wished he could think of the right words to let her know that.

"And I don't deserve the help you've been giving me."

She crossed her arms. "No. You don't."

He took a step closer to her, and she didn't retreat—or make a quick grab for the shears to cut his balls off—so he took that as encouragement. "And I was an asshole back at the ranch. I didn't mean to demean what you do."

Her eyes softened, but her expression was still pained.

"Do you think that, though?" she asked, all her anger draining so that the only thing he could hear now was the hurt. "That what I've done with my life doesn't have the same meaning as what you've done with yours?"

His eyes widened. "Jesus, Ava. *No.* Hearing all that shit about how happy my parents were, though?" He shook his head. "In case you haven't noticed, I don't exactly deal well with the unexpected."

That elicited a bitter laugh from her. "I suppose you've

had quite a lot of that thrown at you in less than two weeks. That stuff Jenna said got to you, huh?"

"Yes," he admitted.

"But you don't want to talk about it," she added.

"Not right now."

"I told you I'm not gonna push you, Jack. But I'm also not gonna cut you slack for how you process your repressed emotions, especially if I get caught in the cross fire."

He raised a hesitant hand toward her cheek, and when she gripped his wrist and brought his palm the rest of the way to her skin, he let out a shaky exhale. "I'm sorry," he said softly. "I don't deserve you."

She kissed his palm, then gave him a pointed look. Hell. What had he done now?

"You deserve so much more than you let yourself believe," she said. "But I can't make you see that, Jack. You have to see it for yourself."

Did he deserve another chance with her? Or a chance to prove the father he'd be for Owen was nothing like his own had turned out to be?

She kissed him, and he heard her breath shudder as she did.

She may have hurt him, but he understood why: Her reasons were born out of love. His had come from self-preservation.

The truth was, it was she who deserved *everything*, and he had no clue if he could be the one to give it to her.

CHAPTER SEVENTEEN

After working on the vineyard for the better part of the day, Ava thought she'd relax while Luke and Walker gave Owen a riding lesson. She thought wrong. Instead she watched, heart in her throat, because her son, who she thought was getting so big, was dwarfed atop a giant horse. Walker rode a horse named Bella, one who was only five years old, next to Owen on Cleo, who had belonged to Jack when he was a young teen. Not that he'd ever mentioned her when they'd dated in high school *or* that she was big enough to eat her son.

Horses didn't eat people, though, right?

Luke kept a steady pace on the ground next to Owen, but he was no longer holding the reins or guiding the mare. Her boy was on his own, and damn if he didn't look good on a horse, like she assumed his father did.

Owen grabbed his Dodger cap by the bill and twirled it in the air like a lasso. "Woohoo! I'm ready to drive some cattle!"

But as soon as the words left his mouth, he lost his balance.

It felt like everything happened in slow motion, but it was over in a blink. Ava burst through the gate, not even thinking about spooking the horses. Her only thought was getting to her son. By the time she did, she couldn't remember how she got from point A to point B—and then there was Owen, upright on the horse again, Luke steadying him back into the saddle.

"Mom!" he cried, a grin spreading from ear to ear. "Did you see that? I almost totally wiped out, and then Luke caught me! And Cleo even stopped, like she knew something was up, and it...was...*awesome*!"

Ava started laughing hysterically as tears sprang from her eyes at the same time. Maybe she wasn't laughing at all, but then again, what did it really matter? Owen was okay. That was the only thing that mattered. Ever.

Walker spun around on Bella and trotted back in their direction while Luke rested a hand on Ava's shoulder.

"I live and breathe this shit, Red," he said. "As long as I'm around when he's on the horse, your boy is in good hands."

Ava had to catch her breath and collect herself before she could respond. By the time she was ready to speak, she knew Luke was right. This was Owen's family, and in the short time they'd known him, they already had his back. And something made her trust that for as long as Owen was in their lives, they would.

"Thank you," she said. "I just—I don't want you to think—it was a knee-jerk reaction, you know?"

Walker and Luke both nodded. "You were protecting your young," Luke said. "No worries. As long as you know now that he's safe on the horse. Safer than any other *Shortstop* I know."

Owen groaned and rolled his eyes, but he was still smiling. He enjoyed the constant ribbing from his uncle, and Ava enjoyed watching it. It was like they really were a family or something. As quickly as the thought made her smile, though, it filled her with guilt.

They had to tell him. She kept rationalizing that she had to know exactly what role Jack would play in Owen's life before telling her son who his father really was. But each second they kept the truth from him was a betrayal of the person she loved most. The ball wasn't only in Jack's court. It had to be in hers, too.

"Jack back yet?" Walker asked, as if he could read her thoughts.

She glanced back to the driveway that was missing his beat-up truck. "Nope."

"He's a man of mystery, huh?" Luke asked.

"More like a closed-off asshole," Walker added, but Ava caught the hint of a smile on his usually sullen face.

"You say 'asshole' a lot," Owen said.

Ava opened her mouth to protest, but then she thought better of it. If adding a few new words to Owen's vocabulary was the price for getting to know the Everetts, so be it.

"He's right, you know," she said with a grin.

Luke tipped his head back and laughed. "Can't argue with the truth."

For a second Walker's jaw tightened, but then his shoulders relaxed. "Well, *asshole*," he said to Luke, "when you're right, you're right."

All four of them laughed now, and Ava forgot *the man of mystery* for a few minutes.

The day's work had gone as planned, right down to learning, thankfully, that the cover crop was doing its job. They wouldn't have to replant, only till—which was still a big job—but it could have been worse.

But Jack had been gone for over an hour now at a meeting in the neighboring city of Pismo Beach. Jenna had already left, and neither Luke nor Walker knew anything about the meeting, either. Jack hadn't bothered to fill anyone in. All they knew was that Jack Senior's lawyer had called and asked to see Jack in person, and he had dropped everything to do it.

The unmistakable sound of tires on gravel broke the laughter and Ava's train of thought.

"Mom!" Owen called as she watched Jack's truck roll up the driveway. "Can I ride for a little longer? I *promise* I'll be careful."

She turned to him, brows raised. "And what about walking your dog?"

Scully, wiped from the day's work, which had included racing Owen up and down the rows of vines, had been passed out on the living room floor when they'd left the house. Ava didn't actually mind walking the dog. She also didn't want to be the mom who said no because, despite knowing Luke and Walker were there, she still worried. It was a prerequisite of mothering, one that seemed to last far beyond the preschool and toddler years.

He looked at her with pleading eyes, so in love with being on that horse. "Ten more minutes? Pleeeaase? Then I'll walk Scully, and I'll even shower without complaining."

She laughed at this, and Luke stared toward the house.

"Go on. I said he was safe, and I don't go around saying shit I don't mean."

Her frantic heartbeat finally slowed. "Twenty minutes," she countered, and Owen's face lit up.

"Thank you!" he cried. "Thank you! Thank you!" He wobbled a bit in his excitement but immediately righted himself. Ava still gasped—and then laughed.

He would be fine. And she? Well, she'd still worry, but then she always would.

* * *

Jack was in the kitchen when she made it back to the house. He sat at the table staring at a business-sized envelope as if he was waiting for it to speak.

"I bet Carnac the Magnificent could tell you what's in there," she said.

His head jerked up, and for a second she thought he might not recognize her.

"What?" he asked, his voice strained.

"Johnny Carson?" she said. "Carnac the Magnificent? It was a bit on his show. My dad has all thirty years on DVD. When Johnny retired, he started over again from the beginning, and when I was old enough to watch with him, I did. It was kind of our thing."

Jack let out a bitter laugh. "Apparently my dad's *thing* is to still keep some sort of twisted hold on me even after he's gone."

Ava worried her upper lip. "You mean the vineyard?"

The line of his jaw flexed and released. "I mean this." He slid the envelope across the table, and Ava moved closer so she could read the words scrawled across it in a jagged script.

For Jackson Everett Junior
    To be read in the event of my death.

"Even when his words were slurred or barely legible, he still managed to get the last one."

She pulled out the chair across from him and sat, resting her palm on top of his.

"So that's why his lawyer called you? To give you the letter?"

Jack nodded. "He had a few other things to go over, but

he wanted to apologize and give me the letter in person. It got lost in a pile of paperwork. He said my father gave it to him days before he passed, like he knew he was at the end. I always thought he was too sauced to even know he was sick."

Ava rubbed her thumb over his knuckles. "You're gonna read it, right?" she asked and felt the veins in his hand tense as he curled it into a fist.

"No," he said flatly. He stood, folded it in half and shoved it in his back pocket. "How's Owen doing with the two knuckleheads?"

He smiled, but she could tell it was forced. She could also tell that the discussion about the letter was over.

For now, she thought.

She slid out of her chair and rose to meet his gaze. "Well, I had a heart attack when he almost fell off of Cleo, but Luke caught him, and Walker was right next to him on Bella."

"Christ," he hissed. "You can tell Luke and Walker to lay off the riding. I didn't invite you here to put your son in danger."

Her breath hitched.

Your son.

He must have realized what he'd said because his eyes widened.

"Jesus, Ava. No. That's not what I meant." He rounded the table so he was in front of her, cupping her face in his hands. "Calling him mine?" he said. "That's a privilege I haven't earned yet."

She got that. Hell, she knew ten years ago he hadn't *wanted* such a privilege. Yet here they were, staying in his home with him. He wanted—*something*. Didn't he?

"Your terms still," he said, a tentative grin taking over

his features. "As far as what happens between you and me while you're here."

If she kissed him now, the subject would be effectively changed. No letter. No talk of them as an "us" instead of a her, a him, and an Owen. But Owen deserved better.

"We're lying to him, Jack. He's out there having the time of his life with his uncles, and I feel like we're playing some huge joke on him. He's a good kid."

"I know," he said softly.

She shook her head. "No. He's a *great* kid. The best, and he deserves the truth. I told myself I wasn't going to give you an ultimatum, but for Owen's sake I have to." He kept talking so much about doing right by her and Owen that she hadn't realized, until today, that they'd missed the mark.

"You're right," he said, his gaze fixed on hers.

Only in his eyes, that storm of blue, could she see his warring emotions—what she guessed was hesitation and fear mixed with his insistence on always doing what was best for everyone else.

"I thought I could wait," she said. "I thought I could let you deal with your dad's death and figure out this vineyard thing, but you're *leaving*. I can't let the month go by only for us to tell him right before you hop on a plane." Owen deserved time with his father *knowing* who his father was.

"Everything this week is your call," he said.

"Okay, then. It should be just the three of us, right?" Not that she had a clue. There was no protocol for something like this, but she figured it should happen without the whole Everett/Ellis entourage. "He has a baseball game Saturday morning. His first of the season. Come to the game, and we'll take him out for lunch after. We'll tell him and take it from there, and whatever happens, the two of you will have at least another week before—"

She didn't want to say what came next, but Jack was good at filling in the blanks.

"Before I move to New York."

She forced a smile, but it felt like her chest was caving in.

They stood there in that heavy silence for several long seconds, the lack of words passing between them saying more than if they'd stated the obvious. Whatever this was with him and her could only ever be temporary unless he gave up his job.

But it was more than a job. It was his career. And it wasn't like he was asking her and Owen to drop everything and come with him to New York. She couldn't, even if he did. She *wouldn't*. Her life—her *future*—was here. So was Owen's.

He reached for her hand and laced his fingers through hers. "I got you something today," he said. "After my meeting."

Her eyes widened, and the change of subject made breathing a little easier.

"It's still in the bed of my truck."

He pulled her toward the door without another word.

When they reached the truck, he lowered the back door and pulled back a small tarp to reveal an easel, a blank canvas, and several tubes of paint.

Ava's hand flew to her mouth.

"I know Owen said the painting wasn't going so great lately, but I thought—I know how much you loved it, and that if things with us had worked out differently, you would have gone to art school ten years ago instead of just applying now. Aaand...I can't tell if you're smiling or crying right now, so if I've messed up again, please tell me. I can take it. I'm apparently on a roll."

Her eyes shone bright. She was sure of it, but not because he'd messed up again. Far from it. So she dropped her hand to reveal a smile. Because despite her and Jack being virtual strangers, he still knew her enough to do something like this.

She threw her arms around him and hugged him close, whispering in his ear, "Thank you." Then she kissed his cheek. "Thank you. Thank you."

He pressed his lips to her neck, and she shuddered. This was exactly what she needed. She'd let her body take over so she could give her brain—and heart—a rest.

"I did good, huh?" he said against her, and it was all she could do not to moan right there.

"You did *really* good," she said, and he peppered her collarbone with more kisses.

This was the language they could speak, one of mutual understanding. And pleasure. They were really good when it came to pleasure.

"Owen and your brothers can probably see us," she said.

He laughed, his warm breath making *her* warm in places he couldn't see. "Nope. They're on the far end of the stable loop. We've got at least three more minutes of being undetected…*unless*…"

He backed her around the side of the truck and up against the driver's side door, which meant they were completely out of sight.

She gasped as he continued where they'd left off, lips trailing to where her cleavage peeked out from her T-shirt. He dipped his tongue between her breasts, and she hummed a soft moan.

"I gotta say," she started, her voice accompanied by small, sharp gasps, "these stolen moments with you are about the sexiest thing ever."

His palms were on her hips, and he slipped his thumbs beneath her T-shirt. Then his hands slowly lifted the cotton up and over her breasts.

"God, I'm glad you don't have neighbors," she admitted, then cried out as he popped the cup of her demi bra down and took her hard peak into his mouth.

"I hate neighbors," he said, his voice rough with what she hoped was a need that matched her own.

She knew they'd have to stop in seconds. Minutes at the most. She wouldn't let Owen and his uncles catch them like this. But hell if she wouldn't take what she could get.

She ran her hands through his golden waves. "Did you have neighbors in San Diego?" she asked.

He nodded, his five o'clock shadow scratching deliciously against her chest.

"Hated 'em," he said before attending to what she hoped wouldn't be a neglected left breast.

She laughed and then cut herself off with a gasp as he flicked his tongue against her nipple.

"You're not capable of hate," she said when she found her voice again.

He lifted his head at this, his gaze studying her for several long seconds. God, she wished she could read what went on behind the storm in those blue eyes.

"They're walking the horses back into the stable," he said. "We should probably—"

She kissed him then, taking her fill in hopes that what he gave her now would tide her over until their next stolen moment. But every kiss made her want another. And she wasn't sure she'd ever truly get enough.

"God, Ava," he said. And he kissed her harder, longer, like he was trying to quench a thirst as deep as a well. "You make me—"

But he didn't finish the thought. He kept kissing her as if this was the last time they'd get to do this.

The hell it was. And hell if she wasn't going to pull some sort of revelation from him, no matter how small.

"What? I make you what?"

He rested his forehead against hers, his chest rising and falling with ragged breaths. "You make me *want*," he finally said.

She sighed and gave him one last soft kiss.

How long had she put herself on the bottom of the list? Owen came first. And that would never change. But maybe it was time to bump herself up a couple of notches. Maybe it was time to let herself want, too.

And hope.

"Well," she whispered softly against his cheek. "I guess that makes two of us."

CHAPTER EIGHTEEN

Jack was happy to give Ava and Owen the guest room, but that meant he'd had to unexpectedly face at least one demon he'd thought he'd avoid—being back in his old room. It wasn't the room so much as climbing that flight of stairs. When he reached the top, he reminded himself that there was no drunk Jack Senior on his arm, fighting off his son's help, but that did nothing to keep the memory at bay. It didn't matter much, just that tonight he'd be more restless than usual. There was also the matter of a chocolate Lab whimpering outside his door. Scully hadn't woken him, only reminded him that it was past midnight and he was still wide awake.

He groaned and rolled out of bed, throwing on the T-shirt and jeans that lay on the floor.

"I'm coming, ya whiny mutt." But really, he was happy for the company of someone who didn't expect any more than to be taken for a walk and maybe play a little fetch with a now tooth-marked baseball. Besides, who could resist a dog named after the Dodgers' former longtime announcer, Vin Scully?

He hadn't confirmed this assumption with Ava or Owen, but he knew there was no other explanation. How had this kid who'd never known him turned out so much like he was when he was young? But if Owen could take after him without the two having ever met, then he could still end up like Jack Senior, couldn't he? There was probably more of a chance after having grown up with the man.

Jack threw open the door, and Scully's whimpers morphed quickly into excited panting and tail wagging.

"You're so full of shit," he told the dog, but gave him a scratch behind the ears anyway.

Luke and Walker's doors were shut, but the master bedroom hung wide open at the other end of the hall. They'd left the room untouched so far—his brothers conveniently too busy to add it to their to-do lists. Luke always had to be somewhere when Jack brought it up, and Walker was usually gone with a six-pack if he was done working the ranch for the day.

Jack knew it was more than just clearing away the last of their father's belongings. After their mother died, Jack Senior held on to *all* of Clare's clothes, her bottle of perfume, and probably even her toothbrush. He'd left all of his wife's earthly possessions exactly as they had been since the day they'd lost her.

He tried to forget about the times he'd successfully gotten a drunk Jack Senior into his own bed for the night, only to find him the next morning still passed out yet clutching one of his mom's old T-shirts like a life preserver. Remembering shit like that tended to stir emotions—like sympathy—that he didn't want stirred. But as he led Scully to the top of the staircase, his stirrings were thwarted as he recalled once again the last time he'd stood on that threshold with his father—and then was knocked violently down the wooden steps—and eventually out of the ranch for good.

"Until now," he said aloud as he gripped the railing much in the way his father had held on to those T-shirts. Like a lifeline.

Scully scampered to the bottom as Jack moved slowly, steadily, holding his breath.

"Damn it," he whispered as he stepped onto solid ground. "Let it go, already," he told himself. But he'd been telling himself that for ten years.

"Come on, boy."

Scully followed him to the front door, where he slid his feet into his boots. The cold night air bit at his flesh, and he shoved his hands into his pockets. The dog ran around the front yard, took a quick piss, and then ran back to Jack's feet, where he stood wagging his tail. He was ready to grab a ball from the back of his truck when someone yelled *"Shit!"* from behind the house.

Instead of a ball, he grabbed a bat and rounded the side of the ranch as stealthily as he could with an excited pooch at his heels. He gripped the bat firmly in one hand, poised to react—until he climbed up on the deck, only to find it littered with crushed beer cans. Luke and Walker had left their lawn chairs abandoned as they poked at something with a stick in the fire pit below.

He dropped the bat onto the ground. "What the hell are you assholes doing?"

He bellied up to the deck rail while Scully leaned down on his front paws, his ass in the air as he still wagged that damned tail.

"Lost a full can in there." Walker stared toward the blaze.

Luke snorted with laughter. "Some shitheads lack the hand-eye coordination needed to open a goddamn can of beer."

Walker pushed his brother good-naturedly, but Luke stumbled too close to the fire for Jack's comfort.

"Consider the can a sacrifice, and get your drunk asses back up here before it explodes or something."

He could see the can. It wasn't exactly in the flames, but retrieving it would be no easy feat, even if sober. He had enough on his plate as it was. He didn't need his drunk brothers ending up in a burn unit on top of it.

Luke and Walker stumbled back up the porch steps, and Scully immediately dropped to his back, tongue dangling out the side of his mouth as he lay in wait for a belly rub. Walker obliged.

"Did I miss the invitation to the party?" Jack asked. "Or is this a nightly routine I'm only now learning about?"

"That depends," Luke said. "Does the party include you filling us in on that meeting you had with Jack Senior's lawyer? I get that you're the most qualified for all that legal speak, but we're not kids. We've been running this place for almost as long as you've been gone, big brother. I think we can probably grasp some of the finer details of what's going on."

Jack found the source of the beer cans—a cooler outside the sliding glass door—and decided he'd rather join his brothers than lecture them, as long as they stayed the hell away from the fire.

"You're right," he said, collapsing onto the bench that ran along the deck's side rail. "I was waiting until I knew how I wanted to proceed, but it's as much your decision as it is mine." He took a long sip of beer and then tilted his head back against the rail ledge. "Thomas—Dad's lawyer—found a buyer for the vineyard."

All three of them were silent for several beats after that. It was Walker who finally spoke up. "Is it a good price?"

Jack nodded. "Best we could hope for, especially without knowing how much crop we'll yield. How to actually turn the grapes into wine. Can we really sit tight and wait for wine to age before even knowing if it's any good? Plus, no tasting room." He scratched the back of his neck. "The deck is stacked against us."

"We could build that tasting room," Walker reminded him. "We get the Callahan brothers involved, and we could get a real good place done for little more than cost."

Jack sighed. "And that would take months more."

"How long we got to decide on the offer?" Luke asked.

Walker stood now and crossed his arms next to his brother. Scully sprang to his feet as well, so he was faced with a line of brotherly and canine interrogators.

"A week," Jack said. "The offer is good for a week."

Walker shook his head and let out a bitter laugh. "And if we sell—I mean *when* we sell because you sure as shit want the hell out of Oak Bluff—you take off to New York, right?"

Jack laughed bitterly. "You act like it's a choice I'm making. I accepted a goddamn partnership. Everything I own that's not in my truck is already in Manhattan." The truth was, the *This is my career* argument was starting to sound less and less convincing even to himself.

"You tell Red about this?" Luke asked.

Jack clenched his jaw and shook his head. "And you won't either. I don't want to tell her anything before I have an answer. She knows about New York, and it's not like me staying was ever on the table."

Because there was that other niggling piece of truth—the one he couldn't admit out loud that had the power to change everything. Ava had never said anything about *wanting* him to stay. Everything had changed since he'd returned, yet at the same time felt like *déjà vu*. She'd pushed him away before because she'd thought it was what he needed, and maybe it was. And maybe it was what he'd thought he needed when he accepted the partnership in New York. But that was before he'd pulled up in front of the Ellis property, before he'd seen his son. Before he'd started falling for the woman he'd never been able to forget.

"I just—I think she and Owen deserve better," he said. Because despite everything that had changed in a matter of weeks, he was still the son of Jackson Everett Senior. He was still the kid who'd put another guy in the hospital when he'd completely lost control. And he was still the man who was terrified of what kind of father he'd truly be when he never intended on being one at all.

Walker scoffed. "Better than what? The son of an abusive drunk?"

Jack rose to his feet so he was eye-to-eye with his accuser. "Yes, Walker. *Hell* yes. They deserve better than the son of an abusive drunk who has no damned clue if he'll be one someday, too. Why is that so hard for you to understand?"

Walker moved closer so their chests almost bumped. Jack knew he was riling Walker up, but hell if he wasn't going to try to make them understand.

"If you're so damn sure you're him, then hit me," Walker said.

Jack's eyes widened. "What the hell are you talking about?"

"*Hit* me," Walker said again, and this time their chests did bump, forcefully. But Jack knew *he* was standing still.

He placed a hand on his younger brother's shoulder and squeezed. "I think that's one can too many for you. Sleep it off."

Walker sniffed and puffed out his chest. "You think I can't take it? You think I'm not man enough to take what you took on our behalf for five damned years? I don't need your protection anymore, big brother. I don't need you to waltz in here and take care of everything like you do—and be reminded of how you *took care* of everything when we were kids." He gritted his teeth. "Leave if you're gonna leave, asshole. Be free of this place. But even the score already and just. Just. Do it."

Jack pushed him back an arm's length, but he sure as shit wasn't going to let this go any further. "There's no score, Walker. Jesus. You don't *owe* me anything, and I sure as hell don't want to be some twisted Jack Senior surrogate for you so you can deal with whatever it is that's eating you. Do all of us a favor and sleep it *off*." It was like he was eighteen again, trying to coax his father to do the same before getting himself pushed down a flight of wooden stairs.

Walker let out a bitter laugh. "You don't have it in you, even when I deserve it. You stand there, beer in hand, yet other than *one* time—after all the hell you took from him for five years—I've never seen you out of control once in your goddamn life. It ain't my kid or my woman. I'd tell them to run as far away from here as they could if it was. It's *you*, Jack, the one who always kept it together—who took every fist or boot so we didn't have to. So don't tell me they can do better. Don't make that your reason for leaving us—I mean *them*—again."

Walker crumpled his empty can and chucked it forcefully over the railing and into the fire. "Screw this," he said and stalked off the stairs and toward the open field.

Jack stood there in stunned silence for several long moments.

"He'll be all right," Luke finally said. "He just needs to blow off a little steam."

Jack realized his free hand was balled into a fist, and although he had to force himself to unclench it, he'd never once considered hitting his brother. "You think the same things he does?" he asked. "That you deserve the kind of treatment I tried to keep from you?"

Luke shrugged. "I think it's a hell of a thing for any kid to watch the brother he looks up to most get abused by the one person who was supposed to protect them all."

Luke's ever-present smile was gone, and Jack felt an ache so big it almost rivaled the years of his life he kept trying to forget.

"We all got our demons to dance with, Jack. Walker's still trying to find his way back to the land of the living."

"And you?" he asked.

Luke winked, but it was forced. "Everything I do is living, big bro." He shrugged. "I don't know. I think you gotta do whatever makes living *your* life bearable." He looked around the deck, littered with empty cans. "I'll get this in the morning," he said, then left his brother alone with his thoughts and a confused-looking dog.

Jack crouched so he was eye level with Scully. "That was ten years' worth of unsaid shit that I guess needed saying, huh?"

The dog lapped at his jaw.

"Is that all *you* have to say?" Jack asked him, and he received another slobbery kiss in return. He gave Scully an affectionate pat on the head and stood. Then he started collecting the empty cans, cleaning up the one mess he knew he could.

CHAPTER NINETEEN

Ava backed into the laundry room off the kitchen as soon as she saw her father's name pop up on her phone. She'd done so well avoiding any verbal run-ins with him all week, but now that it was Friday, she knew she couldn't ignore the call and shoot off a quick text. Owen had his first official game the next day, and he'd want to confirm when and where, despite her having emailed her parents the entire season's schedule.

"Hi, Dad," she said softly. Owen was taking a shower, and Jack and his brothers were finishing up in the vineyard. The crop was almost ready to do its thing—or at least try. But it would take the better part of a year to see if the grapes would flourish. They were close enough, though, that they didn't need Ava telling them what to do anymore.

"*Hi*, Dad?" he said, the hint of teasing in his tone. "You've been giving your old man the brush-off all week, and all I get is '*Hi*, Dad'?"

He was trying to make light of the situation, but both of them knew what was brewing beneath the surface, so she decided to dive right in.

"This week's been good for him—for Owen. You should

see how well he clicks not only with Jack but with his uncles and his great-aunt Jenna."

He was silent for several beats before saying, "Doesn't mean the Everett boy is good for him. Even if I let slide what happened a decade ago, you can't know a man's character after a couple of weeks."

Ava groaned. "This, Dad. This is why you got the *brush-off* all week. He doesn't deserve your judgment—"

But he cut her off before she could reason with him. "The hell he doesn't, Ava. Who was there for your morning sickness, for monitoring your meals when you got that pregnancy diabetes? Huh? Who was in the delivery room when the epidural wasn't doing its job and you thought those goddamn contractions would tear you apart?"

"Dad," she said, trying not to let her voice tremble.

"If he's such a stand-up guy...If he's *not* someone I should worry about entering the lives of my daughter *and* my grandson, I'm waiting to hear how you've come to this grand conclusion. For *ten* years you hear nothing from him, and the second he waltzes back into town, you take Owen and shack up with this stranger—a stranger with a past full of violence—for a week?"

"Dad!" she cried, and she *was* shaking now, but she didn't care. "How dare you judge him without ever taking a second to look past *one* night—one terrible night—in Jack's life, and how *dare* you judge *me* when everything I've ever done has been for the good of those I loved, including Jack Everett. I'm grateful for what you and Mom did for Owen and me. There is no possible way to ever repay you. But enough is enough. Jack made a mistake when he was a scared, messed-up kid. How long does he have to pay for it?"

"It's more than that," her father said. "I don't care if

Everett knew nothing about his son. *He* walked out of your life and only came back by accident, and we're all supposed to rejoice just so he can leave and hurt you again—hurt the both of you?"

"I gotta go, Dad." She heard the front door open and slam shut, followed by the not-so-distant grumbling of what she knew were three tired, sweaty men. "The game is at eleven in the elementary school baseball field. We'll be there by 10:30. Send my love to Mom."

She ended the call and quickly swiped under her eyes, hoping the three brothers were too exhausted from their longest day of work yet to notice she'd started to cry.

"Something smells good," she heard Walker say.

"Too bad it ain't for you!" Luke answered. "You'll be eating good old-fashioned rodeo fare tonight, my friend."

By the time the three men made it into the kitchen, Ava had a smile painted on her face as bright as the yellow, pink, and orange flowers on the sundress she was wearing.

Jack stopped short as soon as he saw her, and his brothers had to struggle not to plow right into him.

"Whoa," he said. "I thought you were heading back here early so Owen could shower and eat a 'sensible meal' before he was carted off to the rodeo."

She let out a nervous laugh. "He's finishing up in the shower, but I don't care if he stuffs himself full of nachos and hot pretzels tonight. It's a special occasion for him— getting to see Luke compete." Her cheeks grew hot, but she didn't care if they saw her blush. It would hopefully distract from her glassy eyes. "The—uh—sorta sensible meal is for you." She turned toward Jack, who still stood there looking mildly stunned.

Walker pushed ahead of his brothers. "If he's not gonna jump at a home-cooked meal, can I send *him* to the rodeo while I stay here and eat whatever it is you got in that oven?"

Luke smacked his brother on the back of the head. "Forget it, asshole. You and Jenna are on Shortstop duty tonight. Now go shower. You smell worse than the stables."

Walker smacked Luke back, but Ava could tell it was all in good fun. She liked seeing them happy, acting like brothers rather than what she'd overheard the other night. She hadn't been able to make out what the three of them were saying, but sound carried through a house with the windows open and no one or nothing nearby to drown out the noise.

They'd been arguing—all three of them—yet Jack hadn't breathed a word of it to her.

Luke and Walker made their way upstairs to rinse their own hard day's work away. Jack, though, just stared at her.

"What?" she asked, first tightening the halter of her dress and then fidgeting with the long braid that hung over a bare shoulder.

Jack shook his head as if waking himself from a daydream. "Sorry," he said. "You're just—I've never seen anyone so beautiful."

She covered her face with her hands, unable to take such a compliment without going completely crimson.

In seconds she felt his rough hands wrap around hers, pulling them free. She bit her bottom lip as his gaze bore into her, so full of heat and—and something she couldn't name.

Damn it, why was this man so hard to read?

"You made me dinner?" he asked, his voice deep and smooth.

She nodded.

"I thought I was supposed to take you out tonight." He scrubbed a hand across his deliciously stubbled jaw. "I distinctly remember Jenna saying, 'Walker and I are taking Owen to the rodeo so you can take that girl on a proper date. Now don't y'all go and mess it up.'"

She shrugged. "Surprise?"

He grinned. "Was this always the plan?"

She shook her head. "Not until today, actually. But you all worked so hard all week, and I know Jenna had some very specific instructions, but it's our last night here, and I kinda wanted to stay in. With you."

Jack's eyes searched the kitchen and the living room beyond. His Adam's apple bobbed as he swallowed. "I never thought of this place as somewhere to take a girl on a date..."

He trailed off, and Ava's blush changed from one born of flattery to one fueled by utter mortification.

"Shit," she said softly. "Shit. I wasn't thinking. Of course this is a terrible idea. I'll cover the lasagna and leave it for your brothers. I'm sure we can find someplace nice to go without a reservation—"

Jack cut her off with a kiss. Her eyes were still open, wide with the horror of her mistake, until the taste of him registered, until the scent of his sunbaked skin mixed with the musky earth he'd toiled in all day enveloped her, and she sank into this man who could flip off the switch of her worry so that all she could concentrate on was the kiss.

"I need to shower," he said, pulling away.

She nodded. Words weren't exactly possible at the moment.

"And then we are going to have our first date in this house because it's about damn time I make some new memories here. Besides, hell if I'm gonna let Luke and Walker get their hands on a home-cooked meal meant for me."

"There's enough for all of you—"

"Red?"

"Yeah?"

"I'm not sharing the lasagna *or* your company with anyone tonight. Okay?"

She let out a breath and smiled. "Yeah. Okay."

Chaos erupted as Owen and Scully came running from the guest bedroom where Owen had gotten himself dressed after his shower. Walker lumbered down the stairs in a red and white flannel shirt and jeans—just the right amount of California cowboy—followed by Luke in full rodeo gear, including the boots and the hat.

"No stitches tonight," Jack said to his daredevil brother, even though he knew it was a pointless request.

"No promises," Luke countered with a wry grin.

"And *you*..." Jack pointed at Walker. "You are on Shortstop detail. He comes home in one piece without needing to vomit from all the shit you're gonna feed him."

Jenna burst through the front door, and Jack relaxed a little.

"And you're on Walker detail...which means you're backup for Shortstop as well."

Jenna gave him a firm salute. "Sir! Yes sir!"

Jack rolled his eyes but then paused when he noticed a bruise on Jenna's wrist. "Don't tell me the chicks attacked again," he said with concern.

She laughed, but Jack could have sworn the reaction was forced.

"No chicks," she said. "Banged it on a doorknob. Never said I was graceful."

Jack held her chin in his hand, turning her head from left to right as he inspected.

"What in the hell are you doing?" she asked.

He dropped his hand, satisfied for the moment. "Seeing if you've had any other recent *accidents*."

She waved him off. "Who's the guardian here, huh? Me or you?"

"That isn't a clear response, Jenna."

"You didn't ask a question."

"Fine," he said, soft enough that the others—now congregating in the kitchen—couldn't hear. "Here's a question for you: Are you still seeing the egg man, and is he hitting you?" His jaw clenched, and his hand balled into a fist at the thought of anyone laying a hand on his aunt—or anyone he loved.

She scoffed, but he could see it. Something was off.

"We went on a few dates. It didn't work out. So *no*. I'm not seeing him anymore, and he's *not* hitting me."

"Jenna…"

"Jack…"

"Don't play games when it comes to this type of shit," he said. "Because if this guy is hitting you, and I find out who he is…"

"I took care of it," she snapped under her breath. "I have been looking after myself too long to be accused of not knowing how to do it."

Jack opened his mouth to ask her one more question, but the two were bombarded by the whole rodeo posse, ready to get on the road.

Ava bent down to give Owen a hug and kiss. "You have my cell phone number, right?"

Owen recited her number back to her.

"And I have it," Walker said.

"So do I," added Luke.

"Same here," Jenna said.

Ava let out a nervous laugh. "Okay, fine. So I worry when I send my son off to a rodeo that's almost two hours away."

"Ninety minutes," Luke said.

"Eighty if we go at least ten miles over the speed limit," Walker amended.

Jenna groaned. "Which we are *not* going to do since *I'm* driving."

Ava kissed Owen once more on the forehead and stood up. "Well, I guess that's it, then."

Owen looked at his mother, then at Jack. "Are you taking my mom on a date?"

Jack gave the boy a single nod. "With your approval, of course. You all right with it?"

Owen looked him up and down. Then he turned his gaze to Ava. "Are you all right with it?" he asked her.

"Yeah. But your opinion counts, too."

Owen shrugged. "I guess if my dad can't come back to be with us, Jack's pretty cool."

Everyone in the entryway went silent. Ava pressed her thumb to the corner of her eye, and Jack wondered if she was fighting back tears because he felt like he'd been socked in the gut.

But Ava smiled and tousled his hair. "Jack *is* pretty cool, bud. I'm glad you like him."

"So...we should head out," Jenna said, and Jack was grateful for the redirection.

"Okay," Ava said. "Just don't feed him too much junk or let him out of your sight, which I know you won't, but there...I said it. I'm a mom. I can't help it."

Luke pursed his lips. "Actually, I'm worried. Something isn't right."

Ava's eyes widened as Luke slipped out the door and

onto the porch. Seconds later he was back inside with a brown cowboy hat that he plopped on Owen's head.

"Yes!" Owen said, pumping his fist in the air.

Jack laughed, Owen's glee contagious.

"*Now* we're ready to go," Luke said.

"Good luck, Luke!" Ava said as they started to file out the door. "Or is that bad to say? Is it like theater where you have to say *break a leg*? Like, maybe it's *break a hoof*?"

Luke laughed. "Good luck works fine. Now you kids have a good time."

Jack and Ava stood at the window and watched Luke, Walker, Owen, and Jenna trail out and into Jenna's car. Once they were out of sight, he pulled Ava to him and kissed her sweetly on the forehead.

"Tomorrow for sure," he said. "I don't want to keep it from him any longer."

Ava pulled back to look him in the eye. "He's gonna be upset at first," she said. "And he'll want to know how much a part of his life you'll be after this week."

He nodded once, slowly. "What about you? What do *you* want?"

She pressed her lips into a smile and splayed her hand against his chest. "I *don't* want to be at the bottom of my priority list anymore. And I want someone in my life who won't put me there either."

He didn't know what to say. She was the one who was good with words. They'd once made him feel loved when he hadn't felt worthy. But her words had also pushed him away at the one time in his life when something had made him happy. When some*one* made him happy.

Was she saying he could do that for her? She wasn't telling him to go this time, but she also hadn't asked him to stay.

Why wasn't she asking him to stay? And if she did, would he? She hadn't given him a choice before, and maybe that's what this all was—him finally getting to choose. Still, he wanted to know what she wanted, because if she *wanted* him, did New York really hold a candle?

Her brows furrowed.

"What's wrong?" he asked.

She shook her head. "This isn't supposed to be how our first date begins. It's a little heavy-handed, don't you think?"

The corner of his mouth twitched into a hint of a grin. She was changing the subject. And if he wasn't in such dire need of a shower, he'd thank her properly, right here in the entryway.

"How does it go, then?"

She grabbed one of his hands, his calloused palm sandwiched between hers. "Tonight we forget all this complicated grown-up stuff. Instead of me forcing that crease to appear between your eyebrows, let me take care of *you* instead of you worrying about everyone else."

He took a deep breath and let it out. "And who takes care of you?"

She kissed his palm. "Oh, I think if I play my cards right, you'll take care of me just fine."

He backed toward the foot of the stairs, their hands still connecting them. "I'm going to take the fastest shower known to man. Then I'm going to eat that amazing dinner you made. And then?" He dipped his head to give her one soft kiss. "I sure as shit am gonna take care of you right back."

Her mouth fell open, and something akin to a squeak sounded from her throat. He took that as a good sign as he let his eyes take one last look at the beautiful woman before him, before he spun and strode up the stairs.

Ask me to stay, he thought. Because he could be a lawyer anywhere. It wasn't about the partnership. Or money. He realized that now. What mattered most was that she still believed in him like she had all those years ago.

Show me that you're not afraid, that you believe I'll do right by you and our son.

But other than working his ass off on this vineyard and giving Owen some pitching lessons, what the hell else had he done to prove he was up to the task—or to prove to himself that the apple fell far enough from the tree?

Not a damn thing.

Tonight, at least, he could tell her all the things he should have said ten years ago, all the words that were still stuck in his throat today.

And even if he did leave, she'd know why he never could have married anyone else, that it had always, *always* been her.

CHAPTER TWENTY

Ava poured the two final glasses of the Ellis Vineyard zinfandel she'd smuggled from home and met Jack out on the back deck. He stood at the far end, his back to her, gazing out into the distance where the vineyard lay.

"You guys did it," she said. "You and your brothers. Twelve months from now, you'll have a viable crop," she added. He turned to face her and took the glass of wine from her outstretched hand. "You'll get a good return after all that hard work. If you decide to become Crossroads Ranch and Vineyard."

He took a sip of wine and tugged at the belt tied around the waist of her dress. "I thought we were forgetting everything for the night."

"Mmm-hmm," she replied, and he raised his brows, most likely at the hint of accusation in her tone. "Were *you* forgetting everything while staring out toward the vineyard?"

He gave her a crooked grin. "Not even allowed a little silent contemplation, huh?"

She raised her glass to her own lips, letting the warmth of the vintage spread through and embolden her.

She set the glass on the ledge of the deck rail and reached

behind her neck where her halter dress was tied in a bow—
and *un*tied it.

"Depends on what you're contemplating."

The top of her dress fell open, revealing her bare breasts,
her nipples hard merely at the anticipation of his reaction.

"Christ," he hissed.

She stepped closer and took his free hand in hers, bringing his palm to rest over one of her firm peaks.

"What?" she asked, feigning innocence. "Remember. No
neighbors—unless you count the cows, and I don't think
they care."

He downed the rest of his wine and set his glass next
to hers. Then he pinched her softly between his thumb and
forefinger, and she gasped.

"I guess I'm still reconciling the girl I knew with the
woman you are now."

He took her into his mouth, and she arched her back as
he licked and kissed up her bare flesh until he was nipping
at her neck, her earlobe.

"Same," she said, though she was nearly breathless. She
wasn't even sure how she was still standing because surely
she'd just dissolved into a puddle.

His teeth relinquished her earlobe so he could speak.
"Does this new Ava," he started, his voice so low and
sexy she thought he might simply *talk* her into orgasm,
"still like to make love under the stars?" He kissed her
neck again, then lifted his head. "It's still your call," he
reminded her.

She tipped her head back and glanced at the glorious
night sky sprinkled with tiny, flickering diamonds. She'd
been with Jack before—even slept with him beneath the
night sky. But they had been eighteen. Kids. She'd never
done anything like this in her adult life before, but she'd

also never wanted a man like she wanted Jack, so she found herself answering, "Yes."

He lifted her in his arms, and she crossed her legs over his ass—that perfect ass she'd stared at more than once as he'd pruned the vines and tilled the cover crop. For a man who'd spent the past several years in an office behind a desk, he was a natural in the outdoors, strong and capable.

He deposited her onto a pillowed lawn chair, and she couldn't help but writhe in anticipation.

He untied the belt at her waist, then quickly found the zipper that ran down the side of her dress. In seconds the garment was gone, and he hummed with what sounded like satisfaction to see her laid out beneath him in nothing but her white lace panties.

He sat on the side of the chair, silent as he ran a hand from her cheek, down her neck, over her breast, and onto her stomach, where he traced soft circles around her belly button—and then along the faded scar that signified Owen's entrance into their lives.

She wasn't self-conscious. She wanted him to explore every inch of her, and that's exactly what he was doing in his perfect, silent reverence that she felt not only with his touch but with that intense gaze—the one thing about him that hadn't changed.

As he pulled her panties down, each of his hands explored her hips, her thighs, his thumbs rubbing over her sensitive skin.

Goose bumps covered her flesh, but they had nothing to do with the chill of the night air. Every sensation was Jack. All Jack.

Once they reached her ankles, her panties were no more. His hands skimmed their way back up her legs, stopping only when his thumbs were close enough to tease another sensation from her—one of pure, primal need.

One thumb explored her crease, and he hissed in a breath when he felt how wet she was.

Ava whimpered and squirmed. "Please," she said. "Jack, please."

That same thumb found her swollen center and pressed softly against her.

Words wouldn't come. She could only gasp and hope he understood that what she meant was *More. God. Please. More.*

He slid a finger inside her, then another, and she was sure she was seconds away from coming completely undone. He moved so slowly, with such control, holding her at the edge without letting her teeter over.

He leaned down to kiss her, his lips as gentle and careful as his movements inside her. They'd been virtual strangers for ten years, yet the way he touched her, kissed her, even looked at her—it was as if he knew her better than anyone else.

He was her first love, the father of her child, and the incredible man she'd always known he'd become. And she was falling harder for the man than she'd ever thought possible.

Could he see that, too?

She wanted him, not only like this but with her whole heart.

He pulled back, and she opened her eyes to find him gazing at her, transfixed.

She reached for his face, her thumb stroking the stubble he hadn't shaved, as if he knew how sexy he looked like this.

"You're staring," she said, then gasped as his thumb swirled around her clit.

"You're beautiful," he said matter-of-factly. "So damn beautiful. And *I* get to touch you like this. I get to kiss those perfect pink lips." Then he did. "And I get to look at you bathed in moonlight and stars."

He slid his fingers out, achingly slow as heat coiled in her belly. Then, filling her with the same sweet agony, they sank back inside, pulsing, reaching just the right place until she feared she wouldn't be able to hold out much longer.

She cried out, dropping her hand from his cheek and grabbing the wooden frame of the chair above her head.

"Oh my God!" She bucked against his palm. "You can't"—she gasped for breath—"be all strong and silent"—another gasp—"and then say things like that." She grabbed his wrist to hold his hand still so she could talk. "'Bathed in moonlight and stars'? That's like freaking poetry."

He grinned and tried to peel her fingers from his wrist, but she shook her head. "You make it sound like it's some privilege to touch me."

He tilted his head to the side, his eyes intent on her form again. "Isn't it?" he asked.

She didn't know what to say to that. Because she wanted to read into it and at the same time was afraid it meant nothing more than how he felt right now. In the moment.

"I was supposed to take care of *you* tonight," she said finally.

He shrugged and dipped his head toward the obvious bulge in his jeans. "I think it's safe to say I'm enjoying what I'm doing right now."

His fingers pumped inside her, and she gave his wrist an admonishing squeeze even as she writhed.

"My call. You—you said whatever happened between us here was my call, right?"

"Yep," he said and slowed his movement.

She tugged at his wrist, forcing his hand from her, as much as she hated to do it. "I want to see *you* bathed in moonlight," she told him. "I want to kiss and explore every inch of you, too."

He didn't protest. So she sat up and unbuttoned his flannel shirt, her fingers skimming his shoulders as she pushed it over his arms. She kissed his neck and the dusting of hair on his chest.

"Stand up," she ordered, though her tone was more playful than authoritative.

He obliged, and she got to work unbuttoning his jeans. They'd both been barefoot, so he kicked them off easily. Then she took her time lowering his boxer briefs as he had with her panties, relishing the feel of his skin beneath her own. Her finger ran along the scar on his shin where the bone had been broken and repaired with surgery. They'd been too frenzied that day in the bathroom, when he'd pulled her into the shower, for her to see it. She'd known the scar was there, but time had let her forget. It was only visible on close inspection. And now they were as close as two people could get with the whole night laid before them to explore.

An unexpected tear leaked from the corner of her eye as she imagined the boy he was, what he'd gone through, and why she always knew he'd have to leave.

Then there they were, the two of them bare beneath the moon and stars. Her breath caught in her throat as she stood to meet his gaze. "*You're* beautiful," she said, her voice breaking on that last word.

He pulled her to him, his erection firm against her, and she buried her face in his chest. "Is this the part where I ask you what's wrong?" He kissed the top of her head, and she could feel him inhale against her hair.

She tilted her head up, not trying to hide the other tears that had sprung free. "You lost so much before I'd even met you," she said. "I need you to understand that I kept Owen from you *not* because I saw you as unfit or unworthy but because I loved you too much to make you stay."

It was the same reason why she thought she couldn't ask him to stay now. He had to want it. He had to want her *and* Owen.

"And when I went to L.A.—I got scared. You had built this life for yourself with someone else. I thought I'd just be taking away what you'd left to find in the first place."

He swiped at her tears with his thumbs, then cradled her face in his palms. "I didn't go through with it," he said.

She nodded.

"It wasn't right between me and her. I could never put my finger on it. She wanted exactly what I wanted—no family—just work. We got along great—"

Ava cleared her throat. "Umm, I know I broke the rules and brought up the past, but I'm not sure I'm *past* the past enough to hear about how great you got along with your ex-fiancée."

And how much you don't want a family.

He laughed softly. "You didn't let me finish. I couldn't put my finger on what was missing *then*." He let out a breath. "Or at least, I wouldn't admit it to myself."

"Jack, you don't have to…" Her heart raced.

"I know," he said softly, then kissed her. "But I want to." He kissed her again, soft, sweet nibbles against her lips, teasing not only her body, but her heart. "She wasn't *you*."

She sucked in a sharp breath, then cupped his face in her palms. "I messed up twice," she admitted. "I should have given you a choice."

"And I should have fought harder for you when you pushed me away. But—" He shook his head. "Shit."

"You didn't have any fight left," she said, finishing his thought. "And I shouldn't have let you leave thinking I was afraid of you. That couldn't have been any further from the truth."

He ran has hands through her hair and down her back. "Okay, Red. Your call."

"Fight for me now," she said, then kissed him. "You can start by making love to me."

In a couple of quick movements, he'd pulled the long pillows from two of the chairs and laid them side-by-side on the floor of the deck. He lowered her down to the makeshift bed, kissing her neck and shoulders as he covered her body with his own.

Then his hand fumbled on the ground toward his jeans.

"We don't need—" she blurted. "I mean, I've been on the pill for a couple of years. I understand, though, if you're worried about...you know...what happened before."

Not like it mattered. He'd worn a condom when Owen was conceived.

He stopped reaching and stilled above her. "I'm not worried." He said the words with such certainty. "As long as you're sure this is what you want."

She nodded and let her legs part, a silent invitation as she marveled at his long, thick length.

He nudged her slick opening, and she sucked in a breath. Then he sank inside her to the hilt, filling her so completely that she cried out with total and utter abandon. A growl tore from his throat as he slid out and in again, harder and deeper than she'd thought he could go.

Ava hooked her legs around him and arched into his chest. She wanted him closer. She *needed* there to be no more distance. But only Jack could bridge that gap by letting her in.

"I loved you too," he said, echoing her words, and her eyes opened to find him staring intently once again. "But I also hurt you without even knowing I had."

She tried to swallow past the lump in her throat.

"If I could take back what I said to you while you stood there with Owen growing inside you—if I could erase what it must have felt like for you to hear me say I never wanted to be a father—I would."

The muscle in his jaw pulsed, and she leaned up to kiss him.

"You're not your father. No matter what similarities you think you share, you're not *him*."

His movement inside her was slow, controlled. Just like his words. Like everything he seemed to do. But he was opening up to her now more than he ever had, and as much as she ached with what felt like an insatiable need, she didn't want him to stop talking. Not when they were so close to—*something*.

He kissed her softly, rocking into her.

"More," she whispered.

He slid out and back into her with such aching tenderness. How had she been without this for the past decade? How was it possible to want anyone else like she wanted him?

She skimmed her fingers through his already disheveled blond waves. He wanted her, too. She knew he did. Maybe they were done walking the tightrope, done fearing that any second they could lose their delicate balance and fall hard to the unforgiving ground of New York versus California, of will he or won't he be a real presence in Owen's life—or even hers. Maybe she didn't need to protect her heart from

Jack Everett. Maybe the pie-in-the-sky fairy tale of school, a career, and her, Jack, and Owen being a family could actually come true.

He kissed her, soft and achingly sweet. "When I left here, I didn't just run from my past. I ran from the best part of my life. *You.*" He cupped her cheek as a tear slid toward his palm. "And Owen, too."

Well, damn it if her vision wasn't completely blurred with tears now. She opened her mouth to respond, but he silenced her with a kiss as he thrust inside her, rocking her to her core. Maybe it was better like this. She wouldn't have to ask him what that meant. Because he could say all that and stay—or he could say it and still leave. Right now, though, as they both teetered on that brink together, she wouldn't be able to form a coherent word even if she tried. But every time she arched against him, she thought the words she wanted to say.

Choose us.

Stay.

I love you.

He'd let this week be her call. She had to let the rest of his life be his. She'd made it clear she wanted him to fight for her. He'd have to decide what that meant because it wasn't her right to ask him to give up something as huge as his career.

At that moment he slid his hand between them, rubbing her wet, swollen center, and even when she called out his name, eyes closed in heartbreaking ecstasy, she still saw stars.

He followed her with his own release, a primal sound tearing from his chest that spoke nothing of the quiet control he wore like a mask for everyone else.

For *her* he had let go.

He collapsed beside her. Still in her. His forehead resting against hers.

She stroked her fingers through his hair. The strands at the nape of his neck were damp with sweat. His eyes were closed, but a soft smile rested on his face. As if he knew she was wondering whether or not he'd fallen asleep, he flexed inside her, and she gasped.

"Sorry," he said, one eye blinking open.

"You are *not*." She retaliated by clenching around his still-solid shaft.

He swore through his teeth, then kissed her hungrily.

"I can't seem to get enough of you," he said.

She knew they'd have to disconnect from one another eventually, but she couldn't bring herself to initiate. Not yet. Instead she hooked her leg over his as he traced lazy circles on her shoulder.

"It might take me some time to explore each and every one of these freckles. Are you sure you and Owen have to go home tomorrow?"

Her heart sank. Their five days were up. But he'd said she was the best part of his life. Owen too. Maybe not wanting them to leave meant he was ready to stay.

"Tomorrow," she said with a nervous smile. "You looking forward to the game?"

He grinned and kissed tenderly along the line of her jaw. "Watching Owen play ball? Hell yes. You know…Jenna and Luke seem to have taken a liking to him as well. I even think Walker tolerates him."

She laughed. "Invite them. Please. It would mean the world to him if you were all there, but after the game…"

"After the game—" He paused and stroked her cheek, then tucked a fallen strand of hair behind her ear.

She shivered.

"You're cold," he said.

"No. I mean yes, but—" There *was* a chill in the night air, and she *was* completely naked. But it was also the anticipation of what tomorrow meant.

He did the unthinkable and slid out of her. She gasped, her sensitive nerves still reacting to him.

"We should probably clean up, put some clothes on. The rodeo doesn't go all night." He kissed her forehead. "There's a towel on the bench if you need one and a sweatshirt of mine on the chair in the office, the room right next to yours. You're welcome to it if you want."

Jack Everett—ever the planner. She chuckled.

"Have you worn this sweatshirt you speak of recently?"

"As a matter of fact, I have."

"So it smells like you?"

He laughed. "I suppose it does."

"Sold. I'm gonna go freshen up and change. We'll put a plan in order for after the game. Then, if it's all right with you, I'm gonna grab those amazing paint supplies you bought and paint that sky."

She felt so light, buoyant. Something had surely shifted between them.

He rolled onto his back, resting his head on his hands. Good *God,* the man was a specimen. Simply looking at him made her want to do what they just did all over again. But he was right. Owen, his brothers, and Jenna would be home soon enough. There'd be another chance for round two. She hoped.

"You know, I never really noticed this sky you speak of before tonight. It's not too bad."

He grinned. He obviously knew she was watching. How could she not? He was beautiful.

* * *

She'd cleaned up and thrown on a tank and yoga pants, then padded into the office for Jack's sweatshirt. It was right where he'd said it would be, hanging over the chair. She held it up for inspection. It was a navy hoodie with UCLA embroidered in yellow and LAW in white.

She brought it to her nose, breathed in—breathed *Jack* in—and smiled. He was *never* getting this sweatshirt back. Tugging it over her head was like having his body wrapped around hers all over again.

She glanced down at the desk, which was maybe a little nosy. He'd been doing double duty all week—working in the vineyard and then catching up on legal work whenever he found spare time. This was his private space.

She should have grabbed the sweatshirt and walked away, but on the top of a pile of folders was one that bore a sticky note that simply read: VINEYARD: OFFER OF SALE.

No more secrets, she'd told him when he'd said he wanted to tell Owen the truth. And he had nodded. He was a man of few words. A nod from Jack Everett was worth a hundred yesses from anyone else.

But here was his final secret. Jack was selling the vineyard.

She'd seen him out there, though. Working with his brothers. He'd enjoyed himself—enjoyed *them*. Hell, he'd gone and told her that she and Owen were the best parts of his life, but now she felt like a loose end. One that would be tied up along with the contract to the vineyard.

Damn him for letting her hope. She'd been all ready to create her own new beginning before he'd forced her straight off the road—and what she thought was her new path in life. Now she was right where she'd been ten years ago—head over heels for a guy about to leave her.

When she made it back to the deck with her easel and

supplies, he was already out there, reclining on the chair where he'd almost driven her to orgasm with his hands. Except now Scully was next to him, sitting with his tongue hanging out of his mouth and his tail wagging as Jack scratched behind his ears. He smiled when he saw her, and she forced herself to do the same as she set up and prepared to paint.

"So you know how I applied to Cal Poly?" she asked with forced nonchalance.

"Yeah…" he said, drawing out the word.

She opened and squeezed tubes of paint onto the small pallet, dipping her brush into the inky black. "Well, I'm still missing one small part of my application."

"What part?"

She forced a laugh. "A piece of art. *Meaningful* art. There's an essay component and everything to prove the piece's depth. It's not like I haven't painted anything, but it's been silly stuff like a bowl of fruit… or Scully catching a Frisbee. Nothing worthy of an essay." Oh, she could write plenty now about that portrait of a boy playing catch with his dad, but it might break her in two now that she was sure he was leaving.

He swallowed. "And classes start in August, right?"

"*If* I bring them a piece next week and they approve my application, I start my art degree in the fall session, right in San Luis Obispo like I was supposed to ten years ago."

He sat silent, still petting the dog, for several long beats. Perhaps he was crafting the perfect response. Maybe a way to tell her that he was selling the place they'd all worked so hard to restore. A way to let her down easy after she'd sworn she wouldn't let his short return distract her from what was important—a real future for her and Owen, whether Jack was part of it or not. And knowing that he was getting rid of the vineyard? She was almost positive that meant *not*.

Finally, his eyes met hers.

"I think that's great," he said. "You put your life on hold, not that it wasn't for a good reason, but I'm happy you're doing something for yourself now."

She dropped the paintbrush onto the easel's tray and crossed her arms.

"Are you selling the vineyard?"

His expression barely even changed. There was a hint of shock as his eyes widened a bit, but just as quickly he composed himself. Mr. Control.

"Maybe," he said simply.

"Maybe?" She dropped her hands to her sides, balling them into fists. "I told myself I wasn't going to fall for you because I knew we were moving in different directions. But being here with you—with Owen and you together— made me think we were moving toward something real. What was this whole week? If the big thing that was holding you back was this deep-seeded fear of what kind of father you'd be, how have you not realized by now what I've always known—that you are a *good* man, Jack Everett? And good men make good fathers. But I'm part of that equation, too. It's more than Owen who deserves honesty. I do, too."

He swung his feet off the chair and planted them on the ground. Then he ran a hand through hair that still looked freshly screwed. Except now *she* felt screwed in a whole different way.

"I'm not keeping anything from you, Ava. But I didn't think there was a point in telling you until I'd made a decision. It's not like we're—"

Her eyes widened.

"Shit," he said. "*Shit.* I didn't mean it like that. I've spent the past ten years living on no one else's terms but my own. This?" He stood and motioned between them. "My decisions affecting someone else? That's brand-new."

She huffed out a breath. "I know. But...but how can we do what we just did? How can you say what you said about us being the best parts of your life while you're planning on selling off one of the biggest reasons for you to stay?" She was pushing him now. Damn it. She'd sworn she wouldn't. But she'd messed up with him more than once by saying nothing. This time she had to lay it all out on the table.

"What happened to you giving me the choice I didn't have a decade ago?"

He didn't mean it like that. She knew he didn't, but the words still stung. She *hadn't* given him a choice before, and now she was pushing him to make the one *she* wanted. Well, she guessed there was no going back now.

"What would happen if I asked you to stay and build a life with us here?" she asked.

"What would happen if I asked you and Owen to come to New York with me?"

Her mouth opened and then closed.

"You don't want to give up your life," he said. "And I wouldn't ask you to."

She threw her hands in the air. "But *my* life makes me happy, Jack. I have Owen, the vineyard. I'm going back to school. I have everything I want—except *you.*"

He stepped toward her, and she took a step back. If he kissed her, she'd let her physical need take over, and she needed a clear head now.

"Ava—you and Owen make me happy. I *want* to be the dad he deserves, and maybe if we all start fresh..."

His voice was so gentle, so earnest, that it broke her heart even though he hadn't left yet.

"My life is here. Tell me that New York is going to make you happier than what I've seen these past two weeks with you and your brothers."

He scrubbed a hand across his jaw. "I've been thinking a lot about happiness this week—and how you and Owen have shown me that maybe it is a possibility for me. But every time I think of giving up this partnership, I think about how selfish that decision would be. New York means that Luke and Walker won't go bankrupt if the ranch falls out of the black. New York means that you and Owen will never want for anything."

She groaned, her hands fisted at her sides. "Owen doesn't need money. He needs a father. And I need someone who's going to put us first and not take the easy way out. If New York is truly what you *want*, then go. But if it's another escape—"

"You say I'm not my father," he interrupted, "but how do you know that I'm good enough for him *or* you? Everything your father is afraid of could be true. *I* didn't know I was capable of what I did to Derek until I did it. And when I saw a bruise tonight on Jenna's wrist?" His chest was heaving. "She swore to me that whatever was going on with that damn egg guy was over, but hell, Ava. If you knew the scenario that played out in my head when I thought about someone laying a hand on her...Maybe I'm protecting you like your father is."

Her breath hitched and she started to form the words, but was interrupted by the unmistakable sound of tires rolling over gravel in the front of the house, followed by the loud hoots and hollers coming from Jenna's apparently open windows.

Scully sprang to his feet and started running in circles in front of the sliding door.

Jack held her gaze for a few seconds more, but she didn't know what else to say.

"What does it matter if I believe in you if you don't believe in yourself?" She shook her head. "You keep choosing the past," she said. "And I'm standing right here offering to be your future." She stroked his cheek. "Owen only has a few months left of school. We'll plan a trip to New York this summer so you can see him. I'll make a long-distance relationship between you and him work, but I'm not up for it in terms of us." She'd end this before her heart broke again because it was the only chance at reclaiming her life.

He wrapped his hand around her wrist, and she felt his jaw pulse beneath her palm. But he said nothing.

She forced a smile. "Maybe you should go make sure Luke survived the night without a trip to the ER."

Then she pulled free of his hold, opened the door, and followed the dog inside.

CHAPTER TWENTY-ONE

The whole lot of them—well, everyone but Jenna, who'd gone home last night—sat around the kitchen table eating breakfast as Owen recounted his night at the rodeo.

"Jack, did you know that Luke can ride a horse while he hangs upside down on its side? And that he can stand on two horses at once... while they're *moving*?" Owen shoved a spoonful of Cheerios into his mouth.

"It's called Roman riding, Shortstop, and your buddy Jack has actually *never* seen me do it."

Ava's eyes darted to Jack's, but he had already hidden his expression behind a coffee mug as he took a slow sip.

"Never?" Owen said. "But, like, he won two hundred dollars last night. That's how good he is!"

Luke shrugged. "But not the belt." He winked at Owen. "I'm good, but I wanna be the best."

Jack set his mug down and looked from Luke to Walker. He hadn't just missed the first nine years of Owen's life. He'd missed much of his brothers' lives, too. Now he was traveling across the country to miss the rest of it, and it all felt—wrong.

What *if* he stayed? He could practice law here as well as he could there. Would Luke and Walker really want that after all that he'd missed? Could Ava forgive him for letting logic make his choices when he should maybe start listening to his goddamn heart?

"Jack!" Owen said after swallowing his food. "You *have* to come next time. And Mom, too. You could do a date at the rodeo, right?"

Ava was the one to look away this time. He hated this tension between them, especially after last night. Damn it, *nothing* had ever shaken him to his core—utterly changing how he looked at his life, his future, the possibilities—like the way he felt when he was inside her.

He should have told her about selling the vineyard. But she terrified him. Because up until last night he'd convinced himself that what was brewing between them was nothing more than residual chemistry from when they were eighteen. That he could live without it like he had for the past ten years. But Ava wasn't the girl he remembered. She was a strong woman now, someone who'd put her own future on hold to raise an amazing kid. She was beautiful, and sexy, and full of so much passion that she couldn't keep it bottled up if she tried. It made him wonder if what he'd been doing since he left had really been living at all.

"So are we gonna watch some baseball or what?" Walker asked, pushing his chair from the table.

He had been sober last night when they'd returned home from the rodeo, Walker carrying a sleeping Owen in his arms. And this morning proved the same. Ava and Owen's presence seemed to be affecting all of them for the better. So why couldn't he pull the goddamn trigger and decide to stay?

"Are *all* of you really coming?" Owen asked. "That's so awesome," he said, not waiting for an answer. "Walker, can you show my friends the pictures you took of Luke on your phone? I'm gonna learn how to trick ride someday. You'll teach me, right?"

His eyes shifted from Walker to Luke. Ava coughed on her sip of coffee, and Jack just watched everything play out before him.

"I'll teach you whatever you want to know, Shortstop," Luke said.

"If you ever take a breath and stop *talking*," Walker added, but he winked at the kid.

Was this what it would be like if he gave up a future in New York for a life he hadn't realized he'd ever want? Family breakfasts, Walker sober, and Luke teaching his son how to ride?

Every puzzle piece fit—except for Ava's trust in him not having any more secrets—and his trust in himself that he and his father shared nothing more than a name.

Ava, silent through it all, finally looked at her phone and spoke. "We should go," she said. "I need to drop Scully at home before we head to the field. We'll meet you all there."

At the sound of his name, Scully sprang up and started spinning in circles, and whatever invisible thread had held them all together in that makeshift family moment snapped.

Everyone was up and moving. Jack piled cereal bowls and coffee mugs into the sink, knowing he'd be the one to take care of them later. Because that's what he did. He took care of things so others wouldn't have to.

He'd sent money to his brothers when he'd finally started earning more than he needed to live on. He'd only allowed himself the barest of necessities. He didn't need any more, and he certainly never let himself want. That was his penance for leaving.

Because he'd *wanted* to leave. That was his one luxury. Ava was right. He'd escaped the life that had tried to break him, taking care of his brothers from a distance instead. It was the only way he knew how to show them what they meant to him without having to be in a place where he'd lost all of his good memories.

But look at what they'd done in only a couple of weeks. They'd created new ones, and with one tiny omission about the vineyard, he'd possibly destroyed that.

They deserved more. Ava and Owen deserved more.

The screen door banged shut a few times as people—and a dog—exited. An engine revved in the driveway, and he guessed it was Luke starting up the truck. But Jack remained in the kitchen—separate, where he was safe. He might have been ten years older, but it seemed not much had changed. Even after a couple of weeks in this house, he still couldn't let the past go.

"You coming?"

He turned from the sink to see Ava lingering in the hallway leading to the front door.

"Yeah. Why would you—?" *Damn.* "Did you think after how we ended things last night that I was just going to cut my losses? I messed up by not telling you about the vineyard, but I'm in over my head here. I don't know how to be the guy you think you see in me, Ava. I've spent ten years convincing myself that everyone was better off if I kept them at arm's length. I don't know how to see myself any other way."

She shrugged. "And I don't know how to want anything less than the world for Owen." She forced a smile. "And for myself."

He watched as a single tear slid down her cheek. Then he remembered Walker begging Jack to hit him. As much as Ava and Owen seemed to bring out the best in everyone around them, his presence had upset the balance of so many lives. The thought of hurting his son, though? It tore at something deep inside him, making it hard to breathe.

"You don't want to tell him," Jack said. It wasn't a question.

She shook her head. "That's no longer the issue. You *are* his father. You have as much right to his life as I do. I'm just asking you to be sure about one thing—that no matter where you are, you'll be an active presence in his life and not simply a signature on a check." She let out a shaky breath. "I have no right to put this kind of pressure on you when I'm the one who created this situation, but he has fantasized about you his whole life."

"And you don't think I'll live up to the fantasy," he interrupted.

She worried her bottom lip between her teeth before she spoke. "Actually," she said, "you'll probably surpass it, which will make it that much harder when you leave."

She blew out a breath and plastered on a smile. The mask she wore for her son. How often did she have to do that? And how much of that was because of him?

"Time to go. Don't want to be late for warm-ups with the team. I'll see you and your brothers there. Is Jenna coming?"

"She texted," Jack said. "She said she had something to take care of but that she'd be there before the game ended." He stuck his hands in the front pockets of his jeans. "I never wanted to hurt you," he said. "Not then. And not now."

"I know," she said. "We kind of messed it up together, though. Didn't we?"

He strode toward her, stopping when he was close enough to hear her breathe. He skimmed his fingers through her hair, and she squeezed her eyes shut, forcing another tear to fall.

He kissed her wet lashes. Then his lips found hers, and she melted into his touch. Were ten years too much to repair when having her this close made everything else fade away?

"Why is *this* so easy for us?" she asked when they paused to catch their breath. "But everything else is so hard?"

He kissed her forehead and then pulled her close, and she buried her face in his chest.

"Because I have a messed-up past that won't seem to let go," he said softly. "And there's no way in hell I'm letting that get in the way of your future."

She pulled back and cupped his face in her palms. "*You* can let go, Jack. You are stronger than anything he ever did to you."

She didn't let him respond. She simply kissed him as if it was the last time she ever would. And he let her. Her fingers tangled in his hair as she parted her lips and invited him inside. He savored the taste of her, her scent, the feel of her skin against his. He held her tight, afraid to let go because this couldn't be it. It couldn't be good-bye.

She pulled away first, and his gaze never faltered as he watched her walk down the hallway and then out the door. He turned to grab his Dodgers cap from the counter and noticed her easel still standing outside on the deck.

He ran to the door to catch her, but she, Owen, and Scully were already pulling out of the driveway and onto the main road.

"What's the holdup, asshole?" Walker called out from where he stood, his back leaning against Jack's truck.

"I'll be right there," he said. And he jogged back toward the sliding glass door to grab Ava's canvas from the deck.

He stopped short once he was out there, eyes transfixed

on what he'd thought would be the unfinished painting she'd abandoned during their argument last night. But she must have come back outside after getting Owen to bed because what stood before him was a replica of the sky under which they'd made love last night. This painting would get her into Cal Poly in a heartbeat. But she'd have taken it if that's what she wanted.

Ava had shown him beauty in a place where he'd only ever found pain.

But that wasn't the whole truth. Was it?

Yes. His last years in Oak Bluff had wiped out any good memories of the place. But there *had* been good here at one point. The realization of it had crept up when he wasn't looking, whether it was Jenna recounting his parents' courtship or the revelation of what they'd built together, not just in that damned spare room but in the ranch as a whole.

Then there were these past two weeks working on the vineyard with his brothers and the only woman who'd ever been able to break through his carefully constructed walls. He'd made new memories in a place he'd thought it impossible to do so.

He'd always thought his past would be trampled to dust the day Jack Senior was laid to rest. But Ava was right. His father was gone, but he was still hanging on to the pain. *He* needed to be the one to let go.

"How?" he asked aloud. "Someone tell me how, and I'll do it."

But no one was there to answer. So he grabbed the painting and brought it inside. But he didn't bring it to his truck.

Convincing himself she'd left it on purpose, he decided to keep it—his best new memory, and the hope that it wasn't his last. New York might be on the other side of the country, but he wouldn't stay away like he had before. He didn't need to anymore.

"So, Red's parents seem nice," Luke said sarcastically as they approached the Ellis clan sitting on the bleachers behind first base. "You piss in their rosebushes or something?"

Jack rolled his eyes. "More like I got their daughter pregnant and then disappeared for ten years."

"Shit," Walker said. "'Not like that's on you. You didn't have a clue."

Jack shrugged. "I'd rather they take issue with me than make Ava's life hell." He side-eyed both his brothers. "Just—don't be a dick," he said before they were close enough for anyone to hear.

"Which one of us?" Luke asked.

But they were within spitting distance of Ava and her parents now, which meant he couldn't give Luke a proper, brotherly response.

"Mr. and Mrs. Ellis," he said in a professional tone. "I'm not sure you ever met my brothers, Luke and Walker."

Luke extended a hand to shake, but Walker simply crossed his arms.

"It's nice to meet you," Mrs. Ellis said with a genuine smile. Mr. Ellis did *not* reciprocate the gesture.

"Luke is pretty big in the local rodeo circuit," Ava said. "And Owen got to have his first rodeo experience last night."

Mr. Ellis narrowed his eyes at his daughter. "You brought my grandson to a rodeo?"

Luke cleared his throat. "Actually, sir, we took Owen on our own so your daughter and Jack could have a night to themselves."

Christ. Smacking his brother on the back of the head

would only fuel the fire. He opened his mouth to play defense, but Ava beat him to the punch.

"Jack worked all day and well into the early evening in the vineyard," she said. "I wanted to give him a home-cooked meal as a thank-you."

Walker scoffed. "Yeah, while we had to eat nachos and hot pretzels."

Mrs. Ellis laughed, but Ava's father didn't even crack a smile.

"Rumor has it you got a pretty nice offer on that broke-down vineyard of yours," he said.

"You told him?" Jack asked Ava, but she shook her head, her eyes wide.

"Dad," she said, her voice shaky, "do you have something to do with that offer?"

He didn't have a chance to respond as Owen ran off the pitcher's mound where he'd been warming up.

"Grandma, Grandpa, did you guys see that curveball? Jack taught me that. Did you know he was a pitcher?" He squinted past them toward the parking lot. "Hey, isn't that Jenna? It's so cool you all came to my game."

Jack turned to see Jenna standing on the curb next to the driver's side of a car stopped on the wrong side of the street, idling behind a stop sign. He didn't recognize the vehicle or the driver. He was about to turn away and give her privacy, realizing it was probably a man she'd spent the night with. But then he saw the guy grab her wrist...and Jenna try unsuccessfully to pull away.

"Shit," he said. She hadn't ended it, and the piece of shit had laid his hands on her again.

Jack ran across the short expanse of grass to the idling vehicle, ripping the guy's hand from Jenna's arm before even saying a word.

Jenna gasped and turned to face him, and Jack lost it when he saw the fresh, purpling bruise on her cheek.

He pushed Jenna out of the way and yanked the car door open, tearing the asshole from his seat. He dragged him around the front of the car, slamming him down on the hood before raising his fist to the man who'd raised his own to Jenna.

"Jack! Don't!"

Ava's voice cut straight through to him. He had one hand around the guy's throat and the other pulled back into a fist poised to beat him bloody. But he turned toward her voice to see all of them crowded in front of the car—Jenna, Luke, and Walker. Then Ava with Owen at her side, the boy staring at him in horror, exactly like his mother had ten years ago.

Ava's parents seemed to appear out of nowhere, her father bellowing as he stepped in front of his daughter and grandson, as if to shield them from what he was about to do. "This!" he cried. "This is why you'll never be good enough for my daughter and why you'll never be the father that boy deserves. You're just like your old man. And I'll be damned if I let you do to Ava and Owen what you did to Derek Wilkes…and what your father did to you."

Jack looked at his fist raised in the air, then at the man beneath his outstretched hand whose lips were turning blue. He let go and stumbled back. "Somebody call the cops," he said, barely recognizing his own voice.

"I'm on it," Luke said, pulling his phone from his pocket.

Only then did it register what Ava's father had done.

He turned toward the gathered crowd and saw Ava with her hand cupped over her mouth and Owen's disbelieving stare volleying from her to him.

"You're—my dad?" Owen asked, the hurt in his eyes more devastating than anything Jack could have imagined.

"He didn't know," Ava said, taking a step toward her son, but Owen only backed away.

Jack's eyes were fixed on Owen, whose own were red as tears streamed down his cheeks. The boy was getting dangerously close to the curb.

"Mom?" He was sobbing now. "You"—he hiccupped, trying to catch his breath—"you always knew? This whole time we were at J—at his house, and—and you didn't tell me?"

Not another step, Jack thought as he watched Owen retreat farther, and the boy stopped as if he could read his mind. Jack straightened and let out a breath as Owen turned his gaze to him.

"Do you...Do you not want me? Is that why you didn't say anything?"

Ava reached for her son, but he shook his head and took another step back, not realizing he was stepping off the curb.

It all happened in seconds. Owen stumbled several extra steps to keep himself from falling and Jack eyed the car around the corner making a left-hand turn right toward his son.

The driver wasn't looking.

Ava screamed.

Jack's only reaction was to run.

Owen was in his arms before he heard the sound of tires screeching, before he smelled the burnt rubber. But it was too late.

CHAPTER TWENTY-TWO

❦

Owen sat, quiet and stoic, as the emergency room doctor cleaned and stitched up the gash in his chin. He didn't speak in the ambulance, either. He simply cried softly. But Ava knew the tears had nothing to do with physical injury.

He walked away from the accident with five stitches. *Five* stitches when it could have been—

Ava choked back a sob. If it hadn't been for Jack...

She cleared her throat. "Excuse me, Dr. Bennett, but have you heard anything else about Jack Everett's condition?"

The woman finished tying off Owen's suture and then straightened to face Ava. "I'm sorry, Ms. Ellis. But last I heard, he was still in surgery. And please, call me Dr. Chloe."

The young doctor pushed her glasses up onto her head and brought her attention back to her patient. "That ought to do it, Owen. And can I just say, you are one of the bravest patients I've ever had."

He pressed his lips into a small smile. "Thanks."

She stood and reached into the pocket of her white coat and produced a raspberry Tootsie Roll pop. Ava was sure this would get a more Owen-like response, but he simply held out his hand when she offered it to him and then set it on the hospital bed beside him.

She pulled her dark brown ponytail tighter and stuck Owen's chart under her arm. "I'll hand this off to the nurse who'll get started on your release paperwork."

She offered her hand for Ava to shake, and she did so, albeit absentmindedly. Now that Ava knew Owen was okay, her thoughts traveled elsewhere. "I'll have someone notify you when Mr. Everett is out of surgery. In the meantime, there's a coffee machine in the waiting room, or I can have someone show you all to the cafeteria."

Ava shook her head. "I don't want to miss any news. But thank you, Dr. Chloe."

The woman smiled and ducked behind the curtain that was their illusion of privacy.

Owen sat with his legs dangling over the side of the bed, head hanging low as he stared at the knees of his still-white baseball pants. Not a mark on them. The only part of Owen that had hit the asphalt was his chin. The rest of him had been cocooned inside Jack's solid frame.

Ava took a chance and sat down next to her son, nudging his knee with her own.

"You still not talking to me?" she asked.

He shrugged but didn't say anything. Still, she took the gesture as permission to continue.

"I met Jack when I was eighteen," she said softly. "He and his brothers moved to our area after the winter holidays, so they were new to school second semester. I was the one chosen to show Jack where his first-period class was, and you want to know what?"

She held her breath, waiting, *hoping*, for a response. Anything to show her that he wanted to know their history—the history of how he came to be—because that wanting meant they were one tiny step closer to forgiveness.

The seconds stretched out before them, and Ava felt the tears pricking at her eyes when Owen finally let out a breath and asked softly, "What?"

She laughed nervously. "He was this beautiful, golden-haired boy with eyes as blue as the ocean. And I think I fell for him right on the spot." She rested her hand on Owen's cheek and urged him, gently, to make eye contact.

He did.

"His eyes were just like yours," she continued. "*Are* just like yours."

"The same blue?" he asked.

She nodded. "And the same sadness." She dipped her head to plant a kiss in Owen's auburn waves. "I know you heard your grandpa say some stuff about Jack's daddy."

Owen chewed on his lip. "His dad hurt him?"

She kissed the top of his head. "Yeah, bud. He did. It's not my place to tell you everything that happened to Jack before I met him. That he'll have to tell you himself. But all I can say is that I would have done *anything* to take away his hurt, just like I would do for you right now. And back then, it meant not telling him about you because he had to leave. That was the only way I knew how to protect him— by letting him go."

"So he never knew about me?"

She shook her head. "I was so young when I had you and so scared that if I told him, he would have stayed. Because that's the kind of guy your dad is. But I didn't want to be the one to keep him in a place that caused him so much pain, so I did what I thought was right back then."

She grabbed a tissue from the box on the counter and wiped at Owen's eyes.

"Did you love him?" Owen asked.

"So much."

He leaned his head against her shoulder, and she let out a shuddering breath. She knew they had a long road ahead of them, but her son would forgive her. Eventually, time would help repair what she'd broken.

"Do you—love him now?" he asked, and Ava let out something between laughter and a sob.

"So, so much," she admitted. "I don't think I ever stopped." She wrapped her arm around him and squeezed him close. "We were going to tell you. After the game. We just wanted you to have some normalcy before we turned your world upside down."

He straightened to look at her. "He—he wants to be my dad?"

Her tears flowed freely now, but she didn't care. Even though she knew Jack was moving to New York, one thing was certain. "Yes, sweetheart. God, yes. He wants to be your dad."

"And Luke and Walker? They want to be my uncles?"

She nodded. "And Jenna is dying to let you know she's your great-aunt."

The hint of a smile fell from Owen's face. "That man hurt Jenna. The one Jack almost hit."

It wasn't a question. He knew.

Ava skimmed her fingers through her son's hair. Yesterday, his biggest worry in the world had been keeping his cowboy hat from falling over his eyes at the rodeo. Today he'd learned that people hurt others—some intentionally, and some who thought they were protecting the ones they loved from greater pain.

"Yeah. He did. But she filed a report with the police after the accident. That man won't hurt Jenna anymore."

Ava remembered the look in Jack's eyes when she'd screamed for him to stop—as he listened to her dad confirm everything Jack feared—that he was a replica of his own father. She'd never be able to erase that moment for him.

The curtain slid open and a nurse walked into their small space with a clipboard. "Just a few signatures for you, Ms. Ellis, and some post-op instructions, and you two are free to go!"

Dr. Chloe popped her head in as well. "Wanted to let you know that Mr. Everett is out of surgery and in recovery. The information desk should have a room number for you within the next hour." She grinned. "It was a clean break where he'd broken the leg before, and the surgery was a success. He'll be up and about in no time."

Ava released a shaky exhale, and, without even thinking, sprang from the bed to hug Dr. Chloe. "Thank you!" she said. "Thank you. Thank you."

Her grateful smile fell when she let go of the doctor and saw her parents striding toward her from the nurses' station.

"They said Owen was being released, and damn it, I want to see my grandson." Her father was storming toward them now, but Ava stepped in front of Dr. Chloe to cut them off.

"Mom…Dad…I asked you to wait in the waiting room. There isn't room back here for all of us."

Her father made like he was about to take a step forward, but Ava shook her head.

"Do you…have this under control, Ms. Ellis?" Dr. Chloe asked.

"Yes," she said and dipped her head back around the curtain. "Back in a sec, bud, okay?" she asked Owen.

He nodded and opened up his Tootsie Pop. She smiled. He'd be okay. She and Owen would be okay.

Ava led her parents back in the direction they'd come from until all of them were in the waiting area and out of earshot of Owen's room.

"Ava." Her mom spoke first. "We're *so* sorry everything happened like this. We just want to make sure Owen is okay."

"He will be," she said. "He's got more than a cut on his chin that needs healing, but he'll get there. What about Jack? I don't see you storming through the surgical wing making sure *he's* okay."

Her father's face paled, and he collapsed into a chair. "He could have killed that man. I saw it in his eyes."

"A man that was *hurting* his aunt...like Derek was hurting me. Just because I walked away from that party with only a few bruises shouldn't have meant that Derek was exonerated in your eyes."

Her father's shoulders sagged.

"You were so horrible to him, Dad," Ava said. "You made him believe in his worst fear when he proved today that he's a better father than most, and he's only known his son exists for two weeks."

Her voice grew stronger with each word she spoke, with what she should have said to defend Jack not only ten years ago but when he'd shown up on the day his father was laid to rest.

"You *knew* what happened to him back then. But did you know he took every beating so his brothers didn't have to? Some kids grow up to be just like their parents. Sometimes that's good, and sometimes not. Deputy Wilkes was a good man as far as I knew, but his son *assaulted* me. If Jack hadn't shown up when he did...Yes, things got out of hand, but try to remember what might have happened if he came looking for me five minutes later."

Bradford Ellis, a man who'd always seemed such a hulking presence, crumpled as his face fell into his hands. It was Ava's mother who spoke.

"He was afraid he'd turn out like his father if he ever had kids. And then today—he saved his son's life," she said.

Ava nodded and her mother pulled her close.

"I couldn't tell him about Owen," Ava said, her face buried in her mother's neck. "I couldn't tell him when the only thing he knew about fatherhood was that his own dad had almost killed him, and he swore he'd never put a child of his own in that same position."

She pulled away from her mother so she could speak to both her parents. "Jack made a mistake ten years ago, but today he is the *only* one who is blameless in this mess. And if you need some sort of proof that he is *nothing* like his father, I think the fact he didn't lay a hand on that guy *and* put his own life in front of Owen's should be evidence enough." She sniffled and straightened her shoulders. "He has a new life waiting for him in New York," she added. "Across the damned country. I gave him the choice I should have given him ten years ago—to decide what part he wants to play in Owen's life. And *mine*. And you, Dad, setting up the buyer for their vineyard and then everything you said? He'll be on his way out of here—and probably out of both our lives—the minute he gets released."

Her father ran a hand through his thick gray hair and slumped farther down in his chair. "I'm—I'm sorry," he said. "You're a mother now. You understand what a parent would do to protect his child…" He trailed off, his eyes darting toward her mother, no longer able to hold his daughter's gaze.

"I get it, Dad. God, you know I do. But I also get that we can be so blinded by this need to protect the people we love that we end up hurting them anyway."

He stood, a once-towering presence now humbled by his own daughter's words. "I never wanted to hurt you."

She pressed her lips into a smile she knew didn't reach her eyes. "I know. And I never wanted to hurt Owen. Or Jack. But guess what?" She shrugged. "I did. I hurt the two people I love most, and I can't undo that. We can't undo any of the damage that's been done."

"Then what can I do to make things right?"

She'd give anything to have the right answer, if there even was one.

"I'm going to go and get Owen. You and Mom can take him to the cafeteria, the gift shop, whatever. Get him anything he wants. And when I get the thumbs-up from the doctor to do so, bring him upstairs to see his father."

"Okay," both her parents said in unison.

She hadn't lost her son. Now she had to make sure that no matter where Jack Everett went from here, she wouldn't lose him completely.

The future she wanted included art school, independence, and finally wanting something for herself. That hadn't changed. But it wasn't enough anymore. Jack had shown her that. And even if it was too late for the two of them, she wouldn't pretend anymore.

If he left, at least he'd know the truth. He was more than the father of her child. He was the boy she fell for when she was only eighteen—and the man she'd loved for ten years.

And that would never change.

CHAPTER TWENTY-THREE

Jack opened his eyes, yet he was sure he was still sleeping, stuck in one hell of a nightmare. Either that or his life had just rewound ten years to the night Jack Senior had pushed him down that flight of stairs.

He glanced around the familiar-looking hospital room and then down to where his leg extended in front of him, wrapped in plaster from the knee down. His bed was only partially reclined, so he was practically sitting up and able to take in his surroundings without struggle. Even Jenna was there, head slumped and eyes closed as she dozed in the chair beside him. Everything was the same.

The only thing off was the livid bruise on Jenna's cheek.

The accident.

Owen.

The asshole who'd been hitting Jenna.

He struggled to sit up but then hissed through clenched teeth.

"Shit!" His arm flew to his side as he tried to catch his breath.

"Hey," Jenna said soothingly as she straightened in her chair. "Careful there, tough guy. You've got a few bruised ribs, but luckily none are broken."

He swallowed with difficulty, his throat raw, and the sense of *déjà vu* continued as he remembered the same sensation following the surgery to repair his broken tibia more than a decade ago.

"But I rebroke the leg," he said, and Jenna nodded. "Owen," he added, growing anxious. "What about Owen?"

All the pieces were falling into place. Why hadn't she mentioned Owen yet?

"Oh, you know," Jenna said, a soft smile spreading across her face. "You were just the heroic dad who put his life ahead of his son's. He got a nasty gash on his chin, but he's all stitched up and hanging with his grandparents in the cafeteria."

Jack exhaled a shuddering breath and let his head fall back against his pillow.

"I knew something wasn't right with you," he said, staring straight ahead. "I knew, and yet I let you go back to him to get hurt again."

"Don't," Jenna said, moving forward in her chair, and he finally met her gaze. "You had enough on your plate, and I thought I had it under control. The only reason I met with him this morning was to end it for good. The other two times—the lip and the bruise on my wrist? He was drunk. I thought if I ended things when he was sober that he would react differently."

Her eyes shone with the threat of tears, and Jack grabbed her hand that rested on the side of his bed.

"Instead he *hit* you."

She squeezed his hand. "I filed a police report, something I should have done after the first incident. But I was embarrassed."

"What the hell are you talking about?" he asked.

She shrugged. "I seem to have this radar that homes in

on guys with serious issues. I thought for once I'd found a good one, you know? He was so sweet, and the first time it happened I made myself believe it was an accident, that he'd had a little too much to drink. I swear, the night of the rodeo, I *had* ended it. But then he called, told me he was getting sober, and Jesus, Jack. After what happened to y'all with your daddy, I should have known better."

He tugged on her arm, and she slid close enough so he could pull her into a hug and kiss the top of her head.

"I spent five years hiding what Jack Senior was doing to us, trying to see the good in a man who'd lost his way until I forgot there ever *was* good in him. Let yourself off the hook. But promise me something."

She straightened to look at him. "What?"

"You, me, Luke, and Walker—we're the only family we've got. You took care of us when you should have been living your life. Now it's time you let us take care of you."

She nodded. "You're wrong about one thing, though," she said, standing.

"What's that?"

"We're not the only family you've got." She pulled open the door and popped her head outside, but Jack could still hear her. "He's awake now."

The door swung wider as Jenna waved and headed into the hall. Before it shut, Ava slipped quietly into the room, barely past the door, leaning against it as it closed behind her.

"Hey," she said tentatively.

"Hey," he answered. "Jenna said Owen's okay."

"Five stitches in his chin, which he sat through like a champ." Ava smiled. "He really wants to see you—when you're up for it."

He scrubbed a hand over his face. "He's not pissed at me for not telling him the truth?"

She laughed softly, but it wasn't a true Ava Ellis smile. He knew those well enough, and it hurt more than his broken body to see what the past two weeks—hell, the past ten years—had done to make that smile harder to find.

"He was upset but more because he thought you left because you didn't want him. So I told him everything I could. No details about your dad, but he knows things were bad for you, and he knows you never knew about him. And—and all those awful things my father said, he knows they aren't true. We all do. Because you could have chosen to walk down that path today. You could have hit that guy and made yourself believe that you were *exactly* like Jack Senior, even though we all know you'd have just been protecting your own. But you didn't do it."

One small tear escaped down her cheek, and it killed him that he couldn't go to her. Then the floodgates were open. She stood there against the door, the tears falling faster than she could brush them away.

"And I promise, my father knows he was wrong, that he went over the line. After what you did today?" She shook her head, her hand flying to her mouth.

Jack wanted to pull her to him, to end this damned cycle of grief and guilt that had kept them apart for so long.

"Come here," he said.

She nodded and took slow, hesitant steps to the side of his bed.

"Sit." He patted the spot next to his uninjured leg, and she lowered herself gingerly beside him.

"You chose Owen," she said. "You chose to save your son rather than hit that man, and I know in my heart that you would always choose to protect him rather than hurt him."

Jack threaded his fingers through hers, and she squeezed his hand.

"It wasn't always the alcohol," he said softly, and Ava's brows drew together. "That night he knocked me down the stairs, yeah. He was drunk. I was trying to get him to bed, and he was trying to push me away, claiming he didn't need help. It *was* an accident."

He blew out a breath as his heart hammered in his chest. It was easier to blame his father's behavior on a combination of grief and booze. But the truth was, drunk or sober, the man who'd existed before his mother's death was never the same man after.

"There were those few times when he was sober and I could tell Luke or Walker was riling him up before he even got to his first drink, and I'd push him to the brink. I'd say whatever I could so he'd lash out at me instead. And then I'd lie to protect him."

He shook his head and squeezed his eyes shut.

"Because he was your dad."

He nodded. "I could have killed that guy today," he said, remembering the rage he'd felt at realizing what that man had done to Jenna.

"But you didn't. You could have ignored everything else around you and let loose on him, but you stayed in control. You stayed in control and you saved your *son.*"

She didn't bring up Derek Wilkes, but she didn't have to. He'd let loose on that guy ten years ago, and it scared the shit out of him to think of what would have happened if Derek's buddies hadn't pulled Jack away. But maybe he wasn't that messed-up kid anymore. He still had a lot of issues to deal with, but he was at the wheel now—driving the demons out instead of driving himself to the brink.

She reached her free hand for his cheek, and he felt her

thumb swipe at something wet at the corner of his eye. "I *love* you, Jack Everett. I loved the boy I met when I was only eighteen, and I love the man you are today." She leaned forward and kissed him, and he tasted the salt of her tears. "You've had my heart for ten years."

He pulled her hand to his lips and pressed a soft kiss to her palm. "I love you so damn much," he said. "Both of you, and I think that scared the shit out of me even more than stepping foot back in that house. Losing you once almost broke me, and the thought of losing you again—*and* Owen? How the hell does a man live with that kind of fear?"

His voice shook with the words, but he let go of that measured control. For Ava and Owen he could finally do that.

She kissed him again. "You won't lose us. Even when you go to New York. We'll figure it out. I don't know how, but we will."

He cupped her face in his hands, which was no easy feat with one tethered to an IV, and tilted her head so her mouth was a breath from his. "Ask me to stay," he said softly, and her breathing hitched.

"But you said—"

"Ask me to stay, Red."

"Stay," she whispered.

"Okay," he whispered back. "But only because I'm in love with you and our son, because I can be a lawyer anywhere—and because the Crossroads Vineyard doesn't stand a chance without your expertise."

She laughed through her tears. "*Our* son. You said *our*."

He grinned and brushed his lips against hers. "Yeah. I guess I did." And then he claimed her mouth with his, sealing the deal and letting go of their past.

The door flew open as Luke and Walker barreled their way through.

"Don't mind us," Luke said. "Ain't nothing we haven't seen before."

"Speak for yourself," Walker said. "Just because they're all happy and shit doesn't mean I have to watch."

"Nurse said you were awake," Luke added. "So here we are with all our brotherly support." He held out his hands as if to say *Ta da!*

Jack cleared his throat, and Ava laughed.

"Hey, assholes," he said, his voice hoarse and throat still raw. "This is actually a private room. You ever heard of knocking?"

But both brothers were already lost in exploring a box of baked goods on a table across from Jack's bed.

"Help yourself, by the way," he added.

Luke read a small card that was tucked under the twine that had tied the box together. "Lily Green sent these over?" he asked.

Jack struggled to sit up straighter, then winced, forgetting the whole bruised rib situation.

"Sorry," Ava said. She kissed him and crawled out of the bed. "I'm probably not helping." She handed Jack the small remote that controlled the bed.

"Actually," he said, narrowing his eyes at his brothers, "you're the only one who was."

Walker plucked a black and white cookie from the box. "And here I thought your buddy's wife only did barbeque," he said to Luke. "You really missed the boat with that one."

Luke shoulder-checked his younger brother a little more forcefully than usual, but Jack decided not to push that envelope any further. Because for a man who'd thought for so many years that he was better off on his own—that his absence was protecting those he loved—he was damned happy to have all this commotion for once. Not that he'd admit it.

That was when he glanced to the left and realized the door hadn't ever shut. Lingering in the doorway was a hesitant Owen, chewing nervously on his top lip like his mother so often did, and staring up at the ceiling in quiet contemplation—just like his dad.

Walker took a healthy bite of his cookie and then turned to where Jack was staring at his son. "Oh yeah," he said. "Shortstop here has been sitting on the floor outside your door ever since his grandparents brought him up."

Ava backed away from the bed, motioning for her son to come closer. He approached slowly, stopping short of leaning against the mattress.

"Hey there," Jack said.

"Hey," Owen said. "Are you—okay?" he asked, his voice soft and unsure.

"I will be," Jack said. "Heard you got some stitches."

Owen lifted his head so Jack could see the underside of his chin.

"That's a badass gash," Luke said.

Walker smacked his brother on the back of his head, and Ava groaned. All of it—the sheer normalcy of it—made Jack grin.

"Your uncle's right, you know. Your friends are gonna think you're pretty tough."

"I didn't even cry when the doctor stitched me up."

Jack laughed softly. "But you know, it would be okay if you did."

He thought of all he'd kept hidden, years of pain he'd bottled up, thinking he was safe if he just got far enough away. But safe was being who you were in front of the people you loved—and having them love you anyway.

"I know," Owen said.

"Hey," Jack added. "I've been meaning to ask you something. You name that dog of yours for Vin Scully, the former announcer for the Dodgers?"

Owen nodded.

"Did you know that he was with the Dodgers longer than any other announcer was with a single team?"

The corner of Owen's mouth turned up. "Sixty-seven seasons," he said.

Jack grinned. "You ever been to a game?"

"Just once. Mom, Grandma, and Grandpa took me after my eighth birthday. New season hasn't started yet this year."

Jack scrubbed a hand across his jaw, thinking of all the birthdays he'd missed. He couldn't dwell on that, though. He couldn't change the past, and he got that now. But he could change how things went from here on out.

"You had a birthday before I got here. Didn't you?"

Owen's eyes brightened. "End of February."

Jack grinned. "You think I could maybe take you to your second game? I hear they got this great new pitcher."

Owen nodded, but then he swiped at an almost imperceptible tear under his eye. "Thank you, by the way, for saving my life. I'm sorry you got hurt."

Jack swallowed back the knot in his throat. "Do you know why I did it?"

Owen shrugged. "Because you love my mom."

Jack glanced up at Ava. "I do. I love your mom. But that's not why I ran in front of that car."

His chest tightened. This was the moment of truth, and as much as it was in his nature to do so, for once Jack wasn't holding back.

Owen looked at him expectantly, and Jack told him the only thing he could—the truth.

"I ran in front of that car because you're my son, and I love you. And I would do anything, Owen, *anything* to protect you."

Owen's eyes widened, and Jack watched as the boy's shoulders relaxed and he let the first tear fall. He threw himself at Jack, wrapping his arms around his neck and burying his face into his shoulder.

"I love you, Ja—I mean—Dad." Owen's voice broke on the last word, and the weight that had pressed itself into Jack's chest for half his life finally lifted.

He squeezed his son close and let out a shaky breath. "I love you, too, Shortstop."

They stayed like that for several long moments before Owen finally straightened. Jack's eyes met Luke's and then Walker's.

"We're not selling the vineyard," he said. "And I'm not taking the job in New York."

Walker laughed, then said quietly, "Damned grapes."

"Yeah," Jack said with a grin. "Damned grapes."

CHAPTER TWENTY-FOUR

Thanks to the titanium rod in his leg, Jack didn't need to use his crutches. Despite the doctor's orders to only walk in the cast when absolutely necessary, though, he paced the office floor, the sealed white envelope in his hand.

"There is no way you're going to put your shit behind you if you don't read it," he said aloud. Then he laughed because he was alone. Talking to himself. Afraid of a stupid piece of paper.

He paused mid-pace when he heard a dog's bark. Then he lifted the shade to see Owen and Scully running past the side of the house toward the back. That meant Ava wasn't far behind.

They were early, and there was no way he would be able to do what he planned to do without reading the goddamn letter first.

"Like a Band-Aid," he said under his breath. "Just rip it off."

So he did. He tore open the envelope and pulled from it a single piece of plain white paper.

The lines were crooked, and the handwriting a barely legible scrawl, but Jack could make out the words well enough to let Jack Senior have the last one and then be done with it.

He could have sat in the plush leather office chair. He probably should have, given his physical and mental state. But even if no one saw him, he had one thing left to prove to his father and himself: no matter what that letter said, and no matter what his father had done, he was still standing.

Well, shit. It took him 'til now to realize it? *No matter what the letter said...*

He didn't need to know what was in the envelope. He'd already closed the door on that part of his past. Now it was time to think about his future.

He tore the letter in half without reading farther than his name on the first line. Then he tore it again and again until it was practically confetti and tossed it in the trash.

A soft knock sounded on the door.

Jack cleared his throat. "Yeah, I'm coming."

"It's me," Ava said. "Owen's out back with your brothers and Jenna. Can I come in?"

Jack's eyes fell to the shreds of his father's words in the garbage can.

"Door's open," he finally said.

"Jenna said you've been hiding out in here for almost a half hour," she said, striding through the door. She stopped short when she saw him, crossing her arms and narrowing her eyes. "You are *right* next to a chair. You know you're only supposed to put weight on your leg if you need to—" Her expression softened, and she took a few steps closer, resting her palm on his chest. "Hey. What's wrong?"

He didn't say anything, just pulled her to him and kissed her until he felt like he could breathe again.

"Hey," she said again softly, her lips still moving against his. "Are you okay?"

His lips lingered on hers for several seconds more until he finally backed away. "I am now."

She glanced at the trash can next to his feet. "Was that the letter?"

"Leave it to Jack Senior to have the last word even from the grave."

"You read it?" she asked.

"Nope. I realized I don't need to. I've already moved on."

His leg started to throb, so he decided now was a good time to sit and collapsed into the chair.

She said nothing at first, then just climbed into his lap, wrapping her arms around his neck. She hugged him tight and he buried his face in her hair, breathing in the scent of her, the woman who grounded him and brought him back to the present when he'd been stuck for so long in the past.

"I don't know if I can ever forgive him," he said. "But I can move on."

She lifted her head and gave it a soft shake. "You don't have to forgive him today. But maybe someday. With more time."

His mom would like that. Wouldn't she? Some sort of peace between them. Maybe. All he had was time, now.

"And I made the decision to stay because I can be a lawyer anywhere. But you and Owen are home."

She swallowed and bit her lower lip, her green eyes shining.

"I can't justify what my mother's death did to him, but I get it." He cradled her face in his hands. "If I lost you like that?" He couldn't finish the thought, so he kissed her again.

"You won't," she told him, an unmistakable quaver in her voice. "Not if I have anything to say about it. But if you did?" She skimmed her fingers through his hair, her palm resting on his cheek. "If by some horrible twist of fate you did, you'd be strong enough for you and Owen to get through it, just like you were for your brothers."

He wrapped his hand around her wrist and pressed a soft kiss to her palm. Then he exhaled a shaky breath, and with it he let go of the fear that had kept him from this woman for ten long years.

"Come on," he said, straightening in the chair. "I have something to show you."

Ava glanced at Jack in the passenger seat of her Jeep and grinned.

"It's killing you not to drive, isn't it?"

"Maybe." His head thudded against the back of his seat, and Scully rewarded him with a sloppy kiss on his ear.

"Owen," Ava said, swatting at the Lab and pushing him back toward her son. "You're supposed to keep an eye on your dog when we're in the car."

Owen laughed. "I watched him slobber all over Dad. That's keeping an eye on him, right?"

Ava's breath hitched at how easily Owen had transitioned from calling Jack by his name to calling him *Dad.* It had only been a week since the accident. But they'd spent every day visiting Jack in the hospital after school. Some nights they brought him dinner, while others Jack took Owen to the hospital cafeteria for junk food and some one-on-one bonding time. She wasn't sure what the two of them did while she waited patiently in Jack's room. All she knew was that the two of them always came back smiling, and Jack brought her back something chocolate each time.

"Anyway," she said, cutting off her own thoughts before she got all teary-eyed, "this is supposed to be your welcome home family dinner." She glanced at Jack in her peripheral vision. "What do you need to show me at the vineyard that can't wait until daylight?"

Jack turned toward the back seat. "What do you think, Shortstop? Should we tell her?"

Owen giggled. "Not yet."

Jack turned his gaze to her as she pulled to a stop alongside the rows of grapevines. "Sorry, Red." He leaned toward her and kissed her on the cheek. "Not yet."

She rolled her eyes, put the car in park, and hopped out of the vehicle so she could speed to Jack's side of the car. But he was already standing on the road by the time she got there, Owen and Scully at his side.

"Did you even bring your crutches?" she asked, angry that she hadn't checked before they left.

Jack shook his head. "We're not going far."

"I hope not," she said. "It's getting dark." She tilted her head toward the sky. "At least it's a clear night."

"Come on," he said, taking her hand. "Shortstop, you got the supplies?"

Owen nodded and opened the back door of the Jeep. "Scully and I are right behind you."

"Supplies?" Ava said as Jack pulled her onto the grass toward the first row of vines. She tugged at the hem of her UCLA LAW sweatshirt—because *yes,* it was hers now— and her hand fidgeted in Jack's grasp. "What's going on?"

Jack stopped at the first plant in the row, the one they'd started on together that first day she'd come to Crossroads. Seconds later Owen was there with a plaid blanket over one arm and an excited Labrador by his side.

"Supplies," he said with a knowing grin.

Jack helped their son lay the blanket down flat—and then redo it after Scully ran back and forth across it.

"Sit, Scully," Owen said, and the dog obeyed, tail wagging and tongue dangling out of his open mouth.

"You too," Jack said to her. "Please."

She sat, but her heart raced. She was already teetering on an emotional edge listening to Jack and Owen talk like they'd been father and son for Owen's whole life. Jack was so good with him already, and her heart threatened to burst each time she saw him simply ruffle Owen's hair. She wasn't sure she could take much more.

Jack gingerly lowered himself beside her, but not completely. He stopped at his knees. No. Scratch that. He stopped at *one* knee while his good foot stayed planted on the ground.

"What—what are you doing?" she asked, but Owen answered instead of Jack.

"He wants to ask you something," he said.

Jack grinned. "It's kind of a question for all three of you."

Ava's eyes burned, and she let out something between a laugh and a sob.

"You know I never even noticed the sky—how you can see the stars out here at night—until you showed me." He almost lost his balance, and she rose on her knees to grab those strong shoulders that carried so much weight for all those years, and steadied him. He laughed. "You showed me that there is something good where I couldn't find it before."

He grabbed Owen's hand and patted his knee, and Scully moved to his side.

"This place doesn't haunt me anymore," he said. "Not if it's the place where you are. *Both* of you."

Scully barked, and Jack laughed. "I meant all *three* of you." He scratched behind Scully's ear. "Hey, Red? You think you can fix Scully's collar before he knocks me over?"

Ava's brows drew together, and she squinted in the waning light to try and figure out what was wrong with the dog's collar, when something sparkled and caught her eye.

She gasped as her hand flew to her mouth. "How did you—? You just got released this morning."

He smiled, then got to work unbuckling the dog's collar so he could remove the ring she was too stunned to touch.

"Actually," he said, pinching the silver band between his thumb and forefinger, "your father called in a favor to a jeweler friend of his."

Her eyes widened. "You talked to my father?"

Jack nodded. "He stopped by after you left to pick Owen up from school last Monday."

She wanted to ask more questions. She wanted him to tell her everything she'd missed when she wasn't at his bedside. But he was kneeling in front of her—on a broken leg, no less—with a diamond ring in his hand and their son standing beside them, grinning.

"And *you* were in on this?" she asked.

Owen laughed and shrugged. "Maybe."

"Ava," Jack said, and she tried to focus, but her head was swimming.

"Yeah?" Her voice shook.

"I know it's only been three weeks…" He smiled. "Well, ten years and three weeks, but I was wondering if you all wanted to marry me."

Scully barked. *His* mind was made up.

Owen stifled another laugh.

And Jack just looked at her expectantly, his blue eyes no longer the storm they'd been all those years ago when they'd met, or when he'd forced her off a country road a few short weeks ago.

"Just to clarify," he said, when she hadn't yet been able to formulate a coherent sound, "in case you need convincing, I love you, Ava. Pretty sure I have since the first day I met you in the school office, even though falling for someone was the furthest thing from my mind." He tucked her hair behind her ear. "You are so strong."

She smiled.

"And stubborn."

She narrowed her eyes at this.

"In a *good* way," he said. "I was convinced that there was nothing good in my life other than my brothers and Jenna. But then you pushed past every wall I tried to put up. You made me feel like I was worthy of someone else's love." She opened her mouth to say something, but he interrupted her. "I'm not done yet."

She bit her lip and waited.

"I love the girl you were when I met you and the amazing woman and mother you've become. I'm a better man for knowing you. For *loving* you."

Tears fell from her eyes and she shook her head. "I hate that you ever thought you weren't good enough. That I made you believe that when I pushed you away," she said with a sniffle. "You were *always* a good man. And you're already an amazing father."

They both looked at Owen, who beamed back at them.

"I'm just following your lead," Jack said. "You were a single mom raising this spectacular kid. I couldn't ask for more but to learn from the best."

"Mom," Owen said. "Are you gonna answer him?"

Ava laughed. And cried. And nodded. Because he

wasn't simply staying. After everything, he wanted her—*them*—all of it.

"Yes!" He slid the ring onto her finger. "Yes," she said again, placing her palms on his cheeks. "I love you." She kissed him. "I have only ever loved *you.*"

"Yes!" Owen yelped, and he and Scully ran up and down the aisle of vines.

"I was kind of hoping you'd say that," Jack said softly as he lowered himself to the ground and pulled her into his lap. "I wouldn't mind hearing it again."

"Which part? Yes, I'll marry you?" She laughed. Then she kissed him for breaking his heart all those years ago, for all the time they'd missed, and for all the years ahead. And in his kiss she felt the long-empty corners of her heart fill.

"I like that part," he said. "But I was kind of referring to what came after."

She smiled and let her forehead fall against his. "I love you, Jack Everett."

"That's the part I'm talking about." He kissed her one more time. "And I love you, Red."

They entered the ranch to whistles and hollers from Luke and Walker and a teary-eyed Jenna, who pulled Ava into a warm hug.

"Thank you," she whispered.

"For what?" Ava asked.

Jenna backed up to meet her with a watery gaze. "For helping bring him back from a place none of us could grasp." Ava opened her mouth to speak, but Jenna kept going. "I don't mean San Diego or New York," she said. "From the moment I found him in that hospital a decade ago, he was beyond my reach."

"And then I pushed him away," Ava said shakily.

Jenna shook her head. "He needed to leave in order to realize that one day he could come home again. I'm just sorry it took him so long to get here."

The two women embraced again, and Ava could feel the shared pain lift from where it had been hovering in the air. She looked at Owen and Luke wrestling with Scully, at Walker sipping a beer, shaking his head at his nephew and brother, and at Jack leaning against the kitchen counter, grinning and taking it all in.

She went to him, pressed her palms to his chest and her lips to his.

"You look happy," she said.

He laughed. "I'm not sure if you heard, but I asked this amazing woman to marry me, and she said yes."

She bit back a smile. "Is that so?"

"Yeah, but I wanted to ask her *one* more thing."

She tilted her head, her eyes narrowing. "You sure do ask a lot of questions."

He laughed. "I know Owen has school tomorrow," he said, "and that you'll have to head home after dinner."

"Mmm-hmm," she said, brows raised.

"Well, it being my first night home from the hospital, I was thinking I probably shouldn't sleep alone."

"Luke or Walker didn't volunteer for the job?" she asked. "I bet Walker is a closet spooner."

He crossed his arms and leaned back, giving her a pointed look. Her hand flew to her mouth, and she stifled a laugh.

"I was wondering if maybe you'd take me home with *you* tonight. But if you think one of my brothers could better care for a man just home from the hospital..."

She swatted him on the shoulder, but all at once the joke

was over. She bit her lip, not sure if the tears would start again once she tried to speak.

"No," she said, head shaking. "I *don't* think they could do a better job. I almost lost you last week," she added. "If you think I'm letting you out of my sight now that you're home—"

He kissed her before the reality of what she'd said had a chance to sink in any further.

"Good," he said softly against her. "A sleepover it is."

CHAPTER TWENTY-FIVE

Jack watched from the doorway as Ava sat on the side of Owen's bed and bent to kiss him on the forehead.

"You want me to sing?" she asked, and their ritual made him smile. He knew his son was still a boy, but he was maturing, and the events of the past few weeks had probably sped up the process. Still, a warmth spread through him to see that for these two people he loved, some things hadn't changed.

Owen's brows drew together as he chewed on his upper lip.

"He gets that from you, you know," Jack said.

Ava turned to look at him from over her shoulder. Not wanting to interrupt a part of their life he didn't quite fit into, he hadn't announced his presence.

Scully pushed past him and made his way into the room where he hopped onto the foot of the bed and curled up at Owen's feet.

"I think I tired him out," Jack said.

She'd left the man and the dog in the backyard when she'd finally put an end to the evening's activities by announcing that it was, in fact, a school night, and Owen had to get ready for bed. Jack had said he and Scully would follow them in soon, but he was stalling, unsure of his role in what had become, to Ava and Owen, routine.

"Mom?" Owen asked, and she turned her attention back to her son.

"Yeah, bud?"

"Could—could Dad maybe tuck me in tonight? I mean, if it's okay with you." He looked up at Jack. "And only if you want."

Owen's tentative tone made something in Jack ache—that Owen could think for one second he'd say *no*.

"I was kind of hoping you'd ask," Jack said, striding toward the bed. Okay, so it was more like *limping* toward the bed, but he still felt steady on his feet. He could do this.

He lowered himself on the other side of the mattress and reached for her hand. She grabbed it and gave him a reassuring squeeze before she rose.

"I'll let you two have some man time," she said with a grin.

Jack raised his brows. "Fair warning, Shortstop. I don't really do the singing thing."

Owen shrugged as Ava pulled the door shut behind her. "That's okay," he said. "It's kind of Mom's thing anyway. Maybe we could think of something that's just ours?"

Jack grinned, eyeing his son's bookshelf where he saw everything from Harry Potter to a baseball card price guide. "How about we read?"

He waited until Owen dozed off against his arm—and then he waited a few minutes more. Finally, after assuring himself he'd get to do this again, he slid quietly from the room in search of his fiancée.

He found her in the extra bedroom, where close to a

dozen finished canvases lined the floor against the far wall. He glanced at the one she was working on and winced.

"That is one hell of an ugly tree," he said. "You ever think about getting rid of the one out back? It doesn't look like it's fruit-bearing... or olive-bearing. Is an olive a fruit?"

Ava sighed. "I've been trying to paint that stupid tree for the better part of a decade. I thought if I could paint it, that it would be the one and only piece of art worthy of admission to Cal Poly. I thought I had to prove something to myself with a stupid tree."

"But now you don't?"

She shook her head. "I already got in, didn't I? With the portrait of you and Owen playing catch that I painted before it even happened."

"Because you knew," he said.

"I hoped," she admitted.

She crossed her arms, paintbrush still in hand. She was wearing nothing but an oversized white T-shirt he guessed was her regular uniform when she worked on her art. The paint-splattered garment slid down her left shoulder, exposing her pale, freckled skin.

Jack kissed it, then smiled as he felt her shiver.

"You boys have a good time?"

He nodded. "I didn't sing, if that's what you're asking. We did some bedtime reading instead."

"Oh yeah?" she asked. "What book?"

Jack gave her a wry grin, and she shook her head. "You read baseball stuff, didn't you? I'm going to be left out of conversations now if I don't know the Dodgers' batting order. I've basically lost my son to his father and vice versa."

She swiped the paintbrush across his cheek, but he grabbed it from her before she got the other.

He raised his brows. "Tell me about the tree," he said softly. "Or I retaliate."

She shrugged. "I have more brushes."

"And I'm not going anywhere. So talk to me, Red." She reached for the brush, but he was too quick, hiding it behind his back. "I'm not *leaving*," he said.

Without the brush to occupy her fidgeting hands, she wrapped her arms around her midsection and blew out a long breath. "I bought this house *because* of that ugly tree."

His brow furrowed. "Why the hell would you do that?"

"Because the last time I saw you—when I told you I wasn't in love with you—" Her voice shook.

He reached for her, but she held out her hand, staving him off for just a bit more. "I have to say this. And you can forgive me or not for all I've kept from you. But in order to move forward from this, I need you *not* to make it easier for me."

It killed him to do it, but he took a step back. For her.

"That's where we met," she continued. "Under that ugly tree across the street from the school. I called you there to tell you about Owen, but instead I pushed you as far away as I could because I knew—after the party and then what happened with Walker—that you wouldn't survive here if you stayed. So I hurt you more than you were already hurting, and now you're here, and you gave me this ring, and you want to *marry* me." She shrugged. "I've been telling you since the moment you got here to face *your* past, but the truth is, I guess a part of me is still stuck under that tree."

He dropped the brush onto the table next to her easel and closed the distance between them. His eyes searched hers for the girl who couldn't let go. "Tell me now," he said, his voice gentle. "Tell me now what you wanted to tell me then."

He swallowed past the years of separation, and he was eighteen again. Eighteen and lost until *she'd* found him.

She glanced out the window toward an innocent tree that had no idea the role it played in her torment.

"Hey, Red. It's okay. Pretend we're there."

She rested both of her hands on her flat belly. "I'm pregnant," she simply said.

Without hesitation, he covered her hands with his own. "I'm gonna be a father."

She nodded. "A really good one. I think it's a boy."

He smiled. "Who'll love baseball, and Vin Scully, and have an excellent pitching arm."

She laughed. "I'd like to name him after your mom." Her voice caught on that last word, and he watched her struggle to hold it together. For him.

"That means more to me than you will ever know." He realized he'd never thanked her for making Owen his, even when he wasn't here.

He kissed her then, and as their lips met, he felt her finally let go.

He scooped her into his arms, her bare legs warm against his hands, and carried her from the room. She narrowed her eyes, and he knew she wanted to give him hell for putting the extra weight on his leg, but he gave her a quiet "Shhh," warning her that if she said anything now, she'd wake Owen. Besides, he was so quick, she was on her back on top of her unmade bed in a matter of seconds.

Jack returned to the door to gently close it, and she rose onto her elbows. "You are terrible at following the doctor's instructions," she said.

He shrugged. "Doc didn't know I was making love to my future wife tonight."

She sucked in a breath, and he shook his head. "No more tears."

"But these are happy ones."

He stood above her and she tugged at the belt loop on his jeans. "Come here," she said.

He obeyed, climbing over her, but she shook her head and pushed him to his side so they were facing each other.

"I get that in the hospital you were hooked up to machines, which didn't leave you much of a choice. But part of this deal"—she motioned between them—"is that you don't get to be an island anymore. You put everyone else ahead of *your* needs. And I love that about you. But you've got people to take care of you now, and you better let them do it."

He tilted his head toward hers, the warmth of their breaths mingling between them. "Are *you* one of these people who want to take care of me?"

She rested her palm on his cheek. "For as long as you'll let me."

He kissed her, long and slow and sweet—at first. But when she parted her lips, his tongue slipped between them and he grew hungry with need.

"I missed you," he said as he came up for air.

Her leg slid between his, and her hand snaked around his back. "I know. A week is too long."

He kissed along the line of her jaw, nipped at her earlobe, and smiled when she gasped. "Not just this week." He rose on his elbow, and with his free hand gripped the hem of her paint-spattered T-shirt and tugged it over her head. *He* was the one who was short of breath now. Because there she was, in nothing but a pair of black panties—and the diamond he'd placed on her finger. He helped her out of the former as quickly as he had the shirt.

"I *missed* you," he said again, his voice rough, and the look in her green eyes was one of complete understanding.

She pulled his face to hers. "I know." She gave him a quick, chaste kiss. "But there's one thing wrong here." She looked him up and down.

"What's that?"

She raised her brows. "You're wearing entirely too many clothes."

He barked out a laugh, only to be shushed by the beautiful, naked woman beneath him. He was out of his own shirt in seconds, but the jeans over the cast were another story. Together, though, they made it work, and soon he was bare before the woman he couldn't get enough of.

"See?" she said. "That's how it works. Letting someone take care of you."

Without warning, she pushed him down on his back and sank over his erection, burying him to the hilt in her slick heat.

A low growl rumbled in his chest. He pulsed inside her, eliciting soft, short breaths that let him know that even injured he could still get the job done.

She squeezed her knees against his hips, tightened her muscles, and slid up and down his length so slowly he thought he might lose his mind.

"This," she said, lowering her head to his so she could kiss him. "This is me taking care of you for the next hour or so."

He raised his brows. "An hour? You think very highly of a man who hasn't been inside you for a week." And who felt like he might lose control in a matter of minutes. But that didn't worry him anymore—letting go with her. He wanted every part of this woman—body, heart, and soul. And he knew without a doubt she'd given all of that to him.

What surprised him now was, after all these years of distancing himself from that kind of connection, it was so easy to give back to her.

She rocked against him, her movement slow and controlled. "We'll just have to do it more than once, then. To work up our staying power."

He laughed, then wrapped his arms around her so the whole length of her body was flush against his. "I love you," he said, his hands gripping the backs of her thighs.

She gasped as he tilted his pelvis toward hers. "I love you, too," she said.

"I always thought I couldn't be happy here—coming back to this place. But you and Owen changed that."

She smiled. "You're really happy?"

She arched her back, and one of his hands snuck between the place where they joined. She cried out as he pressed a finger against her aching center.

"I'm happier than I ever thought possible," he said. Because he never could have dreamed this—a second chance with the only girl he ever could have loved.

"Promise?" she asked.

He kissed her, and her body melted against his.

"Cross my heart, Red. I'm finally home."

Look for more in the
Crossroads Ranch series:

Tough Luck Cowboy
Hard Loving Cowboy
Saved by the Cowboy (novella)

About the Author

A librarian for teens by day and a romance writer by night, **A.J. Pine** can't seem to escape the world of fiction, and she wouldn't have it any other way. When she finds that twenty-fifth hour in the day, she might indulge in a tiny bit of TV, where she nourishes her undying love of vampires, super-heroes, and a certain high-functioning sociopath detective. She hails from the far-off galaxy of the Chicago suburbs.

You can learn more at:
   AJPine.com
   Twitter @AJ_Pine
   Facebook.com/AJPineAuthor

Looking for more cowboys?
Forever brings the heat with these sexy studs.

COWBOY HONOR
By Carolyn Brown

After her SUV runs off the road in the middle of a Texas blizzard, Claire Mason is stuck in a remote cabin with her four-year-old niece. Lucky for her, help comes in the form of a true Texas cowboy...

TOUGH LUCK COWBOY
By A.J. Pine

Rugged and reckless, Luke Everett has always lived life on the dangerous side—until a rodeo accident leaves his career in shambles. But life for Luke isn't as bad as it seems when he gets the chance to spend time with the woman he's always wanted but could never have.

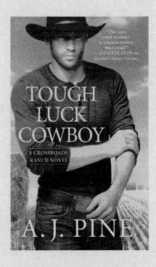

Discover exclusive content and more on forever-romance.com.

BIG BAD COWBOY
By Carly Bloom

When Travis Blake gets the call that his young nephew needs him, he knows he has to return home to Big Verde, Texas. His plan is to sell the family ranch and head back to Austin, but there's a small problem: The one person who stands in his way is the one woman he can't resist.

THE CAJUN COWBOY
By Sandra Hill

With the moon shining over the bayou, this Cajun cowboy must sweet-talk his way into his wife's arms again...before she unties the knot for good!

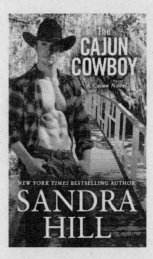

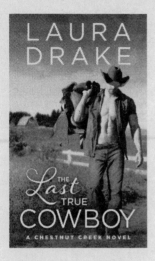

THE LAST TRUE COWBOY
By Laura Drake

Rodeo rider Austin Davis will do anything to win back the love of his life. But Carly's definitely hiding a secret—one that will test the depth of their love and open a new world of possibilities.

LONG, TALL TEXAN
By Lori Wilde

Texas socialite Delany Cartwright is a runaway bride who hopes a little magic will unveil the true destiny of her heart. But be careful what you wish for…

(previously published as *There Goes the Bride*)

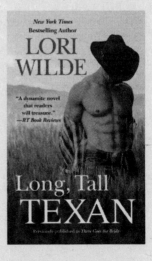

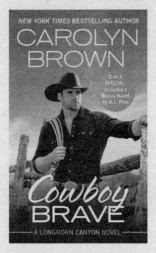